"No novelist has written as woman's struggle for equality ___ ___
— Charles R. Larson, *World Literature Today*

"Farah is one of the few African men who write wonderfully about women."
— Doris Lessing, *New Society*

"Nuruddin Farah has a remarkable ability to see things from a woman's point of view and to express the relationship between mother and daughter, and between women friends."
— *The Listener,* London

"Nuruddin Farah's provocative trilogy is one of the most powerful novelistic explorations of dictatorship since Asturias' *El Señor Presidente* or Roa Bastos' *I the Supreme.* . . . He is a major writer, one of Africa's best, and this splendid and very readable trilogy is the centerpiece of his considerable accomplishments."
— Robert Coover

1992

Variations on the Theme
of an African Dictatorship:
Sweet and Sour Milk
Sardines
Close Sesame

Also by Nuruddin Farah
From a Crooked Rib
A Naked Needle
Maps

NURUDDIN FARAH

SARDINES

GRAYWOLF PRESS

Schroth

Publication of this volume is made possible in part by a grant
provided by the Minnesota State Arts Board, through an
appropriation by the Minnesota State Legislature, and by a
grant from the National Endowment for the Arts. Additional
support has been provided by the Jerome Foundation, the
Northwest Area Foundation, and other generous contribu-
tions from foundations, corporations, and individuals.
Graywolf Press is a member agency of United Arts, Saint Paul.
Book designed by April Leidig-Higgins.

First U.S. Printing, 1992
Graywolf Press,
2402 University Avenue, Suite 203,
Saint Paul, Minnesota 55114.

9 8 7 6 5 4 3 2

Library of Congress Cataloging-in-
Publication Data
Farah, Nuruddin, 1945–
   Sardines / Nuruddin Farah.
      p.   cm.
   ISBN 1-55597-161-X (paper) :
$12.00
   I. Title.
PR9396.9.F3S2   1992   91-40273
823–dc20   CIP

For my brothers and
Martine and Patricia
and Koschin, my son –
with tremendous love

My very special thanks and love to all my friends who have been of great help during these lean years – in particular: Monique, Rosalynde, Jenni & Angus, and Josef & Janine; and to Margaret, my editor, my loving thanks.

P A R T   O N E

· · · · · · · · · · · ·

Being chained is a luxury.

The chained have somewhere to sleep

The unchained have not.

– Ho Chi Minh

All dies! And not alone

The aspiring trees and men and grass

The poet's forms of beauty pass,

And noblest deeds they are undone,

Even truth itself decays, and, lo

From truth's sad ashes pain and falsehood grow.

All dies!

The workman dies, and, after him, the work.

– Herman Melville

In a famished town, as in a cheap restaurant,

there is always a flavour of food in the air.

– Malcolm Muggeridge

O N E

She reconstructed the story from the beginning. She worked it into a set of pyramids which served as foundations for one another. Out of this, she erected a construction of great solidity and strength. She then built mansions on top of it all, mansions large as her imagination and with lots of chambers that led off corridors in which she lost herself but which led her finally, when she chose to follow, to a secret back door in another wing of the building. She stood at a distance; she breathed deeply and took her time. She admired the result.

The silence widened and she entered the door which opened. She roamed about in the architecture of her thoughts. She found she had to repaint everything, to redecorate everything, replaster the walls and paper each pillar all over again. Now she covered every corner with a new coat to give the place a colourful purpose, as meaningful as the vision she had seen, paint fresh as a sweet dream, blue and beautiful here, white and sunny-bright there. To create effect, she marked where the walls met with a warning written in red: *Stop and give heed: He is not all of us!* She walked about aimlessly, stumbled upon a vase full of water and broke it. She ceased moving. Her mind segregated the dead from the living; she stared at the lily which had withered with the same deliberate indifference as the water that, like life, ran away to merge with another form of life. She decided to banish from her thoughts all things which had no immediate relevance.

And upon what she had reconstructed she superimposed a tapestry of patterns she herself had developed, none of which, to the best of her knowledge, had known precedents. This she believed would enable her to introduce fresh turns and curves in the rebuilding of this large structure, the reworking of the designs, the flowers and also the castle: her life!

She would allot a room to each of the names which had presented themselves to her. She would do that before the *ideé-construct* fell in on her like a house of cards. But did she have enough rooms, did she have the space? Would she allow anybody to shift the furniture about, change, say, the position of a chair or a table? Would she let anyone make alterations in her plans or for that matter suggest she change the menu for the day or the week? Would she consult anyone while ordering anything? And who would have access to all of this? Who would the *guests* be?

A room of one's own. A country of one's own. A century in which one was *not* a guest. A room in which one was *not* a guest. . . .

She had a room of her own. She was young and beautiful. By the standards of anyone anywhere in the world, she was well-read, one could even say she was very learned. Professionally, she was a journalist. She had taken a degree in literature, then applied her talent to writing for the press; she freelanced while still a student in Italy and when she returned to Somalia got a newspaper job. Two and a half years later she was appointed acting editor of the only daily in the country. She came into a head-on confrontation with the authorities over the paper's editorial policy. She was sacked. A presidential decree forbade her to publish her writings inside the Somali Democratic Republic. So she directed her talent elsewhere: she decided to translate twenty world classics from six foreign languages into Somali. She was fluent in four European languages, her proficiency in Arabic was good and her understanding of Spanish was tolerably good. But since she wouldn't be permitted to circulate these efforts of hers, since she couldn't publish them because of the banning order, she decided to read them to her daughter Ubax. She gave them to her hot like maize cakes from the oven.

Ubax loved hearing about the Arabian prince in the *Nights* climbing flights of stairs up to the chamber of the waiting princess, the princess with the anxious look. Ubax also loved to listen to an Icelandic commoner buying the favour of the prince with a gift (Medina changed the gift from bear to horse and the snow to sand – "A country spread out," she said, "like pages of sandpaper"), and would happily sit at her mother's foot and wait for these stories to brown like onion in the pan of Medina's creativity, gluttonous as only the very young can be, anxious like hunger, her joyous expressions delightful like the eyes of a young deer. (Her favourite story had been a folktale Medina adapted from Chinua Achebe's *Things Fall Apart,* to which she had given the interpretative title "He".) For two months, for three months, day in and day out, the two were together from morning till evening now that Medina did not go to work, now that she had fewer engagements to attend. And they would wait for Samater and celebrate his homecoming with the re-telling of what they had done, which stories they had told each other, who had come to visit them. Then one evening Samater did not return on time. He did not come home to hear how his wife and daughter had spent their time while he had been gone.

Ubax sensed a change in the atmosphere the following morning: not only did her mother stop baking new stories for her, she became unapproachable and entered into long conversations with a number of elderly men who called. Medina was unbearably difficult and answered to questions only "yes" or "no" and would not say any more. One dawn, two men came for Samater and took him away. Ubax rose with the sun and found her mother reading the daily newspaper which carried a large photograph of Samater on the first page. She later learnt that her father had been appointed Minister of Constructions. When he came home for lunch that day, Ubax was surprised to hear her parents' raised voices; she was sad that they were not prepared to share their quarrel with her for they lapsed into a foreign language and this excluded her. Ubax asked: "What's happening, Medina?" No answer. And there arrived a chauffeur-driven car so Samater hardly needed to use the family car. Life was never the same after that.

Something else took place. An extra hand, a man, joined the household: an orderly who made himself useful as a gardener, a woodchopper and who helped the maid iron or wash clothes. Medina warned her daughter against talking openly with this man. But why? Her mother spoke evil of "informers and *pederasts* and boot-lickers". Then, six months or so later, Medina packed two cases, one for herself and another for Ubax, and moved out. She left a house which was legally her own and moved into another which was in her brother's name. Did she want to underline the temporariness of this move?

Many people speculated as to what had happened, others made up their own versions of what had occurred.

A room of one's own!

• • • • • • • • • • •

Medina was as strong-minded as she was unbending in her decisions, and she guarded her secrets jealously. She was, in a manner, like her father Barkhadle. She was as confident as a patriarch in the rightness of all her decisions.

Samater, however, was as weak in the head as he was in the knees. His mother Idil said it was because he had not grown up with a strong father to emulate or imitate. She was herself, though, as powerful as providence itself. Idil never failed to influence her son's decisions. She bullied him, she pampered him, she encouraged or discouraged him, she blackmailed him socially and every now and again, especially when she feared she had lost him, she jogged his memory and reminded him of what he had been like as a child, she reminded him how she was the only one he had when small and in need and how she had worked the hardest she could in order to send him to school or buy clothes with which to cover his back. But what was he like as a young boy? He remembered being excluded from every sports activity, being made to look after the clothes of the other boys who played football, or at best forced to keep goal or be the referee. And what was he like when he met Medina? He was weak as his voice and went where he was taken, he was the shadow which followed when they turned their backs on the sun. He was bright with a smile as the face of a full moon when others were happy and became sulky when Medina was unhappy. When Medina and he married and returned to Mogadiscio, all their friends derided what might happen when she and Idil met. Medina proved to be the stronger, the more confident of the two. In those days, Idil was living with Xaddia her daughter and so the sparks of her explosive suggestions as to what to do about her son's daughter Ubax ignited no fires of great hostility. She made no secret of the fact that she was sad that Xaddia wouldn't give her a grandchild. With this in mind, Idil consulted an herbalist and a sheikh. What made her sadder was that not only did Xaddia refuse to do as suggested but she said she was

taking pills so that she could not give birth to a child. Idil went insane
with rage. For weeks, for months, she spoke of nothing else. Finally,
Xaddia's husband's father stepped in: he ordered his son to dissolve
the marriage, otherwise he would disown him. The son obliged. Xaddia reacted angrily and threw her mother out. Medina and Samater
took her in. A condition was stipulated: Idil would not interfere with
their lives.

Not long after Idil had moved in with them, it was obvious she
wasn't going to keep her promise. She began to blackmail Samater with
her tyranny, although in Medina's presence, and when she encountered her daughter-in-law's impenetrability, she chose to stay on
guard: she moved about quietly like a guest. When Medina was not
there, however, she spoke loudly, like an overseer, her tongue lashing
away at him, at what he stood for, undeterred by logic or reason and
undeterrable. Their war was the one which ridiculed all social wars.
But would Medina's defence-wall break and one day give in? "No. Not
as long as I have a room of my own, so long as I have Ubax and principles to fight for." A room of her own. A life defined like the boundaries
of a property. Although one thing need be said: it worried Medina that
an overreaction to Idil's tyrannical behaviour could influence her ad-
versely, make her harsher towards herself, unfair to Samater, obsessive
about Ubax. She told herself to calm down. Then she quoted literary
antecedents in Indian and Arabic folktales in which mothers-in-law
terrorized their son's wives and drove them senselessly mad. No, this
would not happen to her. No fear of that. Idil had, in effect, excluded
herself: she hated eating at table with forks and knives; she preferred to
tell her beads in the privacy of her room. And when she was present, if
ever the need arose, Medina and Samater spoke in a foreign language
to exclude her. It was when they drank liquor, poured themselves or
their guests a nightcap, that Idil would turn "tombwards" and talk
about death, about God, about paradise and hell. No one paid any attention to these long-winded sermons.

Then one day she threatened to destroy "all those wicked books in
which you both appear engrossed", she threatened she would empty
"those cases full of wicked drinks". Samater readied to appeal to her
reason and to remind her of her promise not to interfere with their
lives. But before he said anything, he looked at Medina and saw her

stare at Idil in such a way it was understood she was being defied, challenged. Samater changed the topic of the conversation to something of common interest: to their surprise, he broke the news that he had bought plane-tickets for Idil and Medina's mother Fatima bint Thabit so that they could call at the Prophet's Tomb.

Mothers-in-law! The two were dissimilar as the palm and the back of a hand. Fatima bint Thabit, Medina's mother and Samater's mother-in-law, lived as though inside a whale which hardly came ashore: she was Yemeni, a woman weighed down with the contradictions of tradition: she was chained ankle and wrist and foot to the permanence of her homestead. She seldom came out of her house unless it was absolutely necessary, unless she had to answer an urgent call of some kind. She waited for her daughter's visit (Nasser her son lived in Arabia and in any case never liked to visit her) with the patience one in love waits for a kiss or a benevolent word. Idil's background was nomadic and on the whole a lot less rigid than the Arabic tradition of institutionalized mannerisms. She had never learned what it was to be strangled with the strings of purdah, nor had she known only the inside of a home. She had a profession, she supported her own Samater and Xaddia by making maize-cakes on commission from a restaurant. Because of the nomadic nature of her life, and because neither her son nor her daughter owned any property, Idil moved with the lightness of a tree with no roots. Fatima bint Thabit, on the other hand, walked with the stoop of a middle-aged person burdened with the history of generations: she was born in a house her family had owned for nearly a century. Oddly enough, it was Idil who spoke about continuity and discontinuity of cultures, it was Idil who believed that the younger generation, no matter how they tried, were not in a position to think of any "culture-substitute as faultless and whole as the one Somali society had developed in the past few centuries, any substitute with which to replace the traditional culture they appear to have discarded and which they deny philosophical validity." And by the time you were ready to ask her a question, you would discover that she had already moved on, taking refuge in unscientific generalizations; you would find that she had changed residence and had nomaded away, impermanent as Fatima bint Thabit was permanent in her fixed abode. A nomadic family without a fixed homestead married into a house of familial contradictions and genealogical connections as multinational as a constellation of stars; a family whose house had lived through flood, fires, internal intrigues, bankruptcies; a family whose history could be traced to a known patriarchy, whose four generations lived under the same sled-roof.

.   .   .   .

Hours later.

In her imagination. Medina saw the edifice she had built grow, then she noticed that the number of allottable rooms decreased as the number of eligible persons increased. She reread the names. Ubax. Sagal. Sandra. Nasser (if he came). Samater (when he returned from Algiers). Idil. Amina. Atta. Dulman. She knew she had to put these names into some order. She crossed out the names of Soyaan (dead), Loyaan (forced into exile), Koschin (in prison), Siciliano (in prison), Dr Ahmed Wellie (traitor), Xaddia (to be contacted when in town again). She was sure she had forgotten the names of other friends; also, she chose to cross out the names of some people who had been obnoxiously inquisitive and with whom she did not want to have anything more to do. Mursal?

How friends disperse when something happens, like a flock of pigeons hearing the blast of a gun! Most of them stayed safely away from her. For a week, no one called: they all waited to see if it was measles or smallpox before they prescribed their advice. During this period, the phone calls, the contacts were brief. No one pushed her, no one, except one or two whom she had never considered friends, wanted to know more than she was ready to tell them. Once they were sure that she was serious about not returning to Samater, there were more and more phone calls: the callers wondered if she was free that evening for this or that; would she like to go to a late-night party – a sort of an orgy, actually. . . . Some of these men were curiously insistent. A woman called her to say that she had seen Samater in the company of a woman. Medina knew that wasn't true: Samater had been gone a week and hadn't returned. She asked the informant the name of Samater's date and was given the answer: Atta! Medina did not tell the woman who had called that Atta was at that very moment sitting a few inches away from herself.

But why did she leave Samater? Why did she one day pack her two suitcases and leave? Speculation. Suppositions. It was common knowledge that long before Samater was appointed minister, Medina had decided she was not going to send Ubax to any of the state-run schools since, she said, all that children were taught there were the ninety-nine names of the General. Could it be that the Generalissimo pressed Samater to impress upon Medina how politically important it was for her to change her mind – and that, in reaction, Medina packed and angrily left? Another rumour had it that she had taken time off to write a book about the revolution. Or did all this take second place in importance? In other words, was there a secret which Medina guarded jealously? Was Samater in a position to call her bluff? Would the trip have done Samater any good? He had looked broken and was melancholic, given to longer silences, hardly speaking lest he say something he shouldn't, lest he commit himself one way or the other. To draw even with her, he would have to travel a longer distance than he had so far covered. He had had to put his mother in her place for she had been nagging at him more and more; she had now begun to exaggerate and kept reminding him that he was living in *her* house, that he was driving *her* car, that he was dependent on *her* economically, and, worst of all, that he had no bank account of his own and no ideas of his own. To live the life of a man, she suggested, he should be exorcised; he should be helped to become independent; and he should marry a woman of her (Idil's) choice. Or was this all the product of ill-founded gossip? And how did Medina feel about the separation? Did she show any signs of distress? She was slightly shaken, there was no doubt. You could tell from the way she answered the questions. But her distress wasn't half as shocking as Samater's. It was more like a slight inconvenience, a small indisposition – no greater than when her face contorted on account of her period.

A room of one's own. A life of one's own!

Medina now stared blankly into the blinding brightness of noon. She remembered that she had watched that very sun take shape and grow, like butter under fire, right before her eyes. She remembered that she had kept vigil almost all night. Ubax had cried and cried and cried. Ubax had cried for help. Like dawn, Medina stole in on her daughter and listened to her tell a rosary of names. But Idil's was the one name which made the little angel's sleepy lips tremble with a touch of nightmare. Another frequent visitor to the little one's lips was Samater, her father, with whom she spoke and exchanged a dialogue of love. Sagal. Amina. Sandra – whom she detested. Atta – who fascinated her. Fatima bint Thabit – whom she didn't like much because she gave Ubax a hand to kiss whenever they met. And Dulman – whom she was fond of and asked to sing a song: Dulman obliged. Ubax also mentioned Medina's name, in whose maternal syllables she sought permanent refuge.

"Ubax," she now called to her daughter. Warm and yet cold if touched: was this the wetness of childhood? "My sweet flower!"

Ubax curled up in her sleep. She put her small head between her knees. And she spoke. She said to send Sandra and Idil away. Why them? Because Sandra had been the disaster which visited the family, and because Idil had a knife with which to purify the little girl's *ufta!* Medina's hot breath, as though falling on a window-pane, left a film of moisture on the cheeks of the sleeping flower.

"They are not here," she said. "I've sent them away."

But Ubax wouldn't open her eyes and she recalled as much of the dream as she could, a dream in which Sandra said that she herself was a flower in full bloom: "And if I have a child, it would be the centre of everyone's attention, mine included. For this reason, I won't have one." Did Sandra appear and say that to Ubax in her dream?

"Wake up, my sweet!"

A saxifrage which in its day, as nature ordained, pushed energetically through the now-healed scissor-cut. True to life, the little thing on birth had issued a most hideous cry; like a thunderstorm, it made the hospital shake to its rocky foundations. The doctor whom she consulted in Rome had forewarned Medina, had said her delivery would require expert handling. *All wounds heal save that of a caesarean,* she thought now and cursed the memory whose larvae awakened the sleeping germs of a dead sore.

"My Ubax. Wake up, please."

Silence. And Medina let the name of her love sail away, let the name Ubax ride the windmill of her fantasies.

·   ·   ·   ·   ·   ·   ·   ·   ·   ·   ·

A flower of the plains.

"Ubax, wake up," Medina said slightly impatiently.

She kissed her. She waited for Ubax to open her eyes, her arms, then to yawn and finally to return the kiss. When none of this happened, Medina moved as though to go away, saying:

"You asked me to wake you."

Ubax sat up suddenly and said: "I did not."

The sharpness of this challenge did not shock Medina as deeply as her daughter might have expected. But she was taken aback; it was an aberration which, like an ugly reflection in a mirror, made one look betrayed. She asked Ubax to repeat what she had said.

"I couldn't have asked you to wake me up."

"You did."

"What did I say I would do if you woke me up?"

"You didn't specify what you would do when you woke up."

"Let's not fight, please." Ubax turned her back on her mother and went back to sleep. After two minutes or so she tossed and ultimately settled into a comfortable position.

Medina watched her pretend to be asleep; she heard her false, small snore. Fresh as a flower, enchanting as a familiar tale; a flower so charming, so sweet to smell, so nice to touch, pleasant to ogle. *My own daughter. The brightness of dawn. The light of the sun. The sprout of my happiness, my delight, my obsession. My joy. My pain. My life. My death.*

"Aren't you getting up then?"

"What will I do if I get up?"

"I'll read you a translation of a story. Or we can go out together, you and I."

Was that a proposition Ubax liked? She opened her eyes and smiled a little.

"Where shall we go?"

There was a pause. Ubax made it known that she was fully awake. Then she said:

"I want my toys here."

Both fell quiet. The words remained suspended in the air like a hover-fly undecided whether to alight or not.

"I thought you wanted me to read you a story, the one I've been working on. Do you remember? You said you wanted me to read it to you as soon as I finished translating it."

"No stories today. I want my toys."

It seemed nothing else had any meaning this morning, everything else was inessential, unimportant, unnecessary. Today it was the toys which took absolute precedence over everything. Yesterday it had been, "I want to go and play with Abucar, Omar and Sofia," three children of her age who were notorious for the filthy words they made articulate use of, who taught her deprecatory anatomical nicknames for the General. Yesterday Medina hadn't allowed her to play with them. And today? Medina had no intention whatsoever of having an ugly confrontation with Idil, Samater's mother, who had installed herself in the house where the toys were and was expecting this kind of a visit; Idil who, rumour had it, had fired the maid, discharged the orderly and hired a new maid she hoped would replace Medina as Samater's wife. No, Medina wouldn't go to that house, although it was her own. She wouldn't go anywhere near Idil. Ubax might rage for half a day, crying, "I want my toys, I want my toys," but before the end of the day the two would find a way out. It was healthier that way. Ubax would learn better, too; she would cry less, depend less on Medina. They would also have a chance to talk things over. Medina had not yet revealed precisely what had taken place between her and Samater, but she had promised she would. Ubax held to that promise as to a swing, her interest swaying, and meanwhile Samater had gone abroad. "Father is in Algiers," Medina had explained, and that was that. Since in any case Ubax hardly saw her father as much as before he became a minister, his absence wasn't too great a mystery to her.

"You don't want me to read the new translation to you?"

"Which new translation?"

Medina told her which book she had chosen the folktale from and reminded her of Samater's reservations about the way she rendered interpretatively the title as "He" when it should have been "I am Everybody". But Ubax still couldn't remember.

"At your age you should have a better memory," Medina commented.

"You want me to be just like you, remember the titles of all the books I see, remember every story anybody tells me, remember who said what to whom. Leave me alone. I'm only eight years old."

To make her soften like bread dipped in water, to dissolve her rigid expression, Medina tickled her. Ubax kicked her legs in the air, then was quiet again like a child chewing the remains of morning's sweet sleep. Her mother was saying:

"Of course I want you to be like me. But I want you to grow up healthy and independent. I want you to do what you please."

"Why don't you let me go and play with Abucar, Omar and Sofia?"

"When you come home, your language suffers from lack of originality. You keep repeating yourself, saying the same thing. I want you to speak like an enlightened child."

"Why don't you let me go to school like the other children then?"

"Because schools teach you nothing but songs of sycophancy and the praise names of the General. And because I can teach you better than they. I can teach you things that will be of use to you later in life."

She kissed her. Ubax perfunctorily returned the kiss. Medina kept her weight off the bed lest it collapse; she supported herself on her elbows. Her body breathed the delight she now felt in her breasts. They hugged.

"You are a nasty little girl," said Medina.

"You are the nastiest mother ever."

They fell apart. Half-jokingly, Medina said:

"Do you really think so?"

"No, no, I don't. Do you think I am a nasty little girl?"

"No. I was teasing."

"I was teasing you. You're the sweetest mother there is."

Silence. Medina, in a flash, recalled the pain accompanying the pleasure of giving birth to Ubax. The hospital in Rome. Nasser and her father Barkhadle on either side of her. Samater didn't arrive in time because the airlines were on strike. The pain and the scissor-cut; and the complications which had arisen because she was circumcised. But the pleasure was more huge. Ubax was a lily on the shallow end of a swamp, whose water remained still although every now and again a wind stirred the surface, giving the feeling that one need smooth the pimples of the water with caring hands, that one need scratch the scabies of the diseased water. Something which in itself was pleasure-giving – like the pleasure-in-pain of squeezing the pus from a boil which has ripened, or like a delicate touch on the dark rim of a wound which has started to heal.

"Medina?"

"Yes, my sweet."

"What am I to you when you're not teasing?"

"You are the sunflower of my life."

"The sunflower of your life?"

"You nod your turbaned head in the direction of the pathtearing wind," she said, touching Ubax's head and playing with her hair. "How about this: You are the bird which leans against the air from which it seeks support; like the bird, you are the one who upsets and breaks the very air whose support you seek."

Ubax gamefully opened her eyes larger. Then she opened her arms.

In her mother's embrace she cuddled, she tickled, she crooned and felt comfortable being so close to her mother's breasts which were solt as a duck's. Medina was in her housecoat, her body still warm from the morning's tropical touch. But she smelt of cigarettes and this annoyed Ubax who pushed her away saying:

"You've gone back to smoking."

"I only had one."

"You promised you wouldn't. You promised not to smoke again."

"I'm sorry."

"Stay away from me."

Ubax's concert of moods, her symphony of needs and desires, the variations she could play at only eight years of age were worthy of a maestro. Her own father had once said: "A flower chokes on the bountiful waters which surround it. Too much of anything in the end smothers, too much of anything kills. Don't you know when love ceases to be love? You must leave breathing-space in the architecture of your love; you must leave enough room for little Ubax to exercise her growing mind. You mustn't indoctrinate, mustn't brainwash her. Otherwise you become another *dictator,* trying to shape your child in your own image. And you don't want to be that, do you?" To Medina, Ubax's "Stay away from me," her "I want my toys," were but expressions of a need to communicate; they weren't to be taken less seriously than an adult's asking for something, although in the light of her age and her enthusiasm, which wore away like perfume, one might deduce that if refused or defied she would react in accordance with the rules of the game she had learned. Most parents didn't take serious consideration of their children's needful aberrations. And there are a thousand and one commandments of which children are reminded daily and on the basis of which they must act. Any deviation is punishable with the cane, harsh language or no food for the child who disobeys these unwritten rules, which are basically authoritarian, matriarchal and patriarchal. As a child, Medina had suffered greatly. Being a girl, she was not allowed to play with her own brother, Nasser, and her grandfather said she would not be sent to school. But thanks to her father, she was saved from this and worse after her monstrous grandfather died. Samater's childhood had been one long unslept nightmare. His mother flogged him and pommeled him every time he answered her back; he remembered her rising to thrash him when he was twenty-one, before he went to Italy for his university studies. Ubax deserved better; Ubax was worthy of her love. Medina didn't want her to grow up with complexes, afraid that if a parent raised a hand it meant you would be hit. So she took a perverse pleasure in hearing her daughter's refusals, her well-articulated challenges stated in the frankest language and without fear, her defiances uttered plain as truth and her angry "No".

"What do you suggest I do?" she asked Ubax after a silence.

"I want you to promise that you won't ever smoke again."

"I promise, though I'm sure I won't be able to keep to it. In that case, you'll have to come up with a suggestion."

"Don't come anywhere near me when you've been smoking."

"But that's not fair."

"Then promise you'll smoke less often."

"I promise."

In the silence which followed, Medina's imagination grew wings and flew elsewhere. She saw Samater's mother Idil pointing an accusing finger at her and telling her son to take another good look at himself in order to know once and for all whether he was really a man, and if so what he had done with *his manhood*. Did he know that *she* was a woman and wife? How could *she* run things for him? How was it that the family's earnings went to a bank account in *her* name and not his? Who was the head of the family? How could he allow *her* to spend so much money on toys for the girl? Why didn't he let his daughter play with the other children, eat dirt like other children? When his mother Idil had talked for nearly an hour, Samater had turned to Medina and enquired whether or not she realized that she was flooding the girl with her love and understanding, breaking the small girl's dam with her affection. Give the child a chance to live a child's life, he concluded. It was then (Samater had just been appointed Minister of Constructions) Medina said that one reason why she opposed the present dictatorship was that it reminded her of her unhappy childhood, that the General reminded her of her grandfather who was a monstrosity and an unchallengeable patriarch who decreed what was to be done, when and by whom. "I want Ubax to be free of all that," she had said. "I want her to live her life like a dream. I want her to decide when to wake up, how to interpret her dreams. . . . " But Ubax was now saying:

"Are you going to get my toys then?"

"No, I'm not."

"I'll go and get them myself."

Medina let go her arm. "Go. I'll wait for you here."

"You know I can't go by myself. That's why you say that. But one day I will."

"I'm looking forward to that day."

"So am I."

Medina withdrew clumsily, like a defeated army in retreat, and the expression on her face was hard as water which has congealed into a wrinkled coat of rust.

"One day, I will have outgrown you, become independent. Then I will leave you."

"I look forward to that."

She had hoped that Samater, too, would one day say this, she had waited for him to outgrow her, outgrow his mother and breathe with his own lungs, have an affair with another woman, do something unexpected. Ubax, on the whole, was more promising. It seemed she had the nerve to turn a table, cheat a hand, build a lie. Medina was very fortunate, she told herself. No complaints really; she was lucky to have Ubax as a daughter. Think of the others. "Think of Nasser and his wife to whom a tongueless child was born; think of Dulman who did everything humanly possible to bear and give birth to a child; think of Amina who was raped and became pregnant with the children of shame; think of Atta the Afro-American who says she never uses contraceptives but aborts whenever she is with child; think of Sagal who is obstinate as unreason and says she will never have a child; think of Xaddia who wanted no child and her mother Idil who did want one, think of the millions whose children die before their first birthdays as a result of malnutrition; think how fortunate I am to be here with Ubax, an intelligent eight-year-old who acts and speaks like an adult, who remembers bitter quarrels and who, like an adult, passes judgment and condemns." Silent, tongue-tied, Medina withdrew, promising to help her daughter through her toilette if she wanted her to.

"Give me a minute," said Ubax, getting out of bed.

"I give you two. Aren't I generous?"

"You are sweet."

∙   ∙   ∙   ∙   ∙   ∙   ∙   ∙   ∙   ∙   ∙

Ubax had bathed and dressed.

"What do you want me to draw?" she asked. She had to hand all the necessary coloured crayons and paper onto the floor where she had seated herself.

"Anything," said Medina, using her index finger as a bookmark and looking distracted by the question. "Draw whatever you like, anything you want."

They were in the sitting-room which was bright with noon sunshine. Medina was sitting further from the open window, whereas Ubax was right under it, which meant that she would knock her head against it if she got up without taking care. The place was bare save for two armchairs and a couch: Medina couldn't stand the place to be overcrowded with furniture. She held the view that one couldn't think clearly in such surroundings; one's mind bumped into things, was distracted by the material things around. She liked to have the absolute minimum, so that she could pace her mind and walk it up and down the room, with an idea on a leash like a beloved pet, perhaps with a book open or an illustrated marker at the page where she had closed. She didn't mind the intellectual disorder of half-read books lying about, she didn't mind a book on the mantelpiece, a magazine by the bidet, a cookery book by the scales and a tin spilling with pens. It was difficult to turn this place into a tolerable habitat for her brain, since the Indian of the UNDP who had previously lived there had wanted it filled with chairs, divans, couches. When she moved in she had had to wash every nook and corner; she had had to unchoke the place by putting all the unnecessary objects in another room. The walls needed to be whitewashed because of the Indian family's tandoori-stained fingerprints. Thank God Samater wasn't an *arriviste* like this UN expert who had rented her brother's house. Thank God Samater shared her views about the need for internal space within a room's four walls. The world was a room. And it was the state of the room, whatever its shape, in which one drew breath and had one's most private or creative thoughts, it was the state of the room that determined the mental state of the person in it. She looked up at the ceiling, contemplated the open window and the blue sky, and reminded herself that this wasn't actually her place, that she was here *temporarily*. But why didn't she like it? Didn't she have the bare minimum? A few books she hadn't had time to read, a few toys thrown here and there. No, it was very orderly; this house was too bare. It wouldn't give anyone the chance to lose anything in it so that when looking for what was misplaced, one might accidentally discover something very precious which one was not searching for. One couldn't arrange one's thoughts, shuffle them like a deck of tarot cards and deal out precisely the hand one had in mind. But if she had installed herself here *temporarily,* was she going to return to Samater's? What was it that had frightened her off? Why had she moved out? She once told Ubax, answering the question about why she had left Samater, that she was like the man in the proverb who having lost a camel put his hand in his milk container to see if the camel might have entered there.

"Look." Ubax held her drawing up in front of her mother.

"What is it?" asked Medina.

"What's it about?"

"Can't you see?"

"Tell me what I should see."

"A man chasing another man."

"A man chasing a man?"

"Look at his face, the one running away. See how frightened he is. He knows he has no hope. Look at his face."

Medina looked. She didn't see a man chasing another. All she saw was something that might have been produced by a madman retracing the pathways which led to his insanity. She saw a drawing non-figurative, as Islamic art was symbolic and representational: a number of short and long Arabic vowels seemed to shake hands with consonants stood on their head.

"What do you think?"

"Interesting," said Medina, "very interesting."

"I knew you wouldn't like it."

"No, no, I do. I do like it." After a second or two she asked: "Why is he chasing the man?"

Ubax shrugged her shoulders. "You're always talking about people chasing each other. The General, the Security. . . . Now, what shall I draw next?"

"Draw the world."

"How can I do that?"

"Draw the contradictions of the world and its falsities," Medina mused, though she knew Ubax would not understand. "Draw the disgrace on our faces, the pain in the expression of the humiliated; draw the long shadow of your grandmother Fatima bint Thabit; draw the tunnel old age has dug in the bones of your grandmother Idil; draw the indifference on your father's face. . . . "

"What are you talking about? How can I draw all that? Nobody could," Ubax said. "What do you really want me to do?"

"I'd like to go back to my book. Won't you let me read in peace for a while? Why don't you go back to your room and draw whatever you like?"

"You tell me what to draw, then you can go back to your book."

How they tugged at each other's attention, like two clowns grinning their painted smiles at an invisible audience, one in harlequinade tights, the other waving a wand.

Medina reflected for a few seconds.

"Draw Sandra. Draw Sandra in an unguarded moment. Go on."

"That's not fair." There she was again: *That's not fair, that's not fair.*

"Why not?"

Ubax pondered then said: "You're either afraid of Sandra or you hate her, I'm not sure which."

That caught Medina unprepared and she hastily tried to correct Ubax's point of view.

"I neither hate nor fear Sandra," she said, spacing her words carefully.

"Then you're jealous of her, and that's even worse."

"I am *not.*"

"I heard you talking with Samater once. He said that to you and you said it wasn't true. But you are jealous of her, aren't you ?"

"What makes you think so?"

"You said you both hated and loved each other, you and Sandra. That's what you told Samater when I was eavesdropping on you that morning."

"You're a very naughty girl," said Medina.

Ubax had cast her net and caught her mother in it, not Sandra. Medina was undoubtedly uneasy about being confronted with the truth of what she might have said privately about Sandra, the Italian journalist with whom she, Samater, and Nasser had gone to university in Milan.

"I don't hate or fear her," she repeated. "Honest. I swear."

"You've also told me that Sagal doesn't hate or fear losing to Cadar and Hindiya. They are friends as well. But I've seen Sagal's face when she talks about them. You both look the same when you're talking about people you're jealous of. I can tell. Shall I draw what you look like then? Or when you're with Xaddia?"

"No. It isn't the same. You don't understand. You're still a child when it comes to understanding these things."

"That's what you always say to win a point. It's not fair."

Medina took Ubax's hand to reassure her that all was well and that she should not be offended or hurt. She made as if to prepare her lap for the child to sit on, but Ubax did not move; and Medina continued:

"The fact that Sandra is a member of a group which I personally consider unhealthy for her, the fact that she deliberately misinforms the world about what is happening in Somalia – those are the reasons I don't like her. But I certainly don't hate her, and I am not afraid of her. Why should I be anyway?"

"I don't understand anything any more," Ubax said, going back to her drawing. "After all, I'm only eight."

Medina's gaze became distant like a migrating bird. She was seated with an open book in her hand, a book which she could consult like her palm about her pre- and post-Samater days and a present without him but with Ubax. Her gaze was vacant and vague but was asterisked like an annotated horoscope with present, past and future lines which crossed, touched and ultimately joined in ink-stained dots of concentration and with a touch of finality. Ubax squatted not far away, her young angelic face wrinkled with effort over her drawing, a crayon between her teeth, one of which was half broken. She cast her eyes, like a net, in the direction of her mother, hoping to catch a glimpse of that far-fetched look so that Medina would help her: how could she draw, how could she capture and present the streak of guilt in the eyes of a subject which she traced with a pencil? Medina, however, had her worries. Her attention was focused on the life-line of the palm spread out for her scrutiny. That took her to the pre-Samater days. Here Sandra was prominent as the two figures engraved like an incision on her right palm, whereas the line of her ideology mapped the eighty-one crossing the eighteen: O God who art in Heaven, how many are Your names? Only ninety-nine – Amen! Then her nomad eyes were caught and instantly framed by Ubax's stare: would Medina kindly advise her what colour to do the aeroplane?

"Dye it socialist red, my darling," she said to her attentive daughter.
"What?"

Medina searched for signs of irritation in her daughter's eyes and was disappointed not to find any. Neither was there that quizzical look Medina had hoped to produce in her.

"Dye it socialist red, with the red star of victory (and bureaucracy) prominently placed in its proper central position. And in the background trace lightly a crescent, like a half-cup. Don't forget the sword whose blunted edge is good for female infibulation."

Ubax was definitely angry. Ubax was so angry she threw the crayons aside and tore the drawing into shreds small as teardrops. She then kicked at one of her toy trains which had been in the corner and out of her focus. When the noise had died down she went to her mother, defiant as her rage, and asked for an explanation.

"What are you talking about, Medina? Kindly tell me what you're talking about."

"Politics as usual."

·　　·　　·　　·　　·　　·　　·　　·　　·　　·

"Politics in Africa and the Third World," wrote Nasser in the letter Medina was now reading, "is but an insipid goulash of western and eastern ideologies. The Soviets mastermind the acculturation of the African and the Asian as much as the other foreign powers did before them. But I would not say that they are 'imperialists' (though of course that is open to debate): the difference is that the Russians lack the exploitative socioeconomic factors which enabled the other imperialist powers to become who and what they are. As to whether or not one is a 'guest' in *their* ideology, well, let me say this: you can change the ingredients of your cuisine and, if you wish, put more or less salt in it – who cares! Sandra will criticize you or the Soviets, so will your friends the intellectual left. Tell them you are African; tell them the General is a fascist and prove it to them; tell them that the Soviets, the Italian Communist Party and the world's left have become befogged by the General's declarations, the General who laughs at them when their backs are turned and says to his incestuous circle, '*Come li ho fottuti tutti quanti.*' Challenge them thus: why do Europeans grant the decorative title 'Marxist-Leninist' or 'Progressive' to any African who declares himself one when they haven't had a chance to study his credentials? It reeks of condescension. As for the Soviets, they got what they deserved. They led their *little boy* by the hand and introduced him to their friends. They used him; they cleaned his coast of its fish; they had their base, etcetera, etcetera. He used them too. He made them train his clansmen; he used them to build himself a system of security, water-tight as the KGB. Each imagined the other hadn't the slightest idea what they were up to. In the end, it is the Soviets who are the losers. Imagine being laughed at when your back is turned. Imagine the jokes *he* cracks to his incestuous circle. I am not surprised that Sandra completes the incestuous circle. Why are you so uptight? What has Sandra done to make you so angry? Has she elbowed you out professionally? Do you remember the folktale in which an Arab agreed to share his tent with his camel – and you know what in the end became of that Arab? Cheer up. I am coming to see you. First, do me a great favour and call Dulman to warn her that I am coming. Ask her to prepare and wait for me; tell her I am coming to reactivate the lines of communication. Tell her to hold on to the latest delivery, not to send it, but tell her to prepare all the tapes meanwhile, to copy them as clearly and without disturbances as possible; let her know that the last ones received here had noises in the background and I had difficulty selling them. When will I come? I'll take the first available flight. So cheer up.

"So Soyaan is dead? And nobody knows what has become of Loyaan? Someone saw him briefly in Rome in the back seat of an embassy car. He looked ill, this person said, and his cheeks were puffed up. The others are in prison; so is Siciliano; Koschin is broken and foams at the mouth, you say, unable to hold his saliva. And Samater is Minister of Constructions. I suspect you are as hasty as the others. He is the son the clan has come to claim, eh? I am sorry, but as far as I am concerned he was a non-starter. It's not surprising that the General appointed him Minister. The General wisely lends the sceptre of power to those he can recover it from with the greatest ease. And where is he? In Algeria, or back in Mogadiscio? His mother, you say, has taken up residence in your house, fired your maid and locked the drinks chest with a rusty padlock. One lives and learns. You say she's preparing a surprise welcome for him? Granted, that woman is capable of stirring up enough trouble to make Samater lose face, job, honour. Neither of you seems to realize that there is one thing society will not forgive him: for disobeying the authority of an aged mother. Idil represents traditional authority, and it is in the old and not the young that society invests power. If he as much as raises his voice or a finger, the man is gone as a slaughtered cow. But why did you leave him?

"How is Ubax? My son is well, though silent as a closed tomb. His mother and I see each other now and again; we meet when we visit our son. Father is well; I haven't seen him so healthy before. He's in high spirits; he has his friends, his books, all the pleasures which make him forget about his exiled status. He's working on some FAO project. More when we meet. I embrace you and send you and Ubax my warmest and tenderest love."

·   ·   ·   ·   ·   ·   ·   ·   ·   ·   ·

It was a little after midday, and the sun raged like an old man denied his rights, an old man who had nothing to lose or save. Ubax was on Medina's lap, exhausted after a few minutes of kicking a ball about, bouncing it on the ground. And her mother had spun for her a tale of a million and one nights and spread out its fabric, a tale of silky original-ity. Medina had spun for her daughter a tale of cambric fineness, woven out of the threads of her colourful experience and knowledge. But why did she always tell Ubax tales whenever the two were alone and the little one was about to ask a difficult question like "Why did you and Father part?" Why did Scheherazade spin these thousand and one nights of a tale? Was it simply to save herself from that monstrous authoritarian murderer of a king who would have dispatched her to her creator? Did she in any way gain expressive articulable humanity in the telling of the story nightly? Not only that, but she saved other lives, the lives of those many poor women whom he would surely have killed. Scheherazade had been the most inventive of women, no doubt. Medina stitched for Ubax out of her patches of wordy threads a canopy under which the two would tent to protect themselves from the wicked eyes of the vicious, the evil tongues of the mean and the gossipy, the envious lot.

"Tell me another."

"Which one?"

"The one called 'He'."

"The one by Chinua Achebe?"

"Yes. Please."

Medina's eyes became smaller as she concentrated upon the details, the incidents which gave life to the Igbo story. Ubax fell silent and contemplated the sky: she saw an eagle fly further and further into the heavens, purposeful as life. Could she draw that? she challenged herself. Could she capture that? An eagle chasing his catch? Could she?

Whereas in Medina's mind the world was reduced to a room.

T W O

· · · · · · · · · · ·

Sagal was fretful like a fish in agitated water, malleable as a piece of metal under prolonged heat. She would exude enthusiasm for someone or something, then, like a lamp whose wick had dried, the fire in her would extinguish itself and die completely. Sagal seldom finished anything she began. There was no doubt that she was an exceptionally gifted girl. If challenged by her mother or her friends, she could show her worth. She passed examinations easily, made friends with facility, but she forgot things as fast as she learned them. Less than a year ago, she bet a friend that she would win something at the East African Regional Swimming Championship: she was medalled by a head of state whose visit to the country coincided with the event. On another occasion she won for herself and for Somalia a bronze bust of Lenin. Now, in less than a month, she could have the opportunity to represent her motherland at the Africa-Comecon Meet to be held in Budapest. But would she remain level-headed, could she keep a low profile until the moment of departure, would she stay out of politics? Would she follow the advice of clandestine opposition, carry the banner of a banned movement and be the spokesperson of an underground organization? Most important: would her patience stand the test, would she remain faithful to her dreams? Or would she, as she threatened, prime the canvas of dawn with slogans against the General's regime and if caught end up in prison?

"My daughter hasn't the political conviction, courage and maturity to paint the morning with anti-government slogans," Ebla said. "Her political pronouncements are inarticulate. And she isn't artful; all the knots she ties sooner or later come undone. It's my feeling that she hasn't a balanced enough mind to sculpt a living portrait from the clay of her river-bed, but could certainly do that if she put her mind to it." Ebla's smile was light like the water of childbirth, her teeth white like diluted milk. She had appeared vexed and fell silent. There then came a fly big as the summer sun and she chased it away.

"My daughter is faceless like a windmill and spins fast. Her memory is bad, too. Yes, she's spoken to me of her plan to leave on a government ticket for Budapest and her desire to defect to Rome, London or somewhere else in western Europe. But before she is seeded, before she is allowed to compete, she'll have to seal her mouth, train harder for the contest, take part in the activities of the District Revolutionary Centre where one chants the numerous praise-names of the General and where one is as false as their revolutionary password. Possibly she will put in an appearance at the Centre, maybe for a day, maybe two; then she'll vanish, irritable as ever, angry with herself. She'll unchain her tongue and utter the most unpalatable truths. But she will not, I repeat, she will not paint the morning with anti-government writings."

Medina, Sagal's friend and intellectual mentor, held a similar view: Sagal had not the patience to follow anything through to its end. "Sagal moors at a bank of convenience and stays there as long as the waters are shallow, as long as she can swim away at an instant's notice. Docked in comfort, she then goes underwater and resurfaces when least expected. In fact, had I not pushed her and forced her to take herself seriously," Medina would continue, "had I not fetched her, given her a lift to and from all swimming sessions, had I not helped her train, Sagal would never have won either the East African Regional Swimming Championship or the Lenin Medal. Water forms rust, water makes things go rotten, she would complain. Water makes one's mind inactive. Where's she going – Budapest, then Rome? I've never known her to follow a thing through to the end. If she needs help, she knows I am at her service."

Sagal's closest friend Amina showed no sign of surprise when this gossip became insistent as the contractions of labour. It certainly was not the first time she watched her friend filch the dream she had fleshed with inspired fantasies. As always, Amina searched for and found fault with Sagal's plans. "Sagal is a river changing course, country, beds, master and lover. She is the river which floods the farms it has watered. Where will she go? To Budapest, then London? It's not the first time she's talked of that. No, nothing will surely come of it: she will not paint the dawn walls with slogans against the General. But her rivals might, her runners-up might. It's either . . . or. . . . "

Sagal, standing goose-pimpled by the springboard, insisted that she was ready to dive into the water of life. Her body was fresh, like early morning water inviting the splash of children to break its crystal innocence. Sagal: a skimmer of a swimmer! She argued that this time she would hold on to the raft carrying all those hopes and dreams which had been casketed in her all these years. She would cross the water-barrier and reach the other bank which, as far as she was concerned, offered more opportunities to a young girl of her age and background. "How I look forward to putting the sea between myself and the peninsula!" She would drop anchor in Europe and in that clearer waterbed would spread out her lint mattress of talents. She would lie there comforted by the water's ebbing. . . .

"Its like trying to read a child's scribbles on a looking glass," her mother Ebla said one day. "I find your plans clumsy and heavy-handed."

"You wait and see."

"Your plans are as confused as they are unripe. Today this, tomorrow that. You're as easily influenced as a stay-sail. For example, Barbara has offered to help if you need her assistance, hasn't she? Anyone suggests something and you say, 'Right, that's what I'll do.' To go to Budapest as a participant in the Africa-Comecon Meet was Medina's idea; to defect to Rome and not return is Barbara's and I know that. But whose idea is it to paint anti-government slogans? Is it Amina's? Or her rivals whatever-their-names?"

Sagal held her breath and didn't speak; her features went rigid as if she were standing under a cold shower. She did not rise to her mother's provocative statement. Instead she left and hid herself in her room and re-read the letter from Barbara. Its passages flowed in her mouth like melted gold, one sentence leading to another. Barbara: a gem of a friend who in the letter promised she would build a bridge all the way from Europe to Africa. "You are the pillar which shoots out of my life's wreck," she wrote, "a pillar shaky but solid." The letter suggested that Sagal call as soon as she arrived in Rome. If there were visa complications or the like, Barbara would herself join her in Budapest and fetch her. "Come out of that prison whose warden is the Generalissimo. Come, my dearest, come to where you can do anything to your heart's content. Come to Europe. *Come and be what you want to be.*"

Sagal now closed her eyes, hoping to exile from her mind all she did not want to think about. She needed calm, she told herself, in order to take good care of her floating light in a night of forecast storms. However, the instant she started to row alone, the lights went out and she was in complete darkness. She heard the noise of oars combing the waves. And she shouted:

"Who is it?"

.   .   .   .

"It is I," said a woman's voice.

"Did you turn the lights out yourself, Ebla?"

"No, I didn't. It's the usual thing: power-failure."

"Power failure? Every night for the past six months?"

The darkness was very severe: this gave Sagal time to hide all evidence that she had just smoked a cigarette. The first match Ebla struck did not provide enough light to thin the severity of the darkness; she held the burning stick in the air for as long as it would survive the breeze. Then she lit a second. The items in Sagal's room now were recognizable.

"Ah, there!" Ebla spotted what she was looking for.

"What?"

"The lamp."

She struck another match whose flame caught the wick's unoiled end. She set the lamp on Sagal's dressing-table.

"Are you all right, Sagal?" she said.

"Yes. Why do you ask?"

"Why are you in bed so early?"

Sagal hid her writing-pad. "Thinking. Yes, that's it. I am thinking."

"Not about what to write on the walls of dawn, I hope. Nor about your defection to London. You must be careful. In this country, thinking wicked things about the General is criminal. One of your uncles paid for that dearly. Do you know the full story? Do you know why he was punished so severely? Your uncle said the General wasn't God. That earned him a life sentence."

A mesh of shadows lined Ebla's face; some of them started there, as part of her, while others were cast by her headdress or her profile. The deeper shades were caused by a wretched worry, constant in the past couple of years: would Sagal end up in prison? The light of the paraffin lamp chased away the feebler shades of purdah and for a brief instant Sagal could see her mother's now genuine smile as different from the one she had first worn when delivering the warning. Then a waft of wind made the light bow away. A little later, the wick straightened and stood sharp like a crayon.

"And you? Why are you home so early?"

"I'm going out."

"Where? Where are you going?"

"You never tell me where you go or with whom, or what you do, so why should I?"

"Fair enough."

Ebla closed the door. Turning, she winced. She was facing Che Guevara's portrait which now occupied the space on the wall reserved for Sagal's latest favourite hero or heroine. One day, she read her mother a poem by Che. Ebla said she did not understand its significance. How could she? The poem was written originally in Che's mother-tongue; for years, it had lived in the borrowed garments of an English translation which, in turn, was further rendered into Somali. Ebla couldn't appreciate the design and the tapestry of the man's ideas and metaphor. She argued that had someone read her a poem by the Sayyid or Qammaan, or one by an Arab from medieval times, she might have got closer to wrestling with or grasping the poet's intentions.

"How was business today?" asked Sagal changing the subject.

"Bad as usual." (Ebla was thinking: *Is Sagal in one of her quiet moods?*) "And you, my Sagal, what did you do today?"

"Nothing."

"How do you mean? Did you not train? Did you not see anybody about the trip you're planning to embark on? Are you not well?"

Sagal fell silent. She looked fixedly at something in front of her.

Where her stare ended, Ebla found when she followed it, was a wall on which were pinned a number of stills she had selected with care. They showed Marlon Brando in various scenes from the film *Queimada*. Sagal, with endless enthusiasm, had spoken of the film to her mother whose interest and curiosity she aroused by telling in part an untellable tale. Ebla had many questions: who, in the first place, was the hero? What was the revolt that he had led? What were the other revolutions taking place at the same time in other places – in particular Africa? Sagal said her mother's questions were naive and impertinent. Then Ebla said that she had a more pertinent question: why is my daughter taking a perverted interest in faraway revolutions in Latin America, Southeast Asia, South Africa, etcetera? This made Sagal so irritated that she walked away. But Ebla insisted her daughter listen, so she held her by the arm and said: "*Queimada* did not even pass the censor's tight marking here; a heavily cut version was shown for one night only and then, on security advice, removed from circulation and banned the following day. And you did not see *even* the mutilated version. So why must you hold the banner of the revolutionary when you are not properly initiated, why are you at the head of the list of student agitators? Do not hold the banners of banned underground movements, do not tire your arms, but lower your head and be careful."

Silence.

Ebla feared her daughter's inborn violence would awake in her dormant ghosts which had remained locked up and forgotten in the cellar of her mind. She, too, as a young woman, had once rebelled about being chained; she, too, had said NO. Shades of doubt met the dust her feet had then stirred as she left behind her the dwelling of her people. But the air had been purer, and there was no one ready to shoot her for her principles which were all personal. Whereas Sagal was playing with the fire of politics. So by way of advice, she now said:

"The land is mined, and this General is out to kill. Duck at the buzz of the coming bullet; duck, my dearest, before a stray one gets you, duck and dodge. Do you argue that the city is full of walking corpses? We all know it. Who doesn't? And please do not speak of *conscience* to me. I, too, have one. But I wear mine inside me and not on my forehead. I know many men and women in Somalia who wear their *con-*

science inside, pinned to their underthings. Private as one's private parts."

Another silence.

Lost tempers she hoped would be immediately regained. With this in mind, Ebla began to walk back and forth, explaining her position as mother, as one who cared, an older person, more experienced and therefore a connoisseur. Sagal, silent as her mood, had started to replace Marlon Brando's stills with a sequence of Malcolm X and Martin Luther King. "Who are these people?" asked Ebla. Sagal explained in detail who they were. "Forgive and forget." And then they hugged, and then they kissed. Each promised the other the necessary understanding. Whereupon mother spoke in understatements and daughter quoted a poem by an Italian. After this came a needed silence. Then:

"You haven't answered my question."

"What question, Ebla?"

"Are you in bed early so that you can get up early enough to paint the morning leaves with anti-government slogans? Or have you decided to listen to your mother's advice for once? Will you return to the university? Will you train harder for the swimming competitions? Will you stay out of politics?"

Sagal got out of bed. On her way to the record-player, she and Ebla for a second met and touched, like silk passing a hand. Both were tall, mother fleshier, the cheeks of the daughter hollower and her breasts larger. Of late, Sagal had lost weight and Ebla had gained more. "Men in most African and Middle Eastern countries like their women fat. They prefer your size, Mother, you who wear your wealth of fat. I? I would feel like a fattened cow being readied for slaughter if I gained another ounce."

"You haven't eaten, have you?"

"I have not."

Sagal switched the battery-operated player on and listened to it turn, but held the record in her hand while she checked the speed. The record was Stevie Wonder's latest, which she had borrowed from Medina.

"Do you think anyone will believe me if I say that Sagal doesn't know how to make an omelette? A girl of your age and times who doesn't know how to make an omelette! But never mind. That's your affair. Do you want me to cook something for you before I go out?"

"No, thank you."

"Are you on a diet?"

"No, I just don't feel like eating. That's all."

Through the see-through pyjamas, Ebla could see her daughter's pubic hair, wild as a safari, untrimmed-curly and unshaven and shocking (she, Ebla, like most women here did not wear hair on any part of her body other than the head). She could also see the bend of her daughter's well-seated breasts, and the nipples which insisted on pushing through. Above the record-player there was the bookshelf which, despite its smallness, was impressive: Ebla had never seen so many books in one room. It was Barbara who had given her the books and the record-player as her parting-present. Through the see-through. . . .

"Are you in love, Sagal? Is there a man you're in love with?"

"What man is worth falling in love with, pray?"

"Are you or are you not?"

"Don't be ridiculous, Mother. All the men worth falling in love with either live in exile or are in prison. Both categories are outside my reach. That's why I want to go abroad: to join the ones already in exile."

"And if you can't?"

"I'll paint the morning leaves with slogans and go to prison. Possibly I shall meet some of them there."

"You are mad."

The wind's winged invasion shook the room. This coincided with the instant when Ebla was most certain she wouldn't be able to convince her daughter to drop her stupid decision to stage an unorganized single-handed rebellion against the present dictatorship. She went to where Sagal had been standing and leaned against one of the speakers. She stared at her daughter's naked feet whose squat toes twitched obscenely. But what was obscene? To walk barefoot made Sagal feel light and natural, like sleeping in the nude in the privacy of her room. Whereas Ebla believed that a woman's body is her *pudore*: she must wear it with modesty. A woman must not boast in vain about it nor must she take pleasure in the extrovert exhibitionism of those Europeans who, having chased the sun down to its summer abode, delight in catching it, and bathe nude in their triumphant sweat. Sagal saw it differently, "It's the Islamic concept of *cawra* that is my great concern," she would begin. "Yes, I'm referring to the canon laws which decree that to nobody other than her own husband, her brother or other women should a woman expose any part of her body save her feet, face and hands. See? A man isn't burdened with the weight of his body, every cell in a man is not an instigator of sin in another being. A woman's body is tempting sin and Satan dwells in it. A woman's body issues evil messages to the eyes which behold it. A woman's body estranges man from his Creator. A woman's body is better hidden, as a corrupted Arab parable has it, like the reverse side of the moon." Now Ebla interrupted:

"If I pay your fare to Rome, London or any other city you fancy going to, will you promise to stop taking part in these anti-government activities until your departure?"

"You needn't pay, Mother. I'll make them pay."

"But I am willing to pay on condition that – "

"No conditions. You needn't pay. You needn't spend a penny on my expensive tastes and moods. I hope to win first place in the competition and make *them* pay for my trip to Budapest. So you needn't worry about the ticket or any other stupid expenditure."

"What if they catch you while you're at it, painting, tracing the lines of his mouth, his – "

"A long term of imprisonment. No scandals, no trials, never fear. In that case I'll be in this country with you, forever in prison until this dictatorship is toppled by another military dictatorship, and so on and so forth."

Sagal had meanwhile put on Stevie Wonder's *Love Keys* and gone under the sheet again.

Then: "Enjoy yourself if you go out, Mother."

· · · · · · · · · · ·

They had separate rooms and each created a habitat to suit herself. Ebla had Koranic writings on her walls and a prayer rug hung there which, although made in the Republic of China, had the prophet's tomb outlined delicately under Arab inscriptions. Ebla's room was plainer than

Sagal's; she slaked the hardness of the bare walls with smiling photographs of Sagal-as-child, Sagal-as-teenager, Sagal receiving medals of recognition for her swimming and other talents, Sagal of the present miming Sagal of the past, Sagal as photogenic as she was lovely. Ebla's room was larger and was furnished simply. What did not go well with it, according to Sagal's friend Amina, was the double-bed studded, in a vulgar way, with pillows in flower-printed cases. The room, otherwise, was spacious as it was sunny bright. The two had different tastes, too. Ebla was sumptuous in her love: "I am a parent, Sagal is not. Parents are more generous in displaying their affection." When Sagal was small. . . .

When Sagal was very small, Ebla had mounted the child's bed on steady ground, a bedstead supported by legs which took root in the very earth in which the little one had her milkteeth buried. Ebla planned to give her daughter the happy childhood which she herself had not had. She hoped one day Sagal would be able to narrate her own life in capital letters of joy. Perhaps every now and then there would be a slight change in the stage-directions. Some scenes needed alteration, in particular those which told accurately of the tribal courts convened backstage to put Sagal fully in the legal custody of Ebla. Sagal's father, Awil, lost the case which Ebla won. "When an eagle flies off in triumph with its catch, it discovers that the sky has no place where it may alight calmly to pick the bone from the flesh." To give Sagal a firmer bedstead and a securer homestead, Ebla contracted another marriage. Alas, this lasted for only two years, in which period she bled a stillborn babe as yet unboned before the end of the second year. But he was a wonderful father for Sagal. Such a generous soul, too. A soft-spoken man, with cold feet and cold hands but a heart warm as love. Anyway, before his soul bid its body and home for fifty years farewell, he dictated into his will a clause which left to Sagal, to whom he had given his name (it transpired the courts of law had no authority to endow her with his name), a five-room house, precisely the one in which they now lived – the three other rooms were rented out to a large family of seven. Ebla was also left the shop. One day, not long ago, this:

"It is God's mysterious ways which have to do with who is blessed with intelligence, patience or children. You can't say I haven't tried. All my life I've done all I could to make your life the happiest, all my life, Sagal."

"How very vulgar of you, Ebla, how very commonplace! I've always thought of you as special, a mother of a different breed, an older *Medina!* Listen to your gabble, your worrisome prattle. You're as plaintive as Idil herself. Shame on you."

"Shame on whom? You swim as though you are wrapped in water, breathe as though you are the air. I just want to remind you that some of us are mortal and realize we are. Have you ever considered the position of a worrying mother who clutches her daughter as though she were life? Have you ever considered the case of a Dulman who has done everything possible to have a child and failed? Or the situation of an Amina with 'children of shame'? Or even Nasser, with a speechless temptation, a child born without a tongue? Some of us are mortal and know we are, and therefore believe in miracles and in traditions and in the continuation of logical arguments. And besides. . . . "

"Besides what?"

"Medina, too, has had a child and is married."

"I used that as an example."

"I'm doing the same, no more and no less. Somalis have a proverb: *Intuu toggaaga ku kiri lahaa tolkii ha badiyo!* And that is precisely what she has done."

"You're quoting the proverb out of context."

"I'm not."

"Yes, you are."

There followed a bitter argument. Ebla finally made amends; she conceded the point, admitted she had quoted the proverb out of context and then said:

"Come, come, let's not fight."

But at the best of times, when Sagal's mood was a colourful flag in the high winds of happiness and Ebla's business was flourishing, the two would link arms after such an argument and go further into the night which opened up like the teased lips of a vagina. The masked opaqueness of the hour would open like a tunnel of softness to welcome its own breed. Ebla: motherhood of exemplary worth to a daughter with whom she was blessed at nineteen. They would go together through the entrance of the night's starry doors like two feathered doves, proud in their plumage – two vessels of purity. Like egret, like cattle! They would keep pace with each other and together move in the direction of the nodal knot within the circle which their presence created: an image as fascinating as the whirlpool of a herdsman's dust. The slight wind of the night's sleazy feeling, Ebla's silky touch, Sagal's voice a sort of whisper, coming in waves of words out of which one could build a castle of meanings. Ebla, once provoked, would say: "A myth is butterfly-fragile. Brush the silky dust off it and you kill it. So is motherhood. Sure, she and I disagree on a hundred and one things. Of course, we do. Each of us speaks for a generation, each of us is like a clock keeping its own time. What one gains, the other loses. What my daughter does not have, I have. But we are two persons with two different backgrounds and two separate minds. Although the hands of clocks might not point at the same second, there is no doubt the difference is minor, particularly when both are functioning well." Ebla's face would become tense like that of someone from whom a sneeze found no release.

"Like egret, like cattle!"

"Like fish, like water!"

Ebla's fingers were magic-light, very inventive, always thinking of combinations, reviving things. (Just like Nasser, Medina commented.) "Mother's fingers are magic-light like a circus hand's," Sagal would say. "Look at mine: they are so clumsy. They are thick as only the brain-tubes of idiots can be, heavy as though swollen with pus. The knots my fingers tie will easily come undone. Also, I am dreamy, and Mother is practical. And a major difference: children."

"If you had another child," Sagal would say, "what name would you give it?"

"God has not willed it." Ebla's jaws opened and closed.

"If you had a son, let's say – play the game, Ebla, what's wrong with you?"

"Don't blaspheme."

"What name would you give him if you had a son? Come on. What's wrong with you, Ebla?"

She would give in and say: "Dulmer would be his name if I had a son."

Sagal had by then accepted nature's patrimony; her body, like a por-cupine's, shot out quills of femininity, one after another. Her body fi-nally surrendered to the invasion of womanhood, before she even knew it.

"And you, what name would you give your child if you had one? Tell me, Sagal."

"I'm not going to have any child," she answered.

"I used to say that. Before I had you, I used to say the same thing. So what name would you give the child? Play the game by its rules."

"But I am not *you*. And since you don't want me to blaspheme I won't say any more about it. But I am not you, neither are you me."

"It is God who gives, takes and decides for us. He is the maker of miracles. He carved a woman out of a man's crooked rib. He blessed Mary with a marvel of a child by the name of Cisse without her coming into contact with a man. I would certainly be happy if you were to give me not only one child but as many as ten."

"And carry water in sieves?"

"I don't understand. Please explain."

"I'm not an aeroplane out of which pops a parachutist every time one presses a button."

Ebla, saying nothing, unlinked her arm and walked away. Sagal ran after her. And without explaining anything the two joined arms again and walked on as though nothing had happened. Affectionate as pi-geons, their cheeks (and not their hearts) feeling the chill of Mogadis-cio's humidity which was sticky as dried sweat, the two trod on the hem of the retreating night. The mother would every now and again hesitate and hold back; the daughter was brave as her age, bold as the years she had seen roll away (she would be twenty in a few days, and her birthday would coincide with the New Year bonfire festivities): the daughter not only brave but urbane and suave as well. The night's skirt, laundered by the National Security Service, lay spread out like a canvas to be primed with Sagal's graffiti against the General. Right there and then (Ebla would scream: "Sagal, darling, don't blas-pheme!") the mother would pull the under-threaded hemp apart so that Sagal's hasty scratches became unreadably meaningless and insig-nificant. *Basta! I am fed up,* she was thinking. *I shall finance your trip anywhere and do anything else you ask of me. I prefer that to your languishing in a prison here. It would make my maternal heart bleed, and my menopause would advance on me.* But Sagal was saying:

"Our heads and hearts are what will divide us, in the end."

Ebla slowed down. "Heads and hearts, did you say?"

"Whether the seat of reason is the heart or the head," Sagal said. "You obey your heart's dictates; I, my head's."

In the void, Ebla's legs like a sleepwalker's tried in vain to regain the strolling rhythm which had already been lost. Sagal had upset everything by letting her arm go limp, which she did too shockingly quickly, too suddenly.

"What time is it?" she asked.

"What time do you want it to be?"

Fade-out: slow and torturous. The two parted, each went her way.

•   •   •   •   •   •   •   •   •   •   •

It was half past midnight. Sagal was alone in her room reading *Oblomov*, a novel she had borrowed from Medina. She turned a page, then turned her mind away from the page and stared at the title of a book she had promised Medina she would read, for comparison, after *Oblomov:* Flann O'Brien's *At-Swim-Two-Birds*. But why was anxiety for Ebla's return suddenly kicking so furiously inside her like a seven-month-old pregnancy kicking at its mother's ribs for recognition? True, she hadn't worked out in detail how she was going to leave the country, but why this sudden anxiety? Certainly she wouldn't sit up all night waiting to tell her mother about this affair which had just begun to turn sour. If anything, Ebla always heard of her affairs from other people. Perhaps lurking in the fertilized soil of her imagination was a seedy feeling which, although bizarre, hadn't taken shape . . . a feeling, something to do with a premonition, say, a decision. . . . Would she, after all. trample on dawn's laundered skirt? Or carve a child out of a ribless one-night stand, out of the non-starter of an affair?

Sagal started, for suddenly all was bright with light. She switched hers on. The fluorescent tube hissed non-stop, persistent as a dung-beetle's drone. She put the book away, got out of bed and stood in the doorway. The night closed its eyes, while the inhabitants of the city snored away their dreams. Somewhere in the neighbourhood Sagal could hear Dulman singing her most favourite song, "Even Cain killed Abel". Yes, Sagal would wait until Ebla returned. It was unfair not to tell about her most recent important decision. She looked at her watch. It was late. The family of seven, the tenants of the other three rooms, had turned in probably hours ago. Then what was left of the night finally descended between the trees and flowed into the patio; it had spread itself as lightly as a spot of light.

Then there came the noise of a car being braked. The engine stopped. And Sagal heard a woman's voice. The car's engine started again. Thank God, thought Sagal, Ebla had taken a taxi, which meant that Bile hadn't accompanied her home in his car. Sagal often had difficulties speaking to Bile. She would be able to talk to Ebla alone and unescorted. She told her heavily beating heart that it would feel lighter after she had spoken what was burdening her thoughts. But what was that?

The street door opened. Ebla entered, quiet as a hedgehog. She saw that Sagal's light was on, her door ajar, and that she was standing in the doorway waving whispers of welcome.

"Did you have a good time?"

Ebla, badly needing to use the lavatory, excused herself but was hesitating when Sagal said:

"Go, go. I'll close the outside door."

"He's parking the car properly."

"Who?"

"Who else? Bile."

Sagal thought it best not to say anything. She went back to her room and her *Oblomov*. Just before dawn broke, she finished reading it. She had decided to save O'Brien till the next day when she heard the outside door thud shut. Ten minutes later Ebla came to her.

Sagal told her mother of the future she had invented for herself. A future without obstacles, a future beyond the future of a future – what she dreamt of doing and what was going to happen to give meaning to all that she held close to her heart. In plain, simple language, she would defect as soon as the plane hit Rome, Barbara would come and fetch her and they would go together to London where Sagal would register for a course at a polytechnic and would do some modelling to earn some money. What was Ebla's role in this? What could her contribution consist of? Nothing. Just moral support and her maternal blessing.

"Medina gives you what she considers 'the classics' of the European tradition, advises you what to read. Barbara offers you air-tickets. Amina the support I can't give."

"They are my friends."

"You wouldn't want to let them down, would you?"

"Of course not. Nor would I deliberately fail you, Mother."

"You have more trust in humanity and friendship than I do. Friendship, my dear Sagal, is but a thread thinner and less durable than the umbilical, and it snaps when unnecessarily stretched beyond its limits. You must nurse it, walk with care as though you have survived a delicate surgical operation. Times being what they are, you must also be prudent. Do you understand what I'm talking about?"

Ebla's questions opened unfillable holes in Sagal's planned defection. How would she get to Rome in the first place? Shouldn't she wait until she won the swimming competition? What about her rivals?

"I don't want you to misunderstand me: I want to go down in history as contributing to a cause. I'll do all I can to make it a reality. If I don't win the competition, then I'll reconsider joining the clandestine movement. Yes, I'll tie the thread-end of my future to that of the country."

"A clandestine movement?"

"Why not?"

Ebla's worry about her daughter's motives in joining a clandestine movement against the General's regime grew more acute, assumed grand proportions which in a manner of speaking made Sagal worthy of her pride. What were the choices open to her daughter? To take part in and win the championship, then leave; or to join a clandestine movement. In either case Sagal hoped to contribute to a national cause. So why should Ebla be selfish? It was definitely preferable to the situation depicted in the stories travellers to East Africa and Italy brought back, stories poor in human contextuality, anecdotes of horrors of degradation and prostitution; young Somali girls from decent families beating the streets of Nairobi, Kampala and Dar es Salaam like vigilantes without uniforms listening for unusual movements which late-night solitaries create. At least Sagal's high morals wouldn't let her condescend to join that degraded racket of frustrated exiles. To be a saboteur of the ambitious type was preferable. Her ambition knew no limits, her daydreams knew no end, her goals were unreachable. She was never realistic, never walked with her feet on the ground; never woke to reality when she had dreamed.

"What are the names of the two girls you fear may unseed you, the ones you consider your only rivals?"

"They don't matter."

Ebla remembered telling Sagal one day – jokingly, of course – that they could hire a witch to disable her rivals, then she need have no fear and could go to her Budapest or wherever. Sagal had said that was wicked, adding: "You shouldn't think of things like that. I'm going to win."

"Tell me. What are their names?" Ebla insisted now.

"One is called Cadar, the other Hindiya."

"Suppose one wins and the other comes second, what will you do then? How will you accomplish your dreams, your Rome, your Budapest and all?"

"I will dream again and again. Medina told me that Beydan before she died saw a dream in which she wasn't the central focus, and therefore she died. The focal point of the dream is always myself. I'm not Beydan. And I don't dream my own death, neither do I bewitch my rivals. The dialectics of my dream are such that I see the contradiction in the future I invent and what life's reality has in store for me. Besides, there is another door I haven't entered. . . . "

Sagal seemed quite certain of what she wanted. She had never appeared so sure as she did tonight, and that delighted Ebla all the more. But what if the conditional turned out to be the categorical, the dream a hard fact, and Sagal woke already unseated, no longer the champion, no longer rowing in the direction of the lighthouse that had lit her future, but towards a vulture perched on the point of the obelisk? What if. . . .

"You once told me," Ebla said, "on the eve of Soyaan's death, that this regime doesn't kill but makes one's death meaningless."

"Did I say that?"

"Yes. On the eve of Soyaan's death."

Sagal shrugged her shoulders as if to say, "So what?"

"On the other hand," Ebla continued, straining towards her point (for she didn't quite know why she had quoted that), "this regime constructs to order a life becoming a hero or heroine worthy of the nation's respect and love. Soyaan, in any case, will go down in history as a hero."

Sagal held her breath and waited; she stood, so to speak, on the tips of her toes, a marathon-runner ready for the blast of the starting-pistol.

"The mosaic, the collage, the parts from which a hero or heroine can be assembled like a machine have been imported from a foreign country that specializes in consignment orders of the required product after painful research into local conditions. In the same way it is possible to unmake anyone. Just as Medina was offered the pen with which she wrote herself off; just as Samater was appointed Minister of Constructions a week or fortnight after Medina was put under a banning order."

"Wait, wait," said Sagal.

"What?"

"Had Samater refused to accept the nomination, fifteen or twenty of his clansmen would have gone to prison. Or so the story goes. The General gave him an ultimatum; Samater's clansmen were told: 'Convince him to take the ministerial position, or else I will destroy you one and all.'

"'Compromise and accept my nomination or I'll imprison all your clansmen.' That's the politics of the day."

"Why are we talking about all this, Ebla?"

"Because I want you to be wiser than the history you read in books. Because I want you to see well in an ill-lit place. Because I want you to rise when meteors fall. Because I want you to take your humiliations like bitter medicine. I stand by you now. I will collaborate as much as I can. If you tell me to auction the shop, I shall do so. Your life, however, is your responsibility. So do with it what you please. Just tell me what your wishes are so I know. Teach me. Prepare me. Please. But do not torment me."

Ebla got up, her cheeks moist with tears of tenderness. The scene was very touching. Sagal stood up too: the column of filial strength on which Ebla's world rested. Ebla went to the door. After reflecting for a good minute she asked:

"You're going to Medina to talk about your dreams, when it's day?

Or are you going to practise at the swimming-pool? I mean, would you rather I woke you before I go to the shop?"

Her tears spread and stained Sagal's conscience. Sagal was sad she hadn't the courage to share with her mother the secret of her non-starter of an affair. But she decided it didn't deserve her mother's worry as well as her own, so she instantly dismissed the thought. She wouldn't let a Wentworth George of a nonentity make a mess of her life. Her mother would be startled by the foreignness of the name and would probably say: "George who?"

"Dream well, then, my dearest," Ebla finally said.

"Sleep well."

T H R E E

· · · · · · · · · · ·

Poised against the vast emptiness of a door which had just opened, the figure of Sagal was charted like the reflection of a reflection in a mirror. She was swaddled in the bright vapour of noon. Medina looked up from her writing-pad: the day's brilliance dislodged her vision, her general perception of things. But she looked up at Sagal: on her face there was a vague smile.

Sagal thought that Medina looked fatigued, too tired to be engaged in anything she might have wanted her to take part in; she wondered whether her friend and mentor was in a position to give the level-headed advice she had come to receive. What Sagal couldn't have known was that half of Medina's attention attended to a possible phone-call: Nasser had said he would call if he wasn't coming, in case he was unable to get a place on tomorrow's plane to Mogadiscio. The maid had come and gone, and probably wouldn't return for quite a while since she had to queue up for sugar, for salt, for bread and for meat. Medina hoped that Nasser would remember to get her a bagful of cheese and a few bottles of wine; one had to pay prohibitive prices if one were lucky to find them in the open market. And Ubax? There were moments of tension between them when they discussed whether or not Medina would go to collect the toys from the house they had moved out of and in which Idil had taken up residence and full control. Ubax, very angry, went to her room and began talking to herself.

"Ciao, Sagal," said Medina, courteous but firm. "Take a seat."

"Ciao!" But Sagal stood there, taller and thinner; straight as a telephone pole and just as immobile.

"Don't you want to sit down?"

"Where is Ubax?"

"She's been beastly. I asked her to go to her room."

"Poor thing!"

"What about me?"

"What about you? You and Ebla are the same: martyrs!"

"Mother-as-martyr is a traditional concept. We're no exception to the general rule. But you can't deny that we're a great improvement on Idil, on Fatima bint Thabit and a great many others."

"I won't deny that. In fact, I feel it's wrong to speak of you, Ebla and Idil in the same breath."

"And how is Ebla?" asked Medina.

"She is well and having an affair with that awful man Bile. It makes her plaintive, her expression mournful. She knows how I feel about it. As a result we had a minor fight."

"Why ?"

"I'm going abroad, I said. If I can't, I'll paint the dawn with my dreams."

Having said this, Sagal came forward and took an armchair opposite Medina. She watched Medina light herself a cigarette.

"You're going abroad?"

"Briefly my travel-plan is: Budapest, Rome, London."

"How will you do it? Do you have the money, the tickets?" Medina asked.

"I plan to win the national swimming championship, go with the group, then defect."

"What if Cadar or Hindiya wins?"

"In that case I'll write my warnings on Mogadiscio's dawn walls."

Sagal is half-child, half-adult, thought Medina. *To me she is the bridge I crossed yesterday, the muddy and violently wavy river which I swam through.*

"And how will you do that?"

"I've told you how. I'm serious this time."

"Since I don't remember, I'm afraid you'll have to tell me again."

Medina remembered something Sagal had once said to her: that the world is a swimming-pool; you either drown in its overwhelming tide or you swim through and become a victor wearing a watery grin, squinting slightly but nevertheless triumphant. "Life is lived in the parenthesis of diving and surfacing."

"It's very hard for us mortals to follow the trail of your thoughts," Medina added, echoing something Ebla said the previous night.

"What's hard to follow?"

"First you have to win the contest, then get to Budapest, then Rome, then London. If things don't work out according to plan, what happens? You've already reached the highest rung of the ladder when you don't even know where the ladder is."

"My mind is set on a trip abroad. If I don't go, then. . . . "

"Let's talk about all this when you've won the competition. There's no point swimming in a dry pool or counting uncaught fish."

Not only did Medina sound dismissive, she was ready to change the subject and talk about what she had in mind herself. She meant to tell Sagal that Nasser was likely to turn up before the week was out; she meant to ask her young friend if she would like to come for a meal one day to meet him; she meant to suggest that Sagal speak to Amina to tell her to let the present swallow up memories of the past and that they should meet, Amina and Medina, to talk things over and reconcile several facts. Sagal stole a furtive glance at Medina, who was at that moment feeling like a person who had outlived a ruinous trauma, Medina who was counting to herself the names of *the ten* who began with her this arduous journey which they all hoped in their different ways would enable them to give political expression to their lives, their education, their dreams. Some had survived this terrible journey of self-discovery through sheer manoeuvering and tact; some failed the test and ended up unhappy and compromised; others encountered the naked violence of power and died – Soyaan, bless his soul!

As for Medina: "The General's power and I are like two lizards engaged in a varanian dance of death; we are two duellists dancing a tarantella in which they challenge their own destiny. He is as aggressive towards me as I am towards him. He uses violent language and so do I. He calls me 'a dilettante bourgeois', 'a reactionary'; I call him 'fascist' and 'dictator'. Why has he never put me in prison? The General is primitive (to use another aggressive, violent term) in thinking that women are not worth taking seriously, which all the more proves that he is backward and fascist and, worse still, an uneducated imbecile." But she told herself she should be very cautious since she was one of those who survived the ruinous trauma, cautious about what she said, cautious whom she talked to. Sagal? *Sagal is the bridge to an unbuilt future. Now she is the river. Tomorrow – who knows?*

"I've always won, so there's no reason why I shouldn't win this time too, is there?" said Sagal.

"There is Cadar, there is Hindiya."

"Sure, there are Cadar and Hindiya. What about them?"

"And there is *you*."

"Me?"

"One is, on occasion, one's own enemy, the undoer of one's own knots. Sagal, you won't deny, is as inventive as the weather, Sagal changes like the seasons."

"My mind is set on this trip."

"You won by a very small margin last time. And they both seem more disciplined and more determined. Of course, they don't have your inventiveness or your quickness of pace and body movement. But you dwarf your own greatness."

"I'll win this time. I promise you."

"I'm looking forward to that and I'll be the first to congratulate you. But I have doubts about whether your interest in this trip abroad will constantly remain in your vision, like a distant lighthouse to a lost ship."

"Ebla is plaintive; you, doubtful about my capabilities; and Amina is very unhelpful, not forthcoming. Cadar and Hindiya are my only hope of decent survival-of-the-best-and-fittest."

"Cadar and Hindiya, whom you hate as much as you love."

"Don't talk nonsense," Sagal said.

"How are Amina and her child?"

"Growing healthily and happily together after a fashion."

"Tell her to come with you for a real meal when Nasser turns up, will you? I think I've been unfair to her. After all, she was the one who suffered most and whose choice, whether to compromise with her parents or not, we should've respected or at least seriously considered. Tell her I'd like to talk to her, apologize to her."

"Do you know when Nasser will be here?"

"I hope his arrival will coincide with your winning the championship."

"How I look forward to seeing him!"

"You were tiny when he came years ago."

Sagal turned away and the room stretched before her like a road, menacingly empty and unfillable, with undusted corners and un-painted walls; a room dull as the UN man who had lived in it and left it in such a state. Sagal was shocked when she came to help Medina sweep it, clean it, make it habitable. Medina hadn't yet called the con-tractor who said he would come to deal with the ceiling, the roofing and the pipes which leaked; the smell wasn't there though, thank God, Medina had got rid of the odour of curry-powder and the unhygienic stench which reminded one of overdone tandoori, chapatis or puris soaked in the oily broth of oriental cuisine. The rust was there, too, the rust which coated the doors' hinges and made them creak. Meanwhile Medina allowed herself, with tranquil self-abandon, to think of noth-ing but rested her thoughts like the bones of an elderly person bending with the tension of senility.

"I saw Sandra the other day," Sagal said, "in a chauffeur-driven car with a bodyguard seated in front. Just behind her car was the ideologue's car. Master and mistress . . . when I think of one, I auto-matically think of the other."

"When was that?"

"Day before yesterday, I think."

"The incestuous lot," said Medina and thus thought she dismissed the theme.

They fell silent. Their thoughts flowed like a well-written saga, and each lost her hand to a convenor of meetings – the queen of memory: Medina found herself sitting by a fire which consumed ashes of coal; whereas Sagal let her "convenor" lead her by the hand and tell her a few home-grown secrets. She shouldn't have mentioned Sandra's name at this point, something told her. She should not have. Cadar and Hindiya; Sandra and Samater; and now the maid whom Idil had crowned as the bride-to-be of her son. . . . *Two is a number of possible contraries,* Sagal was thinking. One pairs up an unlikely couple and then one is shocked to learn that the match-making didn't work. Those who know one intimately and know all one's shortcomings can do more harm than anyone else. Sandra came as a welcomed guest of Medina's but she overstayed her hospitality and abused it – as her grandfather the colonialist had in his turn done to Medina's grandfa-ther: both became inconvenient to their hosts. In a manner, Atta did the same. Two is the number of possible contrasts that can be paired.

Two is an evil number. One, divine. Three, a crowd? A holy number? A blasphemous number?

"I suppose you saw Atta, too?" asked Medina.

"Yes."

"With Wentworth George?"

There was silence. The ball was in Sagal's court, but instead of playing it she walked away unsteadily like a drunkard, conscious of hostile eyes trained on her back. On the screen of her memory flashed the scene of her single encounter with Wentworth George, that one evening which had bred so much worry in her lately, the one night he thought would allow him to make a claim on her. But Sagal wasn't going to tell Medina how preoccupied she was that she might be pregnant, for that night she had used no contraceptives, taken no precautions at all. Now Medina towered above her, tall, strong and powerful; and Sagal felt weak, small and broken. She sent her thoughts out on random errands and hoped that something would emerge from all her efforts. What did return worsened the situation: myriad thoughts which needed a home in which to roost. And when she sat down properly to sift them, Sagal discovered her head was empty as a tin drum and it beat thunder-like to a detonating rhythm, the known cluster rhythm of a migraine's percussion.

"You saw Wentworth George, did you?" she asked after a little while.

"He didn't see me but I saw him. And I overheard him."

"How was he?"

"He seemed accomplished."

"What do you mean?"

"He was excited that a portrait photograph he had taken of the General is going to be in the newspapers one of these days. He was overexcited."

"And you say he looked 'accomplished'?"

"Professionally, I mean. He didn't look as dejected or deranged as your description of him and he had no problems with the Security Service either. As a matter of fact, he was with a man who just might belong to another extension of the incestuous circle."

Looking up, Sagal saw that Medina's stare had softened. Now what could she say to explain away her silence and her embarrassment at the mention of Wentworth George's name? Should she tell Medina of her weird sensation that she was with child by this man whose wounded soul she tried to medicate that one night, a man for whose state of downtroddenness she had felt sympathy and as if to pacify him slept with him? What if she was pregnant with the child of a man who had accepted to compromise with the General's regime? What disasters one's destiny constructs!

"Do you have any tampons?" Sagal suddenly asked, without thought.

"Tampons?"

"Yes. The city's chemists have run out of them."

"I think I have some reserves. The chemists have run out? How symbolic! Do you need them immediately?"

"Not really. But if you could let me have some before I leave."

Sagal had recovered her mental balance remarkably well in such a short time; she didn't look at all shaken or worried as she had feared she might. She reasoned that everything depended on whether or not she was pregnant, after all, and that she wouldn't know for at least a couple of days. Two is not only a number of possibilities and probable contrasts, it is a number with a private as well as a public utility and mundanity: a married couple; lovers; a two-piece suit; to second a motion or a nomination. Three is in another domain totally: trinity; the three oaths of Islam — *wallaahi, billaahi tallaahi*; the three divorce-pronouncements of Islam which are a man's prerogative; a lovers' triangle; incest with one's offspring; three also means two against one and thus creates a situation of unfairness. Sagal remembered the Somali saying that what is seen by more than four eyes is considered of public knowledge and what is heard by more than two ears is no longer a secret. And the General's power did not only divide to rule but it put together forces of diverse political trends and unified their interest. His power played one off against another. It was this fascist regime's maltreating Wentworth George which made her defy her own rules and sleep with him. Did that mean that now he was accepted, feasted and offered a job by them she wouldn't want to see him, would have nothing to do with him and would never mention his name or have his child?

Medina lit herself a cigarette, striking the match quietly. Sagal looked up and their eyes met; they smiled at each other but remained silent, neither knowing what to say. Maybe a door would open, a door of a possibility neither had considered knocking on; maybe either would crack a joke and would loosen the bowels of the tension each felt. . . . And lo and behold: Ubax was there in the doorway sucking her thumb of solace.

· · · · · · · · · · · ·

"Ciao, Ubax!"

"Ciao, Sagal!"

But Ubax didn't come forward, didn't approach, although Sagal's movements suggested an embrace. Smiles all round. Three faces like the phases of a moon: a young crescent, a half moon and a full one.

"What have you got in the hand you're hiding behind your back, Ubax?"

"Nothing."

"Come and show."

"Nothing."

Medina chose not to challenge, not to insist on being shown. The world, represented by the room's four walls, shifted, the world revolved round the sun, the sun revolved round the universe and the two together gave birth to the image of the wicked serpent biting its own tail. Should she sing the *ninnananna,* the *huuwaayaa-huuwaa* of a lullaby, or should she give way and give up the challenge? The feeling returned, the feeling which had to do with her being the one person who had survived a ruinous trauma, an arduous journey, a disastrous duel; she felt as though she were playing with people who weren't seasoned by time, whose experiences were limited if not shortlived. She was livid. Imagine being one among the few with sight in a blind country. She gave Sagal advice, books, told her what to do about her complaints. She consoled her about her premenstrual complications and her dysmenorrhoea as much as she had to to find scientific answers to Dulman's fibroids and hot flushes; what to do about a child whose eyes don't focus, or a mother suffering from eczema. Why should she have answers to all these when she couldn't deal with her own child sucking her thumb?

Then out of the corner of her eye she saw Sagal had got up and gone to Ubax with whom she exchanged kisses on the cheeks. Sagal bent to speak to Ubax, but the little one wouldn't at first reveal what was hidden behind her back. She dwelt unnecessarily long on the absence of her toys, spoke about the fact that Medina wouldn't let her go and play with the neighbours' children although she used to be allowed to play at least once in a while with the other children near the house from which they had moved. Ubax said she was fed up with it all.

"Yes, but what are you holding?"

Ubax took her thumb out of her mouth and brought her other hand from behind her back. She was clutching a tampon. Heavens! And while stealing a furtive look in Medina's direction, Sagal saw that she had hidden all evidence of having smoked a cigarette.

"What are you doing with that?" Sagal asked Ubax.

"Just playing with it. I was going to dress it like a doll."

A passing flash of sun, like the beam of a lighthouse, fell on Medina's forehead, illuminated it and then vanished. Medina pushed the ashtray under the chair without comment.

"Did you hear that, Medina?" said Sagal, holding out the tampon. "Did you hear what your daughter said?"

"No," she said as though not interested.

"She was playing with this tampon since you won't let her play with the neighbourhood children, won't send her to school like the other children. She says you won't let her act like a child of her age. You've moulded her mind and made her speak like an adult, she says. No toys, no dolls. Tampons."

"Did you say that, Ubax?"

"No, I did not say that."

Sagal smiled sweetly enough to charm a fish out of the sea.

"Don't let anyone misquote you," Medina said. "Speak up. What did you say?"

There was a long silence. Ubax stood straightbacked like a sentry at attention and looked her mother in the face.

"I want my toys, I said." Her voice had assumed a graveness one would never have credited her with.

"But we've spoken about that. Besides, your uncle Nasser promised to bring you some new ones. So please go back to your drawing and show us what you've done."

Sagal looked from one to the other. Medina lapsed into a foreign language to explain to Sagal the ugly risks going to the other house involved: she would rather save everyone the embarrassment of a confrontation with Idil and the new maid/wife. At any rate, she hoped Nasser would arrive with a caseful of toys before tomorrow evening; and by then Samater would have returned from Algiers. She hoped that in the meantime Ubax would calm down. But Ubax didn't. She behaved strangely, went about shouting at the top of her voice.

"I want my toys," she chanted. She burst into tears and sobbed and sobbed and sobbed. Then she felt ridiculous, seeing that she couldn't change her mother's mind; Medina remained as placid as ever. Ubax rushed out of the room.

"Why don't you get her toys for her?" asked Sagal.

"She'll have to learn to live without certain things once in a while."

"I'm sorry about misquoting her. I didn't mean to."

"That's all right."

"Tell me: is it because you don't wish to unseat Idil the queen-mother and earn the anger of her disordered mind? If that is it, I understand. Although one thing needs to be said."

"What?"

"Mother-as-martyr or mother-as-the-all-knower. In the final analysis, what is the difference between yourself, Idil and Ebla?"

"I would rather not go into that."

"Two as an even number is an evil number."

"Please. Let's not go into that now."

Sagal's theory of antinomy inventoried other possibilities. Why would she rather not confront the monster in the den she had dug for herself? The place was her own, the house was in her name, so legally she could call the police and have Idil thrown out if she wanted. Was she afraid of the scandal? It wasn't her own mother and, in any case, she had parted with this woman's son, her husband. "The General's power and I are like two lizards engaged in a varanian dance of death"—the emphasis on power and not on the General; power as a system, power as a function. Was Idil part and parcel of that power?

The sky would fall in on anyone who upset a pillar of society – in this case Idil. So Medina would go about with care; they were like monitor lizards in combat, each dancing the tango of its strategy, chest to chest, face to face. . . . She would rather be like the matador who gives way when the bull rushes at him blind as red blood.

"Theory of antinomy? Two as an evil number? Have you been reading Flann O'Brien?"

"Yes," said Sagal who was up on her feet, a cigarette stuck between her teeth. "I Oblomoved while I read this Irish classic. I never know how to thank you. Ebla thinks evil of you and Barbara when she sees me so engrossed in a book."

"Whose idea is it that you leave the group in Rome and defect to another country, and eventually go to London? Barbara's? Is that why your mother is plaintive? Does she blame me or Barbara?"

Sagal was not listening attentively but had been executing a brief dance. There was silence for a while before she stopped. Medina was very impressed and the gorgeous finale of small gestures and beautiful body movements had continued. Sagal's cigarette dropped from her mouth but rather than bending to pick it up she crushed it under heel.

"Whose idea is what?" Sagal asked.

"Either to write your name into history or out of it heavyhandedly."

"It's mine. Certainly not Barbara's. Can't I think for myself? Can't I initiate an idea?"

Sagal picked up the crushed cigarette and dropped it into the ashtray. Medina waited, not wanting to be accused of being aggressive or envious.

"Haven't you been corresponding with Barbara?" she then said.

"What has Barbara to do with all this?"

"I just thought. . . . "

"You just thought what?"

A faint wind blew in, moist as the monsoon, and Medina turned the words over and over on her tongue like an experienced cook tossing a coal of fire from hand to hand. She was a shepherdess who mustn't lose sight of the goats she was minding for she was in wolf territory. In the end she decided not to say anything. Sagal:

"Two is a number of possible contrasts: you and Idil, on the one hand; you and Barbara/Sandra on the other. Two lizards engaged in a varanian dance of death. Two is an evil number!"

"I think I've lost you."

"My theory of antinomy is concerned with the basic contradictions inherent in the elimination of one's direct rival. You are in a ring with Idil inasmuch as you both have the same aim: to possess Samater. On the other hand, there is Sandra and yourself: professional incompatibility. To confound issues, you talk of political contradictions on her part, about the fact that she, being European and Italian, can never understand the inter-tribal, inter-clannish allegiances according to whose dictates the country is run. Let us go further: there is Atta the Afro-American in another ring not very far, and Sandra is the defender of a title she won as Queen of the Incestuous Circle."

"And you, where are you in all this?"

"I am in another ring and my challengers are Cadar and Hindiya."

"I see."

Here Medina was drowned in a meandering stream of reminiscences, she was flooded with a rivulet of memories which abandoned her on the bends and creeks of a ditch. Would someone fling her a lifebelt? Would someone stretch out a little finger for her to hold on to? And her mother Fatima bint Thabit was there, veiled from the top of the head to the tip of her toes in the dark traditional lengths of *purdah*. Noons in those days were hot and pungent with capsicum; noons in those days smelt of garlic and onions and quarrelsome children. And there was a bedridden monstrosity, Medina's grandfather, who had large eyes and a mouth ravenous as a locust's. His cheeks had pouches like a baboon's and he chewed with tobacco-stained teeth and breathed venom. He was unkind to Medina and to the women in the household; he was the cruellest man these women had ever known. He was the typical authoritarian patriarch. "A woman needs a man to intercede for her and present her to Allah; a woman's God is her husband," he would go as far as misquoting the Koran. She hated him. She had been four or five and Nasser eight or nine and the two plotted to kill him but couldn't for they could never find a poisonous concoction stronger than the venom he breathed. He lived to a hundred and ten, astraddle two centuries in which he played his authoritative part. He was Sandra's grandfather's grand challenger when it came to freeing his slaves: "You free my slaves, and to show gratitude to you and your church they embrace your faith. Before long, my emancipated slaves and I become your chattel. This is not the way it will happen. Give me time to think it over." Meanwhile, he thought of a plan. He asked his slaves, men, wives and children to gather in the courtyard for he said he would like to speak to them. He decided to emancipate them all and he arranged a trip to Mecca, passage paid there and back. He knew that once freed by him they would still remain his slaves. They set forth before Felice, Sandra's grandfather, returned to inquire whether he would free them or not; and then he came back wealthier and titled as Xaaji. Most of his friends and family were gentlemanly about discussing the topic although they had reason to believe he had sold the slaves when they got to Mecca. Felice wrote out a favourable report and sent it to Rome. Gad Thabit and he struck up a friendship of sorts; in their rationale there was no conflict of interests between them. The challenger and the defender became one, Sagal's theory of antinomy would explain.

"You and Samater, for example . . . "

"Yes?" Medina said. "What about Samater and me?"

"I cannot envisage you and Samater as the two lizards engaged in a varanian dance of death. Unless and until your interests converge and focus on Ubax. In that case. . . . "

"I'm listening."

A pause. There was the smell of rain in the wind. And Medina thought of Nasser saying that she shouldn't waste her precious time guarding the eye of the needle but that she should keep an eye on the camel itself.

"Are you with me?" Sagal was asking.

"Yes, I am," Medina lied, not quite hearing but thinking: I *wonder why she never mentions Xaddia's name? Xaddia who is definitely the strongest of Samater's family. Imagine: Medina and Xaddia entwined arm in arm in a dance of death!* Sagal continued:

"My mother and I are two clocks which keep different time. What hers loses, mine gains. We are not two lizards engaged in a pugnacious dance of death. I give way or she does when we come to the decisive hour. Reason: because we don't aim at taking full possession of the same position, neither do we unseat one another like you and Idil, or like Sandra and Atta. You could kill Idil and she would you if she had the chance."

"And why did we try to poison our grandfather, Nasser and I ?" She had spoken with consummate emotion about how much they had hated Gad Thabit and how they had plotted to poison his food, but failed.

"Because he had taken full possession of your young souls just as the General has taken possession of the nation's – and you planned to kill him to recover that for which he would himself crush you."

Medina liked what Sagal had said. She was proud like a teacher whose pupil had finally made it, although she thought it best to keep quiet, lest her voice betray a streak of jealousy and tension. She remembered that someone had set fire to the wing of the house in which she was born. Was Grandfather Thabit behind the conspiracy? He used to say that Fatima bint Thabit his daughter (and mother of Medina and Nasser) had "picked the fruit the Catholic Church discarded. Her life will rot as has the tree whose fruit she has eaten." And why did he need to resort to this violent method? "The fruit the Catholic Church has discarded!" This was a reference to Medina's father Barkhadle who (rumour had it) was found on the doorstep of the church, an abandoned child wrapped in rags, a child whom the church brought up and schooled in the Christian tradition in a country wholly Muslim. He was a foreigner in his own country because of the faith he held. Fatherless like Christ, he would joke. A gem of a father to her, and to Nasser, too, although Nasser wasn't from his own blood; Nasser's father had committed suicide because that bedridden monstrosity believed his prattle of senility should be received as law, that no one – not even his sons-in-law – should dispute his authority.

"There is another thing."

"What?"

"You deny Idil's right to become the principal star; you deny her the authority society invests in her. What is more, you wouldn't want her to invade Ubax's rosy sleep, to prick the little girl's intactness and hurt her to the depth of her veiled soul. Which is, in my opinion, the reason why you left Samater."

"What are you talking about, Sagal?"

"I've reconstructed the whole thing and find it holds."

"What have you reconstructed?" asked Medina.

"Do you remember the episode which so upset you that you burst into angry tears, in fact the only time I've known you to break down? Do you remember?"

"About the middle-aged Somali-American who brought his wife and sixteen-year-old daughter to introduce them to the country of his birth, the poor man trusting naively and paying for it dearly?"

"The poor man whose sixteen-year-old daughter had been circumcised without his consent and who considered his life a great failure and instead of explaining it to himself or his wife simply committed suicide?"

"That was tragic," Medina said.

"I was the bearer of the sad news, remember?"

"Yes. But I knew the man. I went to university with his sister. He was a very sweet person. It was the most hurtful thing; I had not heard anything so awful in years. But I don't remember bursting into angry tears. Why?"

"And a day later, what did you do a day later?"

"How do you mean, what did I do a day later?"

To the fore of Medina's mind came vividly the scene in which she received the tragic news. She had had an argument with Idil over whether or not Medina and Samater should pay so much attention to Ubax, whether they should spend so much money on the girl, on her toys. Idil at some point said that she would take things into her own hands and show them what she was capable of. But Medina couldn't now remember whether Idil was present when Sagal relayed the tragic news. But what happened the following day?

"The UN man moved out of here a day later and you came to get the keys from him. You then decided to move because when I met you the next day, you made an allusion to that effect. And on the fourth day, you packed your things and Ubax's and moved in here."

"That is very clever," said Medina. "The new Inspector Poirot."

"I should think more of Maigret."

"How so?"

"Maigret's approach is more cerebral than Poirot's puzzle-solving technique. Poirot turns up at the right time and so do his solutions to the cases."

Medina was impressed. Shouldn't she review her impression about Sagal as half-child, half-adult, and tell her that she was the only one who came anywhere near guessing why she left Samater? Sagal as the bridge which connected her with her own yesterdays or Sagal as future, a possible replacement. . . . The two faced each other, each thinking slightly about the other. They both looked up. Ubax had returned. She was hungry and wanted to know if they were too.

"Meet you in the kitchen," said Medina.

·   ·   ·   ·   ·   ·   ·   ·   ·   ·   ·

Sagal wore her youth as the season wears the weather. In a manner of speaking, Medina's and her own life histories would travel a small distance together, would go parallel with one other without ever meeting, like two rivers which empty in the same ocean. Each considered herself a one-parent child: in Medina's replay of her recorded past, the maternal voice was hardly there; and when present, it was barely audible, a soft mumble of hypochondria, her remembrances painful as caesarean birth. In Sagal's, it was the voice of the father which was hardly there. Medina was heavy like a word of wisdom; Sagal, light like a *burzelletta*. Sagal's life was full of anticlimaxes and missed appointments and one would encounter Ebla, or Barbara, Amina or Medina or one of her friends in every blind alley as a lone champion cyclist meets an enthusiastic fan urging him on; in most cases, there was Ebla hiding in the silvered side of the mirror; and Sagal, blind like a cave-fish, would swim in the pools of an unplanned future. Her moods, her thoughts, her likes and dislikes would unpredictably give way to furies, rages, changes of direction. "Sagal doesn't give sufficient time for a spider to weave her a solid master-plan of expediency. Neither does she have the calm vision of an ant; nor the internal peace of a duck," Medina would say.

"Medina's timbered construction," Sagal would comment, "has been invaded by white ants and so the structure of her dream has weakened, the underframe has given, the trunk and flooring have become faulty. If you look further you will find yourself that the half-landing hisses with gaps big as a moon twelve days old; the shaft, the banister and columns have fallen in. A life in ruins. But she herself stands firm, this is a miracle, firm and strong as her intentions."

Sagal, in a dug-out canoe, naked and wet with tropical sweat, would in her imagination loosen the chains that tied her hand and foot to a tradition where women were commodities bought and sold, and were sexually mutilated. "I am a river synonymous with its water. I am a woman synonymous with subjugation and oppression." And Sagal's eyes would roll in a vague movement – like a slippery peeled onion. Here the wings of Medina's mind, like a flighty bird's, would stir: her precious regatta would sail past: a loving father, a monstrous grandfather, an entourage of cousins distant and near, Nasser, Samater, friends, her own mother, and above all a life whose formative years were spent in Europe. Medina would finally emerge with a bowerbird's souvenir of colourful feathers. She spoke four European languages quite well and wrote in two; her Arabic was as good as her spoken Somali; she considered the wealth, literature and arts of these as her own; she loved these foreign cities in which she took residence as much as she loved Mogadiscio. Medina was accustomed to receiving the best. In Europe, whether in Stockholm or London or Rome or Paris, she was the beautiful black goddess; in Africa, whether in Mogadiscio or Ouagadougou or Dakar, she was envied for her cosmopolitan ease, her African pride and her openmindedness. At twenty-three she had a degree in literature, and had published the occasional piece. The wind would comb her hair; a touch of hand would smooth her wrinkles of unnecessary worries; Nasser or her father would telex the money she needed; Samater would dial a number and have her served anywhere. Was anything wanting? Was there anything she would miss? She would confide in her father, in her brother or in a close friend like Sagal. "I fear the descending knives which re-trace the scarred wound, and it hurts every instant I think about it." She experienced the dolorous mixture of pleasure and pain at the age of twenty-four when she brought forth a flower of beauty – Ubax. What pain! What pleasure! There were infibulatory complications, she bled a lot, she had second, third and fourth labours. . . . "If they mutilate you at eight or nine, they open you up with a rusty knife the night they marry you off; then you are cut open and re-stitched. Life for a circumcised woman is a series of de-flowering pains, delivery pains and re-stitching pains. I want to spare my daughter these and many other pains. She will not be circumcised. Over my dead body. Ubax is my daughter, not Idil's."

The sun was now overhead. Medina looked at her watch, then at Sagal and remembered that the maid had not returned from market. Maybe there was no meat, no flour, no sugar or no rice. The telephone rang. With visible anxiety, Medina went to answer it. It was not her brother Nasser but another man, a colleague of Samater's. He wanted to know what had happened, why she had left Samater, whether there was any likelihood of them getting together again. But then he asked if he could take her out to dinner. Medina hung up on him. It was the umpteenth time a colleague of Samater's or a mutual friend had called. It seemed they had been waiting for the chance. Who did they think they were? Then just as she took a seat near Sagal, the telephone rang again. She asked Sagal to go to it. No, no. Not Nasser. Another colleague of Samater's. What did he want? Would Medina like to go to a party? Did they never tire? "Tell him I am not here." Sagal went to misinform the man. The outside door opened. The maid returned.

·   ·   ·   ·   ·   ·   ·   ·   ·   ·   ·

"I don't know if you care to know but they say a man has sandwiched himself between you and Samater. Love at first sight, *un colpo di fulmine,* fast as a thunderbolt."

"They who?"

"The gossip-spinners."

"Do they give the man a name, an identity?"

"They haven't as yet."

"Stupid idiots."

At this point, the maid came in. Medina and Sagal fell silent and looked up. The maid's expression was flat as the tray she brought. The poor thing had stood under the sobbing shower of dust for two and a half hours in a long queue and had come home with only a kilo of sugar and another of flour. Would Medina get her the red ration-card for VIP homes, a card issued only to ministers and other dignitaries' wives and which exempted them from joining queues for essentials such as sugar, oil, flour and foreign cigarettes? The maid set the tray down, and moved about impatiently. Did she want to repeat her request, remind Medina to call on Minister So-and-so? Medina thanked her in a manner which made the maid understand that she was being dismissed. The maid went out. Medina bent forward a little, put three spoonfuls of sugar into Sagal's cup of tea and one into her own. They were silent for a while. They heard the door of the kitchen slam.

"They say. . . ."

"What do they say?"

"They say that the man was a hair in Samater's soup, a hair which lay quietly on the scummy surface of Samater's oily soup. Then one day, not long ago, they say, Samater decided to disturb the sleeping quietness of this hair. The man suggested you left. You packed and came here. And that was that."

"Morons!"

As if on grains of gravel, Medina's teeth gritted with rage: why in heaven's name did *they* always think that when a woman leaves her husband there must be a man ensconced in the night's obscure corners of love? Grains of gossip, a sandstorm of it. Medina's mother, Fatima bint Thabit, was of that opinion, too. "Don't hide anything from me, Medina. Just tell me who the man is. I am quite sure there are few men in this world as understanding and loving as Samater," she said. Grains of gossip. . . .

"They say. . . ."

"What do they say?" Medina demanded.

"That the tyranny of a mother-in-law frightened you and like a hen you left your hatching-rank. You could only feel secure in your father's nest. So you packed and left. They looked for a meaning where there is none and provided one."

"This is not my father's house, it is Nasser's. And the one I moved out of belongs to me."

"I know that but they don't."

"Imbeciles!"

Tiny little irritations such as an itch of the eye or a persistent twitch of a nerve, Medina thought to herself. Something foreign enters the eye and edges itself up and up until it crowds in on the pupil which studies the best way of ejecting the foreign thing: like an insomniac, the eye turns endlessly within the limited space; like a wound, it burns; like a nose infected with flu, it runs. The eye becomes red with pain. And loses sight. Grains of gravel. . . .

"They say . . . !"

Silence. Would any of the gossip-spinners understand if she told them why she had left Samater? A question of principle; loyalty to a cause, to ideas, ideology and movements. . . . No, it would be beyond them. Then:

"What do they say?"

The wind, like the hand of a human, opened a window in the clouds. Medina used the entrance and fell into a quiet trance. Awaking, she found her feet firmly on the ground and was thinking: what *they* touch turns into dust and dies; *their* tongues are wicked and malicious. She was indisposed to consider some of these people as her friends, in particular those who imagined they were in a position to exploit the situation, the males who had hidden in the sweet niceties of friendliness all these years but who now came forward and offered to date her. What about her women friends whose tongues were sharper than evil?

"Whereas I say – "

"You? Sagal, even you? What?"

"I think there is only one hypothesis which can possibly explain why you left Samater."

"Tell me."

"Yes, I've thought about an explanation."

"Go ahead and tell me."

"Will you tell me if I am right?"

"I can't say anything until I hear what you have to say. So go ahead and give me your explanation."

Medina struggled against the temptation to accept a cigarette from Sagal who had lighted herself one. What if Ubax came back from the kitchen and found her smoking? Medina shook her head and pushed away the packet of cigarettes, after debating with herself whether or not to give Sagal as she had promised the unsmoked cartons she had in her bedroom. Now Sagal was saying:

"You left because Samater's mother Idil insisted on having Ubax circumcised. You know that Samater isn't strong-headed enough to stand up to his mother's provocations."

Medina's eyes grew bright with the small smile her lips opened into. But what was the good? She wouldn't say whether that was right or wrong. Why did people bother so much about things that were actually none of their concern? Why did people spend hours and hours analysing other people's lives? Why did they gossip so much? Samater, let it be said, had saved himself from all this by leaving for Algeria Would the fog have cleared by the time he made a stop-over in Rome to catch a plane homewards? What explanation would he offer Barkhadle about Medina's mysterious disappearance?

Medina's face was stern. She was angry with herself for having allowed herself to be dragged this far. But she received solace from the fact that it was she who helped Sagal to formulate these ideas of hers; that it was she who lent her books to read; it was she who refreshed the young brain with new seeds, new ideas. What struck her was how confident Sagal sounded, how certain she was of her convictions. She spoke like a philosopher who just hit on a new theory – the theory of antimony! There was more to come:

"I prophesy a reunion between you and Samater."

Medina didn't know whether to laugh or sigh, she certainly could think of nothing to say. Mouth agape, she stared at Sagal whose voice was assured.

"The question is whether you will go back there (and this may be preceded by his throwing out his mother which in turn will mean him losing his job as minister) or whether he will come here to live under your tutelage."

"And why would he throw his mother out?"

"Because he will realize that he is the subject of your and Idil's quarrel when he returns and she tells him she has arranged a replacement wife. He will rebel, he will fight. She will emotionally blackmail him. And he will throw her out. Then he will come here. I prophesy this."

"But need he lose his job?"

"The scandal will unseat him. I needn't tell you, you know this for a fact: in an authoritarian state, the head of the family (matriarch or patriarch) plays a necessary and strong role; he or she represents the authority of the state."

"That is very, very clever. I am proud of you, Sagal."

There was a self-congratulatory smile on Sagal's face.

And Medina, since she wasn't going to tell anyone the real reason she had left Samater, let Sagal believe she had guessed right. *Why not appropriate Sagal's version and make it work? Everyone would believe it.* A self-congratulatory smile spread across Medina's face too.

F O U R

. . . .

Samater held his hands in front of himself and studied them like a palm-reader. Then he dipped them in the basin in which he had rinsed them, and let the running water wash away the foamy remains of the soap. His glance fell on a black ant which was caught in the overwhelming tide. Samater turned off the tap. In the quietness which followed, he gave hints to the ant, hints by which it cleverly understood the subtle meaning of his moving hands: it followed his suggestions up a wall of wavy water, down a small depression with less or no pressure. Like a child's paper boat, the ant floated to the rim of the sink. Then something quite unexpected took place, as sudden as an attack of hiccups: Samater thoughtlessly turned on the tap. Not only that — his facial expression hardened, he seemed a person upon whom a nightmare had called: it was in his eyes, his distant gaze, and the sweat which coursed down his face. Then he saw what he had done and he turned off the tap. A second later, he decided to throw the ant his hand as a bridge. Its trembling legs climbed wristwards, with a gait as troubled as had been the water a moment before. He took his hands completely out of the water and held them there safely. And the ant started to feel freer, like a prisoner in a prison yard where the air is fresher than that of the cell. The ant knocked its head against the metal strap of his watch a number of times; and when it couldn't go beyond this impediment went along it, up and down it, then round it, round and round until it finally became so dizzy that it fell to the ground. Samater watched the black ant run away as fast as it could.

. . . .

He took his hands out of the water. He grinned at his own reflection in the mirror on the wall. He watched his lips move, he listened to the unspoken secrets of his thoughts, he rehearsed responses to the questions he imagined people would want answered now that he was back. In a moment, the telephone would ring. Perhaps someone would want to hear his version of the story. He wondered what replies Medina had given, what she had said. With studied tact, he had been able to leave the VIP lounge of the airport before giving anyone the opportunity to corner him and ask questions. But he had a ready-made response, just in case: "Medina has moved because she is writing a book." A book? What about? For this he had prepared a neat answer: "I suspect you would do well to ask her that yourself."

Now he soaped his face. But he hesitated about whether to shave or wash first. His memory then went hurriedly over what had happened from when his plane landed. He remembered that as he descended the steps of the aircraft he had been met by two ministers who whisked him off to the VIP lounge where all the vice-presidents of the Republic, a dozen or so ministers and a number of journalists already were. To his query – "But who is the red-carpeted welcome for?" – one of the ministers who had taken him there teasingly answered: "For you, Samater. Everybody has been waiting for you." Subsequently he learnt that the carpet had been unfolded for the Napoleonic Fleet of the Central Empire whose plane was late by half an hour. By then, Samater's eagle-sharp eyes had picked out new faces among the Security men and the hangers-on. Someone informed him that these were replacements for the ministers who had lost their makeshift jobs in the most recent cabinet re-shuffle. The man continued: "Congratulations, Samater. You've been reconfirmed as Minister of Constructions." Then other colleagues came to shake his hand and wish him well. Someone suggested he go and pay his courtesies to the vice-presidents who were looking in his direction. One of them asked him point-blank what presents he had bought him in Rome. (As a general rule, every minister brought back gifts for the wives and the ministers of all three vice-presidents and special presents for the Generalissimo, his two wives and mistresses.) Samater did not dare tell the truth and therefore kept quiet. Then all three vice-presidents burst into laughter which was tinged with bitterness. An indescribable pain tugged at the centre of Samater's being, but he swallowed the sour taste in his mouth and excused himself, saying that he had better collect his baggage, go home, wash and shave. Leaving the airport grounds, his car crossed with the General's entourage. The Emperor's plane large like a vulture came into view, its tyres out ready to land. When he had arrived home, he found the place quiet as a tomb. Someone had put everything in order and left. There was no maid, no Idil and no orderly. Where had they all gone?

He resolved not to answer the telephone if it rang. He soaped his face a second time, but didn't put the blade to his chin. He changed the razor. He told himself that his mother was monstrously unthoughtful to say that Medina's and Samater's marriage was as untraditional as it was un-Islamic and imperfect. Was she mad?

Idil disapproved of the wedding whereas Medina's parents did not, although it was Idil and not they whose mouth was monthly buttered with the ghee from the couple's combined earnings. Medina managed the affairs of the household. It was in her name that accounts were paid or debited. She hired the servants, the occasional handyman, the gardener; she negotiated with them, dealt with them. Samater was not in the least interested in any of this. Also, he was disorderly and was not good at keeping accounts. He never worked out to whom he owed what or remembered whether the milk-woman was paid according to the number of bottles delivered. Add to this the (humiliating?) fact that the house in which they lived belonged to Medina. Idil, when she spoke about it, was inclined to take a hostile view. "What kind of a son have I ended up with? A man dependent upon a woman? And what are you a minister for? How many more months will you hold this important position, occupy the throne of power? Why don't you use it? Why don't you get richer while you can, amass the wealth that is yours by right? Or have you taken to heart what the General says about socialism? Look at your colleagues. They've changed house and wife and mistress." But would he listen to her? Silence. Without losing his calm, Samater would speak from behind the book he was reading and remind her that she had promised not to say seditious things about Medina. He would warn her that he would not tolerate it. "Do you know any man in this country who trusts his wife with a delicate matter such as administering his financial affairs? What if you die today? You have no bank account in your name, there is nothing which belongs to you legally, your name will not enrich me a cent. Turn this over in your head and think of me and your sister and your clan." Silence.

Samater's throat would choke on his inability to speak his mind. He was never able to answer back as he should: good breeding told him to hold back. Would he forgive himself if he angered the woman who began him, the woman who begat him and gave him the loan of life? He would ask Medina to silence her with more money. Where would she like to go? To visit the Holy Stone? "Here is a ticket to Mecca and back, may Allah bless you while you are in His abode, may He protect you with the benedictions of your visit. What else do you want? A home of your own?" And he bought her a house, half-stone, half-mud. For a week, for a fortnight she would chain her tongue with the fetters of compromise. Then she would change strategy and theme. Now her favourite topic was "Ubax and her toys". She would observe that what Medina and Samater paid for Ubax's toys could feed a family of three in Mogadiscio. Why should they alienate the little girl from the other children in the neighbourhood and spoil her with these expensive machines? She would grow saner if she played with the dirt like others of her age. "Toys. Colourful pens, each thick as an adult's finger. Expensive tastes developed for her poor mind. In my opinion, you've made her think of herself as a boy. Look how you dress her, in shirts and jeans; look at the way she walks, just like a boy. Listen to her answer back: she never hears what I tell her, she isn't interested in what I might say. That's very irresponsible, un-Islamic and untraditional. Why, you will probably say that she won't be circumcised like the other girls. Whoever heard of such a sordid thing?" And Samater's eyes had turned grey, the colour of dead embers, lifeless and lightless. "Leave. Leave this very second, leave or else. . . . " Medina intervened, Medina who almost always appeared on the scene when a situation demanded her presence, Medina who patched things up, going from mother to son, from son to mother. A week later, the topic was "Samater, Medina and their books". They cost so much, these books. One day, she threatened, they would wake and find them all gone. She would burn them. Life was a tightrope fixed right above oneself and astraddle the sword of ghenna. Then not long ago, maybe a fortnight before Medina left, when in a bad mood Idil said that one day she would take Ubax by the hand and have her circumcised.

"Life is a kiln in which one bakes one's experiences: some are taken out half done, some underdone and some undone," Idil would say. "I can tell you one thing: Samater and Xaddia are the half-dones."

Samater was now moving about the house uneasy like a guest.

His unplanned movements took him finally to the kitchen where the cups felt recently used, the kettle handled, the stove lit: in fact, the whole place felt abused. He wondered who it was that had moved the table from its original position, who it was that had worked hard at changing the appearance of the place. Certainly not Medina. Probably not Idil, either. But who?

The kitchen walls were semi-naked: someone had replaced the calendar and the newspaper-clippings with publicity pin-ups of the General and reprints of his quotations. Medina's labelled bottles were gone, too. So were Ubax's poses for the camera, and Medina's cookery books. Did Idil think that by removing this or that object, changing the position of the bed and the pillows, she would cancel all the signs which indicated Medina's presence in this house? But there was another thing which he noticed: the maid's room smelt different; it smelt less like the maid's, it was too dry for his nostrils; and the clothes hanging in the cupboard suggested someone taller, someone of modest taste. Also, the maid's hall of mirrors and her cabinet of cosmetics, the nail-varnish, the *kuxl,* the *xinna,* the facepads: all had vanished. The occupant of the room had a plainer taste, something like a nun's. Had his mother fired the maid? And the orderly, why wasn't the orderly here? His mother didn't like him either. The maid and Medina were close, and at times Medina lent her dresses, jewellery, encouraged her to attend evening classes for which she paid. Samater could never tell why Idil didn't like the orderly. The question was whether Idil had exploited his and Medina's absence to sack the maid and tell the orderly to report back to army barracks. Something told him that his mother had done just that. Everything, indeed, seemed stamped with her signature. "Her thoughts travel one way," Medina said of her. "Like rain, they travel only eastwards." He surely wouldn't let her get away with this, he told himself emphatically. Maybe he should ring Somali Airlines to find out if Xaddia, his sister, was in town.

Oh, think of the angel and the devil appears fleshed in his proper garments! There under a container of home-ground coffee was a note Xaddia had signed, a note which talked of strained nerves, near fistfights with Idil and what she called "mother-migraines". But there was an NB whose contents Samater found quite intriguing for it spoke of a certain Wentworth George who'd called at least three times the same day to invite Medina and Sagal to a party. Xaddia had written: "Perhaps out of this rubble will rise the ghostly evidence of some interesting tale. Is there a man on the scene?" Samater had never met this Wentworth George, but was sure as life that there wasn't any man hiding in the perfumed love gardens of Medina's secrets. Possibly Wentworth George, he thought, was given the number by Sagal or a mutual acquaintance of Medina's. Or else he was an American or an Englishman passing through town whom Barbara had asked to call Sagal and Medina. He neatly folded Xaddia's note and tore it into pieces which he threw in the bin. He was at peace with himself. He turned his head away and reminded himself not to lose control. He was inarticulate with self-questioning.

In Algiers, now he remembered, a woman had asked him if he was married. He had given much thought to the question and had answered: "Separated. My wife and I are separated. Let me explain. When things come to a nasty collision, traditionally the wife leaves her husband's household and returns to her father's or her brother's, or, if neither is there, a male relative of hers. Positions and conditions are negotiated between the husband's and wife's clans, and the wife is brought back to the house." The French woman had appeared fascinated and inquired whether he thought his wife would be re-negotiated for him by the orators of the clan. "No, no," he had said. "My wife is a tough negotiator herself." A day later, he took the woman aside and told her the whole truth. But why had his wife left him? "She is planning to write a critical book about the revolutionary government in which I am a minister. You see, we don't agree, she and I. I believe that my being a member of the cabinet helps give a human touch to these contradictions. She needs to distance herself from me and my compromised position. Do you understand?" he had asked. Of course. Who wouldn't?

He filled the kettle with water through the spout. He lit the gas stove. Thanks to Medina he knew how to make a kettle sing any tune and was an expert at the art of dishwashing. He placed the kettle on the fire and went and opened the fridge: meat, vegetables and milk-bottles. No beer. Earlier, he had noticed that somebody had removed all the hard liquor and hidden it away. His mother and her councillors had forgotten that his duty-free shopping bag would contain a bottle of whisky, another of brandy, a bottle of Algerian Maskera, and a vodka. He closed the fridge. Would it break a heathen's heart if he admitted that he had never set foot in a kitchen before he went abroad? He had never cooked anything nor had he ever made a cup of tea until he was in Europe. His first attempt had resulted in a near-fatal accident because he forgot to turn off the gas. His mother used to say that a kitchen was a woman's territory where men had no business. No wonder she was shocked to learn that not only did he cook meals for Medina and Ubax, he was also the official dishwasher of the household when the maid was not there. "I shun the company of other women because of these shameful things," she complained.

He made himself a cup of tea. Sugar. Lemon. Then vivid memories of his childhood, the smell of burnt maize cakes (his mother was a professional baker) and the charcoal taste of the unsold *canjeera* on which his mother fed him and his sister. But his mind was astir not with the dust of the past but that of the present. He walked out of the kitchen carrying his cup of lemon-tea and was half-delirious with thoughts. He walked down the sunlit corridor and entered the bathroom.

The telephone rang.

• • • • • • • • • • •

In less than five minutes the telephone rang five times. But nothing would make Samater change his mind, make him pick it up and answer. He had no wish to speak to anyone before he had gathered his wits, like a robe, around himself, had washed and shaved; not, at any rate, until after he had solved the mystery of the missing maid, the orderly and his mother. What if it was someone trying to get a message to him? In that case they should ring and leave a message with his secretary. Unless the caller was his secretary; or Medina wanting to know if he had any money and if she should send him a cheque. What if it was the Presidency? Hell, they could send a car and a driver like that time when the General sent for him because Samater was the only Somali who spoke fluent French and could be trusted. Pity is no national characteristic of the Somali; but that was precisely what had happened when it was discovered that the Minister who led the Korean delegation spoke perfect Italian and the General could speak to him alone. Samater became redundant.

Now he filled his lungs with air: exhale, inhale!

Of late, Samater spent the first puffs of his early morning energy fruitfully: he lifted weights and built his muscles. He sweated the brain in order to warm it up for a boring day whose seconds, minutes and hours ticked with false grins, silent nodding heads, congratulatory whispers, bass voices of caution (*the Security's walls have ears, so mind what you say*) and of falsification. This – would anyone believe him? (Medina did) – coincided with the General's "To All Ministers" circular in which it was suggested that all the General's men should be physically fit and mentally agile. They should be men who could hold any giant enemy safely at bay. The General's men (and Samater was one of them) should serve as the pillows of the nation's head, the midwives of the nation's undelivered pain as well as suppositories of the country's constipated economy. Awake and alert, the General's men would stand united against the common enemy. Asleep in the early hours of dawn, they would remain divided by their dreams. Just as the brain must discard all that is harmful to its growth, the body, too, must get rid of the morning mistiness. The bounty of dawn would go to those in whose eyes the morning's fog had cleared. In short, the General's men should lull the nation to sleep while they sang his praise-names. They should also be the first to get up. As one of the General's wise sayings had it (this gem hadn't figured in the collected works): *Mens sana in corpore sano.* (Samater here choked on his laugh.) Anyway . . . ! For a good five weeks, every major street of Mogadiscio, every asphalted road in the city, had a board on which this wisdom was copied by the sign-writers of the Revolution. But no one dared tell the General that the quote shouldn't have been given in large capitals of plagiarism. A month later, one of the Pope's representatives teasingly mentioned it to one of the dictator's cousins who was himself a minister in the government. The next day the nation learned what would become of sign-writers who put into the mouth of the wise President something he had never said. The signwriter was sentenced to five years' imprisonment.

"One. Two. Three."

The veins of sweat opened and poured out. In a little while, he would stand under a cold shower. His pores would close. He would dry himself with that big towel which once belonged to Medina's father Barkhadle. Then he would beat it like an egg: he would look at it move like jelly, but like the white of an egg transparent on the flatness of his palm. . . . "There: the germ of my waste," he always said to himself, when he emptied himself of all that energy. But need he resort to such infantile methods? In Algiers, did he not try to take the French woman to bed? In Algiers, the local women were vulgarly veiled, shrouded in the shade of puritanism; they were clothed in the tradition of the Casbah, they looked at him from behind a screen of eyes. And they talked of a revolution! *We mutilate our women when we circumcise them in Somalia. In the Middle East, they exclude them from partaking in the hubbub of living.*

"Two. Three. One."

He agreed with Medina that in Somali power-politics there was no room for women and that in a set-up such as the General's there was no hope for them. Women had to fight for their rights as in other societies; women had to inform the misinformed public about important issues such as female infibulation. But what was he doing in a dictator's cabinet? "If I leave, what do you think will happen? Who do you think he will replace me with? At least every now and again I may make him change his mind about one thing or another, every now and again. I suspect the advice I give softens the military regime's harsh intentions. I believe that our presence acts as a controlling force, as a rein. Is this a revolution? No. The General's regime is a facsimile of the fascist left anywhere. To complete the picture, you must superimpose the tribal motif on the tapestry of African politics."

"Three. One. Two."

He paused for a minute and breathed heavily. He supported his weight on arms shaking from exhaustion, but he was tired and weak in the loins. He got up. He walked about for a while to allow the blood to circulate more freely. Now he fought hard against a thought which struggled in him like a bee held prisoner in a cup. *Truth must be owned,* he finally said to himself. *We the intellectuals are the betrayers; Thee, the so-called intellectuals, are the entrance the foreign powers use so as to dominate, designate, name and label; we the intellectuals are the ones who tell*

our people lies; we tell them that we cannot bake our bricks in home-made
kilns whose fire has died. And when the fire of enthusiasm has diminished,
what do we do? We don't replace the kiln but those who work it. Then we ex-
plain and tell more and more lies. We are the ones that keep dictators in
power.

He went and showered. When he dried himself with Barkhadle's
towel, the door-bell rang.

"Who is it?" he shouted.

A woman's voice: "It is I."

·　·　·　·　·　·　·　·　·　·　·

The woman who came in looked at Samater but walked past him without saying anything, her eyes downcast and shy. When he shouted at
her, like a drill-sergeant at a private soldier, asking her to tell him
where she was going, she turned, calm and composed as the secret defence weapon she knew she had. Her stare stirred the sweaty blood in
his groin. His arms were folded across his chest and he was wrapped in
a towel big as a *matrimoniale* bedspread. He took his time, and she
hers. He looked her up and down; her skin, he noticed, was in dire
need of one of those ointments with which she might have smoothed
the scar of a nomadic background recently abandoned. Her feet domi-
ciled in the shapelessness of a pair of Chinese rubber sandals like
animals in a zoo. The blisters on her feet, the thorn-scratches on her
forehead, her elbows became part of the general trend and shape of her
wear.

"Who are you and what are you doing here?" he asked.

The woman smiled when she saw Samater preoccupied with his
towel whose knot had come undone. Her gaze stopped at his loins. He
avoided confronting her eyes and therefore saw that she was carrying a
bunch of keys in her free hand. He wondered why she hadn't used
them. He would ask her. But when next their eyes met, her hard stare
dissolved. Things then began to fall into place: the clothes which he
had seen in the maid's room were surely hers, and in all probability she
was the person who had used the kitchen a little before his return. But
where had his drinks disappeared? Or should he take up this and other
issues with his mother when she came back?

"Are you the new maid?"

She appeared offended by the question, but Samater did not understand why. She set her shopping-bag down on the floor. While doing so, the red ration-card dropped out. She bent to take it.

"Are you the maid's replacement?" he persisted.

"Who?"

"Jiijo, the other maid, our maid."

She stared at him and her large eyes turned like ball-bearings.

"Will you answer my questions?" He shouldn't lose his temper, he told himself. Not with her anyway.

"Yes, I will."

"Who are you?"

"I am your cousin," her voice trembled. "I am not a replacement for the maid. I am your cousin."

Suddenly he felt cold. His arms crossed and uncrossed nervously. Finally, like a woman surprised in nakedness, he covered his chest with his hands. She said, having picked up her shopping-bag from the floor:

"We didn't expect you back today, otherwise we would have prepared ourselves adequately. We thought you wouldn't be back for at least another week."

"We who?"

"My aunt and I."

"Your aunt?"

"Your mother is my aunt. Remember: I am your cousin."

"Yes, of course!"

A shudder of anger ran through him. He held the frame of his body up like a door with one hinge missing. He was thinking: *I must detribalize this house.* He remembered something similar to this which took place not here but at his sister Xaddia's a year before. His mother had filled Xaddia's place with tribeswomen and tribesmen of hers. It was during the worst period of the famine and all the malnourished clansmen and clanswomen who managed to run away from the camps specially erected for them went and were given shelter there as though Xaddia's was a rehabilitation centre.

"Where is she?"

"Who?"

"My mother—er, your aunt."

"She should be here any instant."

It was an hour later. The sun searched the width and breadth of the sky for a cloud behind which to hide. Idil had made herself comfortable like a queen in her residence.

"Who is this woman?" Samater asked.

"She is your cousin. Your uncle's daughter."

"And where is Jiijo, Medina's and my maid?"

"Don't mention that woman's name."

"Did you fire the maid, Mother?"

"Yes."

"By whose authority? Who do you think you are?"

"I am your mother."

He was irritated. He was angry. He was so enraged he was afraid he would do something unbecoming of a son. He walked up and down like a wounded tiger. His eyes were red: he was livid.

"I want this woman out of here. Immediately," he said

"No. She will not leave. She has every right to be here where I am. She is your cousin, she is your blood."

"I want her out of here, I said."

"You will have to force me to do that physically and I am sure you won't. After all, I am your mother and I want her to be where I am."

"I give you half an hour. I'm going to shave. When I come out, I want her gone. If she isn't, I shall throw her out myself. And if you say as much as a word about it, I shall throw you out too."

A cautious silence; then:

"No respect for your mother?"

Her short hand went into her bag. She took out her knitting. She chose the thread, but then changed her mind about the colour and selected another. Idil murmured a small prayer of *Faatixa* before she put needle to cotton thread.

"And before you leave," Samater continued, "since leave you must, I want you to remember what you've done with my beer, my whisky, my brandy and my gin. Also you must tell me what you said to the orderly, and whether you paid the maid. I want you to explain to me the story concerning the bidet."

"What order do I follow?"

"Never mind what order."

Idil balanced her knitting-sheath between her fingers and closed her left eye as though she were a shooter about to pull a trigger.

"No one will drink any liquor in this house as long as I am here. It is my duty as your mother and as a Muslim to remind you of your religious responsibilities. You can drink in the company of your sinful friends or in bars. But not here."

"I will drink where I please!" he shouted as loudly as he could.

"Not in this house."

The new maid had come soundlessly to the door and stood there. Samater's voice went up like a curtain and disclosed a number of hidden tremors as he continued, pleased that she was there to hear:

"Yes. I will drink where I please, and when. I buy these drinks with my own money, and I like drinking here, and this is my house. Let me live my life the way I like it. Let me pay for my own sins, face my God myself."

"Not in this house, no."

"This is my house."

"No, it isn't."

"What? What did you say?"

"I said, it isn't. It is Medina's house. It isn't yours."

Idil used the needle with the hooked end as a toothpick. Squinting at him, she went on:

"First, get yourself a house out of which you can throw anyone. 'I buy these drinks with my own money.' Why not save it towards a down-payment on a house while you can, eh? This is Medina's house. Don't forget that. You cannot throw me out."

Samater, angrier with himself, shot out of the room.

·   ·   ·   ·   ·   ·   ·   ·   ·   ·   ·

He had not only challenged her authority, he had offended her and hurt her pride, too. But it wasn't the first time he had come so near to hitting her. *How easily children forget! How easily children forget what they've always known,* Idil thought. "Look at them now, grown-up, their noses dry, their clothes clean and washed, and, thanks be to Allah, healthy as the sun in a clear sky. Small and helpless, they wake you up, tire you, age you faster, force you to change your sleeping and eating habits, make you subject yourself to all sorts of humiliations. When children cry at the oddest hours, when they break dawn with their shrill scream, they ask for you, the mother, off whom they live and on whom they grow like wreaths of greenery on your tomb. Then as soon as they feel the muscle of independence roll in their arms, as soon as they are adults, and their noses are dry, their clothes clean as laundered money and they don't make water in their bed . . . the words they use to pin you in your place, what words – words of ingratitude! There is nothing like the ingratitude of the young. How they forget the pain of love, the pain of delivery, the pain of being opened up to let them come out, head first then the rest of their body; how they forget the pain of being a mother, a parent! To the one to whom you are a parent, Somalis say, remember he or she is not your parent. And Samater, my son, between thirty-three and thirty-four, Samater, my son, a minister – no respect, none whatsoever for his mother. Such a frail child he was, and sickly, too, with a nose running a stream of mucus round the clock." She had carried him tied to her back wherever she went, like the fruit a tree carries on its bough. In those days, there were no maids to wash his clothes; come to think of it, there were no clothes to wash, for they could never afford to buy him anything. They were so poor that he shared the edge of her robe when she carried him and was naked when on the ground, eating mouthfuls of dirt. Then she obtained a commission to bake *canjeera* and maize-cakes for a restaurant owned by a man who – the truth must be told – had easy access to her. With the money she earned from these ventures, she bought her son clothes and was later able to send him to school so that he would become a clerk in a government office and bring back a monthly stipend. How children forget what in fact they've *always* known!

"Yes, yes. I've heard that a million times before," Samater would retort. "Different versions of the same story, tinged with the blood of sacrifice, mother-as-martyr. But you must know that when you invest in something one of the possibilities is that nothing will come of it. Parents here invest in their children. They believe that they are closer to their Creator through the intercession of their offspring: three male children assure a parent a place in paradise. So much the better if there is money. If only you'd realize you cannot remind me of something I've *never* known. But if you see me as an investment, haven't you presented your accounts, haven't I paid my dues, hasn't my sister Xaddia? When I was small and you were my only help. . . . I know the story, I've heard it a million times."

"You will hear it again and again. It is the only story I know and I tell it to myself often. It is the life you imposed on me. Had I known it would be you, I might have thought a million times over, I might have thought of bleeding you to death. Your father had just died serving the Italians."

"One doesn't forget what one has *never* known."

Of course! He had forgotten ever having seen those housepigeons which made ugly noises as they pecked at one another's feathery bottoms, quarrelling over crumbs of bread Idil had thrown to them. Those were straw-thin days. They lived in a thatch hut that wasn't theirs. And like the poor anywhere they had no relatives – and now guess how many uncles and aunts they had? She was twenty, poor, with a child suffering from kwashiorkor and diarrhoeal diseases. They sat by the funereal fire she had built. When they were slightly better off, when she had earned enough money from the baking ventures, the dead husband's brother demanded the right of *dumaal*. Xaddia, the only issue of that union, was born. Years later, she obtained a divorce from him.

"Yes, I've heard that, too."

"There is a lot you haven't heard, a lot I haven't told anyone. But it is high time someone told you that your life consists of trivia: 'my beer, my whisky, my books, my maid, my orderly'. Out of your mundanities, you should be in a position to do what a minister can, mint something worthy of your station. You should be in a position to say: 'my house, my car, my bank account, my farm, my land'. The rest is absolute trivia. Yes, absolute trivia."

Samater would here explain himself in condescending bisyllabic abbreviations, in effect saying that his and Idil's life's exigencies wouldn't converge . . . there was no cultural continuity, the line was broken! She would continue:

"One shouldn't search for my past in the manifold cultural contradictions of your present and your future. I've collected and eaten the fruit of the tree my parents planted. I am what and who I am. I am the product of a tradition with a given coherence and solidity; you, of confusion and indecision. I have Allah, his prophets and the Islamic saints as my illustrious guides. For you, nothing is sacred, nothing is taboo. You are as inconsistent as your beliefs and principles are incoherent. What is more, your generation hasn't produced the genius who could work out and develop an alternative cultural philosophy acceptable to all the members of your rank and file; no genius to propose something with which you could replace what you've rejected. You are the children of our apprehension; you are the protagonists of your indecision. After all, you are a kin of Cain's blood-brother."

The thick thread of her past wouldn't pass through the eye of her needle. His mother's tongue would wet the thread, then roll it against her fingers to thin it. Meanwhile, Samater would borrow another alien concept and vision and draw a humpbacked camel-bird. *Maanshaa Allah!*

"There is no pleasure like remembering the pain of the past," Idil said, "and nothing like being ashamed of your past. How much pain your father caused me you can never imagine. No, no, not physical pain. He never hit me, never lifted a finger to strike me. No. He just didn't have the guts to shout at anybody and I used to groan inside, wish that one day he would beat me like all the other men beat their wives, that one day he would out-shout the other men or even out-shout me, his wife. He was a *si-commandante*. You? You are like your father. Medina has larger testicles than you. Just as I had bigger ones than your father."

Idil's ball of thread rolled away. And she looked up when she heard someone's footsteps approaching. She then began to thread-draw in her mind a past with patterns different from the one she had the intention of re-narrating.

•   •   •   •   •   •   •   •   •   •   •

The maid gave the ball of thread to Idil and asked:

"Do you think I should leave? Samater is not happy about my being here. What do you say? Do you think I should?"

"No, you are not to." Idil counted the number of holes she had to jump in order to form a pattern.

"What was Jiijo like?" asked Asli, the new maid. "Was she good-looking, was she good in the kitchen, was she Medina's and Samater's favourite maid, and why?"

"She had opinions."

"What? A maid of inferior status with opinions?"

"I don't like maids who serve you a plateful of their opinions. Neither do I like them when they dress better than their mistress. Jiijo, for instance, dressed better than Medina and at times even borrowed Medina's dresses or jewellery without asking permission."

"All the maids who belong in this city. . . . "

"She was from the River people."

"Oh, my God! What is this world coming to?"

"I wonder, too."

"She probably charmed them, bewitched them."

"It was scandalous. You would be shocked if you saw her. She spoke to Medina and Samater as though she were their equal."

"A woman from the River people!"

"Of course, you are not a maid. You're the daughter of my cousin. You mustn't think of yourself as a maid but as the future wife of Samater and therefore must behave like a person worthy of that title. Yes, Samater's future wife. But when one is a maid, I always say, one must behave like one."

Asli was uneasy. She repeated to herself: *You are the future wife of Samater and therefore must behave like a person worthy of that title.* She wished she could get up, but the burden of this secret held her to the floor.

"What I always say is this," Idil continued: "we can tell the world what pleases the ears of the world. But facts are facts, and God is God. It is all in the book. Allah says it very clearly in His book, the Holy Koran. Clear and distinct as the Sacred Word."

"That's true, *Xaajiya* Idil!"

Silence. Asli appeared struck by the gale-winds of what Idil had said and was profoundly thoughtful. Idil was mysteriously buoyant. She was saying:

"He is a minister now, clean, and always in the choicest of wear for he can afford it. He is one of the most highly educated men in this country, and among the most intelligent anywhere. He is one of the best architects ever to have graduated from his university in Italy. But I used to say to him when he was much smaller, I used to tell him – "

The door of the master-bedroom opened and closed. Idil and Asli had time to exchange a look, and:

"Yes, Aunt. When he was small. . . . "

"When he was small. . . . "

"When I was small. . . . "

Panic-stricken, like a flock of birds the words of her thoughts dispersed at Samater's appearance on the scene; they dissolved inside her head. With a needle penetrating the air as an apostrophe pierces the meaning of a word, Idil stared up at him. He had on a pair of trousers pressed as though hurriedly (Asli would have to be taught to do better than that, Idil thought) and a Mwalimu shirt. The maid felt the weight of her presence and left.

"Yes?"

•   •   •   •   •   •   •   •   •   •   •   •

"Yes?"

He was silent. How could he throw out the woman who begat him, how could he throw her out on the streets like the greasy dishwashing water women empty into the undug sewers of this city? How could he? A hunchback, in the end, gets used to the discomfort he carries like a rucksack. He moved up and down like a horse held by a rein. The woman who began him in the first place, the woman who begat him, the woman for whom he had become too large like a child in last year's clothes, looked up at him every now and then and waited for him to ask her pardon. But that didn't seem to be forthcoming today. The umbilical love had snapped, he had outgrown her like a weaned child his mother's breasts. Now she said:

"I shall become one with your shadow so as to feel no pain when your rebellious youth tramples all over me. I will whisper my inner secrets to my rosary, and will be as immobile as a prayer-rug."

Like the hole, he thought as he paced up and down, which grows larger the more you take from it . . . a life of compromises. He would pay her handsomely, he would ask Idil to go back to Xaddia's and leave him in peace. And the new maid? He'd keep her for a few days, then fire her when he had decided what to do with the house, and with himself. But he wouldn't lose his temper or be rude. He cleared the lump in his throat. A smile moulded itself on his lips.

"I've had a thought," he said.

"Yes," she said. "I, too, have given everything another thought."

A seed of suspicion already sown?

"You know that I've always disapproved of your marriage to Medina."

Blades of grass which cut and hurt?

"The whisky, the brandy, the beer: all these are secondary."

"Come to the point, Mother."

"I shall bless you, and God will bless you, too. I am sure of it."

"What is all this, Mother? What's this blessing for?"

"Take her as your wife. I've already asked for her hand from her father who's given it. Asli is a very good girl and I will bless you and God will bless you, too."

"Asli?"

"The new girl."

A high watermark, certainly. He didn't think the inundation would hit a point as high as that. He could not launch into any discourse.

"What do you think?" she said.

His tongue was jelly-cold and unmoving in a mouth which had opened but wouldn't close. After a long while, his tongue thawed in the warmth of a certainty that silence might be taken as acceptance.

"I want her out of here," he said. "I shall pay her a month's salary, and her bus fare back to wherever you got her from. That's what I want, Mother. No blessings."

"And what will I say to her father?"

"Ask for his pardon. Give him back her hand."

He moved towards the door. He was not in the least agitated. He was, as a matter of fact, surprised that he hadn't lost his calm. He turned.

"And you, too, Mother, I want you out of here. I don't want to find you in this house when I return."

On the way out, he met the maid bringing in an armful of fuel for the New Year's bonfire tomorrow. She gave him way, her eyes downcast and shy. He didn't say anything to her. A new year – this?

F I V E

He kneaded the softest part of her body like dough. He oiled his hands and, with tremendous care and tenderness, massaged, thumbed and squeezed the hard joints. His expert fingers, at times, descended like a hawk hunting on the wing and, at others, crawled like a many-legged insect on a plateau of uneven smoothness. He touched, he pressed, he tickled. He helped orchestrate the rise and fall of her body's temperature. With equal facility, he conducted his hands through a series of annotations: a scar here, a cut too low or too deep there, a burn which his memory couldn't date, another which marked where the blade met the shoulder, then a medicinal burn near the spine. Nasser knew his notes well enough, he hardly needed to improvise a move.

"Do you think Samater will go as far as that?"

"You mean will he throw Idil out of the house?"

"I mean dare he throw her out?"

"I think he will if she insists on him marrying her choice."

"I don't want to be present when that occurs."

"His sister Xaddia threw her out because she planted a seed of discord and hate between her and her husband and finally made them part. But Xaddia is decidedly stronger than Samater and she fears no scandals, she doesn't hold a political office as he does. Xaddia flies with Somali Airlines; she is hardly in town, she prefers to be out of Mogadiscio."

"What if he marries the maid Idil wants him to?"

"What if he does?"

"You mean you're not in the least threatened by this marriage Idil has arranged for her son?" asked Nasser in disbelief.

"No, I don't feel in the least threatened by Idil nor by the marriage she's arranged for her son."

"Why did you leave him then?"

"Everything at its proper time, Nasser." Later, she would tell him the story Sagal had told her, the one Medina had made her own.

She looked up at him. He was muscular and hairy, a shade lighter than she and two inches taller. The curtains of an open window, like the colours of a popular football team, flagged down the incoming dust just as it beat the outgoing wind with great pomp and show. Nasser stood up to close the window, but Medina insisted that she wanted it open. She then accepted the pillow he passed to her. First she buttoned her half-undone underbodice; then she made herself more comfortable by lying straight on her back. Looking upwards, she took in the ceiling, the electric bulb white with light; then Nasser. She wondered what people would say if they saw him massage her back when she was semi-nude. She abandoned herself to her thoughts and found herself in a thick forest of inhibitions. Tradition told one how to behave, what to do and what not to do. The fact that she even considered what people might say worried and at the same time surprised her. When had she ever worried about what others said? Whatever had become of her personality, the strength of her weakness, the undeniable fact that she was almost always a woman among men, sharing things with them, drinks, reading the same books as they, borrowing or lending them ideas? Was she not the only woman member of the underground organization which so far had sacrificed Soyaan and Koschin? She turned to look Nasser in the eyes. His face broke into a gentle grin. And this brought her to an open field: the forest of fearful inhibitions and bourgeois preoccupations cleared. She paid him several years' arrears of sisterly affection. But he was remote again and she couldn't reach him. Was he irrationally wondering whether he needed to come? He had come with the impression that Medina's barbecue of nerves could do with a cooling, nursing touch, that his visit would stand her on her feet again. He believed (mistakenly?) that he could gather up her crumpled parts as one cupped into one's palm breadcrumbs off a tablecloth. She admitted that this was a difficult phase; that she felt, every now and again, as though she were the sole survivor of a traumatic incident. Nothing more than that. Nothing less. . . .

He was asking a question: "How did Ubax take it?"

"Ubax's needs keep me in constant check. I find I need her more than she needs me. We are passing through a phase at the moment and on occasion she is difficult. But so are all intelligent children."

Silence. She should have known better than to make reference to "difficult", "intelligent" children. Nasser's gentle smile stiffened and he shifted slightly, though he knew she didn't mean it. He changed the subject.

"What about Fatima bint Thabit? How did she take it?"

"She says that I am black and sinful as my un-Islamic thoughts. She always puts the blame squarely on me, and in the same breath admits that she doesn't know what to say. Then she says I don't tell her enough, that she receives all my news and yours, too, from second-hand sources. As for Samater: she's always held the view that I'm not worthy of his love and trust."

"Whereas Idil believes you're the evil that has lured her son away."

No comment. Her eyes caught and held his stare until he blinked. She wished she could give him in a single phrase the hint which would open a door, give him access to her most intimate secrets. He was patient and he would wait. She was tactful and wouldn't play, he hoped, unintelligently. Here again: the varanian dance of death? He knew for example why she had lost her job. He saw the editorial changes she had made and wondered how she got away with it. Imagine what a daredevil she was, editing the General's speech. Only a mad person would use the space reserved for the General's daily wisdom to the nation as stop-press, said all her friends. He knew this because they had corresponded; they used Xaddia as the message-conveyor. But how much did letters tell? These letters catalogued her secrets which in turn she was certain were filed away in the reservoir of interpretative memories. Why did neither use the postal services? Letters were, in many instances, opened for security purposes. She preferred to hold in her tight embrace those intimate secrets she couldn't trust to her letters unless their carrier was someone she had faith in.

"How is your son?" she finally asked.

"Yusuf gurgles his words less and doesn't filthy himself as often as when you last saw him, three or four years ago, I think. He appears to have resigned himself to this state of speechlessness. He silently stares into the eyes of the void."

Medina was uneasy and wished she hadn't asked the question. She rehearsed to herself something to say by way of consolation but her tongue was glued to her palate and she was speechless herself. Nasser went to the window and partially closed it.

"When he stares at me I tell myself that perhaps he will surprise us all one day," Nasser said, "speak something comprehensible after all these silent years. His concentrated look is vividly intact like the desert at dusk and with his communicative smile his eyes become clear like camomile tea. Forgive me, but it is on such occasions that I see God in him."

Had what he said disquieted her? Why did she look away as if avoiding his eyes? She told herself that Yusuf's condition was perhaps in keeping with what Fatima bint Thabit believed, the very concept she had aptly described as "the inescapable logic of the truth that is Allah!" Understandably someone like Fatima bint Thabit or Idil whose upbringing was basically traditional, she suspected, might search for and find religious responses to scientific inquiries. Medina was so embarrassed she couldn't recall how old Yusuf was and didn't dare ask.

He was older than Ubax by less than a year, but precisely how many months she wasn't sure. Because Yusuf never expressed himself verbally she couldn't tell how developed or mentally undeveloped he was; he was like a tree whose rings never made complete circles so one couldn't tell its age. She once said to Samater that people with a deficient organ or with a face ravaged by famine or tropical diseases of malnutrition made her feel uncomfortable: she didn't know what to say to them, whether to preface her conversation with an apology for God-knows-what, an apology on behalf of humanity, common sense, etcetera. But when she looked at Ubax who was whole like a goddess, she would prattle with excitement and her tongue would loosen. She confessed that her mind couldn't make the metaphysical leap nor did her scientific reasoning supply her with the courage to face the naked reality of life's inadequacies. She envied her mother Fatima bint Thabit, she envied Idil who, with blind faith, believed in maxims like: "All mysteries lead to one major mystery: Allah!" Again the scene shifted and she saw on the stage of her memory Anna, Nasser's wife, head bowed in supplication, watching Yusuf whose tongue was out in concentration like that of a dog. Ubax was there, Ubax who young as she was could gargle a few confused meaningless nouns, and was saying *ga-ga-ga, ma-ba-ma, ba-ma-ba,* wrapped in the autumn leaves of the season. And Yusuf, toothless and speechless and foul, like a man in his second childhood with jaws constantly in motion. Anna would stare monstrously in Ubax's direction, then at her son, and she would remain silent where others might have spoken: science-as-doubt, a mystery not yet demystified.

"How is Anna?"

"She is devoted day in, day out to Yusuf."

There was a pause. Anna not only envied Medina her Ubax but everything; to her, Medina was "a full-bodied miracle, and Ubax a dream-child". Think of the angel, indeed. For Ubax entered there and then, very excited and thrilled at the toys Nasser had brought for her. She had little interest in anything else: she was engrossed in the mechanical movement of a toy whose head tossed backwards and forwards in clockwork obedience. She wound it and waited until the head moved no more. She then unceremoniously went away. Nasser's and Medina's thoughts raced in opposite directions (*Should I tell Ubax to ask after her cousin Yusuf?* she was thinking. And he: *Sandra, where and how is she?*) but joined after a little while, travelled together for a certain distance, then again parted company.

"How far has Sandra prostrated herself for the catch?" he asked.

"I would say surprisingly a great deal."

"In '68, one wouldn't have thought so, would one?"

Medina regarded her brother with a gentle look.

"Sandra is a lie told over a hundred times. One becomes weary hearing it and in the end doesn't even bother correcting it. But of late she has become scarce. Her visits are rare, like the eclipse of the moon."

"Yet when she came to the country you were the sun whose light she borrowed from and in whose light she saw everything," said Nasser. "She was your guest for a while, wasn't she? Why are her visits so infrequent?"

"Her infrequent visits are ominous. Samater used to (jokingly?) invoke the spirits' protection whenever I told him she was coming. He saw an apparent link between her visits and what happened to one of us immediately she was gone. She was the one who broke the news to me that I was appointed acting-editor of the paper; again, she turned up on the morning of the day the Security served on me the writ that banned me from publishing anything in the country. She was having a meal with us when an unidentified voice mysteriously telephoned and said that Samater was to be appointed Minister of Constructions."

Nasser opened the window fully and let the breeze enter. "So that explains the tension between you both. You never thought highly of the ideologue anyway."

"It is the group whose company she keeps that I disapprove of."

"You speak as though you were her chaperone."

"She is with an incestuous circle which draws its members from the General's clan and those related to this tribal oligarchy through marriage. She is a naive European who believes everything Somalis tell her. There is no tension between us. There are contradictions which have bred frictions, and frictions which have made her speak inconsistencies, and inconsistencies which have given birth to misunderstandings. But it is her membership in the incestuous circle of which I greatly disapprove."

Nasser surrendered himself to his unruly memory which stretched across continents and years to recall when he, Medina, Samater and Sandra were enviously referred to as "the incestuous foursome".

"Atta is the Afro-American girl who's joined Sandra's circle lately?" he asked.

Medina was taken aback for she couldn't remember even telling him about Atta. His long strides took him across the room and back. He closed the window, then opened it. He was proud that he was still in command of the situation. Medina now said:

"What makes the whole thing absurd is that the regime is very security-conscious and paranoid, and doesn't tolerate Somalis coming into unauthorized contact with foreigners, in particular those from Western Europe or the USA. But the members of the tribal oligarchy have the General's absolute trust and can afford to introduce into the country anyone they please. As a matter of fact, any foreigner they vouchsafe for is issued a visa or given a job. Some come as mistresses, others as collaborators in business or as accredited newspersons. Atta is one such foreigner brought here as a mistress by one such tribal upstart. Sandra completes the circle Atta began. Result: the two hate each other."

A pause. Then, as if on cue, Ubax called out to Medina to come to her room and see the castle she had constructed from the plastic squares her uncle had brought. Nasser thought of saying something about this constant need of Ubax's to be assured of her mother's presence, but decided it would be superfluous. Meanwhile Medina began saying:

"Do you remember how Sandra used to make all the fuss in the world when you or I or Samater made unwarranted remarks about Italian politics? Do you recall the heated argument she and I had in the piazza of Vigevano? 'You have no right,' she told me, 'to discuss internal Italian politics, since you don't understand it.' At Vigevano you kicked me under the table, you pinched me, tried every means to stop me hurting her, for she had just aborted the child you impregnated her with and you said in Somali that I should be tolerant, forgiving and understanding. I obliged. I shut my mouth. Years later, guess what? An identical situation in reverse: Sandra, Samater and I in Somalia. Sandra this time is hysterical with power and she talks longwindedly, nonsensically about Somali politics, so I challenge her. I ask how come she is discussing internal Somali politics? I tell her she doesn't understand local Somali politics. I remind her of Vigevano. She raises her voice; and I, mine. She loses her temper; and I, mine. Then Samater, ingenuous as only he can be, kicks me under the table and tells me in Somali to be tolerant, forgiving and understanding. And do I oblige? Do I shut up?"

"I bet you didn't!"

"You bet. There was Atta. She and I cornered Sandra. I told myself I wasn't going to be tolerant or forgiving or understanding all my life. No tolerant Nasser and no intolerant Samater would let her off the hook this time. I insisted that she answer me."

"What was her answer?"

"She said my mistake was to look for her in the mirrored history of her grandfather's colonialist and paternalistic attitude to the African. And she went on: 'I am a Marxist and as such have the right to share my acquired experience with a government which calls itself Marxist-Leninist. I don't interfere in internal tribal politics. How can I? I don't even understand it. What I do is work with my Somali comrades towards the day when these tribal allegiances will have no more significance. Collaborate with the government as Marxists, yes. As Marxists,' she said, 'regardless of colour, creed or country, we try to exploit the contradictions for the benefit of the masses.' I think I called her *faccia tosta!* But there was nothing doing. Atta had already risen between us and awoken the dormant racial tensions. I shouted: 'Peace, peace, let there be peace among the races.'"

"But you do remember, don't you, that you quoted the Sayyid's poem about the Italians when we were at the piazza in Vigevano, the poem that goes: 'It is you (the British) who lead to pasture these weaker beasts / Can I distinguish between you and your livestock?' How she hated you whenever you quoted that or any similar poem. Although on the whole, I would say, '68 was great fun."

The fabled year of '68, precious to Medina, Samater, Nasser and Sandra as a sip of vintage wine! He remembered the long, unbroken, Ginsbergian cries; the columns of *bandiera rosa;* the *commizzi;* the long nights in the piazzas; the brown bread and the cheap wine; the hope of an orderly future, a leftist, socialist future for mankind; and Sandra shouting at the top of her voice against social *imperialismo* and *egemonismo;* and the autumn of Prague; and Medina who considered herself "a guest" in that ideology, a guest in Italy and now a guest in So-malia too; and Samater who, like a bad conscience, reminded one of where one had failed; his silence, his yes-that's-right and his holding the flag when everybody's limbs had tired. . . .

The telephone in the other room rang. Medina ignored it. Nasser said he was going to unpack. Medina said she would go to Ubax's room. They agreed to meet later in the kitchen to make something to eat.

•   •   •   •   •   •   •   •   •   •   •

He unpacked. A caseful of liquor; another colourful as an assortment of Italian wine bottles from Tuscany, Umbria and Lombardia; a third full of pharmaceutical odds and ends, pills, tampons, malaria tablets and other items Medina had asked him to acquire for her; clothes and more toys for Ubax; gifts and a parcel for Dulman. Asked how he had managed to pass through customs with it all, he shrugged his shoul-ders. She pressed him to answer. He rubbed his thumb to and fro against his forefinger – meaning money, bribery. Medina left it at that. She knew he must have paid in dollars.

"I'm embarrassed by my expensive taste," she said.

"Nonsense," he said.

The breeze in the room whose windows were wide open stirred and planted the field her brain walked with rows of thorny hurdles, curved as undotted question-marks, and she could hear Idil's accusing voice and plaintive menace, Idil talking about her expensive taste. Medina's face was sweaty like a mirror somebody had breathed on. She wiped her forehead. She put on the table in front of her whatever items she had been admiring and sat down herself. Nasser sensed the approach of a significant moment: he dropped what he had been doing and took a seat and listened.

"Four months or so ago", Medina began "two friends of mine (you've met them but probably you won't remember them) came to Somalia on a visit, having been away for twenty years and meanwhile become American citizens. They brought with them their daughter aged sixteen, a gem of joy, American as they only make them in that enormous continent, American as ketchup and Coca-Cola. The primary idea of their pilgrimage was to introduce their daughter to the country of their birth. The secondary idea was for the husband to check the data for a book he was working on, on the life of the Sayyid; and the mother, a fashion-designer, thought she would study the possibilities of taking back to the American market Somali goods such as the guntiino, the dirac, etcetera. . . . "

Her silence crawled up his spine like an insect which has found its way into one's bed when one's reaction is half numbed by sleep and the darkness of the hour. Her silence gave a Hitchcockian touch to the story she was telling: the curtains blew in the wind; a door opened and slammed shut somewhere in his roomy brain; a silence deep as the night was opaque; another door opened (he remembered the anecdote she once wrote to him about Amina who had been raped by two men and the political exploitation made of this and the hush money paid by the government), the door creaked and shut in strict obedience to the powers of nature.

"On arrival, they were gently asked to hand in their American documents and to collect them from the Immigration Office in a couple of days. They were told this was the normal routine. I bet that's what they told you when they instructed you to hand in yours."

"'Go to the Immigration Office in three days and you can have it back,' was what the officer said," Nasser enjoined. "Three days."

"When they went to the Immigration Office three days later, the officer told them that all Somalis must be proud of being Somalis and that the Revolutionary Government found it necessary to inculcate this idea into everyone. The fact that a Somali should return to his country sporting an American document was absurd and a sort of neo-colonial behaviour which the Revolution wouldn't tolerate. Our friends couldn't understand the meaning of what the officer said. He explained to them in poor bureaucratic terms that their passports had been confiscated and that they would be issued new Somali documents provided they applied for them in accordance with the laws of the Democratic Republic. The officer went on to say that they should be proud of their own nationality and should feel grateful if their request was complied with. Bewildered, they came away. They went round and sought advice. They were told this was absurd. They then began to knock on all the possible doors. They moved Kafkalike from one office to another. They finally went to the American Embassy and were told to return in a few days' time. But as they were leaving the embassy, they were stopped, frisked and taken to the Security Service Headquarters for further interrogation. They were asked to explain what they were doing at a *foreign* embassy. The officer, after a while, condescended to remind them that since their American passports were confiscated, did they not know their *foreignness* ceased as a fact? Now (you've realized by now, I hope, unless you are slow) they were being accused of spying for the Americans. They were held for a month untried; they were tortured daily: 'What secret, national information did you give to the American imperialists ?' Then they were inexplicably released. They were dumped in a car and frogmarched into a hall where a tribal chieftain presided. The tribal chieftain told them he had negotiated for their release. They were at last the sons of the clan which had given them birth. They were lent a house and supplied with all the material needs an American might require. During this period, the husband called me one day wondering if we could meet to talk things over and so that he could introduce his daughter to Samater and Ubax and me. We fixed the date, the hour we would expect them for lunch. That day we waited and waited and waited. At nightfall, when there was no sign of them, I asked Samater to use his little influence as minister to find out from the Security what had happened. We were sure they had been stopped on their way here and taken away again. But we wished we'd never made the inquiries."

"What happened?"

Her eyes were encased in thoughtfulness and were fixed as those of a painting. He would wait and make no comment. He wouldn't be unreasonable. A long pause. Then she changed the rhythm and the style in which to tell the remaining part of the story:

"Rumour had been spread that the husband was antirevolutionary: he had published an article or two in the US, apparently under pen-names. Someone he had trusted betrayed him, I think. . . . Then the tragic news."

"What tragic news, Mina?"

"The tragic news about the family."

"What happened? Were they executed, put against the wall and shot?" he asked.

Her voice was worldly, flat and noteless:

"The powerful have other ways of humiliating a victim. It broke me. The news broke me."

"What? Will you please tell me what?"

"She was sixteen, healthy and jovial. She was many things other Somali girls of her age were not. She was American. And her tongue rolled her r's like chewing-gum, her teeth were dentist-trained and her palate and stomach were unseasoned for the piquancy of Somali cuisine."

"But tell me what happened," Nasser said.

A theatrical silence. A gentle sigh. A suspense dramatic as life.

"The women hired by the newly-stipended chieftain plotted. One night, while the parents were asleep in their room, they dragged the girl out of her bed, tied her to the bed-post, gagged her mouth with a cloth and circumcised her. Poor thing."

"At sixteen?"

"Does it matter whether a girl is six or sixteen?"

"I am sorry, I didn't mean that."

"That is the same exclamatory remark Samater and every man to whom I've told the story made. 'At sixteen!' What if she were six or seven or eight, would it make a difference? Wouldn't you be just as horrified? Of course not."

Nasser was embarrassed. The silence was unbearably long. Certainly it was a horror story the like of which he had not heard in years. The violence of the fascist state chasing the poor man from pillar to post until he is securely tied to society's aggressive tradition. How much can resistance see one out of a given difficulty?

"They cut tragic figures, didn't know how to take what had happened to them. The crack in the glassy superstructure that had been the heavenly dream they imagined their daughter would wake up in became bigger, a crack whose leakage they could stop with their collective suicide. . . . "

"They committed suicide?"

"The two of them. They committed suicide when the tribal chief who had interceded on their behalf said why the girl had been circumcised: to marry her to a man of the clan."

"And the girl? What became of their daughter?"

"When she regained consciousness, she was told that her parents had gone back to America. The chieftain who was in the General's pay and was her uncle then introduced her to a man he had chosen for her. Poor thing! Not only was she not ready to be consumed like a meal, she didn't even speak the language. They converted her to the Islamic faith, and she is held prisoner somewhere in Mudugh. All this, someone told me later, was done in cahoots with the Generalissimo. The tribal chieftain knew about it. But no proof."

Nasser was lost in the turbulence of terror the story created in him. He felt small as an ant but had no hole in which to hide. Medina felt smaller and sadder: in her mind she blindly ran and ran and ran, until she came up against a wall huge as the Himalayas. When she could go no further, she stopped to reason. She decided to open up for her brother the portcullis which had remained locked since the day she left Samater, a portcullis at whose entrance a spider had woven a web.

"When Sagal who brought me the news had left, in came Idil. She saw me choked with tears. No one had ever seen me in such a state before. She enquired why. I told her. Her eyes brightened as though she had seen a meteor with the devil at its heels. She said that was what she had planned: she said she might one day take Ubax by the hand, as if taking her to the hairdresser, and have her circumcised. I vowed I wouldn't let her go anywhere near Ubax and that if she so much as exchanged a word with my daughter about this I would murder her. When Samater came home I repeated everything to him, and do you know what he did? I was still in that broken state."

"What?"

"He chuckled and said I shouldn't worry, that he would speak to her. Of course I knew he wouldn't dare. By then Ubax had begun to see Idil in her dreams, Idil carrying a knife in her hand every night. It was on the morning after the UN man came to hand the keys over to me that, during a very lucid moment, I saw the mirage which I thought would quench my vengeful thirst – yes, the mirage which finally led me here."

They were silent for the time it takes a person to change a carried weight from one hand to the other. Each shifted ideas about in his or her head. He appeared not to have accepted her explanations: *too simplistic,* he thought. He looked dissatisfied, unhappy that she seemed in no need of his mending abilities, that she wasn't "a barbecue of nerves" his cooling touch could cure. She held back; and she didn't need him. Which was why he would go and call on Dulman tomorrow; for Dulman was a woman of needs and fears – Medina, of secrets treasured and nursed with care.

"Shall we prepare something to eat?" Nasser said.

Medina was delighted he had changed the subject. "Yes, let's," she agreed.

·   ·   ·   ·   ·   ·   ·   ·   ·   ·

The kitchen was large. Its walls were furnished with shelves lined with bottled spices from India, China, the Middle East as well as Africa; tins of imported tea and cans had been laboriously labelled according to their contents. There were also some colourful containers full of dried fruits and medicinal herbs. The Indian UN man and Medina had come to an arrangement: she gave him a global sum of two hundred shillings for these. But she didn't pay him in cash. No. His wife had broken the washing-machine and the repair fee came to roughly two hundred and fifty shillings. Medina was now busily washing a pile of plates while Nasser arranged the wine bottles in a corner, arranging them as though they were to be the targets of a ten-pin bowling game.

Inside Medina hissed her rage, like a gas-stove at low combustion. She had an unmistakably long face: someone with whom she had spoken on the telephone had apparently said something which annoyed her. Ubax came in and asked:

"What's wrong with you, Medina? You said you'd come and that I should wait for you. Then you go to answer the telephone and forget all about me."

"I'm sorry."

"Who was it?"

"A silly man."

"What did he want?"

"Nothing."

Ubax's elbows curved wide at her sides like a bird's wings: a pose of challenge and of defiance. Nasser opened his mouth to speak but Ubax's stare made him tonguetied; he was used to Yusuf who never spoke, never challenged, never questioned, never answered back. He wasn't prepared for this confrontation. At Ubax's age he would never have interrogated his mother as Ubax was now doing.

Ubax tugged at Nasser's trousers. She indicated the glass she was holding and made signs that he should pour some wine into it. At first he wouldn't. He sought Medina's approval. He got it. He poured un dito of white wine into Ubax's glass. She protested, insisting that he give her more. When he refused, she took her glass and, grumbling, filled it up with water straight from the tap.

"The men who telephone me insistently," Medina said, lapsing into a foreign language her daughter couldn't understand, "make me feel like a cow rolling in the sand of its heat, a cow which displays its pinky lust like a peacock to all and sundry. They phone me one after the other, these silly tribal upstarts, call to invite me out, to be their date; they ask me to join the incestuous circle. The telephone hasn't stopped ringing since I moved here. They want their incestuous circle to grow large as their insatiable lust. They invite me to join the circle Sandra and Atta have begun. And I refuse."

Nasser, avoiding her eyes, opened a drawer in which he found a cheque made out to Samater and signed by Medina. He wondered if he should remind her of the other cheque he had found inside the *Espresso* which was in the toilet, the *Espresso* whose article she had read avidly and underlined. He remembered her once mentioning that she and Samater had an account together which was in her name since he had more faith in her administrative capability than she in his. Moreover, whenever someone came to him with some heartrending demand, when any clansman or clanswoman came asking for a tribal contribution, Samater didn't know how to turn them away empty-handed; whereas every clansman and clanswoman knew they had no chance with Medina.

"Who are these men anyway?" asked Nasser.

"You don't know them. They are tribal upstarts, *nouveaux arrivistes.*"

"But who are they?"

Medina turned to face Ubax whose questioning look she knew she should answer. It was obvious that she was nervous, that she was withholding something. She gesticulated as she was about to speak and forgot the soaped plate she held in her hand. It dropped and broke. Silence. Nasser gathered up the half-moons of the broken plate and put them in the bin.

"These men are the new upstarts of the tribal oligarchy," she said. "They have arrived with the same suddenness as the wealth of petrol-dollar countries."

Ubax helped herself to more of the wine. Neither of the adults said anything to her. Medina took a seat. Nasser wondered what Idil would say if she could see her granddaughter drinking wine undisturbed. Medina continued:

"These are the *nouveaux arrivistes* whom the tribal oligarchy has recruited from the various clans in the General's favour to fill positions which have fallen vacant through his imprisoning the *titolari* or on account of these people choosing to remain in exile. One can recognize them by their showmanship."

Nasser recalled seeing a couple of men who fitted the description. And, of course, he had met them in Jedda and in Rome. He had been shocked to see them behave as if the embassy in Jedda or that in Rome belonged to them. With one or two, whom he had known before the boom of tribal power, he had even dined at the Cicerone Hotel in

Rome. He agreed with Medina that sudden wealth created a certain in-coherence in one's lifestyle, just as sudden power did; sudden wealth turned one into a spendthrift: one discovered that one had spent the money before one's fingertips felt the silver lining of the banknotes. It was like a running stomach: one sensed the sudden, unexpected emptiness.

The telephone rang, filling the kitchen with its insistence.

"May I answer it?" he asked.

Medina was in two minds whether to let him or not. Because he was over-indulgent and too protective towards her, she feared he would be unnecessarily rude to the caller. She watched him stand up and set down his glass on the table between them; she watched him go out but neither encouraged nor discouraged him. He was back in less than the minute it took to drain her glass and pour herself some more wine.

"Who was it?" she asked.

"No one."

"What do you mean, no one?"

"When *he* heard my voice, he hung up on me."

"How do you know it was a he?"

"Only tribal upstarts are as susceptible to influences as that, and fearful of the inevitable confrontation."

They now heard Ubax softly sobbing. They looked at each other, then at Ubax. Her sobbing, like a deliberate alteration of speech technique, gave force to her protestation.

"What's wrong, Ubax?" Nasser said.

She blew her nose. "The same thing. It's always the same thing."

Medina's forehead, puzzled, was lined with open-ended rows of wrinkles. The veins of her hands, Nasser noticed, crossed like the routes of a metropolis and were swollen. He turned to his niece:

"What are you talking about?"

"Medina and Samater always talk in a foreign language when they don't want me or Idil to listen. That way they needn't bother about me being there and don't have to tell me to go outside to play, like other parents tell their children. They speak Somali when they want to shut Sandra or Atta out. Now you are doing the same thing, Uncle Nasser, and I don't like it. Medina and Samater can't say I haven't told them. And now I'm telling you: it's unfair."

"What do you suggest we do?" It was true that her presence was sometimes inconvenient.

"Since you don't want me around, I'm leaving to give you and Medina the chance to talk about these men or about politics. Please call me when dinner's ready."

She went out of the kitchen. Behind her she left the weight of a complaint neither could dismiss easily. They were silent for a long time, not knowing quite where to begin or what to do or say. Finally Nasser rose to prepare dinner; and Medina went to make peace with Ubax.

·   ·   ·   ·   ·   ·   ·   ·   ·   ·   ·

An hour and a quarter later:

"I don't guarantee you'll eat well," he said. His eyes were clear as the vegetable soup he had made; his gaze was as vague as the pale circle of a young moon.

Medina and Nasser were alone in the kitchen, for Ubax had suddenly doubled up in exhaustion and couldn't manage even any of the soup. While Medina was telling her daughter a personalized version of the Arabian Nights, Nasser had searched for a neutral subject which took into account her barbecued nerves. He thought he would for a change altogether omit mention of Idil and Samater, as well as Ubax, nor would he allow their conversation to breathe life into Fatima bint Thabit's hovering ghost. This was easiest, he decided, now that he knew (or thought he knew) why Medina had left Samater. But something haunted his mind, like an irritation which wouldn't clear. Why did Medina herself not speak to Idil if she knew that Samater wouldn't? Why? Granted, she sought the quiet her house couldn't offer and so left and moved here; she sought a means of filling her house with her *absence,* in the same way that Xaddia did; she sought the easiest method of making herself the subject of everyone's conversation. In this way, she was sure that Samater and Idil would talk about her and would eventually come to a head-on clash. She hoped they would come to an agreement or a disagreement; she hoped they would decide on their own whether they felt the presence of her absence as much as they had sensed Xaddia's. Medina had once told Nasser that she was *the stranger* in Samater's and Idil's life; indubitably her presence made them behave themselves, and they hardly fought when she was there. For years, she said, she had been *the guest* who forbade them to speak their minds, who made them postpone their confrontation, postpone it until *the guest* was gone, until they were alone and could speak to each other as mother and son. Every topic, every discussion between them could trigger off a quarrel. But what did Medina hope to get out of this confrontation? Idil disapproved of everything Samater represented. This was no secret and they both knew it. Suppose, however, that Idil won more rounds? Suppose she won the present round – the one in which she suggested Samater marry a maid of her choice? Did Medina not realize that a confrontation with Idil meant a direct challenge to tradition, to the General's generation? Could she not see Sandra, the Ideologue, etcetera, among the spectators, pleased either way, not caring whether it was Samater or Idil who won? For this was a fight they had themselves won on points, with Medina the loser in any case.

Nasser took a sip of his wine. He looked up. His eyes met Medina's. She tasted the soup. Her gaze neutralized his worried appearance.

"They eat well who are less religious," he said.

She took another mouthful. "Less religious or irreligious?"

He went on as though he hadn't heard her challenge, as if the distinction did not concern him:

"They are less inhibited and less worried about whether or not they offend the sacred sense of diet." Nasser uncorked another wine bottle – a Chianti – and passed it to her to pour. "A Muslim, a Jew, or a Hindu each has but a few items which the scriptures have not forbidden. Add to this the fact that what is not tabooed by religion is forbidden by tradition."

She had filled two glasses with wine. She was thinking about Samater who was probably poorly provided with any drink unless he went out of the house in which Idil, the self-proclaimed protector of tradition and religion, ruled with the iron fist of a dictator. Medina was convinced that Idil hadn't thrown away the liquor but had sequestered it somewhere, and wouldn't bring it out until Samater swore he wouldn't touch it; tight-fisted as she was, Idil would never waste all that money, nor would she know how to sell the alcohol if she wanted to. Medina remembered how easily she could orchestrate Idil's moods to make her look ridiculous to herself whenever the topic led to what one should drink or eat. For Medina would simply confess that she had been brought up on "the meats and milks of infidels" and had no choice but to follow the habits she had developed. "How can you eat the meat of pork or drink liquor? Does your conscience not prick you?" Idil would finally tire and give up. Whereas there was an understanding between Medina and Fatima bint Thabit that so long as these forbidden foods were consumed in her absence the matter did not concern her; which meant perhaps that Fatima bint Thabit did not pretend to have power over her daughter's decisions.

Medina sipped her wine. Nasser served the first course.

"They do not eat well whose eating-habits remain private and unvaried," he continued. "In Somalia, men have the best part of the meat, women the entrails of animals and the leftovers. They eat the same thing day after day and are therefore uninventive; they are not promiscuous in their thoughts. Homogeneity in gastronomy is a disadvantage."

"How do you mean?"

"Chinese cuisine, Indian and Mediterranean peoples' foods are richer and more varied than, say, the untravelled kitchens of Zambia or Australia. Parmesan cheese is as great an invention as cotton-wear or silk."

"Wait a minute –"

"Add a dash of garlic salt and you change the texture and taste of what you eat."

"Garlicky food, I would have thought, knocks one down with its pungent smell and heavy flavour and makes one lethargic and belchy. Which reminds me of something Stendhal said: that everything tastes flat and lifeless to a person who comes from where the seasoning is high."

Nasser looked at her suspiciously for he did not believe she had quoted the Frenchman correctly. It was also his opinion that she had quoted him out of context. He sighed. He dipped a slice of bread in his soup but didn't manage to get it into his mouth before half of it dropped off onto his trousers. Medina gave him her paper serviette. A little later, all that was heard was her munching noise which alternated with the movement of Nasser's Adam's apple. Then someone turned a key in the front door and opened it. Medina explained that it was the maid who had just returned from her evening class. Nasser remembered Medina writing him that she helped pay for the classes.

"She is unlike all other maids I've known," said Medina. "No, she won't come unless I call her. She'll go straight to her room and prepare for bed."

"But the poor thing is probably hungry." He had taken a second helping.

"She is very private and very quiet and won't come in here so long as we are here. When we've gone, she'll steal into the kitchen like a thief and help herself, then cover things again the way she found them. The maid Samater and I had was noisy and nosy. Though she was great fun to be with."

Nasser reluctantly took his seat. He felt a question surge to his throat, a question about Samater, about the maid, about Idil and, naturally, about Medina, too. Undotted in its unutterability, the question stayed in his throat and tickled the nerves of his larynx like the two-day old stubble of a beard. His wandering gaze focused on Medina and he wondered if she sensed his uneasiness. Should he wait, like the dry hot earth waits for the cool rainy season? Should he wait like a calf for its mother? Or should he push her a little, jerk her memory and shake it as children do a fruity lemon tree? Suddenly he cleared his throat as though it had been irritated by the touch of passing dust.

"The maid at Samater's –" he said.

"What about her?"

Someone had told him there was something between the maid and Samater. But now he hadn't the courage to ask if there was a grain of truth in the gossip he had heard in Rome. The question remained poised in the unfleshed status of the unspoken. Nasser drew the curtain on all that should have remained private and unuttered.

"Yes, Nasser. What about Samater's maid?"

He was quiet. The stage was bare. He couldn't people the ring with a Samater confronting an Idil, traditionally a favourite and possibly the winner, an Idil who considered herself the defending champion; and among the applauders he saw Sandra and the Ideologue. Round after indecisive round Medina's absence from the scene filled the air with wedding bells, a shower of confetti and a feast thrown in honour of the champion. This put "the stranger" in the place where "the stranger' belonged; and when the guest was gone, the mist of misunderstanding cleared. But what if the decisive confrontation did take place and the son took things into his own hands, floored his mother and then threw her out? Did that not mean he would lose his job? And then? Imprisonment? Were things likely to happen that way, or did this show that he was too prone to the same fears? Suspicions and paranoia that the whole country suffered from? Meanwhile, Medina couldn't tolerate the silence and she gently steered the conversation back to people's eating-habits and was saying:

"When researching for an article on the Sahelian drought, I read everything I could get my hands on: books about malnutrition; statistics of infant mortality; the policies of the American and Soviet administrations on the starving millions in Africa and Asia; the tactics of the European governments in taking away Africa's wealth yet helping not at all to impress on the puppet regimes the seriousness of the situation—since the economic intelligence the multinational companies gather could easily have informed them of what was to come. The USA sells to the Soviet Union at a prohibitive price the wheat the starving Third World needs in order to maintain its hegemony. And think of nature or God. Rain causes the outbreak of a hundred and one types of insect about which we in Africa know little: grassland termites compete with cattle and man for whatever scarce pasture is available; tsetse flies account for two-thirds of the annual (potential?) production in Africa; armyworm moths; sorghum shootflies. Hardly worth our scientific effort how insects are eaten as food – the Turkana peoples have an ant-delicacy they prepare for their most honoured guests. We know very little about the insects and the plant hormones and the livestock ticks. Obviously we cannot find solutions until we know what and who we are dealing with. The American and Soviet and European governments might silence the crying mouths with rice- and milk-powder. Africa's malnutrition nourishes the multinationals, and the unstudied three hundred odd insects."

She stopped. She looked tired and sad and she held her head in her hands. She was slow in coming to the point.

"The hand which feeds has power over whom it feeds," she said. "The absence of one presupposes the absence of the other. *Guarda caso*: the only time a woman in the Islamic tradition is given the right to 'divorce' her husband is when he is unable to provide her and her children with the food and clothes they need. *Masruuf* and *marasho*. The multinational of the metropolis or the oligarchy of the presidium open or close the taps of provision."

A slight pause. Then:

"During the 1974/75 famine here in Somalia, for example. . . . Planeloads of starving northerners were brought and made to settle in the greener southern regions. Others were forced to become fishermen. The government's propaganda machinery exploited this, the news was carried on the front pages of several international papers, there were FAO delegations and UNESCO's aid mission and a planeload of tourists. When the government had collected as much money as could be got from raising the hopes of international foundations or philanthropic Scandinavian organizations, the General lost his original enthusiasm and the helpers who had been sent there were disbanded. It's since been written off as a project which has failed."

Another pause. And:

"As far as I am concerned, this enabled the General not only to make money out of the misery of these starving millions, money with which to finance the security services, but he has also made revolutionary publicity out of it. What's more, he has been able to break the pockets of resistance which were strong in the north. The famine has enabled him to divide families in order to rule them. Just as I am quite sure the Soviet intelligence service was aware of the threatening drought long before it occurred but chose to wait. I see this as a continuation of the same barbaric methods as were used by the Americans when they caused famine in Southeast Asia. It's easier to negotiate from a position of power with a hungry country; it's easier to rule a starving family. There were signs of this drought as early as 1972. Haile Selassie used hunger as a controlling force in the Ogaden, Wallo, Sidamo and other provinces. The strategy has remained the same: *starve and rule.*"

Nasser was going to pour her some more wine but she raised her hand and shook her head. The brief pause became a long silence. He hadn't the courage to share with her the juxtaposition of notions and suppositions that furnished his mind. But perhaps it was better to let her finish. She was much closer to these things than he. All he could have done would be to try to correct her thesis slightly, improve on it here and there. One couldn't be as categorical as that.

Why had she left Samater? To make him see how much in need of her he was, she would wait until he came crawling on all fours. *Starve and rule.* Or had it all started with a small notion, with her saying that she wanted to change the position of a chair, which in turn required the shifting of the bed and other furniture, as she had explained in her letter? Yes, did she want to be the centre of everything? But she wasn't able to conduct things from the position she held, and events took their own course. The original notion was small but essential as original sin; then Cain came for the kill; and Idil's plot thickened as Nasser's soup. *Waxaan dhuuso mooday miyaa xaar igu noqday!* She was the mistress whom the dog dragged along as the leash stretched and stretched. Again she changed the subject:

"Incidentally, for tomorrow's festival of fires would you like to come with me and Ubax?"

"Where are you going?" Nasser asked.

"We plan to spend the day with Fatima bint Thabit."

He was reluctant to say anything at first. He drew his eyes up like a bow-string, then narrowed them as though about to aim at a target. A smile light as margarine covered his face and spread downwards to the chin, producing a softening effect on his features which had gone rigid at the mention of their mother's name.

"I plan to spend the Neyrus with Dulman," he said. "I intend to talk to her about the underground theatre and business. In any case it's preferable to spend the first day of the year with someone one cares about."

Medina decided not to risk asking. Was it the hand-kissing ritual he couldn't stand? (He'd said something to that effect once.) One inclined one's head when kissing Fatima bint Thabit's unringed fingers and Nasser often spoke of how he loathed himself for doing that. Medina managed to keep her distance, managed to remain *formal* with her mother, no bowing of head, no touching, no kissing. Ubax didn't like the hand-kissing either.

"Dulman told me she gave you some tapes for me. Have you had a chance to listen to them? Do you think that aside from their artistic worth one can also sell them?"

"I haven't had a chance to listen to them. They're in the other house.

I'm sorry, I clean forgot about them. Perhaps you could call Samater, if he's back, and ask him to bring them over or something."

"I don't want to see Samater at this point."

"It's risky anyway dealing in these underground tapes."

"I hold a foreign passport. All they could do is deport me."

"They've confiscated your passport just as they dispossessed the American family whose story I told you. If I were you, I'd prepare myself for the worst."

"You don't need to be that pessimistic."

This halted their forward movement and diverted their mental direction elsewhere. She looked sad. Was it because she was remembering the tragic story? She appeared broken and weak. She looked like an upturned chair, malpositioned and ugly. She went out of the kitchen.

•   •   •   •   •   •   •   •   •   •   •

"Life is a pot which your struggling feet break when you are born," Nasser would say. "All your life, you work towards the moment when you can mend the pot. To do this is next to impossible. But when you succeed, you become the happiest person on the face of this earth; and you join the ragged, dented edges of your broken halves and make them whole again. If you are fortunate, you meet another person whose broken half has the same dents, the same jagged edges as yours. You fall in love the instant you meet this other person. Then with the passage of years, the dents show differences in the tincture and texture; the two halves will no longer fit, they won't form a whole when put together. Yes, the moment has come, the inevitable has taken place, the hour of parting has arrived. Each must search for another person whose pot's dents are similar to his or hers."

•   •   •   •   •   •   •   •   •   •   •

Nasser loved mending broken things regardless of whether, once mended, they served any purpose. If, for instance, while taking a promenade, he spotted a branch about to fall off its parent tree, Nasser would stop and with dedicated patience try to see what could be done. He wouldn't leave until he had put it into the least hurtful position. He had been known to bury dead birds. He used to come home carrying a stray cat with a bruised leg, a bird with a wing nearly gone, or a hopeless animal spending its last wind. He used to fight with any child who chased or stoned dogs. And Fatima bint Thabit would say: "If you touch a dog just don't come home; dogs are impure." One day he asked her why, and her answer surprised and shocked him: "A dog bit off a chunk of Adam's foot: that's why human beings have insteps."

A broken glass. A limping bird. A sick mother with a child, weak with the complications of underfeeding. A dog's panting tongue of painful loneliness. A cat with a wet nose. "You can find God in these or similar helpless creatures," he would say. "God is not in mosques made beautiful and covered from wall to wall with Saudi donations of silk. Neither is He in the church on whose starry chandeliers dwell the saints' eyes. God lives in the crack of a mirror, the broken wing of a bird. He is in the lungs of a dog running away from the children who are stoning it to death. We run from the duplicate fears of the shadow we most fear, don't we? When a machine cuts off a worker's finger, it is in that finger, if restored, that you can find God: He is in the fold of the hurt joint of the finger, He is in the pained scar of memory."

Uncle Saleh would comment: "Nasser is a collector of oddities, human or animal. He collects the corpses and the wingcases of cockroaches. But why does he do all this? Because he hasn't friends and cannot make them. In a way, this gives him a chance to gather his missing parts." And he would punish him; Nasser would be made to starve. His uncle would bring him the Koran and he would be asked to chant it hour after hour, late into the night. Medina would steal into his room with food, Medina who, because she was a girl, was never asked to read a verse of the Koran; Medina who, because she was a girl, was allowed to go into the kitchen without being reprimanded. (It was much later when they joined Barkhadle in Europe that the two could be together when they chose; and Nasser could collect what trivia he wished; and Medina could read the Koran if she so pleased.) But he used to confide in Medina: "When I grow up, I shall kill Grandfather and break Mother's neck and will not keep it as a souvenir, neither will I permit anyone to mend it. Or else I'll give her a broken feather. That is what she deserves."

What did Nasser find in all this? Did he find solace in comforting a startled child? Did he find consolation in touching the nerve of a dog's need of companionship? Sandra said: "He feels superior, the one and only person who has this hidden talent for restoring things to their original order and state of being. He thinks he is great when he is standing right in the centre of a hospital of oddities. He fears the feeble cry in the middle of the night, the feeble cry of the helpless weak." But Medina would intervene, Medina who had known him longer and who loved him more than anybody else. What did these people know about him? She would say: "Nasser finds the state of these people, animals and objects interesting. He somehow sees a resemblance between man's mental condition and these people's or animals' abject misery."

But what about Fatima bint Thabit? What was their relationship like now that Nasser was grown-up, with a wife and child? "Medina is black with un-Islamic thoughts but does visit me now and again. She comes and asks after my health, and is willing, if asked, to provide for my meagre needs. Nasser? Do you know he did not call on me until he was ready to leave, last time he was here? His wife, poor thing, with her beetle eyes and the tongueless burden Allah presented them with for a child, plucked up enough courage to visit me. She was sweeter to me than he; just as Samater, in his own way, is a lot kinder to me than Medina."

Now Nasser was seated in the living-room, with a drink in his hand, waiting for Medina to return. These worries misted the windows of his memory but he was in a snow-covered land, a Europe which had been under a winter's siege. Then the night wind brought him a waft of Dulman's voice, Dulman his favourite singer and the woman to whom he felt very close and in his own way loved. He would see her tomorrow, he hoped. He promised himself that they would build a fire together, they would welcome the New Year together. Dulman was a barren woman, a broken woman; she was much more in need of his mending abilities than Medina who could still hold her head high and who had her saxifrage which survived the weight of walking feet. Medina had numerous open doors to enter, whereas Dulman waited for only one door to open, a door into and out of which a pram could be wheeled. Nothing else mattered to her. Only children. Her fibroids did not hurt as much as the absence of children from her life.

A little later, the air was soaked with soot. Medina looked outside and watched, with intensity and passion, the stars which were spaced like dice cast with meaningful deliberateness. Would tomorrow's flames offer a response to the question Medina's leaving Samater made everyone ask? Would tomorrow's New Year festivities bring Sagal's rivals closer to the championship? Would tomorrow's *Neyrus* tell Dulman that she would no longer be barren and would soon be with child? Would tomorrow's *Dabshid* soak Samater's roots with new hope? Would Idil, who had burrowed in the fringes of the mined area and dug at the most dangerous spots, get away with it? Would the sixteen-year-old survivor of the Somali-Americans grow without complexes, would she feel light as wood-shavings, escorting the wind like a starred flag?

Nasser listened to the heavy baying of the night outside. He would not admit that he saw a vague similarity between his case and that of the Somali-Americans. Since he had handed his own passport over to the Immigration Officer, would he, too, be told, on going there in a couple of days, that he was to be issued with a Somali travel-document? Somehow he doubted that this would happen. And so in silence they sipped their drinks, their minds alight with the bonfire of the hope the New Year festivities might bring to everyone.

PART TWO

I am like the crescent moon: my cup is not full.

– Moamed Iqbal

When the bread is scarce, there is hunger.

When the bread is bad, there is discontent.

– Bertolt Brecht

. . . .

A galaxy of charred stars in flight. A deposit of the day's tears in smoke, tears of ash sprinkled on the year just ended. The year's blessing was expressed in burning ashes light as dead leaves, which flew and floated here and there and in the air like dust and fell like dusk. Ebla had suggested to Sagal and her friend Amina before she left for her shop that they keep a pail of water within reach in case the fire went out of control like the neighbour's. There was no need to remind them of what had happened to the neighbour's child and thatch hut. The news had travelled faster than the flames which reduced the child and the hut to ashes powdery as talcum; the news had travelled faster than the wind which gave chase to but couldn't catch the devil in the flames. Sagal was, however, doubtful whether the child would have survived another season had she not died in the fire. She had been a poor little thing, very bony, and had suffered from every malnutritional disease before she was a year old. All her life she had been ill and had never known a day in which she did not vomit, did not suffer from diarrhoea, did not cough. If she didn't cough, she had some disease her mother had no name for. Kwashiorkor. Xerophthalmia. Bronchopneumonia. Sagal had talked to the mother on several occasions, tried to convince her to take the little girl to a hospital. The woman said she didn't have the money with which to buy milk for her child, no milk and no food – and how could she speak of medicine? Did food come before milk and medicine before both? Of course. But now the death of the child made holes in Sagal's heart, holes small as maggoty brown millet. A young fire extinguished . . . and the old not yet!

"How old was she?" Amina asked.

"Less than a year and a half. Maybe a year and four months. You couldn't tell her age, because malnutrition had disfigured her body and she was such a small thing."

"The first year is crucial. Death waits for children at every angle and leaps out at them. Three hundred thousand children each year. That's a lot for a country with a population of less than four million. Poor Somalia!"

"But this one died because that stupid mother of hers left her alone in the hut and padlocked the door without telling anyone the child was inside."

"She would've died from measles, TB, scurvy or pellagra before her second birthday. What difference does it make? Where did her mother go, anyway?"

"While the house was burning, someone said, the mother was in a long queue, getting a kilo of meat and one of rice to cook a meal for her husband who had sent word that he would come for lunch. Hold your comments, please, till you hear the full story."

"Go on, then."

"Her husband, whom she hadn't seen for a long time, had invited himself to lunch. Excited over this, she went and stood in this long queue. She probably was of the impression that they would reconcile once they met, that they would arrive at a compromise."

"Stupid woman," said Amina. "How could she stand in a queue and leave a child like that?"

"You don't stand in lines, nor does Medina, so please spare your naive comments. Of course nor do I. Nor Ebla. We're of the privilegentsia, one way or the other."

Sagal looked away and stared at the fire whose glowing grin welcomed the New Year. A little later, her eyes travelled to and dwelled on dusty crossroads at one of whose junctions Amina had parked her car. Her thoughts: the burning line of lightning in a dark night; she remembered two nights as dissimilar as two versions of one anecdote. Astir in the ground of one of these nights, the distant noise of thunder in the air; whispering conspiracies; trousers being unzipped; shoelaces being forcibly undone; and the sight of blood; the smell of rape. In the background of the other night: things moving as subtly as ants feeding on the destruction of a foundation; here the scene is more jovial, there is a party going on, the hour is late, the night is advanced, and there are a few couples on the floor soaked in the sweat of early morning lust. The heroine of the anecdote doesn't know the man's surname nor is she bothered about it. The first night sowed two seedy stars on the surface of the sky; the harvest is late; the heavens are clear as a pool; the moon is reflective like a mirror. The heroines of the two nights are young as the clouds which would, on the morrow, wrap themselves round the sun just born. Two nights, one long, long ago; the other just under four weeks away. Amina and Sagal: the heroines!

"And my mother Ebla keeps nagging at me, says I must give her a child. What future is there for a child born now, under the tutelage of the General, Father of the Nation, General Warden of this Prison – what future?"

Amina was silent. It may have been a bad idea of Sagal's to talk frivolously and glibly about such things; but Amina wore a sour grin for a long time and looked dismally unhappy. It was regretful that she had made her friend unhappy. To make amends, Sagal decided to confide in Amina her preoccupation that having slept with that man – what was his name? Wentworth George . . . well, truth must be owned – she was probably pregnant. She recalled something Ebla said once about the politics of resistance: that the weak, in order to punish the powerful, undermine their own activities, commit silly mistakes and in the final analysis, unless they are cautious, become their own victims. True to form, Sagal took it upon herself to recruit Wentworth George for their camp. It had crossed her mind that this would earn Medina and Amina's admiration and respect. She had hoped, if she succeeded, to get a well-done pat on the back, a slap-of-the-five Afro-American style and a tell-us-how-you-did-it! Now, however, she was in no doubt this wouldn't come about. The man, it seemed, had been seen very often in the company of *the enemy*. There was a rumour that his freelance work would appear in the daily paper. Not only that, the man had become a frequent companion, and therefore a friend, of the Ideologue and Sandra. If Sagal told either Medina or Amina of her predicament all she would extract from them would probably be a drawn out sigh. Yes, that was more like it. She would, in addition, get their you-stupid-little-thing, why-did-you-do-it and a heartrending look of sympathy and a silence filled, like a magician's sack, with clues to heavenly mysteries and solutions to the problem at hand.

"Are you all right, Sagal?" asked Amina.

"Yes, I am. Why?"

"You don't look all right to me. Your painful expression speaks for you."

No comment from Sagal. The children of the village had come closer to Amina and Sagal's fire, there was more noise than before. Some of the girls drew lines on the dusty ground and began to compete among themselves to see who could jump furthest or skip more squares without touching the ground with both feet. The boys, who were excluded from this, started their game of football in the dusty courtyard nearby: other smaller girls crouched on the floor and played *shanlax*. Games of childhood, children's lore and literary riddles such as adults didn't have answers to. Folktales which made the universe a place worthy of one's love and logic and understanding. Why did the lion fall out with the hyena? Songs. Fairytales. *Kabacalaf and Huryo. Dhag-dheer.* Look and listen. There were other girls chanting a nursery rhyme. . . . *Guun guun, Guun saar/Tan mahee, Teeda kale keen!* The fairyland of childhood from which Ubax was probably excluded – perhaps not, thought Sagal. Or was she really? She had no time to answer that. Amina was saying:

"So you've decided to train for the swimming competition. Do I also understand that you've already been twice to the Orientation Centre? How do you feel about it all? And how do you rate yourself? I mean, what are your chances of winning? What about Cadar and Hindiya who are seeded second and third?"

Sagal's eyes were still as a monument's. A very long pause. What were her chances? Did this not depend on whether or not she was pregnant, did it not, in the end, depend on her state of mind? Her chances were meagre. But could she tell her friend? Could she tell Amina that she had been deeply impressed when she trained with Cadar and Hindiya that morning? She had been so impressed she thought they should have been seeded first and second and she third. Could she afford to be honest with Amina? Well? In that case, she should tell Ebla and Medina, she should speak to them about her predicament. While Amina was waiting for her answer, something which attracted everybody's attention occurred: another thatched hut in the neighbourhood was ablaze. All the children rushed away in the direction from which the noise came. This gave Sagal a chance to skirt round the question. She decided to lead the conversation in a roundabout way to houses burning in conspiratorial fires.

"Did you know that there was a family conspiracy to burn the wing of the house in which Medina was born? Medina, just born, nearly died in that fire. It is believed that her grandfather was behind the plot. Did Medina ever tell you?"

"I know."

"Did you also know that Nasser's birth was greeted with a flood?"

"The flood is of an elemental nature; the fire may have been conspiratorial." Amina was quiet like a child just tucked in. And Sagal continued:

"For instance. Who burnt Giuba Hotel? Who set on fire the ten thousand quintals of sugar in the factory store? The Security? The manager of the Jowhar Sugar Factory because his administration justifiably wouldn't account for the embezzlement of government funds?"

Silence. Then Amina's eyes lit up like a lantern.

"It all began with that mythical theft, didn't it?" she said.

"I'm sorry?"

"Prometheus, the rival of Zeus, who stole a live coal and taught mortals how to make use of it. These conspiracies of a Promethean grandeur: one's liver is thrown to the vultures."

The mist upon the window of Sagal's memory would not clear; she couldn't remember what she had in mind when she led the conversation to "conspiratorial fires", to Medina's grandfather or the burning of Giuba. Prometheus, the rival of Zeus, the stealer of fire, the demi-god who was generous enough to share with man the secrets and the power of fire. That's it: the power! Now:

"The corporal has been nominated chauffeur-in-residence. He drives the Mercedes of a man considered to be of tremendous importance in the party. The corporal sits at the wheel of power. He has come to this village once or twice to show off, to display the marvel of twentieth-century technology to the children of the village. The children were terribly excited. They forget that they knew him as a corporal who drove an army vehicle, Russian-made and very battered too."

"At the entrance of the palace of power stands a corporal at attention and he gives way as the fire-eater walks by, and as the lantern-carrier goes past. Is this what you mean?"

First she nodded. Then:

"The compass-needle of power jerks to life; it points at a three-digit figure, gains speed, its head well-balanced, reading the meter; the figure becomes a four-digit one; the foot-pedal pumps new energy and makes the blood of the thermometer rise higher and higher. But neither the party-man nor the chauffeur-in-residence can read the computerized dials of the Mercedes, nor do they understand the meaning of the numbers the indicators show."

"What is the point you're trying to make, Sagal?"

"The privileges granted to the chauffeur-in-residence are numerous. He lives in the servants' quarters of the party man who's issued a red ration-card that exempts its bearer from queuing to get a kilo of sugar, of meat or oil."

"What has the corporal done with the red ration-card?"

"He's given it to his newly-acquired mistress. The ironies of life play high-handed jokes on one, don't they? And there is the other wicked side of the story, the version which has it that because the wife heard that her corporal of a husband gave the red ration-card to his newly-acquired mistress, she decided that she would go, stand in a long queue and meantime set the house and child ablaze. Why, they say, she stood in that queue long as death when she knew that the child was inside, too."

"Poor child!"

"Anyway, she put a padlock on the door and didn't tell anyone that the child was inside. Which is what she used to do whenever she went out to get something."

"I don't believe it."

The fire was still warm although it had become less expressive. The ash had gathered into a pile and stood aside; on the fringes, it had grown wrinkles like tree-rings.

"Poor who? Poor child or poor parents? Not only has this tribal oligarchy robbed the woman of her husband but it has also denied her all possibilities of survival. And the husband? The regime has reduced him to someone without dignity or integrity. And don't talk to me of the fire brigade. What kind of fire brigade is it that has its headquarters ten or so miles from anywhere?"

"A Promethean intervention is in order!"

Silence. Sagal was thinking: *We are the bark a tree has discarded and another cannot wear.* Then the wind of her imagination began to shake things so wildly she felt as though she were merely a branch of a tree. There: the wild fields of a future emerged from behind the greener courts of others. And in this future of futures, she was with a child, a child of her own flesh and blood, a child so sweet and smiling she reminded her of Ubax. Her mind scattered the seeds further afield and (what a pleasant surprise!) harvested a future of delight. Unlike her friend Amina, who always dreamt of having the island of happiness to herself, Sagal wanted to be among the very people who had begat her island of unhappiness; she also wanted to be with Medina, Ebla and her close friend Amina. Had she not always said she wasn't going to have a child, that she wouldn't condescend to having anything to do with childbearing? But so had her mother. And when she bore Sagal, she wasn't sure whose child she was.

What about her future as a swimmer? What about her future anywhere? Would she defy nature, her ambition, her wants? Would she, like Amina, have a child in order to prick the nation's conscience with guilt? Now her future, it seemed, chose to separate itself from the rest; it stood out, giant as ambition, large as a dreamt wish, but like promised goods not yet delivered. She was telling herself the story – *her story!* A woman, without taking the necessary precautions, one night made love to a man she had not met before that evening. And then? A hesitant pause came after this. Had the well of her imagination run dry? Why didn't she continue? Her double told her other double that she shouldn't *judge* but that she should *narrate;* certainly, she shouldn't blame *the reason* or *the act* itself, for both were noble in themselves. Whom should she blame then? She intended to serve a cause. It was sad that that was the wrong night; or that her constitution arrested the flow of life; or that all these, in turn, had agitated the waters of her future; or that she betrayed the hope and trust others close to her had invested in her. She had miscalculated; that was all.

She noticed that Amina had got up and was waving to a small child at whom she grinned like a visiting queen to her vassals: Amina's grin was condescending and her waving hand, her manner suggested hesitation coupled with condescension A look at the child assured Sagal that she had correctly understood the relationship just forged between Amina and the newly arrived child. A thought: was it not Nietzsche who spoke of childhood as the tragic door through which every adult has walked? Somalis say every adult camel was once a two-year-old infant. Is tragedy seminal in the outgrowing of one's own childhood?

Then she looked at the fire which, she realized, unless fed with more fuel would die prematurely. The ashes had turned greyer. The sun, meanwhile, had begun to crown herself with a halo of brightness; she surrounded herself with a congregation of clouds.

"Shall we go in? asked Amina.

But she did not wait for Sagal to say anything. Amina collected some of the things the two had brought out and went in. Meantime, Sagal emptied a bucket of water on the fire, kill it lest it claim another young life.

• • • • • • • • • • •

They went inside, leaving behind a bed of ashes upon which lay the ghost of the slaughtered year.

Sagal decided not to tell Amina the worry with which she woke up: that she would miss her period. She took a soda out of the fridge and passed it to Amina who was sitting on the edge of the bed which she herself lay across. The ugliness of the unmade bed disturbed Amina, so she suggested she make it while Sagal put on some music. They listened to John Coltrane without speaking. Coltrane. Cabral. Stills from *Lucia*. But neither was thinking about distant revolutions or films. Sagal was thinking about the little girl who came to her in the form of a sad image of a bereaved mother kneeling by the tomb of her dead daughter: she quoted to herself a poem by Al-Zahawi, the Kurdish poet, the sad lament of a mother on the death of her little angel. In the first lines of the poem, the daughter does not know why she is in this world, why, indeed, she has visited this discontented world; in the last lines, she doesn't know why she is leaving it as though she were an intruder. A little thing born astraddle the bridges which connect life and death; a little thing which came not to stay. An *abiku*! Amina? Amina was thinking about a secret – yes, a secret which had to do with writing on walls and a purge.

"Coltrane is such a marvellous poet, isn't he?" said Amina.

"Yes," she nodded.

Her mind drifted like wood on a stream. Another poet, this time, a local one: Abdi Qays, one of Somalia's finest living poets, singing psalms of praise to his daughter, to whom he makes a promise: to build for her a love-castle. Further along the road, Sagal's memory picked up and immediately dropped the name of Nur Ali Qonof. The beauty of innocence, the verity of this beauty. Imagine how innocuous: little girls whose ankle trinkets rang like bells on their running feet. The poem in'question was Tagore's. Then Yeats's "Prayer to My Daughter," which Medina had translated into Somali. And in the palace of her poetic-memory? She saw little girls, chattery with joy, who held the world's heart in the glowing smiles of their teeth. But when these innocuous things grew up, when the Kurdish girl, the Bengali girl, the Irish or the Somali grew into womanhood – what would be their lot? In Somalia, fifteen per cent of them wouldn't live to celebrate their first birthday. Was that the tragedy of which Nietzsche spoke? And what if they survived? At eight, they are circumcised; at eighteen or before they are fifteen, they are sold into slavery. Then another barbarously painful re-infibulation awaits them. If they are good Muslims they go to heaven, where Allah will assign them their usual job – that of serving men! They will become the houris whose business it is to entertain the men in heaven. But what about the Kurdish girl, the Bengali and the Irish? When little, they would probably remain bouncy as a waterfall; but when they grew into womanhood. . . .

"About sacrificial fires and myths, did you know?" Amina was saying.

"What?"

"That it was the two lips of the vulva of a woman. . . . "

"Go on, I'm listening."

"Yes, that it was that slot in which two sticks were rubbed together and that friction made the first fire. That's why Hindu women burn themselves at the funeral pyre."

They fell quiet. Sagal knew that it was the wrong version of the Hindu myth but she didn't bother to correct it. Through the open window she could see the sun travelling across the blue sky. Amina was now immersed in the waters of her flooded brain and was saying to herself: *I am come from yesterday; I've broken a barrier and have arrived in a land of no return. Yes. I am come from yesterday.* Her tongue did not stumble on the illogicality of the statement. Her past was a large holdall into which anything she could not carry was thrown. Now out of the hole rose the ghosts of the three men who had raped her, although in actual fact, whenever she thought about them, their three faces were moulded into one whose eyes stared at the wound he and the others had inflicted upon her. Then the cut, the knives, the blood on her thighs . . . her lips trembled as she saw the men unbutton their trousers. The rapists had names and she knew them, and therefore she appealed to them, begged them, "Please, no, I am not *he,* nor am I my father. . . . " But what pain, what pain, what pain! She had been a virgin, she had been circumcised . . . what pain, what pain! "We're doing this not to you but your father," one of them had said to her, the one who had gone to the same school as herself, the youngest of the three. *"Not you. Your father."* The rest of the sad story is stained with blood, Dracula red, blood on her legs, a knife by her side, and pain, what pain! They took their turn. The obscene blood of rape smudged their unzipped trousers, then the smell of dawn and nausea. "We're doing this to your father. Tell him that." Hours later, a young shepherdess found her. By then, the sun had dried the morning dew. The shepherdess went and returned with help. "Whose daughter are you?" the villagers asked. She told them her father's name. The two men rolled their eyes in wonder. They went and informed their men. In turn, the men assembled and whispered to one another. The men decided they would have nothing to do with the daughter of that great conspirator. "Do you know how many innocent men of our clan your father has sent to prison, how many he has sentenced to death, and how many his men have tortured?" said one of them. The men walked away. She had no energy to appeal to them. She lay where she had been raped, and her tongue, with difficulty, licked her scorched, aching lips. Then an elderly woman arrived and there were several other women with her. The women disobeyed the men's instructions: they carried her with them, washed her and fed her. When they asked if she knew the men who had raped her, Amina lied and said she didn't. The elderly woman said: "The pain is ours, the fat and wealth and power is the men's. I am certain your father will not understand – but your mother will." The women put her on a bus back to Mogadiscio. The city was shocked. Then the impasse . . . the political dilemma: what course of action was open to her? This was a suicidal challenge made by three young men to meet the General in the ring. Yes, the implications were far too great: people would hear, people would speak; maybe others would try to do the same sort of thing, maybe the government would be blackmailed and ransom fees asked. And all that publicity, think of the publicity it would be given. "This rape is political," her father had concluded. *"But which rape isn't?"* Amina had challenged. For by that time Medina had procured for her a copy of Susan Brownmiller's *Against Our Will:* by then, Medina had made her read Fanon, Richard Wright and Eldridge Cleaver. But her father had strict orders: "The case of your daughter," said the General, "must be isolated; it must be treated as though it were devoid of any political significance; it must be dealt with as having no political implications whatsoever." Her father, a major and a government minister, had no choice but to obey the General's orders. Loyalty to the Revolution. He would do it for the good name of the Revolution. He called Amina and said to her:

"We'll give you a ticket to go anywhere you like and we'll pay for your university anywhere in the world. This is the best we can think of at the moment. In a few months, in any case, people will have forgotten about it."

This shocked her. "Forget what? What will people forget?"

"That you've been unfortunate. People will forget the disgrace that has befallen you."

"People? Who cares about them? And who is the 'we'? You and Mother?"

"No. The General and I. I haven't spoken to your mother. I've spoken to the General. His instructions are clear: no publicity, no scandal."

"Where are they? Does the General know where they are?" she asked.

"Who?"

"The three men who raped me. Where are they?"

"One of them is in prison."

"One? Only one is in prison? Where are the other two?"

"We thought we could not hold three men for rape. It wouldn't stick in the courts. And we did it to minimize the scandal. So we let two of them go."

"Yes, yes, but where are they?"

"They will have crossed the border with Kenya by now, I believe."

"And you think all this will have been forgotten in a few months? You and the General think so? You underestimate me, Father. You really do. Just imagine: you helped two of the men who raped me go scot-free."

"In this country rape is not punishable as other crimes of violence. The characteristic compromise arrived at is usually that the rapist marries the victim, accepts her hand in marriage in the presence of the elders of his and her clan. I am sure you wouldn't want to marry all three, I am sure you wouldn't wish to marry even the one who is in prison. That's why we suggest that you leave the country and leave behind you the unfortunate disgrace.

"I need time to think this over."

Amina consulted her closest friends, namely Sagal, Medina and Ebla. Her father went back to the General for further instructions. A month passed. There were new developments: Amina was pregnant and the third man had been set free. To further minimize the scandal, the government arranged for him to go from Hargeisa via Aden to Rome on a pre-paid ticket. Not much progress on Amina's front. One day Ebla said:

"You're pregnant. You don't need legal advice if you want to keep the child. First, you must decide what you want to do. If you want to you can move in with us."

"It seems to me those men were intent on embarking on a suicide mission," said Amina, her voice rich with characteristic sadness. "Yet not only have they survived, they've done well by it. I promise I won't make it easy for them to forget what they've done to me."

"The offer still stands. You can move in with us. When you want."

"Thanks, you've been very helpful," said Amina.

"Now go and talk to your father. Remember: we'll stand by you, come what may."

She went to her father. He wanted to leave but hesitated, and she exploited this instant of indecision. She knew he wouldn't say anything of importance until he had conferred with the General. She told him that she was pregnant, adding:

"It's not you or my mother who's carrying this child. There's no need your talking to the General or to my mother. I'm the one with the child. So you can speak to me."

"*We* can still come to a compromise. We're still willing to finance your trip anywhere."

"I accept nothing short of your bringing all three rapists here for a public trial. I want everyone to know. I want every Somali to see the political significance. I want everybody to know that every rape is political; that the powerful rape the weak."

"Give me time to think it over," he said.

Further consultations with the General resulted in a government reshuffle in which her father was given no portfolio and no cabinet post. He was appointed ambassador abroad. Whereas Amina, Medina and Sagal had consulted one another on the issue and come to a decision: Amina should be helped to keep the child. Ebla reminded them, however, that they should think seriously about the child, too; they should think of the religious implications, the name of the father, of Amina's relationship with her own parents. Did Ebla wish the child aborted? "No, I wouldn't want to kill an unborn child, that's murder," she had said. Finally they all agreed that Sagal and Ebla would take her and that Medina would contribute to providing for some of her needs and the child's. During this period they went about together, sometimes a foursome, sometimes a threesome, with Amina in the middle, and on occasion with Ubax holding on to her little finger. There rippled through the expectant mother bubbles of delight which ran inside her like a comb through an unkempt head. Evening walks. The pleasure of company. A life made meaningful. Medina: books and gifts; Sagal: the warmth of welcome and friendship; Ebla: the mother of understanding. In this way, Amina read Ann Sexton's *Unknown Girl in the Maternity Ward;* Medina also lent her Brecht's *On the Infanticide of Marie Farrar* "whose sin was heavy, but whose suffering was greater", and in her mind Amina eavesdropped on the small child being choked, saw with horror the child being wrapped in a laundered sheet and dumped in a dark, cold shed. Then, like driftwood her memory had washed up, she remembered Barbara Malcolm's poem in which a mother gives her child a gun to "sleep wit and dream 'bout" because the time was ripe for revolutions. No doubt Sagal, Medina and Ebla had built a motorway of possibilities for her, solid as cement, with flyovers and pedestrian passes and zebra crossings, with a network of possible byways to take. They had thought of and provided red lights of caution, the yellow's awaiting danger and the green signal of please-pass, don't-stop! And in a cross-country trip, a year and a half ago, with Sagal on one side, Ebla on the other, Medina behind them and Ubax, too, Amina acknowledged the pleasure and escorting pain of being a mother. She gave birth to twins, both girls, one of them already dead, the other alive and well, and kicking, and crying. A week later, Amina's mother's maternal instinct made her return to Somalia to visit her daughter in Sagal and Ebla's house. She was received warmly, although not so much the news she brought: Amina should move back into her father's house and, since neither he nor her mother was there, she should stay and take care of it. Sagal and Medina suggested she shouldn't. Amina's mother and Ebla saw things eye to eye, talked to each other as one mother to another. More deliberations and nights longwinded as the repeated arguments of yesteryear. The joy of having delivered that kicking force on to the warm palms of friendship wore out. And many a night, Sagal and her friend awoke just before the dawn because Sagal (this was the name given to "the girl of shame" who survived) wouldn't close her eyes or her mouth. Advice. Counter-advice. Ebla: "If I were you, I'd take up your parents' challenge, move into the house, use the car he is willing to give you, and the money as well." Medina: "I would prefer you not to abandon the hope which has sustained you and held us together. So many women find themselves between one sunrise and another surrendered to the street hyenas of body-commerce; so many are humiliated, so many wives beaten daily and so many are rendered helpless by the fact that they are under-informed and they know not what is happening. Now I would ask of you only one thing: don't humiliate us. I suggest you don't return to your father's. If you do, it's the end between you and me, and I will never speak to you again." Sagal was rather conciliatory, but not as determined as either Ebla or Medina. Then a day before she was due to leave, Amina's mother came and:

"Here is the key to the house, here is the key to your car and here is an account in your name in the bank. If you don't want to move into the house, you can let it and use the money if you need it. Take care of yourself and of Sagal, my love. Take care of the house, too."

A week later, Amina and her small Sagal were in a car with the baby's pram and their things. Sagal senior was sad that her friend had moved out because she thought little Sagal's after-midnight cries disturbed them; she was also sad that Medina had decided never to speak to Amina again.

·　·　·　·　·　·　·　·　·　·　·

The sun floated like a paper boat on the watered horizon of the New Year's noon mirage. And Sagal, alone while Amina had gone to the lavatory, couldn't decide whether to take as mere coincidence the fact that most of her friends and people to whom she was close had either no children at all or had daughters. A higher percentage of her age-group who had children were blessed with daughters. Would she have one herself? Would her mother and her friends stay by her? Should she tell anyone who the father of her child was? Was it necessary? And should she tell *him*? Would all this create complications that would upset her plans to travel to Europe? Would it stand in her way? Her mother had given birth to her when married to two men, although that posed no legal problem: the prophet's tradition assigned the issue to "the owner of the bed," the one to whom the woman was legally tied first. Medina had confided in her that she had planned secretly to abort but had been discouraged by the doctor; she had never talked to Samater about it. The father of Amina's twins was technically unknown. Perhaps, Sagal thought now as she heard Amina's footsteps returning, it was best not to tell Wentworth George about the child inside her.

But was she even pregnant?

·　·　·　·　·　·　·　·　·　·　·

The sun had built pillars of rays. Meanwhile, the youngest child of the woman tenant in the three rooms Ebla let out had swallowed some keys, so there was a great racket until the mother decided to take him to hospital. When the noise died down and the two friends were alone in Sagal's room, Amina said:

"I forgot to tell you some very important news. I don't know how I could have forgotten."

"Don't tell me. Let me guess."

"So you already know about it?"

"Samater has thrown his mother and the new maid out of the house."

"That I didn't know. Has he?"

"Tell me then. What is it?"

"Someone has written something on the walls of dawn."

Sagal was literally at Amina's feet and was jumping about excitedly. Her reaction to the news her friend had brought was quick like a drop-kick. Her eyes were far and dreamy like a lotus-eater's. But why had she not told her this before? Amina could see how thrilled her friend was to receive the news. Perhaps she feared that Sagal might do something rash, had feared the news might throw her into a tantrum of a sort. As a matter of fact, one of the reasons she came to spend the New Year's first hours with her was to make sure she kept her from doing something thoughtless. Was that why Amina and Ebla had whispered something to each other before Ebla went away? Amina said:

"Someone told me this morning that perhaps this isn't a single case of unorganized protest which can be easily isolated; this person believes that it isn't as futile a protest as one might think. It seems it was planned to the minimum details of execution."

"Tell me more."

"They wrote their first words of warning on the walls of Hodan. Then on the recently whitewashed walls of the main post office, opposite the Soviet Embassy. The third wall they used is the one opposite the American Embassy. And they signed 'Dulman'."

"And what did they write?"

"'Down with the one-man, one-tribe dictatorship!' 'Down with the General's regime.' But these weren't written by the same hand. The power of the written word is immense."

"What language did they write these warnings in?"

"Somali."

"Note the irony!"

They remained quiet for a few seconds. Amina wasn't quick to note the irony but when she did, she smiled. *Our dear General: thou art blessed: blessed be thy script: blessed be the Peoples' name, Amen!*

"Has there been a purge?" Sagal said.

"Yes. Early this morning, they took some fifty young men and one woman for interrogation. Then they returned and without ceremony took with them the men who owned the walls on which the writings had appeared."

"Fifty-odd men and a single woman?"

"Yes. Fifty-odd young men and a single woman," Amina repeated.

"Does anybody know the name of the woman? Do you?"

"Yes."

"Who?"

Amina's eyes were not inflamed with enthusiasm as Sagal's had been. Indeed, her face looked fireless and her lips wore the crooked smile of someone stifling a sob.

"Who?" Sagal asked again.

"Do you really want to know?"

"Yes." Up Sagal's spine and into her head crept a suspicion: was someone close to them involved in this whole business? Medina? One of Amina's cousins?

"I'll tell you then."

"Please." She now appeared more relaxed, like a sheikh who had sneezed and said *"Alxamdulillah!"* Her heart rushed through its ritual beating, quick as the drop of tropical storm.

"Cadar."

"Cadar who?"

"Cadar Cali, of course."

Sagal stared at Amina in utter disbelief. "What about Hindiya?" she said then. "Was she involved in this, too?"

"Yes. They came for Hindiya later. Which means that they are actually the only two women swept in this purge."

"You said only one woman, and fifty men."

"They came later and took Hindiya. The third purge was expressly for Hindiya."

"Heroines! Heroines."

Amina was silent. Sagal seemed weak like a moth, she seemed fragile as a myth. Cadar Cali and Hindiya. Her first and second most feared rivals when it came to swimming. Cadar Cali and Hindiya! The two girls who had done as well as herself in everything at school and who challenged her in everything, the two girls who had taken her boy friends away from her – Cadar and Hindiya at last heroines of a movement and Sagal a mere spectator? The nation was speaking about *them;* the city of Mogadiscio was mentioning her great rivals with absolute reverence; everyone, young and old, powerful and powerless, would be uttering their names with due respect. Whereas to the General would go a garland of youthful girls, to Cadar and Hindiya would now go the heroines' medals. Their names would arouse euphoria in the hearts of those who knew and loved them; their names would ring rhythmically like the jubilation of a football crowd chanting for its team. *Mortals like me can do nothing to challenge them any more,* thought Sagal. *They are in the General's prison. They are the only two girls taken and this will make them stand out with prominence. Nothing I can do can change this. If anything . . . perhaps. . . .* But she could think of nothing that would destroy the image of her rivals without their physical destruction: no, she didn't want them made martyrs, heroines whose names would stir into life the lips which uttered them; heroines for whom the nation would build a statue when the General was no more at the reins of power. But how could she destroy the image of her rivals? Or should she do something either was incapable of doing? One thing was certainly out of the question: Sagal wouldn't take part in the swimming competition now. There wasn't any other girl worth competing with; there was no honorary title worth competing for any more. What would she do then? The smoke which had entered the room hung over them like a knife. This surely wasn't the best the New Year could offer somebody who had waited for it and nourished fat hopes on a future now as lean as the mother whose child died in the fire.

There was a very long silence.

•   •   •   •   •   •   •   •   •   •   •

As soon as Ebla returned, Amina cooked up a story of how her daughter wasn't well and she should get back. But not before she had exchanged knowing smiles with Ebla and promised to call on them soon unless, of course, Sagal wished to go to her place. Now Ebla was saying authoritatively:

"Some of us choose to carry the lantern and stand right under it, remaining under its staring eye, until we become one with the spotlight.

Some of us believe that it makes one a hero or a heroine, and we love being watched, shadowed, suspected of one thing or another until we are as heavily guarded as a nation's powerhouse. Remember the story you're fond of telling? The one in which the third person to light the match becomes a target enabling the enemy to spot him, aim and hit him – do you remember that? You are the third!"

The light in Sagal's eyes dimmed.

"As far as I am concerned," she said, "Cadar and Hindiya have carried out what they planned and have succeeded in standing in the lantern's light. Need I repeat that writing their graffiti on the walls of Mogadiscio's dawn has earned them everyone's respect and admiration?"

"I wouldn't say so," said Ebla.

"No?"

"They got caught. How can you talk of a successful execution?"

"That was perhaps the whole idea: to get caught, to become the theme of people's conversation, to become heroines. The opposers of a dictator are the potential makers of a people's history of resistance. The sacrificial element of history martyrdom. . . ."

"I would say they succeeded if they wrote their message and got away."

"The most fascinating aspect is the element of risk – "

Ebla interrupted her: "Somalis have a proverb: mothers of cowards seldom have reason to mourn."

Suddenly they looked at each other and fell silent, for they heard the signature-tune of the midday news. Each held her breath as they listened to the headlines. There was no reference whatsoever to the morning's event, which meant it would not be mentioned in the detailed broadcast either. Ebla returned to her salad, Sagal to the sugared yoghurt which she ate like soup. The woman tenant whose child had swallowed the keys had just come home to a set of hungry children. She moved nervously to feed them.

"Why didn't you tell me that Abucar had swallowed a bunch of keys?" Ebla asked.

"And what would you have done?"

"I would've prepared something for the other children."

But Sagal was thinking about the small child who had died in the fire. Life gave limited choices to some. She invented a future for herself and the child inside her. But was she sure she was pregnant? The future she invented had spacious rooms, in one of which was a small cot for a small child, and above it stood a woman aproned, with a feeding bottle in her hand. The woman couldn't tie her apron on account of her advanced state of pregnancy and there wasn't a child in the spacious rooms with large windows and high ceilings. *Since no child chooses a parent, perhaps I can choose my own child. Or is it destiny which has chosen me?*

"Incidentally. . . ."

"Yes?" Sagal asked.

"Your birthday present."

She received a parcel from her mother with head slightly inclined. And her rigid expression dissolved into a gentle smile. She would be twenty-one tomorrow, twenty-one dreamy years. . . . She would be sad if she missed her period which was for once due on the same date as her birthday – and what a coincidence! But Ebla had intended to ask if everything was all right, to inquire why her daughter wasn't flat on her back with the pain which heralded her period and wrung her inside like a cloth. Sagal was thinking: If the apron didn't tie, would she be as free as the clouds, free to go where she pleased, spend the night with whom she wanted? Her mother, Medina and Amina would want to know why she hadn't taken precautions. *"He breathed like a drowning man and I pitied him, so I slept with him."* No, no, that wouldn't do. She had to think of something else. Why not tell them the truth? Why not tell them? "The man was a foreigner and was very unhappy. Yes, a foreigner, and therefore a guest of my people and country. A brother from the West Indies. Professionally he had a tough time because whereas the Italians who came the same day as he get their permits through Sandra etcetera, this man couldn't get one and naturally couldn't work without a permit for they had confiscated his cameras. And you know how over-sensitive and nervous brothers from the diaspora are when in Africa. Also the man was very, very lonely and had no friends, had never been here before; a brother in need of help; a *guest* of my country and people. I thought I could recruit him, yes, that I could make him see things the way I saw them; that I should earn his confidence; that I should attract him away from the General's circle. In short, I felt it my national duty to keep the man company for that one night, and so I slept with him. In the end, as we parted, he said how stupid he was to mistake a government for a people." What should she say to her mother? Should she share these thoughts with her? Was this something Cadar and Hindiya were capable of conceiving?

The sun's rays entered through the window and played a symphony of colours on the rugs which Ebla had spread on the floor and on which she now stood to say her prayers. The signature-tune which marked the end of the afternoon's newscast was played, then came the national anthem (how could anyone call that thing Somalia's national anthem? Perhaps not many people knew that it was composed by an Italian and that there were no words which could be sung to the piano music of the man's composition).

Sagal silently tiptoed out of her mother's room.

There were waves of smoke thin as vapour where a fire had fed on several weeks' waste and garbage. And a whirlpool of smoke joined the
day's otherwise unregistered weather. Logs of burnt ash lay lifeless. As
if handwoven, these ashy geometric shapes suggested to Medina's
imagination a coming-together of primitive forces that were native in
her. She thought of them as urns which one sacrificed to quiet the cry
of the outgoing year. The year's harvest was smaller than a barber's
daily crop of hair.

"Neyrus! Dab-shid!" she said out loud.

She looked round and saw that she was alone. Ubax had gone with
the other girls, many of them her cousins; Ubax, who had at first refused to go with Medina's cousin's daughters. She complained that
they all played games she didn't know and in which she couldn't take
active part and she didn't like the fact that they lapsed into Arabic every
now and again. Eventually, however, a girl her age whom she knew
and had always liked came, and Ubax accepted to join the others.

"Dabshid! Neyrus! The fire which burns!"

And when her mother Fatima bint Thabit asked where Nasser was,
Medina had lied for him: she said he was on his way and would be
there in an hour or two at most. But she knew her brother wouldn't be
coming, that he had fixed another appointment with Dulman (and this
certainly worried Medina: the Security would shadow him if he went
there alone, she had warned, and she offered to go and collect the tapes
herself). He had said he looked forward to seeing Dulman. He had
served Medina tea in bed, with toast and orange *presse,* fresh as nature.
Before that he had bathed Ubax and given her breakfast, too. It was
while Medina was propped up with the pillow against the wall and enjoying the day's first meal which her brother had served with love that
the telephone rang. He answered it. When he heard a woman's voice

he passed the receiver to her. No, no, it was for him. Dulman. Yes. Dul-man wished to speak to him to tell him he shouldn't visit her. This she did in a flash, saying what worried her was that it was something she would explain to Medina one day – but the urgency was there in her voice, a voice helplessly reaching out to someone. Nasser spoke later about purges and of the dawn writings on the city's walls. He said Dul-man sounded broken and that he would go to her place at the same time as Medina went to their mother's. Had Dulman told him anything else, whether she knew who the Security had rounded up? Two girls. Not Sagal? No. Cadar Cali and Hindiya. Then Medina had tried to get Sandra on the telephone. Her manservant answered and gave another number where she could be contacted. But Medina decided against calling Sandra at the Ideologue's; it made no sense talking to her about the graffiti on the walls when she was at the Ideologue's.

"Neyrus!" she sighed. "The fire which purifies."

And out of the ashes rose a half-burned piece of paper with some writing on it. Medina made no effort to read the writing. Instead, she stared at the dead ashes, asking herself whether dead human beings aroused so many things in the heads of those around their corpse. If you touched these ashes, she thought, you would deform their natural shapes. She should leave these marvellously sleeping angelic figurines in peace, she shouldn't disturb their quiet repose. If she went any nearer, her breathing would stir the fire's nerves and make its cells pulse with powdery life; and the ashes on the immediate surface, like the topsoil, would react; some would fly upwards and then settle as separate grains; and the live fire-bed, red as a traffic light, flashed mes-sages like a pilot's cabin in which green lights exchanged computer-winks with yellow and red knobs.

"Dabshid!" And in Persian: "Neyrus!"

A temple of fire built to honour and commemorate a year spent un-willingly like the last penny in the clutched hand of the poor. And those who built this temple of fire-worship would hope to smoke the wounded stump of the outgoing year. This was the day, she told her-self, when people made as many fires as there were hearths available. The past was ransomed. The past was burned. It was leapt over like the traced squares of hopscotch. The year was compartmentalized, and something put into every chamber. Why all this fire, why all this smoke? "The smoke of the festivities blinds the devil," explained the traditionalists, not quite realizing that it was with the importation of the Islamic morality from Arabic that concepts like prophet, Allah and Satan came. But never mind. People built fires as tall and as big as they could make them, to each according to the means at his or her disposal. Fires as wide as the Ganges, in which to wash away not the day's sweat of labour but the sins of mankind. Whether child or adult (at least in the south), everyone would leap over the fire and make a wish.

Now the children's chatter silenced her thoughts. Ubax and a dozen others. But where was her mother, where was Fatima bint Thabit? Why had she gone into the house and not returned?

"Neyrus!" The fire that produces the birth of the world. Fire as divine; fire as demoniac. Years begin with the rekindling of a new fire and the extinguishing of the old.

The new year's first burials melted into a fiery extravaganza of future dreams. The shadow the fire made, she thought to herself, was such that it offered no one any shelter. But the smoke shot upwards straight as a chimney, then broke at the waist like candlelight in a breezy room. On a day like this, the astrologers would sit in front of fires to trace and re-trace, in their savant's creative vision, the map of the earth's plentiful pockets of rain. They would foretell what would happen the following year. They would prophesy what the harvest would be like. They would whisper hope in the ears of those women who came to consult them: for single women they would smell marriage in the air; the burning fat of wealth for the poor; an easy birth, a boy and good health for young mothers heavy with a bed's brief enjoyment; promotion and transfer to Mogadiscio for a soldier in the army. The year's flowering of new hopes buried in the warm ashes of the burnt year. In Ethiopia, they build an effigy and tell how the year will fare according to the way the effigy burns!

"Dabshid! Neyrus!"

She pricked up her ears. No. There was nobody coming from behind her. And in front of her was the wing of the house in which she was born, the wing which flew up in smoke within precisely two hours of Medina's birth that night so very long ago. Her mother, her grandfather and all her uncles and aunts gave this incident a greater symbolic significance than it had for her. But then they remembered that on the day Nasser was born there was the flood which killed two small children. Medina had a simpler explanation: since the room which caught the first lick and wind of the fire was in the wing where Fatima bint Thabit had been secluded for the last few days of her laboursome pregnancy, was it not possible that somebody, possibly with the consent of the bedridden monstrosity, set it alight? Her mother would smile and shake her head as if Medina were a pupil who gave the wrong answer to a sum. "A boy and a girl. Water and fire. Don't you see the contrast, the elements of life which complement each other? A boy conceived in the full swing of normalcy; a girl conceived in the concealed darkness of tradition. I loved your father and the fire of love consumed my heart; Nasser's father's father asked for my hand and was given it long before I saw what he looked like. I am sure you will tell me that you know better than I, but. . . ." She looked up and her eyes fell on the wing in which she was born, the one which caught fire that night so very long ago – thirty-three years. But why did she not enter? Why did she not follow her mother? The door was pushed open and Ubax waved to her; Medina grinned at her daughter and her two friends. (She blamed herself for not knowing half of her nephews or their names: they were so many she lately ceased to bother remembering their faces or their names or their birthdays. Imagine: a cousin of hers, two years younger than she, had nine children.) Ubax and her companions disappeared and Medina returned to her musing.

"Neyrus! Dabshid! *Karakorok*: an Australian aboriginal myth – a crow which brought down from heaven a flaming firestick in his bill from the sun, a flaming firestick as a gift from the animal kingdom to that of Man, a gift man never acknowledged properly. *Karakorok! Dabshid! Neyrus!*"

Then she picked up a stick and pushed a pellet of goat's dung into the fire. As it burned, the dung became small as a bullet; the organic fabric of the original piece was reduced to a greyish, powdery ball of ash. Would the remains of a cremated sati, a woman who believed that her ashes would rejoin her former husband's mortal constitution, be reduced to that size, too? Such faith in a future. Medina looked up and saw a little boy had joined her.

"Hello!" she said. She picked up the two-and-a-half-year-old child who had crawled out of the door Ubax and the other girls had left open. With a tissue she wiped clean his stained cheeks.

"What is your name?"

The child's answer came in a rhythmic *da-da-da*. Medina looked over her shoulder and saw a woman. She knew this was one of her cousins but as usual wasn't sure what name to give her. The woman, although younger than Medina, appeared aged and wrinkled; she was very fat, too. Her dark purdah's neck-strings tied round her waist, she came grinning at Medina.

"That's my son," she beamed. "His name is Nasser."

Medina looked up at the child whom she was holding with a fresh interest. She saw that she needed another tissue with which to blow the child's nose, otherwise the dangling menace of mucus would fall on to her own dress. But that was going to be enormously difficult, if not impossible. Her handbag was a few paces behind her, for one thing; for another, it seemed that the child's mother wanted to speak.

"If you would hold the child, please!" she said, giving Nasser back to his mother, and moving in the direction of her handbag for a tissue; but she was too late: the mother had already wiped it off with the edge of her own dress.

She went and took a seat by the fire.

"Aren't you coming in?" asked the cousin.

"I am waiting for my mother here."

"Outside? She is inside. Why don't you come inside?"

"She told me to wait for her here," she lied.

But she wasn't thinking about the woman, nor about her own mother: she had relegated both to the fringes of her brain. She was thinking about the fact that among her mother's people, among the Arabs in Somalia, infant mortality was much, much less than that of the Somalis. Another thing worth noting was that even among the Somalis there were more malnourished children in the urban areas than among the nomads. This, in a way, helped her to postulate that the figure of the malnourished Indian in East Africa was a great deal lower or practically nonexistent. Or why not! Among the Somalis, the River people's children suffered less from malnutritional diseases. How so? She decided she would write an article on this, perhaps with the collaboration of Nasser. Now she should simply wait for her mother. She then sat upright and listened for her mother's footsteps, determined not to give her a chance to come upon her as softly as death from behind, as quickly as fire. But why did she always do that? "You, Medina, are the fire which nearly burned everything at birth; Nasser is the water which almost drowned us all. Why, I am quiet as a shadow; I am the shadow which doesn't get wet and which isn't consumed by fire."

. . . .

"Er . . . what's-his-name was here," said Fatima bint Thabit.

Medina started. The fire in her eyes died, so did the flame of her fantasies. Since she wasn't quite sure where her mother's voice had come from, she waited. It had been their commonest game; and they played it civilly. Her mother would steal in upon her "light like the night's sudden tropical darkness . . . quiet as a shadow . . . a shadow which doesn't get wet and which is not consumed by fire". But Medina was prepared for it this time. She had waited and waited and held her breath and for a long while thought of nothing else; although between one pensive moment or another, precisely when she was looking up at the sky and watching the clouds separate like friends wishing each other well – zak! Her mother spoke too loudly and too suddenly from within shooting range, said something which made Medina wonder, ask herself if she had heard correctly. As always, her mother came in on her unannounced "like dawn". Now she didn't turn (this was part of the game), nor did she move her head, otherwise she would see where her mother was and that would spoil the essence of the game, but, after a long pause, asked:

"Who?"

Her mother was breathing clumsily as though she was asthmatic. Medina got up and turned like a person with a stiff neck. Her mother was very, very close; the two were nearly touching. Medina almost fell backwards and into the fire as she moved out of her mother's heavy breath. She then received her mother's extended hand, bony but long and aristocratic – just like Nasser's. Her eyes, black and round like olives, were clear, with bushy eyebrows – just like Nasser's. The children, among them Ubax, came into and out of view, leaving behind them a noise which dragged on for a while after they had disappeared.

Medina and Fatima bint Thabit fell apart as if they were two adolescents caught at a sex-game by their parents. Then:

"And he talked of bidets," said Fatima bint Thabit.

"Who talked of bidets?"

"Er . . . what's-his-name?"

She was very elegantly dressed. She put on her best when she knew that either Medina or Nasser was coming to visit her. She didn't bother much about Samater. She used to tease him and say that he should have been an artist, he was ever so sensitive, ever so likeable even in his rags. One day somebody asked her why she dressed up when her daughter or son was visiting and her answer was that it gave them something to talk about. High cheekbone-structure, an upturned nose, an imposing figure, yes. She wasn't as tall as her children but was paler: her experience didn't include exposure to the sweaty sun in a hot climate: she was in the "dark tradition they call *purdah*" and she hardly set foot outside the precincts of the family household. Sixty, if an hour, healthy for her age and her veiled condition. She had either bruised an ankle or twisted it, she wasn't sure. But then she was never sure of anything, she never took a determined position, had never fought over a question of principle or anything which required high ideals or abstract thoughts. "The tradition of my people encages me in a four-walled prison and makes me the exclusive property of a man. The same tradition, or an abstracted borrowing from similar ones, exempts me from being circumcised in the same way as the African woman, whether she is Somali or Kenyan or Togolese."

"Who was here, Mother?"

Fatima bint Thabit squinted with concentration. She took the seat by the fire, the one Medina had been using.

"Who else? What's-his-name!"

Her doubts about everything were deep and dark like the pupils of her eyes. "A woman mustn't be sure of anything ever," her father used to say. "A woman, like any other inferior being, must be kept guessing, mustn't be given reason to believe that she is certain about anything." Was this why she wasn't sure why Tayib, Nasser's father, took his own life? The light of life, sure as a star in a cloudless sky, would flicker every now and again and then die out.

"Who?"

"He was undoubtedly very unhappy."

"If you don't tell me who, I won't know."

A pause longer than the sun's shadow. And:

"Samater. He came very early. He said he was on his way to the office. His eyes were red from sleeplessness and he looked very unhappy. He came to wish me a good and happy New Year."

Medina's wandering gaze took in all that could be referred to as the outer courtyard and the dirt track which had been tamed by the walking feet of Abu Bakr. The gate was larger now than when she was small. Here and there were small clusters of bushes, shrubs and tufts of monkey-feeds. It was in this very place that Medina had played as a child herself; it was here that her mother wanted her to bring Ubax; naturally, the grass-blades of Medina's childhood weren't there but the earth of which she had eaten her share as a crawling infant was as rich as ever. But wasn't her mother satisfied that there were those nieces and nephews with pock-marked faces, and the house was always alive with children's chatter? What Fatima bint Thabit wanted, in short, was for Medina to return to where she had cut her first teeth. "If you are not with Samater, a wife to a caring husband, then come back here and be the grown child of your own mother." She said that in fewer words. Medina had said that parents don't ever know how ridiculous they are in the eyes of their own children. And her mother challenged it with: "Do children ever?" Then there had been silence. Now Samater's name turned up like hidden treasure. Medina asked:

"That's a beautiful necklace, Mother. Where did you get it?"

"Do you like it?"

"Yes."

"A gift from Algiers. Samater brought it this morning."

"That's lovely."

"Do you remember who gave me this dress?"

"No. Should I?"

There now, each was deep at sea, the oars of each hit rockbottom, for the waterbed was rocky and their memories wet like rain on a desert. Fatima bint Thabit was uneasy because she didn't want to talk about those things Samater had confided in her. He had opened his heart to her, she thought. Since neither Medina nor Nasser told her anything of any importance, the fact that Samater had gone to see her and had spoken ill of his own mother made her believe he had entrusted her with a secret she shouldn't part with. But she was pleased that her dress and necklace had provided the opening cues.

"What was he talking about the bidet for?" asked Medina.

"Did you order a bidet for the house?"

"Not for the one he lives in. Did the shop deliver it there? I ordered a bidet for Nasser's house, the one I'm living in."

"The luxuries some people indulge in!"

"How do you mean?"

"Well, now you have two bidets in your house, and probably none in Nasser's."

"Why two?"

"His mother Idil thought it a godsend and said that for a long time she had been thinking that no good Muslim should touch anything a non-Muslim (that is you) touches or uses. This is the bidet the maid and I will use to make ourselves presentable and pure before we prostrate ourselves before our creator."

"You cannot beat that, can you? The woman's use of symbols is overpowering! And who pays for the bidet? In whose house is she? From whose plate does she eat? An overpowering woman."

She stifled a laugh. Fatima bint Thabit's semi-aristocratic mannerisms ("She hasn't class or style, has she?" she shocked Medina once by saying. "Idil hasn't the same as I, eh?") saved her from making a mess of the scene with a gesticulation the movement of her hand suggested. The hand then rose as though from a plateau but remained balanced and immense before Medina's eyes, standing between Medina and the sun, large, shielding, and elegant like an eagle wearing the season's feather. It was on such occasions that Medina thought Fatima bint Thabit was Nasser's mother and not hers. Her mother was now staring at history, she was looking at what was nearly a hundred years old, a building in which generations of Medina's mother's family lived – the Thabits, the Abu Bakrs and those who married their sons or daughters. Medina was weaned from the familial breast before she was five and didn't feel the closeness others did, she couldn't see them as they saw each other all related circumferentially to one another through the Grand Patriarch.

"I wouldn't say that to a child of mine," said Fatima bint Thabit. "It is barbarous and uncivil."

"You wouldn't?"

"Perhaps because I was exposed to the promiscuity and heterogeneity of thinking and background earlier than she, although ironically I am the veiled woman who is chained to the string of her purdah, the string which strangles one, and she, yes, she the free Somali nomad, let loose on the world like a street dog. She roasted her heart when she baked maize-cakes on one of these commissions for these restaurants. Do you think I am unfair?"

A cute little thing came into view, a little girl who wouldn't approach any further. Perhaps somebody had pushed her from behind to begin with. Fatima bint Thabit encouraged her with words like, "Come and greet your aunt Medina." The embarrassed little thing came and took Medina's hand as though it were a microphone she would speak into. Medina unceremoniously withdrew her hand, held the little girl's chin and kissed her on the cheeks, and then gave her her own.

"Give her your hand," said Fatima bint Thabit, "not your *cheeks*."

"What?"

"Your hand and not your cheeks. Don't spoil things for the rest of us. Come on. Give her your hand like any other parent would."

"But. . . ."

"In a world of equals, you embrace and shake hands without need of inclining your head as to a king or a queen. But children are to parents what vassals are to kings: the head must be inclined, the child should bend head, back and body, then receive the hand of his parent or her parent and kiss it. Whereas when you kiss someone on the cheek you look him in the eye and you might zoom in on him with your powerful lens and catch the person's indecision in the flicker of the lids, or see a tear forming in the loving eyes. Do you think a king or a queen would love to see that happen? Or a parent?"

She had half a mind to argue about what her mother said, but saw that the poor child had withdrawn a little distance from them. Medina was content with keeping to the generality of her undeveloped argument:

"I see things differently, Mother. I don't see myself as the tyrant parent towering above a trembling child, hand half-raised in such a way the child doesn't know whether I am about to hit or give or just want to offer a pat on the head."

"That is it. You must keep them guessing."

"You remind me of somebody I know!"

"Is your child your equal?"

"Of course. My child is my love and you can only love your equal."

"No, no."

"I remember something my grandfather used to say: 'A woman, like any other inferior being, must be kept guessing, she mustn't be given reason to believe she is certain of anything.'"

"That's right. Children must be kept guessing. They must never see you in your weakest moment. A child is an inferior being when it comes to that. As for the half-raised hand about which the child isn't sure. . . ."

"But that's precisely the same concept as the General's. The masses must be kept guessing. The masses are inferior, they cannot in any case understand how a government functions, they cannot appreciate this or that. No one is sure what will happen; no one is certain who will come knocking on your door; no one must be in a position to know in advance what will take place. It's the same thing coated with the ideological sugar of political expediency. Can you not understand something as simple as that?"

"That is politics and I never understand politics."

"But you do."

"No, I don't."

"But you do, you do, you do."

"There's one thing I understand. Yes, there is one thing."

"What?"

"Neither you nor Nasser is willing to incline head, back, and body to kiss your mother's hand. You keep your distance, and Nasser hardly visits me. But Samater is *an incliner of head, a bender of body, Samater is.* He doesn't in the least feel inhibited, he does it so naturally. He kisses my hand."

"The General has trained him."

"Perhaps his mother is to blame."

"No. The General is who I blame. For everything."

Fatima bint Thabit got up and without saying anything took a foot-track which went round the ancient building. But where was she going? Of course, thought Medina, of course. To visit the family burial place just behind the ancient building.

●　　●　　●　　●　　●　　●　　●　　●　　●　　●　　●

Mounds high as sand dunes, ringed with a cactus here, a desert shrub there. The stones placed to mark the tombs had browned as dust. In total reverence, Fatima bint Thabit knelt before the mounds one at a time, beginning with the one which carried an inscription no longer legible. Medina didn't need to be told whose tomb it was; she knew it was Abu Bakr's, the man who had begun this family, who had crossed the sea and cast his eyes and anchor on the pearl of his choice, namely Mogadiscio. He was the man who laid the foundation for the house whose history was the history of the family. He had been strong as a poet. A giant of a man, though Medina couldn't bring herself to believe that he was as giant as they said; the man had come from Hadramout, an island peopled with sarong-wearing midgets. Fatima bint Thabit went from Abu Bakr's burial-mound to that of Gad Thabit, her father. She looked back and saw that Medina hadn't inclined her head even a little. She continued her visits and uttered brief prayers for the souls of the smaller members of the family who were buried there, the souls of the little boys, one of whom was born the same year as Medina. The girls were discriminated against as usual and weren't buried there; they were buried outside the family cemetery. As a matter of fact, most of them didn't have a stone to mark their tombs. Fatima bint Thabit turned to look at her daughter again, but this time there was a vague smile on her face. She then got up and, supporting herself on her stick, came towards Medina.

"You refuse to incline your head and bow even before the dead. You make me wonder. You make me think of things wicked as your soul. How can your refuse to bow and prostrate yourself before your own grandparents?"

The sun was overhead and it flattened Fatima bint Thabit's features, making her look older and aged. The dark rings under her eyes were sharp but thin, rather like a line drawn by a child. She came level with Medina, then passed her without saying anything.

She entered the building and Medina followed.

The door opened to a courtyard which in its turn was open to the sky and other doors of other rooms, one of which they entered. The room was bright with sunlight and was also very noisy since nearly a dozen children, among them Ubax, were playing there, climbing on one another's backs and then the beds, hitting one another, playful, joyful, excited and shrieky. Upon the adults' entering, however, everything hushed; the children, with the exception of Ubax, got off the iron beds which they had unmade with their playfulness, and filed silently out, heads down, eyes averted. When all the others had gone, and her grandmother and mother stared at her, Ubax felt slightly awkward, she felt as heavy as her head which she now lowered as she, too, went out. Medina was tempted to say something but chose to look the other way, then at the ceiling.

"Come, come," said Fatima bint Thabit to Medina. "Enter."

"Yes, yes."

A maid served them coffee.

. . . .

The walls were olive-brown and fingerprinted with a generation of touches, of adults and of children whose hands left smudges like baby stains of chocolate taste. The room smelt like a kitchen; there was a whiff of garlic in the air. The ceiling stared back at Medina, a ceiling solid as were its dyed beams. The window was large and somehow its size contradicted the rest, although the walls were thick as solid stone incised with love. On the wall opposite her was the photograph of Gad Thabit, her grandfather, wearing his favourite silk *jelabi* which he had bought in Mecca, at which sacred place he claimed he had emancipated ten of his father's slaves (although rumour had it that he sold them). The photograph, she remembered her grandfather boast, was taken by the Vice-Governor-General, Signor de Felice, Sandra's grand-uncle. Medina was then too young to ask whether it was de Felice who had forced him to emancipate his slaves. Sandra held this view and generally boasted about it. Not only that but she showed Medina and Nasser her grandfather's correspondence in which he more or less said that Thabit was the "hardest nut he ever broke. The man says," the letter went on, "some men are born to be slaves, and some are born to be masters. The fool, the die-hard fool! So I confiscated all his property and put him and his son in gaol and I said I wouldn't release them unless he signed a writ that he would free all his slaves. Oh, the man's pride, *dio mio!* Then I thought of a compromise: the colonial government would pay his trip to Mecca on condition that he took his slaves with him and freed them there. We knew he wouldn't. But even if he sold them elsewhere it didn't matter to us, so long as it happened outside our jurisdiction, so long as we earned ourselves the trust of the enslaved. This was about the only compromise which the two other hard nuts had accepted. And so he went. As we parted he said jokingly that he would return with the commission. Do I believe the rumour we heard had any foundation? Probably he sold them in the free market, who knows! A fool unlike any I had seen before. Anyway, when he returned I took a photograph of him. The man's pride, *dio mio!*"

"More coffee?" asked Fatima bint Thabit.

"No, thank you."

Fatima bint Thabit poured herself another cup.

"I asked Samater this morning when he came whether there was any truth in the story about his marrying the maid his mother brought from Mudug. He said there wasn't a grain of truth in it, that it was gossip. Did you know?"

"That he would marry a maid?"

"Or something like that."

"What can I say?"

"Don't you care whether he marries or not?"

"It's not that I don't care."

"Not that you don't care? What do you mean?"

"I do care! That is the honest answer."

"I have a strange feeling that the two of you are playing with us, teasing us. But has it ever occurred to you that you might have exaggerated this time? Has it ever crossed your mind or his that this might be a very expensive joke? He will probably lose his job as Minister. And who knows but you may lose him; or take him back into your embrace a different man, a man broken, prideless, needy, with a running nose: a potential suicide."

"I must admit it hasn't occurred to me."

"I am sure as I am of God's existence that he will lose his job before the week is out."

"How do you know?"

"I saw him in a dream last night. He was in rags, he looked worn out and on the brink of a nervous breakdown. You know dreams don't explain or justify things, but I couldn't see how a poor man in rags was on the brink of a nervous breakdown. The two never go together. What counts is what he said."

"What did he say?"

"He was very unhappy in the dream, just as unhappy as he was in real life when he came to call on me. Have you no pity? Have you no sense in you? Why? Why?"

"Now, now, let's not – "

"'In the permanence of her homestead,' you used to say, 'my mother stands in the shade of her purdah peeping through holes in her heart.' You used to add that I am one of *the excluded* and you were of *the included*."

"Yes?"

"You are a prisoner of your principles and your secret dreams, Medina; I am a prisoner of a tradition, that I won't deny. One is always a prisoner of one thing or another: a prisoner of acquired habits or a prisoner of the hope which chains one.

Then there was quietness. And in the doorway was the figure of an elderly woman who wouldn't approach until Fatima bint Thabit told her to (as if she were one of those helpless children, thought Medina). The woman's appearance jogged Medina's memory, reminding her that the family had once dealt in slaves. Indeed the woman, who was from the River People, was a residue of "the family's greatness and claims to royal blood in Hadramout," Fatima bint Thabit would say. The woman, short and busty, was ten or twelve years younger than her mistress Fatima whom she always referred to as *"hiindo"*. Now she bowed as she came nearer, smiled as she curtsied, and stooped as she approached. She was a beast on all fours, submissive, obedient, child-like, a rememberer of a past Medina did not share. While still on all fours, she went and kissed Fatima bint Thabit's hand.

Medina shouted:

"Do I not tell you every time I come here – "

"Yes, yes, you do, but she is a prisoner of her status," explained her mother.

Medina did not speak her thoughts. Fatima bint Thabit turned to the woman:

"What is it? Is something bothering you?"

"They've come," said the woman. "Shall I say you're not to be disturbed?"

"Who?" inquired Medina. "Who has come?"

There was no need to answer her question. The women had already begun to file in one by one, women who had come through the street veiled but who now peeled the purdah off, and who were no longer ghostly-looking and mysterious. One by one, they bowed to kiss Fatima bint Thabit's held-out hand as though it were the ringed middle finger of a Pope; then each woman tapped her index finger on the valley between her breasts, a gesture of heart-touching sincerity which was accompanied with a soft murmured salutation of good will. But as soon as they came to Medina's part of the room, they fell into uneasiness which, for an instant, offended her. It seemed that Fatima bint Thabit was a person worthy of their respect whereas Medina was of no consequence. A little later, the six women spread out evenly like evening birds migrating with the light; three came and joined Medina and the other three went and sat by Fatima bint Thabit. For a while, nobody knew what to say. But Medina was aware of one thing: she was conscious of those devouring eyes of envy, the women's hard stares focused on her. They believed they knew every secret of hers; she could bet her last secret that they knew the precise date and hour in which she left Samater and naturally had heard both versions of the story: his and hers. But how, how did they know? These women generally went out once a week, and on this away-day they traded the latest gossip and their veiled profiles exchanged whispered intimacies. A life with a given coherence, a life lived in a caged existence, it was as though these women "lived in the innards of a whale which hardly went ashore."

"Do you remember me?" asked an extremely shapeless woman who was dressed in the brilliant colours of the exhibitionist. "Do you remember me, Medina?"

Medina thought but she couldn't recall who this woman was, though she did not want to risk offending her by saying so. Her mother saw this, noticed how the others were thrilled at seeing their *diva* fail a banal do-you-remember test: she couldn't allow this to happen, she would intervene, enter and take part in this. Right on cue, Fatima bint Thabit said:

"M'dina!"

Silence, and they all looked at Fatima bint Thabit. There was pride in her voice as she pronounced her daughter's name. It was the way she mouthed the syllables and fitted them as though they belonged to one another by her merely speaking them; it was the deliberate omission of the "e" between the "m" and the "d", making sure that her daughter at least got the hint: that her name was not Mina as Nasser and her close friends whether European or Somali called her. Of course, this was beyond the present audience of veiled simpletons. They would not understand. But that was the point: create a link, a secret passage to which the others had no access, a secret link between mother and daughter. Then again:

"M'dina!"

She bit the "m" this time and held it between her teeth, but eased on the "d" like a lioness playing with her own cub. This let her make the distinction: Mina – the pillar as target, the target as a symbol of Satan. The story was that when Ibrahim was instructed to sacrifice his son to God, Satan offered to help little Ismael to escape. This happened three times, and each time Satan was hit with the stones of Ibrahim's faith in God. Mina, the place where this took place, is marked with pillars which the faithful pelt with stone. Mina is in Mecca. Her daughter's name was Medina, and she was born a Muslim although she had decided to die an infidel. Medina: the city of righteousness. Mina: the place where pillars are stoned, a symbol of Satan. Note the distinction, if you please!

"Of course she remembers you, Anisa. How could she forget?"

"I thought she wouldn't remember," the woman said.

"Anisa? Of course I remember," said Medina.

"And this is my sister Zuhaira," said Anisa.

Her memory ticked these names which were listed in its roll: but other than the names, what could she remember? Nothing. Two little girls who played with her years ago.

"We also met when you came on a holiday from your university. Don't you remember? We are the twins. You are a year and a half older than us."

Yet they looked as if they were in their late forties. Never mind, thought Medina now and asked:

"Married? You're still married. I remember you had some problems with your husband."

"We never talk about things like that anymore."

"Children? How many do you have now?"

Here Medina's mother interrupted: "Eleven children between the two of them."

"Eleven? Heavens!"

She looked from one to the other, then to her mother, and back at the one who spoke. Anisa; then Zuhaira.

"I had eight and she six."

"That's fourteen."

"Three dead. Before their second birthdays."

There was another pause.

"Malnutritional complications?"

She didn't rise to that. She simply said: "Two of mine and one of Zuhaira's."

Another pause.

"We know you have one," said Zuhaira.

"And Nasser has one, *Alxamdulilah* for everything," said Anisa.

"He is here, isn't he? He came yesterday, didn't he?"

"Yes."

"How is he?"

"He's fine."

"And his son?"

Fatima bint Thabit, who had closed her eyes, opened them at the mention of her son's name but waited until she was sure they would listen to her attentively. She cleared her throat and that made them turn to her. Then she made her contribution:

"Allah manifests Himself in a lot of ways."

"*Alxamdulilah!*"

Something in Medina's mind became dislocated, the toothed wheels of time were unevenly matched and the head of the screws were too large for the jaw of the spanner: the real became a threat, and the unreal was like an accident in which someone else died and she didn't. In this way, these women's pasts became the nightmare which stirred the dust of the untrod pathway. One of those who was sitting on the same bed as her mother asked:

"Is it true that you're writing a book about the revolution?"

"A book?"

"You left Samater, we heard, because you are writing a book in which you criticize the Revolution. And since you couldn't live in the same house as a man who was a member of the cabinet of that regime he thought that you should part. Is it true?"

Had the whale come ashore? she wondered. Certainly she was de-lightfully shocked that they were asking intelligent questions, that theirs wasn't a banal inquisitiveness, indeed more intelligent than a congregation of Samater's colleagues who talked about nothing but women, money, trips abroad, presents for their mistresses and wives and, more significantly about their obsession: age. Who was older than whom, who went to school before whom. . . .

"But how do you know about it?"

The women consulted one another and giggled.

They were sure they had asked the right question. They were certain that she left Samater because she was writing a critical book about the General's regime It was her "But how do you know about it?" which confirmed their suspicion. Perhaps, she could let the thing hang there like a question mark suspended Spanish-like upside down and with-out the dot for ornament. She looked at her watch, and suddenly pre-tended she was in a hurry. She said something about keys and Nasser not having one and the fact that she hadn't cooked anything. She really must go.

"Aren't you staying for lunch?" asked her mother.

"I'm sorry, but I clean forgot that friends are dropping in for lunch and Nasser doesn't have a key to let himself in. So I really must be on my way."

Unceremoniously, she rushed out of the room without kissing anyone's cheek or hand. *When the whale is ashore,* she was thinking to herself as she walked down the corridor to take Ubax away, *the stays are laced tighter, and mouths are closed.*

"Ubax," she shouted to her flower.

Silent as the most modern of fetters, the elderly servant of the River People came into view and wondered if *"hiindo"* Medina wanted anything. She appeared stooped with a bow suggested and an inclined head.

"There she is," said Medina pointing to her Ubax. "No thanks. I was calling to Ubax. Come, darling. Let's go. Thank you, thank you very much. Come, darling, come, Ubax."

"But, Medina . . . ," Ubax started.

"Come, I said. Come."

She took Ubax's arm and walked away.

"We're going home?"

"Yes, darling. We're going home. Will you sit properly?"

Medina drove through Villagio Arabo and once or twice sneezed in allergic reaction to the pungent odour of garlic in the air. Ubax grumbled and said that she would've loved to stay with her playmates. Despite her daughter's mild protest, Medina's tension eased and then loosened like a sarong. With her right hand, she managed to ruffle Ubax's hair, Ubax who now smiled, whose eyes dropped like the purdah of a woman who has just entered her own house. She braked brusquely at the change of traffic-lights from yellow to red. Four women in veils crossed the road and Medina noticed that their ankles and toes were ringed, their wrists decorated with bracelets. The lights changed. Medina changed gear and moved. Her mind changed continent, travelled to India where purdah was as widespread as tyrant mothers-in-law. At least, she told herself, festivals such as Holi gave women a chance to release their tension once a year, to drop their veils, and shout freely, and paint the men they found in the streets with colours as red as their menstruation. What did the Arab and veiled Muslim women have for letting the steam out of their enraged system? Nothing. What's more, in India again, a holy fire is built for the young

virgins, and toothless men sit in the fire's shade, gumming groaning
prayers to Kanya and Lakshmi's wealth. She turned a curve and
braked. She parked.

"We're home, darling. Wake up," she told Ubax.

Ubax's face was long. Medina bent forward to touch her.

"Leave me alone."

"All right, all right, sweetheart."

Medina said she would go alone. But:

"Wouldn't you like something to eat?"

"No."

"But what's wrong?"

"See this."

"What is it? Let's see." A small scratch whose blood had dried. "A
nail scratch. Perhaps while you were playing one of the girls scratched
you. It's nothing. Do you know who it was ?"

"That father-fucker of a girl."

Medina held her breath in surprise. "What did you say?"

"That father-fucker of a girl, I said."

"Ubax. I want you to reform you language. I want you to say you are
sorry."

"All the other children speak that way."

"You are not like all other children. I don't want you to speak their
language. Now I want you to apologize to me."

Medina fumbled for her cigarettes and matches. She lit a cigarette.
Ubax took this as the ultimate point their fight could reach.

"But I want you to be like other mothers. I don't like being singled
out as the daughter of Medina. I want you to be like the mothers of the
other children in the neighbourhood. And as you always say, the petals
of your daughter's love will wither if it comes into contact with
smoke."

Medina was so shocked she choked on the cigarette. Then she realized what she had done and immediately stubbed it out. She sum-
moned up the resources of her courage and will.

"I'll try, if you will try, too," she said holding out a hand to her
daughter.

"I'll try."

E I G H T

The stick of a blind man sees, Nasser was thinking to himself, alone, going to Dulman's house; *the stick of a blind man guides, it taps, it touches, it
feels, it tells its carrier and dependent where things are in relation to him.
The blind man holds his stick upright, then diagonally, then horizontally and
finally upright again. It helps him gain new perspective on things, things
which generally start as a mere hinted contour, a mezzanine elevation, a
landing's twists and turns, or a trap of some sort. The earth's surface is read
like a book in braille: the stick sees a small hole in the ground; the hole ob-
structs the stick's movement upwards or downwards, as irritating as the grit
in Medina's rice, which her tongue busily sorts from the grains, Medina
whose eyed tongue, flat against the floor or the wall of her mouth, sees,
tastes, takes its time as it travels up and down the blind molars. The stick of
the blind man sees. . . .*

"Jaalle?" said a man to Nasser, a man he had never met.

"Yes?"

Nasser's grin was thinner than a glint as he squinted at the sun, then
at the man. The man chose to be silent, and the two walked side by
side. But what did the man want? Was he one of those Medina had
warned about, one of those suspicious looking individuals who, she
said, would come up to anyone with whose face or name they weren't
familiar, and try to engage them in a conversation so as to extract information from them, whether for or against the régime? How well Medina had described the encounter which would take place: it almost
seemed she had planned it; it was as if she had known how or when it
would happen. "Middle-aged men, with two-day-old growth of beard,
their hair unkempt, trousers baggy, their general appearance shabby in

the sort of disorderliness you would associate with the city's newly-arrived, and they walk with the ease of a pederast scouring the streets they've always hunted in. They engage you in meaningless conversation, ask the silliest of questions, and at times they imitate the cliched detectives in thrillers who have unlit cigarettes in their mouths and ask for a light." But the man, who in Nasser's mind matched Medina's description of the category of Security he belonged to, was quiet, saying nothing. Then he fumbled for something in his pocket, took out a packet of cigarettes and asked for a light. Nasser didn't answer immediately: the man's artlessness offended his pride. As a result he felt cheap, like a prostitute being picked up. He was sure everyone in that dusty street was watching them, that the women were nudging one another in the ribs as they saw "the pederast pick up his choice"; he was sure that the children who had been leaning over the New Year's fire stopped because they too had noticed what was happening. The "picker" and his "victim" gravitated towards each other, circled each other like wrestlers, faced each other like duellists and each thought the other was indeed the "victim, the one marked as dead", and each, as he narrowed his eyes to aim, willed the other out of the way.

"No, I don't smoke," said Nasser.

"You don't want one?"

"I said I don't smoke."

"And you haven't any matches?"

"No. But you can light from the New Year's fire whose flames are enriching the odourless wind. Here. There. Cheap as a prostitute."

"That's true. Fire everywhere. Cheap as petro-dollars." For an instant, the man's eyes appeared to dim as though they had run out of the oil of curiosity and sensitivity, but then they ignited with life again. He made no attempt at stopping to light the cigarette in his mouth. Did he think he was a small child who would rather wet himself than miss the details of the tales being retold? He made certain he did not leave Nasser for the moment it took to bend double and light his cigarette. Now Nasser was sure the man was as thick in the head as was his skin. And from Alto Bondheere, Nasser could see the sea foam and fume high as the sky and he thought the salt had rubbed the wave's wounds and healed them. He stole a brief side-glance and struggled hard against in-

volving the man in conversation; but perhaps he should ask if he knew
how to get to Dulman's place.

"Dulman, the famous actress?"

"Do you know her?"

"Is there anyone who doesn't!"

"Are we going in the right direction? Will this road take us to her
house?"

"Why didn't you tell me earlier?"

"Why? I thought. . . ."

The man stopped, squinted his eyes and wrinkled his forehead: he
overdid these gestures of concentration in order to earn Nasser's confidence. The man smiled victoriously, thinking himself the winner of
this round because he had something worth reporting back to headquarters. He had the most significant news that any "pederast" could
have picked up that day: that Dulman, Lady of the Revolution, was visited at her residence by Nasser, a man who was undoubtedly
antirevolutionary. The man smacked his lips in triumph; he believed
he had won without striking a blow.

"May I lead the way?" he asked Nasser.

"Of course."

They turned and moved in the direction from which they had come.
Every now and then the sun would come out and lead a drove of
clouds like a herdsman his cattle, then it would stop, wait for them and
become one with them, merge into the dusty haze they had stirred;
with the sun hidden, everything became lightless like the weak eyes of
a senile person. *The led and the leader. Who sees what or whom?* Nasser
was thinking as he followed the man. *The General, tyrannical as Diony-
sius was blind to reality, has sculpted a cave of ears which echo the secrets of
his prisoners; it is a pity the blind are never in a position to read the lips of
their interlocutors, nor the deaf to hear what they see; but generals have
their systems, and philosophers their logic.*

"How long have you known Dulman?" asked the pederast.

"She's a good friend of mine."

"Where did you last meet her?"

"In Arabia. Why?"

"Is that where you come from?"

"I live in Jedda. You certainly are inquisitive. Why are you asking all these questions?"

"You live in Jedda and you are here on a visit? I am just being friendly," the man said, smiling the winner's grin. "Is anything wrong? I am just being friendly, that's all."

"I live in Rome part of the year, and in Jedda the rest of the time."

"You speak our language well for a foreigner."

"Actually, I'm not a foreigner. I was born here."

They passed some children and women leaping over a New Year fire. The man, Nasser saw, sniggered at the sight; perhaps, being a northerner, he found it silly that these southerners held so strongly on to their heathen traditions of fire worship and New Year sacrifices (in the north they threw burning sticks, invoking Satan's unholy names as they did so). But he preferred to say nothing, walked ahead of Nasser.

"Dulman has recently been made Lady of the Revolution," the man said. "I suppose you know that?"

"Yes, I know," Nasser said. He was enjoying this perverse conversation. What harm could it do him ? In the end, his foreign passport would come in handy. Or would it?

"You haven't seen her since, have you?"

"No."

"Have you heard the song with which she won this honour?"

"No."

"It's a wonderful revolutionary song."

Suddenly the man stopped. He cleared his throat and prepared to sing a few lines of the song with which Dulman had won the honour and the title. His voice was rough as sandpaper and it grated in Nasser's ears:

"He is the guarantor to God,
He surely is that,
His machine is made to order
To fulfill a need, the nation's and God's"

The man's supplicatory look, asking for a comment on the song and the singer, received Nasser's silent indifference. The man repeated the chorus. The children had stopped jumping their fires, and the women who were beating the sleeping devil from their mats held their up-raised arms in mid-air and listened. One or two boys applauded, while the others whistled and booed. Nasser was amazed at the thickness of the man's head, and his artlessness was, strangely, very embarrassing. *But then it requires a certain kind of a man to join the General's Security Service, doesn't it? Just as it requires a feebleness of character to become a minister in this régime.* Nasser stepped back. The man again led the way as he led the conversation, too.

"If you live part of the year in Jedda and the other part in Rome, does that mean you don't often come to Mogadiscio?"

"That's right," Nasser said.

"And when were you last here?"

"Six years ago."

"You're the right man, then. What do you think of the Revolution?"

"I haven't seen enough of the country. I came only yesterday."

"Do you mean Dulman never spoke favourably of the Revolution?"

"This conversation is becoming ridiculous. What has Dulman to do with all this? I said I haven't seen her since our last encounter in Saudi Arabia, I forget how long ago."

Silence. They walked on. The sun burnt the day's minutes, seconds, while Nasser waited for the man to challenge him with another provocative question. Then the man's rigid look relaxed into a smile: he realized he had picked a heavyweight; he realized he wouldn't get away with what he had taken on unless he bent double and lifted his weight slowly but surely, little by little, up and up until the strands of his arms' muscles wove the geometry of his strong physique. Otherwise, his spine would snap, and all this weight-lifting would amount to nothing.

Nasser surprised the pederast with a question which unbalanced him, Nasser who had nothing to lose asked:

"Are you with the Security?"

"Why? What makes you think I am Security?"

"Your gait and your mannerisms."

"How do you mean?"

"You seem to me a man undecided whether to use the butt of a gun or the sweetness of a smile in order to get what he wants; and yet you act like a junior officer in an outfit a size too large for you."

They stood facing each other for a long while. Nasser was happy that his voice had that cutting edge in it, as sharp and alive with challenge as chili. Then a child running away from her mother came and stood between them, looked up at Nasser appealingly: from the little girl's eyes hung down, like onions, two huge drops of unshed tears. Nasser turned to the girl's mother who approached and promised she wouldn't beat the child provided she went with her. The little girl wouldn't believe that. But her mother swore on her own mother that she wouldn't. And the little girl took the hand which dropped the cane with which she would have been beaten.

When the two were gone, the man pointed at a door.

"That's Dulman's house." He did not wait for Nasser to thank him, but said before he left: "I am sure we'll see each other again."

Nasser went and pressed Dulman's door-bell.

. . . .

A young girl, probably a relative of Dulman's, had shown him in and left him alone in a room wide and bright with sun, bare save a table and chair and the tape-recorder whose ejector button had been pressed and then not closed. Waiting, he decided to conduct himself on a tour of the few photographs which dressed the walls with the calmness of authenticated history. It had been a year since that night in Jedda when he had thrown a party in her honour. Apparently she had won an honorary title since, and these were the photographs taken to commemorate that occasion. Soyaan had been posthumously knighted "The Hero of the Revolution" and Dulman "The Lady of the Revolution". Nasser's eyes moved from one photograph to another. His heart throbbed like the pulse of a high fever as his gaze caught and read the caption: "The Mother of the Revolution Gives the Title of Honour to the Lady of the Revolution." He imagined that Dulman must have felt betrayed by this distinction: the *Mother* of the Revolution as opposed to the *Lady* of the Revolution. She would certainly have preferred, he told himself, to have earned not the title of *ladyship* but the pleasure and pain of being a mother, period! She had never groaned a child's labour, she was a barren woman, and was between thirty-seven and forty and therefore less likely to become a mother who was wet with the milk of maternity and who smelt of a baby's burp and *dilq*.

Dulman, the *gablan!* She believed she was the victim of desecration, that there was a "dark curse on her femininity", as a sheikh had said.

"The knot of this curse can only be untied after the sheikhs pray for her." And she laid for the sheikhs a series of feasts month after month after month, and a string of decades was dedicated to every bead in the rosary. They called her a woman of quality. They feasted their belches with pronouncements of gratitude and *alxamdulilah,* and touched their foreheads in reverence to the Allah who gives generously: they told beads of benediction. But she remained as barren as before. Not only that. Coincidentally, as these expensive prayers drained her finances and as she took more and more loans to meet the sheikhs' demands, the star of her fame fell suddenly like a meteor. She was bankrupt and heavily in debt. None of the National Theatre producers offered her parts in the plays being produced. And it was at this most disastrous period that she accepted to go on a tour in the Middle East organized by the Ministry of Information and National Guidance. This was a tour all the famous singers had declined. But she had been heavily in debt and it didn't matter much to her whether she sang the General's syco-phantic lyrics or the devil's, as long as there was a clause in the contract that she would be paid handsomely and that, after the tour was over, she would leave on a government pre-paid trip and consult the most well known gynaecologists in Europe to make her bear a child now that "the Koranic glands couldn't give birth to her dreamed-of off-spring". The Middle East tour was a disaster in every sense of the term. The exiled Somali community in Saudi Arabia had organized itself into smaller units, and every evening a given group would go and boo and whistle at the performers. Once or twice, she received threatening phonecalls. And one evening, someone telephoned and talked of a time-bomb which would explode: the theatre-hall was emptied in time by the Saudi Arabian Security. Understandably, Dulman's popularity with the Somalis in general and those exiled in particular touched rock-bottom. Nasser met her during this disaster-prone tour. Crying on his shoulder one night, she said that he was the one a fortune-teller had described and that she would bear him a child if he slept with her. Nasser obliged. Nothing came of it, just as nothing had come of the thousand times she believed her womb would hold, fertilize and bring forth a prediction. Four husbands. She had consulted a traditional doctor in Lagos when she was there for the Black Arts Festival. "She thinks she owes the world a child," said one of her husbands. "What is more, she is confident that in her there is the Mahdi whom she must bring forth. She's mad, obsessed with birth, and never for one second have I heard her speak about death. A real pathological case." But did she have anything to say to that? Yes, she said to Nasser: "My woman-hood faces moonwards. I shall not suffer waiting: I shall suffer if I despair. If I were an ambassador's wife or the mistress of one of the powerful, who knows? I might have found a doctor who would do something so that before my menopause I bring forth a prediction." That night, they came to an understanding: in exchange for payment, she would send him taped versions of all underground songs.

He turned when he heard the door open. Dulman.

"Ah, there you are," he said.

"Nasser, Nasser, could you not wait? Why did you come today?"

"Why?"

"Trouble. Terrible trouble. And I am frightened."

She caught him by the neck as she kissed him, like a nonswimmer clutching whatever comes along, like a drowning person holding on to another whose warmth is reassuring. She caught him by the neck when she kissed him, as though she would hang her unfulfilled life on him like a cloth to dry and leave it there forever. She was cold and she collapsed senselessly and grasped him; he held back his weight lest he too lose balance and fall on top of her. She kissed him on the neck again and again: he struggled like a dead chicken before its last twitch of flesh. Then she let him go and took in a deep breath. There was deep calm, as if a rainstorm had just stopped. She moved away from him and took a chair. She indicated that he should approach.

"I thought you would not come today," she said. "And yet feared you might."

"I promised I would."

"People always make promises and never keep them. That has been my principal grievance against my people. Once it used to be *qawl sharaf*, but does that mean anything any more?"

"I promised and I am here."

Had her inner strength begun to succumb after a few encounters with the naked forces of authoritarianism? It appeared that she was not ready to receive him. Had he disturbed her peace and quiet? Was somebody with her? Should he ask whether it was true that the second

Vice-President of the Republic was the one who had installed her in this villa, with telephone and watchman facilities?

"You look well," she said.

"You look super, too."

"When did you come?"

He remembered the encounter he had had with the Security man on his way to her place and wondered if he should tell her. Maybe she could just telephone and have anybody removed – no sweat! But he did not understand why she was tense, why the air in the room was dense, heavy and unbreathable. This made him uneasy and he thought the best he could do in the circumstances was to give her the gift some fans of hers had sent her through him and the letter which accompanied it. So, very clumsily and without any preambles or niceties, he said:

"Here is a gift I've been asked to bring to you."

He held it out as though it were a bouquet of flowers, he smiled at her, he was friendly. She looked worried, deeply concerned about something, and clasped her hands behind her. She was suspicious. Her cue now: life's theatre of realities, and people remembering others upon whom they shower gifts. She was used to being presented with watches and necklaces when on stage, which would be returned to their owners when the play was over, when the feast was finished. Did she think this was another gift which somebody would return to withdraw and reclaim like those watches, necklaces and silk shawls with which actors or actresses were ornamented temporarily and only when the play was on? Or was this something else special – a gift for keeps? She rose to her feet. Her long dress, ankle-low, swept the floor. Hush. This was life's stage. She strolled up and down, saying nothing, like those seconds when the audience hushed and waited for her to begin to sing her most famous song, the one entitled "Cain in Love with Death". Hush and listen to the silkiness of her stride. "Cain in Love with Death" had been Hadraawi's most accomplished piece, Hadraawi who was undoubtedly the best poet Somalia had produced in the past decade. But she preferred Abdi Qays, another excellent lyricist; she said Qays's lyrics were easier to learn, understand and identify with. She strolled up and down silent as a needle at work, although she gave the impression every now and again that she would break this quietness with the sweetest song anyone ever heard. He remembered how the exiled Somali community in the Middle East had nicknamed her the Um Kalthoum of the Horn of Africa. Finally she sat down.

"Specifically who has sent me this gift? And is it for keeps?"

"There's a note signed by those who sent the gift to you."

"Who?"

"Here is the note. Read. You can read it yourself."

He dropped the note on her lap. She picked it up and turned it as though it were a very hot potato she should wait to cool before she took a bite of it. She unfolded the note and held it away from herself like a long-sighted person. He thought she would perhaps say that she had forgotten her glasses and would he kindly read it for her – something very many Somalis say when they don't wish to confess that they don't know how to read. However, Nasser was certain she had learnt how to read Somali, she had made a promise she would learn. In a subsequent letter, she said she had. But now she squinted at what someone had scribbled on the paper in front of her, she shook her head, she passed the note back to him. "I can't," she said.

"What?"

"I can't read. I don't know how to."

"Read!"

"I can't."

"Read in the name of Allah!"

Her eyes popped out like someone seized, possessed by fear. And she chose to remain silent. It was he who now strolled up and down, started quoting to himself Allah's first contact with the Prophet through Gabriel. *Read, read in the name of Allah. Read in the name of the One who created you out of coagulated blood.* The manna and before that the Torah in five books of voluminous and copious instructions. The Arabs call the Jews "the people of the book". The Arabs refer to their own language as that of the Koran. This was certainly a very interesting distinction. The people of the book. The Arabic "language" is given supreme importance over the "people" who speak it. *Read, read in the name of Allah.* But can one read before one writes? With one single stroke, with a very simple order of divine imperative, Allah willed the Arabs to become a people, yes, a people with a written tradition. *Read in the name of Allah, say My name after the angel Gabriel who's brought to you the divine message of literacy.* Mohammed was an *ummt* and he read.

"Are you going to read it to me?" She held out the note.

"You told me a lie."

"No, I didn't. When I returned from the Middle Eastern tour, I set my mind to learning to read and write and in a fortnight I did just that. In those days I used to receive fan-mail and I needed to know how to answer these letters. Then a few months later, when the fan-mail stopped coming, I learnt to forget to read and write. It's as simple as that."

He wasn't moved by what she said for he didn't share the view that you could learn to read and write as you pleased, which was a theory Medina held to, a theory which classed the Somali generally as "non-bookly". *Read,* he was saying to himself, *Dulman dear, read in the name of the Almighty who is generous in His providence and who might remove your vaginal calcoli without your sensing the least pain and who might invest in your fertile soil a child,* a Mahdi.

"You think it is as easy as that?" she said.

"What?"

"It's not a question of learning the alphabet. It's a question of changing, becoming somebody else. It isn't very easy. You don't change between sunrise and sundown of the same day. It takes ages and a great deal of patience to become a literate people."

"Why is it so frightening?"

"Why is death so frightening?" and she paused. "I suspect because we fear any change."

"Why?" (He noticed one thing: she was talking about death.) He listened.

"I suppose because one loses contact with what one knows best and doesn't know what death has in store. At my age, it isn't easy to adapt to new things."

"At your age? You talk as if you were ancient."

"The only change of status I wouldn't mind would be to become a mother. That doesn't frighten me. And it wouldn't so much require a change; perhaps a challenge."

They were silent again. A young girl came with a tray on which were soft drinks for them. Dulman patted her on the head lovingly as she set the tray down. Then she saw that she had dropped the note. The girl bent to pick it up, but Dulman told her not to bother by shaking her head. Nasser accepted the drinks she passed to him. The young girl returned with a chair which she placed in front of him before leaving. Nasser sat down. He had a sip of his orange.

"Doesn't it frighten you that you might die illiterate?" he asked.

"I am not 'illiterate'. Medina has explained this to me. But why are we talking about all this? Let us talk about you, about us, eh? Why are we discussing whether I am literate or illiterate? We can even forget about the gift these people sent with you and their note."

"Through the irony of history," said Nasser, "an illiterate 'prophet' changed a people from being oralists and forced them to belong to the written tradition. That was Prophet Mohammed. And through another irony of history, an illiterate general who models himself on God has tried to do the same thing."

The sun's weak light forced itself feebly through the window. A waft of windy smoke also came in. Dulman coughed. Nasser wondered but didn't dare ask why there was no fire lit within her compound. Was it because she did not think a fire was worth building, a fire in whose flames one could read one's future?

"Well, well. Tell me then," he said.

"What?"

He nervously jumped up and stood in front of the window, then turned around, was silent for a while. After what felt like a century he said:

"How have you been?"

"Fine, very fine. And you?"

"Fine, very fine." He came back but didn't take his chair. "How is work?"

"What work?"

"Your theatre work, plays you are in, how are things generally with you?"

Her face dead-pan, she said: "I've been out of theatre lately. Didn't Medina tell you?"

"I didn't ask her. What's happened?"

"Hard to explain."

Her eyes were cold like metal, lifeless. Then: "Let's talk about you. How is your business?"

He said nothing. She remembered what he had said to her once: that one's life is rendered meaningless or meaningful in relation to the persons or things one is involved with. She watched him push the parcel he had brought from Jedda towards her; she watched him pull the tape-recorder towards himself. He pressed the ejector and saw that there was no cassette in it. His voice sounded affected when he spoke:

"Since you can't write and you don't read, you use this, tape everything straight from the poet's mouth and then learn your part, is that it?"

A shade of sadness had covered his face. She wondered why he did not want to believe that she had no more to do with theatre, that playwrights did not write parts specially for her.

"You're dependent on this machine and not on your own memory to learn your parts?" he went on. "You are dependent on the twentieth century's advanced technology, do I understand?"

She stood up and smoothed her dress. Tall, clear-skinned and beautiful, she had an attractiveness of features which had matured with her. She was heavier on the hips and downwards, and her eyes were dark as Nasser's were clear. It was when she smiled that her eyes' wrinkles showed how old she was. Nasser believed she could remove her props of age and mask of beauty whenever she wanted; it was as easy for her as undressing before a near-stranger had been, a near stranger whom she imagined would carry the seed which would multiply in her womb and flaunt the actress's splendour. She said, her voice calm as her delivery had been rehearsed:

"Some of us have been catapulted into the centre-stage of a century we actually don't belong in and have nothing in common with. Some of us have been forced by circumstance to accept conditions and the dictates of the century's needs. It's like living all your life in natural darkness or in an area bathed in moonlight. Then suddenly powerful electric bulbs are switched on and you become the spot on which the light falls, upon whom all the world's eyes meet."

She raised her eyes to the ceiling, where a beetle was whirling noisily in the heart of its own drone, turning round and round upon itself in such a way Nasser thought it would bite its tail like the symbolic snake.

"Like that beetle," she said pointing upwards with a half raised arm, so that Nasser saw the sweaty wetness of her armpit. "Just like that beetle."

"I don't understand."

"It whirls in the pulse of its drone and nothing else exists aside from it. But the whiteness of the ceiling exposes its nakedness and turns it into the spot on which our eyes fall."

"I still don't understand," he confessed.

He concentrated on the bore in the ceiling's paintwork, the dents the beetle made more prominent: the fringes of the century and the centred spotlight were one and the same for him. He thought of how Europe looked to the America it had catapulted into the central position of the whirl blast; European intellectuals looked to the Africa they had cast in their imaginings. *Is that what she means?* he asked himself. But she was watching the beetle put its drilling head in the impression it had made wider and hollower. She thought that perhaps they weren't at all catapulted into the centre-stage; perhaps nobody switched on the floodlights to drown and melt the thickness of the tropical darkness. Unless they, too, were willing, no person in the world could push them into any position or make them take nonsense from anyone. She pulled the tape-recorder towards her, pressed the ejector and then closed the shutter by pushing it into place.

"Some of us belong only partly to the twentieth century," she said. "And I believe we have the right to use its technology as much as an African dictator makes the right or the wrong use of a given ideology. It is the technology and the political contradictions rocketing from the catapult of which I've spoken that victimize one."

Nasser nodded his agreement. In the brief pause which followed, he began to hum to himself a tune Dulman had made famous. But she was thinking about her nomadic background, reminiscing about what happened when she first arrived in Hargeisa. The first difficult years. She was passing through the worst patch when one night she was discovered by one of the most talented poet-playwrights, Ali Sugulle, with whom she slept twice. She went from one hand to another like a bill of lading, she slept with every one of them, she chewed *qaat* with them, and *geerash'ed* with every one of them. From Sugulle, through

Hassan Mumin's thick, hairy fingers, through Mustafa Hagi Nur and finally through the then director of Radio Hargeisa: she became a member of a troupe called Walaalo Hargeisa. Folk-plays in Somalia don't require acting talent. And theatre followed the same zigzaggy lines as
that of Egypt. Almost all the theatre- and cinema-debutantes were recruited from those men and women who'd become famous as singers
or entertainers. The most significant parts of the plays are the lyrics
sung by the hero or the heroine. These songs are worked into the un-
scripted theatrical pieces which are no more than bravado of the wild-
est kind. The songs make or break the plays. Although of late
Hadraawi's surrealistic and sophisticated plays, seeming to combine a
touch of sophistication and an appealing set of lyrics, had become very
popular, so popular that the General had to banish him to the provinces.

He had a sip of his orange.

"What is it that is hard to explain? What's happened? Why aren't
you given any more parts to play? Why are you out of theatre, Dulman?
Will you tell me?"

"I became too famous, too important and the General thought it was
time I was cut down to size, made irrelevant like last year's joke."

"I thought they needed people like you. I thought they would buy
you, pay any sum to have you rally for them. Isn't that what you did for
them when you sang those grotesqueries praising him like a God?
What was it? Let me try:

"He is a prophet
His name is Mohammed
He is an *ummi*
But made his people read and write?"

She smiled as one would at an adult who asked a childish question.

"The General used us when he needed our rallying for him; also because some of us were more famous than he when he came to power.
But we were like a shade tree others had planted. Meanwhile he proved
to everybody how cheap we all were, how we changed uniform, how
we sang his praise names as we had never sung anyone else's before.
And he did one thing: he created his own troupe of sycophants. In
other words, he planted his own tree long before we realized ours had

become shadeless. He created younger actresses in our places, younger and therefore more willing to please. Let to the powerful go a garland of youthful girls."

"And where do you stand?" Nasser asked.

"I was made to stand on carpetless ground, I was made to realize how powerless I am. I was accused of having collaborated with Hadraawi on an underground play."

"And so?"

"I'm sure you've heard how before *he* goes on a trip abroad he leaves behind instructions to put hundreds of people in jail, that his juniors should terrorize the country. When he returns and has been here a day or two, he releases those whom his men imprisoned. But he doesn't do that without getting his message across and so he gathers those who've been unjustly put in prison and says, 'I've had a chance to reprimand my security officers for having done this to you and it will never happen again. I hope we've all learnt a lesson: that without me these will pillage and loot and rape your women and put you in jail one and all.' Then everybody goes away, he hopes, grateful that *he* is there. The same happened to me."

"He called you and. . . . "

"A black Security car came early one dawn and I was bundled into it and driven to his office where he was waiting for me. I wasn't sure whether I would be given a place in the cabinet or sent straight to jail. He spoke longwindedly, going over what had been said about me, then about how he was trying to save me from this self-destructive instinct of mine. He asked me *to choose between two things:* either join his enemies, the anti-revolutionary reactionaries (and he named rival clans of his own clan) or else rejoin his. He said he had cleared with my own tribespeople and they were pleased with what he had decided to offer me: I could go anywhere in the world, consult any doctor anywhere, the government would pay for all my expenses."

"Was it you who chose Geneva?"

"He hinted at it himself. He said that his sister-in-law, the wife of Ambassador So-and-so, had a successful one in Geneva."

"What other conditions aside from joining his group did he set down?

"A number of other things."

"What?"

In another room, a telephone rang but stopped after one or two star-tled rings. She laid her hand on the unread letter, then took it away from it and looked at him.

"There is a thought which returns to me like the refrain of a familiar song, something you said that one night when we were in bed together, alone with God. You believed, you said, that we actors didn't quite un-derstand what acting was all about, and then you listed the famous American and European theatre theoreticians and practitioners of the art. I think I said that we did so long as we maintained a rapport with our audience, so long as we believed and the audience believed we spoke for them, so long as there was this contact with them. You gener-alized that Somalis didn't understand what theatre was all about. Is that right, Nasser?"

"Please go on."

"The thought which returns to me like a refrain is that Somalis are the only people who've actually understood the meaning of this art. And I'll tell you why."

"Please."

"Actors perform, they act: they pretend to be what they are not in real life. And when you do that exceedingly well and they like you, Somalis don't only applaud, they come up to the stage and ornament you with their golden watches, necklaces and shawls, *pretending* to give them to you; the audience, everybody in the theatre sees they've done that, and they, too, receive applause for their generous act, and their friends pat them on the head and congratulate them. When the play is over, these *actors* come and re-claim what they gave you in pre-tence; these *actors* come to reclaim in private what they gave in public. Actors and actors and actors."

She was silent for a few minutes. Then another waft of smoke en-tered the living-room and they were reminded of what was taking place outside: the New Year's feast of welcome. Nasser wondered how Medina was doing, how she was getting on with his mother (he looked at his watch and thought she probably hadn't left for home yet), and he flattered himself he was different from those who might have gone to his mother's place on a day like this. Dulman was saying:

"Once a Sudanese singer – I think it was Wardi – came to Mogadiscio and was decorated with necklaces, watches and all sorts of other gifts. As soon as the evening's event was over, he locked them up in his briefcase and was about to go to his hotel when he saw a crowd of women waiting for him. It took the wind out of him. From then on, it became a National Theatre policy to tell all visiting artists of this great pretence. What is more theatrical than that?"

"The Greeks, for example. . . . "

"They cannot have it the way we do. No other people can. Perhaps the Egyptians. But don't let me get carried away, let me come to my point. Politics is another thing in which we are 'theatrical'. The General says Somalia is socialist, and when you ask anyone in public what Somalia's ideology is, the answer is that we are socialist. We pretend we are socialist, we buy the thing we sell to the world. But are we socialist? We say we are when we are in public or when we are with those who don't know that we're *pretending,* that we are *acting.* As soon as the curtain falls on the stage, as soon as we are alone, the mask drops and we talk about the tribal formation of the General's régime, and we come to claim our share of the loot."

She fell quiet again. Nasser grinned, tickled at how certain she was about all that she had said. He looked at his watch, for his stomach had begun to grumble.

"The unread letter is here," he said, "and here is the unopened parcel. Will you please accept the present I brought for you?"

"I really couldn't."

"But why?"

"In Riyad, in Rome, in Geneva, in Nairobi and Abu Dhabi, everywhere I've visited, I saw Somalis who live in shockingly obscene misery. Not poverty, no, but just an abject misery which loosens my bowels and makes me throw up when I think of them. I saw them go from the small hovels they lived in, I saw them assemble in bars to gossip. In the country's ancient tradition of nomadism, one met one's peers and talked and listened to poetry or to gossip in the shade of a tree: that has been replaced with bars when abroad. I saw them move like migrating birds. They would be in one of these bars for hours and hours, there primarily to talk about the General and what he had done to them, but they never raise a finger, never organize themselves into unions and never rebel. Do they still live in that abject misery? Do they live in utter fear of being deported for not having their papers in order? Of being returned as penniless as when they walked to freedom? Of being extradited from Saudi Arabia en bloc? Do they?"

"Nothing has changed."

"Then how could you expect me to accept their gift?"

"Because they send home money to their wives, children, parents and their school-going brothers and sisters here; and because the gifts which they send are accepted by everybody else."

"Evidently I've seen the misery these people live in and their mothers, their brothers and sisters haven't. Otherwise, they might think harder before accepting a penny earned honourlessly in Saudi Arabia or Nairobi, Abu Dhabi or Kampala."

There was nothing he could say. Then he remembered the message Abdullahi Dheere had asked him to deliver, but decided it wasn't the right moment for that sort of message. He found he could think of no reason with which he might exonerate the people whom she had condemned – for in a way he agreed with her.

"Can you explain why Somalis live miserably abroad especially wherever there are a great number of them?" he asked. "And why do they hate one another so much that they avoid each other?"

"Because the 'theatricality' and the 'feast of the masquerade' are shorter abroad; in fact it takes longer to wash off a soap-stain. And then they become humourless, tongue-tied, they do not know what to say to one another."

The white of Dulman's eyes turned whiter than menstrual gauze. He began to see sense in all she had said; he began to see sense in the analogies she had used. But he was disappointed that she was more determined than he had known her, and she appeared confident of her decisions; she knew what she liked, what she hated. And the doctor she had consulted in Geneva had told her, he knew anyway, that there was nothing any doctor could do for her. So probably this helped her to be more determined, helped her to face life with courage – and alone! She saw him look at his watch once or twice. Now he got up.

"I am very sorry to hear that you won't act or sing any more."

"There are others," she said without any emotion.

"No, no, they aren't as good as you."

"Perhaps better. Some are. At least one of them is."

him, then pumped his heart which beat against his chest. He heard the name again.

"Mina! What are you doing here?" he shouted.

"Come, come," she said opening the car door for him.

"What's happened?"

"Get in. I'll tell you later."

N I N E

. . . .

A bird in ascendance, moving upwards as though answering a call, collided with another in mid-air. This produced a heinous squeal, and with a nimble turn of wing each gave way to the other. No doubt it was painful: the upheaving, the uprising of those very wings and the soul which parted with the body of the feathered, the soul of the beaked. Then the tortured cry, the wounded groan and the descending bird's return to the earth of the living-dead. The night was tattooed with the day's graffiti of smoke, and a cloudy shape resembling a shark sporting a long tongue of fire and red lust inched its way further and further into the inner stomach of the heavens: the tongue would rip all that came its way into slices thinner than a drizzle.

Another bird rose from the plateau of dusk and flew high over the thousand fires of the New Year festivities which burnt coal-dead the corpse of the past year. This bird seemed in a hurry, and it flew westward, bidding farewell to the day which was ready to migrate elsewhere.

. . . .

Samater's thoughts, like ashes, floated above a layer of heavier air, but he sat where he was, as if nailed to the chair. He had waited and waited for his sister Xaddia to come or call. In all probability her plane was late; this was normal, as normal as a strike in Italy. He had waited so as to tell her why he had thrown Idil out; he had waited to explain himself, tell her why he decided to move out of Medina's house and into a hotel. But now his tongue stumbled on the phrase "Medina's house": it had never crossed his mind he would use the phrase. Of course, Xaddia wasn't there to hear him and no one else had. He thought it best not to tell anybody that he had taken a room at the Caruuba Hotel and hired a car for a week, that he had opened an account at the bank; and that he had decided to begin afresh with the smoky air of the New Year. He was also going to do something he hadn't done since he married Medina: date another woman. He was disappointed that Xaddia hadn't come to hear him unburden his chest. He looked at the pile of letters and personal things in front of him. He would put all in a polythene wrapper, he would carry it in the boot of his car and, on his way to the appointment, buy himself a pair of underpants, toothpaste and tooth-brush, a comb and perhaps a shirt and shaving things. And before the day was out, he would hand in a letter of resignation. Tomorrow: an-other life and another bridge already crossed.

He was up on his feet. The framed portrait of the General stared down at him from several angles, a portrait made handsomer and younger by the photographer. Should he bring it down and tread on it, break its glass? And what would that get him? He remembered the night he was dragged out of Medina's cradling arms of cosiness and love, when there was that loud knocking on their door and he went to answer it. And the two men who came to him. The black car, the same car the Security used to take prisoners away in. He recalled the unreal things which happened: how a number of his clansmen came one after the other; how they begged him to accept the cabinet post the General offered him; otherwise, if he didn't, they would all go to jail, lose their money. "Our life depends on the decision you make," they had said. And Medina had said: "When have I ever decided for you? It is your life." He doubted if she understood the tribal tensions in one who had grown up in a clannish community. They were his cousins, his people, his friends. His mother's pressure; *his* ideas. Xaddia was never there to comment, Xaddia a big absence in his life from when Idil caused the breakup of her marriage; and all those cousins and tribesmen who were one's family in a tribal society. . . . Meanwhile, the General im-prisoned thirty of his tribesmen. The elders of the clan came and begged him to please the dictator's whim. "Our life depends on your decision," they had said. And Medina again and again and again: "When have I ever decided for you?" The following morning he took the oath of allegiance to the regime. That was six months ago. Now he would undo all he had done. No Medina, no mother, no house, only an account in his name, a room in a hotel, a woman to date. He would resign. He was determined to do that. To hell with the rest.

He tied a string round his letters and his personal things, made sure he had emptied the two drawers. He undid his key ring and left the office keys in a drawer. Then his eyes dropped in awe: a photograph of Medina and Ubax smiling at him from a framed glass in his drawer. He put the photograph in the same polythene bag and told himself that Medina would definitely be happy when she heard what he had decided to do. Medina was the one person who didn't like anyone leaning heavily and dependently on her. A hired car. A bank account. A date for the evening. A room in a hotel. Perhaps the choice of hotel wouldn't go down well with her; she never liked Caruuba. Well, never mind. It might be well worth telling her that he had moved out, so that she would take necessary precautions and see that a night watchman was hired. No, no. Any contact with her would be seen as weakness on his part. No telephones, no calls and no messages. And no mention of her name either.

He descended the stairs, having closed all the doors, and came to the shed where he had parked the car. The night-shift peons *jaalle'd* him, bowed and opened the gate to him. He put the polythene bag in the car-boot. He sat for a long while behind the wheel and he took in everything around him, for he wouldn't come back as "Minister" tomorrow. As he drove to meet Atta, his date for the evening, he thought: I *am the manbeast, the half-animal....*

He turned right, easing up on the accelerator. The car coughed his hesitation, but before it completely choked on it, his right foot descended determinedly and made it shudder like a horse intent upon shaking a rodeo breaker off its back. Then the ride was smooth as the inflow of oil on which the engine fed. A day up in smoke, he started to say himself. But had he already lost the game? He was certain he had done right: by taking a hotel room, he had saved himself the embarrassment of telling a maid that he hadn't money for the day's or the week's groceries; on displaying the room key, he could eat anything, invite anyone and have everything transferred to the bill he would receive when he decided to check out. They were fidgety, the manager, the receptionist, they all were nervous. Apparently, word had already reached the General, whose ears were pricked for anything which took place anywhere in the Republic, and there was a message from him: *Come and see me when you can.* That didn't entirely explain the manager's restlessness. Later, one of the gate-attendants whom he had bribed told him that two Security officers had taken rooms on either side of him. Now he turned left. He was on what served as an imitation of a motorway, what he and Medina referred to as the Outer Circular Road. And he accelerated. He unbuttoned his shirt: the wind was fresh and sweet. He sat behind the wheel and drove on and on and on. Above him, he hoped, would remain the faithful sky, always there wherever one went – whether cloudy, starry or clear. The sky was bathed in tears and on the horizon the wind had shuffled the clouds about like a pack of cards and there was the astrologer's shark, dead as a wishbone and large as a loom weaving a fabric of hope, a fabric with which the New Year would cover its shoulders. On the further horizon, a little to the left of the dead shark, there was his mother's corpse which buzzed with the flies of decay, flies big as vultures eating it down to a skeleton.

Careful. Slow down. Change gear. Don't press the accelerator. Back to first. Then neutral. Poor thing. Samater got out to have a closer look at it. A crane had been knocked down and run over, a crane whose long neck, long legs and bill mapped the circumference of its struggle with life before it gave up its spectre of a soul. A crane was a bird he would not have thought would smash its skull against the windshield of a car. A bad omen, he thought, as he came back to the car and opened its door. There lay dead (he wouldn't move for he trembled) a bird whose soul wouldn't fly god-wards. What he found very disturbing (which explained why he trembled) was that his own nick-name was *shimbir* - the generic Somali name for feathered vertebrates. Should he take that as symbolic? He started the engine. He changed gear. Press. Release clutch, brake. He was on the road again, thinking, remembering, reliving the immediate present, the remote past and the uncertain future all at once. He would begin from the time he threw the "bundle of rags and rage" out. Yes, he would start with that.

He threw Idil and Asli out of the house. He arranged a taxi to come and collect them. Had he not said he would throw her out if the new maid was still there when he returned? As she was bundled into the taxi, Idil had said: "Careful, careful, be gentle. I can walk. You needn't push me or manhandle me. I am rags in whom dwell life's rages. But I will make you regret. I will make you regret." Then she waved to the maid to follow her: neither took a thing, they left empty-handed. Just as the driver was about to move, she had touched him on the back to say to Samater, her son: "Children outgrow their parents; men outgrow their women; women outgrow fashions; and the year, the seasons. Unlike the seasons, the years, the men, the women and the children, unlike all these, tradition stays and wins in the end. You have done something you shouldn't have. And I will make you pay." The taxi was to take her to Xaddia's. Half an hour later, Samater went to his office. Then phone-call after phone-call. A stream of tribesmen called. Samater said he wouldn't see a delegation headed by a chieftain, he told his secretary to turn them away. In substance, the phone-calls were similar: *Have you gone out of your mind? What has become of your experience as a man of the world? You need a doctor, you are mad. You are sick in the head.* One of them predicted he would lose his job. Another threatened to have him fired. A third spoke of how Stalin, when the most powerful man in the world, was forced by the politics of the day to visit his aged mother in Georgia. There was also a recurring theme and imagery which was basically Islamic: it was about the mythical man who, because he wanted to earn society's and God's benevolence, carried his mother on his back all the way to Mecca. Another recurring image was how the clan was united against him, how the clan would ask the General to unseat him.

Slow. Careful. A sign warned drivers of a checkpoint a hundred and fifty metres away. Slow. A raised arm flagged him down.

"Yes?"

"Simple formalities."

A soldier would ask you at gun-point to open the car-boot. Another would take down names of passengers, car number; reason for journey and destination, formalities to which the residents of Mogadiscio were used like heavy cigarette-smokers to morning coughs. Particularly on a day like this, they would be tenser and ruder: possibly this was a sympathizer of those who had written on the walls. But there was a weird silence: the corporal tugged at his companion's sleeves and whispered something which made them both look away as though they were stifling laughter. Had the news already reached them? What version had they heard? Samater, however, was still in his car giving right-of-way to another.

"If I were you, I would register," said the corporal. "Things aren't the same. There have been minor disturbances and a purge. We apologize for the inconvenience."

"That's all right."

It was only when he was on the road again, alone with the wind and with his thoughts, that it dawned on him that the corporal and his friend had not been forewarned by the Security, nor had they heard the news about his mother. Had they heard about Medina? Here he pressed the accelerator pedal of his brain: greasy thoughts, thoughts sooty from the filthy track they had travelled before they came to him (meanwhile, he had a fleeting glance in the rear mirror of his face caked like a mudguard with the earth of travel). He felt nude as a eucalyptus tree, standing solitarily on a sandhill. . . .

The night had spread itself gently, methodically; the moon held the space it had conquered; the stars beckoned to him like a lizard to the fly it plans to trap.

One thing led to another. He remembered when he last set eyes on Medina, how she was bent over a notebook with that engrossed look on her face, for she was translating a tale she had found in Achebe's *Things Fall Apart* and which Samater suggested she faithfully call "All of You". She said that she should give it a more subtle, more suggestive title. One needn't be faithful to Achebe's rendering of the Ibo tale more than to one's own reaction to it. What title would she give it? *He.* Just that? "He"? Yes. *"He"!* And she spoke in the rhetoric of philosophical dead-ends, she quoted Camus, Sartre, Crane and Virginia Woolf; she talked about the humiliated position of women. He had been late for something or other, and she pecked at him like a mother-pigeon. *"He is the tortoise that is all of you, said He to the congregation of Birds!"* (Achebe) The day before that, the week or the month before that. He would do anything at her command. For example:

"Pick that flower for me, Samater."

"If I do, the tree will die, dear."

"Pick that flower, I said."

"And let the tree bleed its white sap?"

"It's the flower I want. I am not interested in the tree."

He stopped thinking, then stopped the car. He said out loud that no dialogue of that kind had ever taken place between Medina and himself. Why did he make all this up? Was it because he wanted to justify what he had done today, justify first to himself and then the rest of the world? He was perspiring, trembling as he had when he saw the dead crane on the road. No, no. What she used to say to him was this: "A flower serves as the humus for the soil of my love for you. Yes, you are the fertilizer. That's why we've given our daughter the rose-name of Ubax." They would make love there and then, under the running shower. He would peck at the flowery privacy of her soul. "Do you know why they nicknamed you 'bird'? You are like the crow which in Egyptian mythology is said to have forgotten how to walk. The crow-as-deity." The qua-qua of the crow (here she would suggest that he re-read Lucky's long monologue in *Waiting for Godot* or Ted Hughes's sequences on the waaq-waaq): a hyphenated word pregnant with sacred significance, invocative of an ancient god of Puntland – waaq! It filled your mouth as you uttered the name of the deity, a qua-qua of the Speechless one, a waaq-waaq pecking at the sensitive nerve of the princess. "The crow," she would conclude, "was the god of all before He became the foreteller of death and ill-fortune – which is why we stone it away from our roofs. You are my unstoned crow: so love me, be with me. Do peck at the flowery divinity of my womanhood." But there was another version, wasn't there? How when Prophet Mohammed was emigrating from Mecca it was the crow which led the chasers to the prophet's hiding place shouting, "Waaka, waaka," which in Somali means, "Here he is, here he is." Upon becoming victorious the prophet laid a curse making the crow darker, and Muslims from that day onward looked upon crows with disfavour.

He had at first had difficulty adopting his nomadic ways to her uninhibited sophistication. "You will have to change your nomad ways," she would say. "These are the gift of the seasons: a mat of autumn leaves, and a mattress of snow bright as life, as spring. Then the period of stasis; and the flowers blossom. Think of me and my seasons of fertility, my periods: a moment of stasis: a moment of indecision and no more." She made him read the world's classics, introduced him to music, jazz, and to cinema; she took him to see *The Bicycle Thief, Casablanca* and a series of Chaplin classics. She helped him with his English, with his French. She took him by the hand and led him through life's unread guides. It was then that he said Medina was a grey-eyed stork, gobbling words, that she believed it was books and learning that would save the world from imminent self-destruction. His Somali friends in Milan, whose company he no longer kept, called him all sorts of names. This helped wean him entirely from them. They became a foursome, and at times a threesome. Medina and Sandra. Nasser and Samater. He was the groomed hope of this association. Quiet, soft-spoken, a man of no outspoken opinion, he listened, he learnt, he read what he was given to read and seldom disagreed with anyone to the point of breaking off the friendship. "The man's inner energy is enormous," they used to say to one another. "He is a well of patience."

Now he started. He looked at his watch and saw he would be terribly late unless he drove faster. He fumbled about, started the engine: the usual cough, the usual kick of combustion like a camel refusing to rise up and go. The night was raven black; the road stretched in front of him straight as his mother's linear-thinking: this is good, this is bad; this is evil, this is not. He changed gear. He changed the subject. He combed the grey hair of his past: Milan. Medina. Nasser. Sandra. Above all, Medina. As she sipped his "sugar-disaster", the tea he had made for her and Nasser when he returned their invitation and meal, she talked about Descartes, Nietzsche, and Sartre. She was impressive, she was wrapped up, like a souvenir, in colour-patches of her (then) bright taste. Medina's father had been an ambassador. Several eastern and western capitals had seen his name spelt rather too boldly in their newspaper columns. He was once referred to by a journalist as "the man who made his country famous". Medina, talking about her past, put it this way: "I prostrated before the powers of femininity at the age of thirteen in a hotel in Stockholm, looking like an over-nourished pet. I stood on the kerb of a cobbled street waving to the chariot which carried my father away into the winter silhouette of a Scandinavian night. Nasser was at school in Milan." That night, Medina washed away the first trickles of her monthly pains. At fourteen, New York women's magazines welcomed her as the daughter of the most well-known African ambassador at the UN. Paris, a year later, pampered her with token presents, a hand-delivery of "Joy" perfume signed by the master himself. Nairobi's *Nation's* gossip-columns had her dating the son of a Kikuyu chief, a young Oxbridge graduate who was the playboy about town. Mogadiscio's tongue, the shape of a sickle, cut her in two. Samater asked – but why? "The Somali is a brother-killer: he is Romulus closing the gate of the city in Remus's face; he is the brother who plots the assassination of Joseph. The Somali is sororicidal as he is fratricidal. He is jealous, competitive and will do anything to achieve his end. However, the Somali is never patricidal. Never in the history of power-struggles has anybody seen a Somali kill his father or mother for wealth or power. To his age-group, his equals, he would raise a finger of rivalry in the act of challenge, he would raise a wet finger against the wind and say: "I dare you to hit me before this finger has dried."

Would that explain why everyone was shocked when the story about him and his mother was circulated? The members of the clan were so shocked they couldn't forge a united front to face Samater. If he beat his wife till she spat blood, no one would stop or condemn him, no one would release God's wrath upon him. Medina was his equal, the same age as he, so he could kill her in combat and nobody would say a thing. His mother? No.

He looked at his watch again. He was already half an hour late. Would Atta wait? He was almost always late for appointments and it was Medina who kept reminding him of this or that meeting with this or that person. If she were with him, he wouldn't arrive a second before or after the appointed time. But if she were with him, there might have been another confrontation between Atta and herself – like that day when she came to their place for lunch, yes, the last lunch they offered as a couple. Atta spoke of "returning to cultures one is part of, native to". Medina had challenged: "Return to what, pray? I understand if you say the Afro-American has returned to his continent. But culture isn't a lamp-post you can go back to. The dynamism of culture is far swifter and stronger than the European holocaust of invasion which tore you from your mother-continent. I am, as much as you are, a contribution to a culture. You to the American; I, to the Somali. I make as much of a contribution to Somali culture as the camel herdsman." After which, Atta asked: "But why did you return to Africa, Medina?"

"Nothing to do with culture. Like an elephant, I've returned home to die." And she looked very serious.

He turned a blind bend in his thoughts. He hooted as he turned. Another bend, a little to the right, a little to the left. Slow. Watch out, there was a car in front. Its rear-lights from that distance resembled a baboon's bottom callouses. Be careful. A little to the right again. And out of the night emerged a man with a paraffin lamp in his hand. Samater braked.

"How many are you?" asked the roving waiter.

"There's an Afro-American waiting for me. My name is Samater. I wonder if you could tell me whether she is here?"

"The *Negro?*"

"Yes, the Afro-American."

"If you would follow my lamp, please. I'll take you to her."

•   •   •   •   •   •   •   •   •   •   •

Under the arched canopy of a thorny acacia whose overhanging roofing had been hoisted up with sticks, under the holes like cats' eyes in the roofing, Samater half bent so that a thorn would not blind him. He saw Atta lying straight on her back, she lay quietly on a straw mat on the sandy floor. Was she sleeping? Like an infant who might fall off a high bed, she had pillows on either side of herself; her dress had rolled away from her. There was a paraffin lamp, by the light of which he could see the details of her sex. Such a quiet sleeper, he thought. He checked that the roving waiter who escorted him had gone away and was relieved to see that he had. The lamp entertained a host of moths which danced frenziedly, tossed and flung themselves like voodooists at the height of ecstasy. Otherwise the place was quiet and she was still asleep. For background noise, there was Dulman's voice, keeping the clients company, Dulman singing one of her "Cain" sequences. Such an angel when sleeping, he said to himself again. (*"Cut out the cliches, please*," said Medina's "voice" to him.) He turned away from the lamp and its ecstatic moths, turned his back on Atta – for there came a brain-storm of memories, there appeared Medina who struck him thought-less for a second, and the fire between his thighs no longer burned with lust for Atta's sleeping sex, Medina who. . . .

Atta groaned as she turned. But there was no significant change in the posture in which she slept, snoring a little, nose blocked perhaps because of dust and smoke. She was still on her back; she was like a boat floating down a quiet stream with a thick bank of vegetation, a boat carrying the tidings of its occupants across a hundred centuries of distorted history. Samater remembered that he had found Medina in more or less the same position and from there everything followed; he slipped in with her because she had invited him. Was that true? The story differed every time he re-told it. When the mood of the moment permitted, he would say that a very seductive hand had taken his and dragged him in; on other occasions, he would say he had found her shouting for help, she had had a scary nightmare which coincided with his re-entering the room. Medina was the heroine in all the versions he cared to tell, Medina was the one who decided what to do and when. But dare he go anywhere near Atta who would in all likelihood wel-come him in, open her legs wider apart, guide his fingers up the curled lips of her womanhood and with her free hand conduct his member in-wards? Could he rise to the raised wet finger of challenge? He backed up and explained the difference between the situation in which he had found Medina and now that of Atta. He had known Medina almost five months and they had already dealt with the preliminaries. Add this: the room was his, she had borrowed it from him for a week when he had been gone for his practicals. Listen to his mother Idil: *If Medina hadn't seduced him . . . !* Well, had she? He hardly knew Atta, you couldn't tell with these Afro-American women, she would possibly say nothing, she would possibly help him, make him commit himself bod-ily and then scream a cry-wolf of I-was-raped. But if he raped her, his mother might then render unto his "manhood" what was always his . . . *a full man!* Or would she? He dismissed the thought.

Atta turned. Perhaps she felt the weight of his clumsy and nervous movements. He had come closer to cover her bare bottom before wak-ing her. But now he hesitated because she might open her eyes just as he was doing it, and then the cry-wolf of I-was-raped! Mogadiscio had gossiped about her promiscuity, had spoken about her brief flirtation with one of the vice-presidents of the Republic and the General himself. Mogadiscio had talked about these things as lightly as it discussed the affairs of the General who was supposed to keep a number of mistresses all over the country. Of one thing Samater was sure: Atta and the Ideologue had something going and that was why she and Sandra spoke ill of each other. If he, Samater, slept with her, what was the worst thing that could happen to him? Nothing. After all, he was determined to resign as Minister.

Slowly but surely her eyes opened like a flower responding to a caressing dawn breeze. She took him in first as part of the surroundings. Then, quick as an acrobat, she sat up and covered herself as best she could. Both were silent for a while. Then a gentle smile broke like the liquid of an egg on her moist lips which she had licked.

"Have you been here long?"

"Fifteen minutes."

"Why didn't you wake me up?"

She acted as though concerned he had come upon her in that state. She got up and dusted her dress, smoothed it with her hands.

"Such an angel when sleeping," he said.

She gave him a light kiss on the cheek. She turned away, walked to the straw mat, which she lifted and tossed to shake the dust off; the pillows dropped to the floor and he went and picked them up.

"I am sorry for being late," he said.

"I've never known anyone to be on time save Medina. In America we have C.P.T. So you don't have to apologize. I carry reading material with me just in case I have to wait or something. I am Afro-American; you, African."

She sat down but was restless at first. She searched, like a Yogi, for a posture in which to meditate, eat and talk to Samater.

"What did you bring to read this time?" he asked her, sitting down. "I'm interested."

"*My Country and My People*. Volumes II and III."

"A good read, I bet you think it is."

She didn't say anything for a second or two. Then:

"Can we change the subject to something less personal?"

"Of course."
But they fell silent.

•   •   •   •   •   •   •   •   •   •   •

Samater raised his glass and they drank thirstily to each other's health.
She was a great drinker, a great eater, and a greater appreciater of national foods. He had asked the waiter to bring them a crate of cold beer
and a portion of rice and meat "for six persons". The waiter held his
breath for he had half a mind to inquire if they needed four extra
glasses. Samater corrected himself and said they wanted "six portions
of food and glasses and cutlery for two". Seeing that she was a foreigner
and wouldn't understand the language, the waiter took the liberty of
saying that he once served a German who ate the amount ten Somalis
would eat. Samater sipped his drink like a sparrow while in the same
second she opened and emptied a can of cold beer then tossed it aside.

•   •   •   •   •   •   •   •   •   •   •

She was a friend of a friend of a friend: that was how Medina and
Samater had met her; that was why they had invited her to a meal. And
she talked about New York and Boston and boastfully about her affair
with a well-known black poet. Atta's "blame of fate" rested on the fact
that she was the last guest Samater and Medina had together entertained to a four-course meal. Medina sat at the head of the table, Atta at
the other end, with Ubax to Medina's right and Samater to Atta's. She
had invited herself to lunch. After all, she was in the land of her brothers and sisters, where she could eat the African soil like a child unat-
tended and survive, and she knew how to eat with her fingers and everything, no worry, no sweat, no problem about cutlery, no formalities
about the number of guests at table – equal numbers of either sex and
that sort of bourgeois whitey thing; she was a sister, vegetarian prefera-
bly but if that was difficult she would eat what she was given, she ate
anything that didn't eat her, as one of her Ethiopian friends in Boston
used to say ("Oops, he was Somali not Ethiopian – what am I saying?"). . . . Would she like someone to pick her up from where she was
staying? No, she had transport, there was a brother, so sweet, who had

arranged everything for her: a trip into the hinterland ("so very like what I imagine my great-great-grandfathers lived in, so *natural,* untouched by the white man's civilization"), a trip up north ("*Hargeysha:* the entwined legs of the qaat-chewing rite, and I enjoyed myself, sat rib to rib with the governor of the region – what more could I ask for?") and another to the Crash Programme ("the kibbutz of organized co-operatives and they sang and sang and praised and thanked the General – it made me feel more grateful to him than before") and to the Young Revolutionary Centre and the Orientation Centre. There was nothing to do but give her the address and tell her how to get there. Before she hung up, she said she would be there bang on the nose, punctual as the West requires.

And she was. The bell rang – but she had already walked in. She was promiscuous in the bear-hugs she gave the maid and the orderly (mistaking them for Medina and Samater), then kissed Ubax; when finally the misunderstanding was cleared up, she greeted her host and hostess in Swahili and was shocked that not only did they know less than she but they weren't even enthusiastic about learning the language or teaching their little daughter to speak it. At table, Atta praised Kenyatta, Haile Selassie, Senghor and Kaunda; in the same breath, she said that the General was the greatest African leader she had ever had the pleasure to shake hands with. The Somalis? Great people, beautiful people. She had Somali friends in Boston, Nairobi and Kampala and loved them all. A longwinded speech about the group in which she said she was a militant, she finally volunteered the name of the radical group of which she said she was an active member. Medina wanted to know Atta's politics. Atta wouldn't go beyond giving the initials of the organization and without translating them went into a tirade about sisters and brothers in the struggle. And every time Medina steered the conversation *to* something more concrete ("What position does Amiri Baraka hold in connection with this or that?" or "How have brothers and sisters in the struggle reacted to Cleaver and what are they doing to isolate persons like him?"), Atta would push *it* aside, like a health food eater pushing away iron forks and knives, and would go on and eat but not answer the question. Good breeding forbade Medina to challenge most of the naive theories Atta put forward; while Samater and Ubax watched her with obvious admiration, looked with amusement at the way she ate and the huge amount she took every time she helped herself. Medina broke through her wall of defence finally; that was when the conversation about "the dominant and the dominated cultures" took place.

"My race remembers sufferance."

"Remembers? 'My race remembers'?"

"Yes. Remembers," Atta said.

"One remembers what one has forgotten."

"I don't see your point."

"*Our* race is still suffering today, in Africa, in America, in the Caribbean. One doesn't remember the pain one is suffering: one *lives* it," shouted Medina.

"I still don't see your point."

"If the Jews remembered Auschwitz, then they would behave differently towards the Palestinians. I have my misgivings about this collective racial memory of which you speak."

Jiijo the maid at this point walked in and changed their plates; Medina's had been untouched.

Atta then went on:

"One doesn't forget centuries of suffering. My race remembers this suffering, my race hasn't forgotten it. I remember this suffering, this pain. *Therefore I am.*"

"Same as Soyinka's poetics?"

"Who?"

If she didn't know Amiri Baraka, Nikki Giovanni, Don Lee, Audre Lorde, Jayne Cortez, if she didn't know or read any of these, she wouldn't know Soyinka either, thought Medina.

"A Nigerian writer who speaks of chains and racial memories in a way not dissimilar to the way you do. No race has memory of pain, sufferance and chains, just as no race has a monopoly on intelligence."

"But the Jews, the 'Chosen People', have done just that. They write copious history books about Auschwitz and they also tell the world that the brilliant physicists, poets and writers are Jews."

"In Auschwitz it was humanity which suffered, not a particular race. Hitler and his system of repression wouldn't have cared who the victims were. The same is happening in Palestine, in the US, in South Africa and other places. No race has a monopoly over pain."

"*My race remembers. I insist.*"

"This is similar to dreams. There aren't any collective dreams. Each of us has his or her own dream, each of us suffers in his or her own way. And when some blacks are suffering, rest assured that others are doing well. You suffer because you are a human being, not because you are who you are, not *because you are black.* And if it were my own people making others suffer, I would suffer too."

Atta simply repeated what she had been saying before.

"Do you see this little thing here, my daughter?" said Medina.

"Yes. Such an angel."

"She was born Caesarean."

There was pain on Atta's face.

"Do you think my husband suffered as much as I did?"

"Of course, not."

"And do you know why I suffered all this pain? Do you know why I needed the Caesarean operation?"

"Tell me."

"Because I am circumcised. Do you know what that means? Infibulated."

There was more pain on Atta's face, a heavier layer, laden with fear too. She stopped eating for the first time and began sucking her fingers clean.

"I suffer this humiliation, this inhumane subjugation of circumcision; you can never know how painful it is unless you've undergone the operation yourself. But must every woman in the world suffer this act of barbarism in order to know the suffering it entails, every woman whether she is Arab, Malay, African, American? A great majority of Africa's female population suffers complications arising from infibulation. It's not racial. Suffering is human."

Ubax was angry that they were speaking a language she didn't understand and therefore could not participate. Then they were all silent. After a while, Samater translated all that had been said, or, rather, summarized it for her. Ubax's comment was that if Atta didn't like whites at all perhaps she shouldn't be invited on the same day as Sandra – which was what Medina had actually intended to do. However, Sandra was away, anyway, on a trip with the Ideologue. ("Lucky you," Ubax had said, in response to Samater's patient explanations.)

·   ·   ·   ·   ·   ·   ·   ·   ·   ·   ·   ·

"How's Medina?" Atta was now saying.

She had a way of asking the wrong question at the wrong time, of unbalancing anything which had been delicately constructed. He should have raped her, Samater thought; it would have gone well with her character: the pain of being entered dry, the suffering, the humiliation. Unlike Amina who gave birth to the children of shame, maybe Atta was prepared for that eventuality since she had come with nothing underneath. *I suffer. Therefore I am.* And she would abort. Yes, he should've raped her. "It is the element of surprise that is so shocking about rape, it is being caught unprepared, unaroused, dry, the stick being pushed in a door which, given time and the necessary caress, might have opened on its own," said Amina. "It is the head-on collision of two vehicles involved in an accident that kills: it is the shock, the un-preparedness," she had continued. You couldn't catch Atta unpre-pared, he said to himself, watching her open and drink the second to last can of the crate of beer. She had four children "back at home". Their fathers? "Afrika." Details? One was Igbo; one Mandingo; one Hausa speaking; one Swahili-speaking. And now? "I am hunting for the undelivered Hamite in me." Yes, he should've raped her. But since he didn't, he should try this:

"How's Sandra? Have you seen her lately?"

Atta's lips curled with anger, lips above which sprouted faint traces of moustache. She reminded Samater of those Sicilian women, ancient as their mourning dresses which they wore year in year out. Did he not remember she had asked him how Medina was?

"That bitch! That *white* bitch!" she cursed.

And in the brown complexity of his eyes was a labyrinth from which the unguided was barred: there, inside the most private part of his brain, was the trace of a victor's smile.

"But what has she done to you?"

"I've always known this: black men in power blindly trust the white chicks they sleep with and let them run the country's affairs for them."

"What's happened?"

"She's a communist and ideologically of the same cut as the Ideologue, she says. She makes no bones of what others feel. She has power in her closed fist."

"But. . . . "

"She's invited at the government's expense a large delegation of her friends. She has government cars at her disposal, she has the Ministry of Information telex at her fingertips. There is a total news black-out until she has filed her item and sold it the world over. Absolute monopoly. The white bitch."

She opened the last can of beer.

"*Hoodi, hoodi!*" announced the waiter his arrival.

"At last," she said.

"At last," he echoed, his voice relieved.

The arrival of the food opened a parenthesis which both felt wouldn't close until they had eaten. Her munching noises were watery and in a short while his mind was moving on marshy sand. She was one among many men, floating with an arkful of Hamites . . . her choice all the more difficult for she wanted every prince she met, whether from Nigeria, Somalia or Zululand. But the coast whose waters they travelled was aromatic with the smell of burning incense and something told Samater they were on the coastline of Puntland. "My race remembers what Medina's has forgotten," she was saying. And she was promiscuous and generous with herself and said: "Let Africa multiply." She charmed everyone in sight. She received the guesthood of the host in all its forms, the call before midnight, the warm bed, and she was peaceful in her own mind. An arkful of Hamites, all men, all going underwater on account of that white bitch who had bewitched them and who talked about "ideology" as a unifying force. And the sons of Ham's land fell for that sort of thing just as the Negro accepted that he was inferior because the white man said so. "A hundred years ago the African was a savage in need of the white man's civilizing mission; now the African needs technology, he needs the white man's ideology; now we are all human, equal and human before the sacred word of Marx and Lenin. They would always get round to you: all this technology, all this ideology, all this white-woman thing are one and the same: to hold on to the reins of your power." And she made love to ribbons of medals because they belonged to an African warrior. Then she made love to *him* as he peeled them off. She said that she had come to Africa to light the candle of the pharo. And why had she come to Somalia? No answer. She had come to Somalia to set aflame the cabinet's thighs, said the malicious tongues of Mogadiscio. Viva the power of women over men whether white, black or African! CIA, many said.

When they had finished eating. . . .

. . . .

The moon which he saw through the holes in the roofing was crowned with a light veil of clouds. The sky's eyes were deep wells of reflected light, silvery like a mirror, grey like the day's smoke. Once they had eaten, he thought, they would leave, she in her government-loaned car and he in his hired one. He wasn't willing to speak to Atta about Medina, about what had happened between him and his mother or whether he would resign. But a slight irritation grew inside him like a cyst: why should he not try it on her? Since they were within arm's reach of each other, he would touch her with a hand supposedly gone astray. If she picked it up from there, well and good; if she didn't, nothing was lost. Then he would start a verbal courtship. A car on hire. A new bank account in his name. A room in a hotel. A night out with a date. A prostitute picked up on the street wouldn't fit well with the rest.

"A beautiful night," he said.

"Lovely."

"Your coming to dinner made it more beautiful."

"Thanks."

His hand touched her. She took it casually, held his finger slightly too long and then let it go. He lay on his back and used one of the pillows. She put her head on his stomach, her feet touching and playing with the sand near the lamp. Without any effort or pretence, his fingers ran over the silkiness of her lips. She bit them, she kissed them, she opened her mouth so that he would put them inside to be played with, sucked and loved. Then she sat up.

"Do you know what time it is?"

"Why do you want to know what time it is?"

"The night is young as a calf, isn't it?"

"Old as a toothless cow," he said.

"Have you ever seen one?"

"What?"

She had stood up, half-bent so that the thorns wouldn't enter her eyes. She was behind the paraffin lamp and tugged at a hanging branch of the acacia.

"I used to think before I came here that Somalis rode camels like the North African Arabs. In fact, my mother warned me about it. She said I could do anything I pleased but never ride a camel."

"Why ?"

"One of her brothers on secondment to a British detachment in North Africa during the war broke his neck while he was on one. A few bedouins found him half-dead and instead of helping him killed him. My mother said that the Somalis might do likewise."

He went and quietly stood behind her. He held her neck in his hands and pretended he would strangle her. When he let her go, he didn't wait to see the reaction on her face but leaped over the lamp (he made a wish she would follow him) and, slightly stooped, stopped right in the entrance to the acacia canopy. But before he knew what was happening, she was hanging playfully on to his neck like a friendly monkey. She ceased playing with him and challenged:

"Can you lift me off the ground?"

"Lift you off the ground?"

"Yes, muscular man that you are. Can you?"

"What in heaven's name for?"

"Just like that."

The question which had occurred to him before and which occurred to him again was this: how come an American, supposedly the enemy of a socialist revolution, was not the first suspect but got everything she asked for? Did anybody really know who this woman was? His thighs weren't on fire any more. His head was aflame with worrying questions. She moved about like an acrobat, demonstrated her muscle, showed off her Mohammed-Ali agility of body.

"If it will make it any easier, I can make myself lighter," she said.

"How?"

"By taking off my clothes." she said, "Are you game?"

Dare he? Could he ever meet a challenge with a challenge?

"What do you bet?"

"Anything."

"Anything? Be specific. What?"

"If you lift me, you've won *it*."

"I've won it? What?"

"Me!"

He flexed his muscles. "Are you serious?"

"Or do you want me to lift you off the ground? You are light as a bird. I am afraid you will fly off into the unreachable if I lift you up."

She moved in his direction. He backed up.

"If the Ideologue could, I don't see why you can't," she said. "You seem more muscular, stronger and more of a man."

"You mean the Ideologue. . . . "

"And two of your three vice-presidents. *Power loves pussy.*"

"Two of the three vice-presidents?"

"One of them would come if you massaged his feet. For real!"

She took him forcefully by the elbows and they wrestled; he wouldn't let himself be taken in that manner, tactlessly. Medina didn't do that sort of thing. Medina wasn't violent and neither was he. If the Ideologue and the two vice-presidents liked it that way, that was their business. In any case why should he believe her? For all he knew, she might be lying. But they stopped wriggling, she stopped struggling and was in his arms, her body warm against his, her breasts under her light cotton dress beating the drum of her need to be taken: like sea to sand, flat and generous and willing. He disengaged from her embrace.

"Wait a minute," he said.

They fell apart. He moved a foot or two away so that he could breathe freely without another person's lungs and breasts warm against his cold, lifeless manhood.

"What's wrong?" she asked, perplexed, standing beside him. "What have I done?"

"Nothing," he said, but his voice betrayed him.

"If you'd like me to come gentle, sweet, licky like those super-sophisticated women you might have met in Europe, well, say it. I, too, can do it." And she touched him. She helped him out of his trousers.

"Please," he said, shrinking from her touch and unbuttoning his shirt himself.

Then the night was bright with a sudden light – as if a falling star had shared its last instant with them. What the hell was that? There was no movement for a while. Then he heard one of the waiters explain something to a client whose car wouldn't start. Perhaps one of the waiters had gone past near them carrying a paraffin lamp.

"Shall we go then?" she inexplicably asked.

"No, no. Let's stay for a little while.

"All right."

She came closer, put her hand under his head and kissed him. This time he didn't shun her touch, nor did he free himself. He let her lead his hand downwards and upwards, making him touch her intimate parts. She took off her dress and lay across him completely naked. Again there was a sudden brightness. Samater was sure this second time: he saw the hands of the photographer disappear into the night. He was certain he recognized the man. It was Wentworth George, the man who had done the portrait of the General.

"I think we can go now," Samater said calmly.

"I thought you were enjoying it."

"I am. Let's do it in my hotel room."

He told her where to meet him and that if he was late she should just park her car within view of the Caruuba Hotel. He gave her the number of his room and wondered if another photographer would be awaiting their arrival, with a taperecorder to register all that was said as well. He was quite sure Medina would enjoy listening to his bugged secrets.

PART THREE

The centuries follow one another perfecting a small
wild flower.
– Rabindranath Tagore

A dog starved at his master's gate
Predicts the ruin of the State.
– William Blake

A man is infinitely more complicated than his thoughts.
– Paul Valéry

The scream

vomited itself.
– Ted Hughes

The crows maintain that a single crow could destroy
the heavens. Doubtless that is so, but it proves
nothing against the heavens, for the heavens signify
simply: the impossibility of crows.
– Franz Kafka

T E N

. . . .

The sun was pale and sickly-looking. Like a dying invalid, it became weak, it grew meek. All around it gauze-thin clouds bandaged the sky's azurine sores. Then it continued to climb up the rungs of time. Medina, with a gaze contemplative as a sage, saw time past in time present: lighter shades of darkness ensconced in the shades of stronger colours. Time past, thin as the topsoil of the Sahelian desert, lifeless, dead before it took life fully into its sandy veins.

But the air was familiar to her, the place too. So was the warning written in red: *Stop and give heed – He is not all of us!* She was back in her own surroundings, she was the bird in the nest – what with Samater gone, what with the stories circulating that he had been seen with *that* woman, had taken *her* to his hotel room and that they had spent the night together. Medina was back where she knew best and so was Ubax, happy that she had her toys, her room, her drawings on her walls. Ubax had asked her mother what all this was about; why had they moved out and then in, what sense could she give to all this? Medina apologized for the inconvenience and promised that it wouldn't happen again.

"You have your toys. Are you happy now?"

"Where's the maid, where's the orderly?"

Medina noted that Ubax did not mention her father's name. Ubax didn't give her time to answer her question, for she was gone, eager to touch and play with her toys again. How she looked forward to seeing those toys and her room again! But where was Samater? Did Medina know? Unsolicited reports had reached her that he had resigned as minister, and the question in everyone's mind was whether or not he would be sent to jail. The smoke and dust raised by yesterday's purge had begun to settle as most of the arrested youths were let go with a warning after an affidavit was signed by their tribal chieftains and their parents that they would not in future take part in any uprising against the regime and would not write on the walls. A few of them had not been released, among whom were Cadar and Hindiya and another friend of theirs.

Medina looked up: Ubax had returned and it seemed she had something to say, something she had forgotten to ask.

"Yes? What's on your mind, my sweet?"

"Where's Nasser?"

"Nasser is at home, the other home, his home, I think."

"And Samater? Why are they never together?"

Medina pushed the notebook in front of her, anticipating that Ubax would ask further and complicated questions. Her face held the smile properly and waited.

"Do you think it will ever be the same again? Samater. You. Me. Nasser. And Sandra. Will it ever?"

"I don't think it will ever be the same again."

"I saw him last night. I really did."

"Who ?"

"Samater. In a dream. I'll ask him where he has been when I see him again, why he hasn't come to see me, and what he's been up to. I have the right to know: he is my father and you won't tell me a thing. You speak on that telephone, talk to other people about him in languages I can't understand."

"But, my darling, what did he look like in the dream?"

"He looked worn out. He had been in a fight, he said."

And Ubax was gone. Medina couldn't concentrate now. Time present retreated like a shy child, whereas time past emerged, brave and bold and dominating like a dream.

•   •   •   •   •   •   •   •   •   •   •

A long draughty road such as is only seen in dreams. Medina, Samater and their Ubax together again, a threesome of rejoicing, a family reunited after whatever it was that had pulled them apart, and each held the hand of another. Along the long draughty road were the carcasses of the sea's waste which someone had laboriously fitted into urns of burning incense whose smell lined both lanes of the road. There was no portrait of any self-appointed power-usurper and neither were there boards on which handsomely paid sign-writers drew sycophantic graphics of adoration. The shore was strewn with the corpses of those who had died in the civil uprising, there were the half-dead birds which trembled with the last twitch of breath since in each still pulsed the desire to live, although they lacked the will to try. "There's nothing as disturbing as watching a dying crane," said Samater. "It maps the circumference of its struggle, with bill pointing in one direction and long legs the other: it has the shape of the African continent stood on its horn, dead like a bugle whose holes are clogged up with sand." They walked, happy and threesome; to the right was the sea, and to their left sand-dunes prominent as the flagposts of a residential palace. There came and went torrents of sand which blocked their way. But somehow they miraculously bypassed the obstructions; at times, they flew over them; and twice, when this was impossible because of the height, they simply went under the impediment of sand. Then the two of them went ahead, and Ubax, who found children to play with, stayed behind for a while. Here they made love and they came once, twice, thrice coincidentally, and they tried a fourth and fifth time although on both occasions neither would come as the other groaned with the pleasant pain of life, and they changed position, he went on top of her, a position they hardly tried, and he arrived quick as a shot. They were full of energy like dawn, and Medina was fertile like the moist morning.

Time present in time past like a playing-card in a pack shuffled by an expert, time past as borrowed from a scene in a dream. And they were still in the water, the two of them out in the blue deeps of the Indian Ocean, and their Ubax splashing and playful in the shallows of safety. Then they heard Ubax shout for help, and they went to her lightning fast. And they found Idil, large as a monster and bosomy, with her large milkless breasts flat on her mound of a chest.

"Why are you here, Mother?" asked Samater.

"I've come to stitch the cicatrice of nature."

Medina lapsed into a foreign language, which Idil and Ubax couldn't understand, and said that she would kill Samater's mother with the

same knife she had brought "to purify her innocent grandchild".
Samater suggested she wait.

"What is the knife for, Mother?"

"What knife?"

And Idil turned. Samater, sudden as death in an accident, struck Idil
so hard she fell into the water and was dead instantly. Her corpse floated huge like a whale. Samater pulled her further and further into the
deep zones of the ocean and buried her in the secret womb of the sea.
When he swam back, Ubax had returned to herself and Medina was
horny and hot with lust and they began to make love energetically.
"Come, come now, come into me, let me fold you inside me, my leaf,"
she said. The sea, dark and green and black, opened up and swallowed
them whole, greedy as love. And Samater dove in and read the con-
tours of her womanhood, his lust enlarged her sex like a speculum.
They came and came, again and again. Then they floated together like
Ubax's paper boats, up and down the waves they had created, following the sea's will and whim, both as submissive as desire. "Come," said
Medina, "let's go and wash in the sun's rays and the earth's sand." But
when they came out, there was no Ubax. "We've visitors," said
Samater. *Hush, and hear the secrets of another soul, the dreams, the desires
of another person.* Time passed as if in a deck of cards re-shuffled, Medina cut and Samater dealt the cards: Ubax disappeared and in her place
was Sandra, pale and sick. Sandra was ornamented with jewellery and
was in front of a Hindu temple talking to a *sunnayase,* suave and gentle-
faced, a small affable man from Kerala who spoke with a scandalously
shocking accent mixing his v's and w's and mispronouncing his t's.
Two of his front teeth were missing. His skin was the most beautiful
Medina had ever set eyes on, smooth as ivory, and ebony-beautiful.
The man had a book open before him.

"What do you see?" Sandra asked the *sunnayase.*

He took her palm, then contemplated her eyes but said nothing for a
long while.

"You'll be amply rewarded," Sandra promised.

"You have said dat before," the Sunnayase said.

He consulted the book. He had another look at her palm.

"Sun and low," he finally said.

"Son and love?"

He nodded his head. "Sun and low."

"What? S-o-n and l-o-v-e?" she spelt it.

He shook his head. She tried again:

"Do you mean S-o-n i-n l-o-w?"

He shook his head again. "I mean s-u-n and l-o-v-e."

She jumped about noisily with delight at this. But the man's cold look suggested she should apologize. She didn't. She sat on the floor, her legs crossed and placed under her heels.

"Where?"

"Vhere vhat?"

"This sun and love?"

The *sunnayase* was silent for a minute or two. He took her palm gently. Then:

"Sun and love. I see plenty of both, I see in the asterisked trenches of your palm rivers of sunshine and love. I see them light up and darken. You'll leave Milan before the year ends."

"And where will I go?"

"You'll go to Africa."

"Africa, how lovely. Where in Africa?"

"For your safe conduct, there is an umbrella already pitched in a land where your grandfather served as an officer of the Italian government."

"Somalia? I'll go to Somalia, to Medina and Samater? Incredible!"

The *sunnayase's* eyes shone in the reflection of Sandra's solar delight and love and he grinned.

"Is there a man? A man under the pitched tent in the sun? Is there love?"

"Many. Many, many of them, more than you've ever known or seen in Milan."

"How many?"

"It depends on you."

"On me?"

"The most powerful men of that country will prostrate themselves before you. You will be wined and dined and dated by the most powerful in that country."

Sandra crouched in front of the *sunnayase* in reverence and in gratitude. She took his long-fingered hands in hers and kissed them worshipfully.

"I'll write immediately to Medina, one of my best friends, and tell her of my decision to visit her. Medina and Samater, two close friends. They'll be delighted."

The scene above spun like a whipping-top, cylindrical and pointed at the bottom; it turned on its axis like the world, like time clocked, pendular and oscillating between a known past and an unlived future. And there they all were, a foursome: Sandra, Nasser, Samater and Medina at table with platefuls of chowder in front of them, with the sea roaring in the distance. Milan. Vigevano. Like lighter shades of dark ensconced within the deeper layers of another. Then, almost too unpredictably and suddenly, time present drew the blinds on time past when. . . .

"Where are you? Ubax was saying.

"Here. I'm here, love."

With her left thumb in her mouth, and her right rubbing her eyes redder, Ubax came to the kitchen from where her mother's response had come.

"What are you doing in the kitchen?"

"Cooking."

"Cooking? But who's coming?"

Medina pointed at a piece of paper on the kitchen table. "A *guest.*"

"Who?"

"Read the note yourself."

Ubax picked it up and squinted at an arrangement of the alphabet which made her feel illiterate.

"It's foreign."

"It is not. It's Italian."

"But that *is* foreign." Ubax folded her arms across her chest, defiant and angry. The pupils of her eyes radiated the flame of her rage; why was Medina so stupid and stubborn? Italian was foreign, and she, Ubax, didn't know how to read it and she hated those who spoke or wrote or asked her to read languages she couldn't understand. Medina granted the point, but:

"Can you guess who is coming?"

Ubax was quick: "Sandra."
She received a kiss from her mother.

⋅　　⋅　　⋅　　⋅　　⋅　　⋅　　⋅　　⋅　　⋅　　⋅　　⋅

A cloister of red flags. A column of student resistance. A pillar of raised fists. A bridge of linked arms. A banner of sickles. And a sea of youthful faces. Medina. Sandra. Nasser. Behind them, like a child holding on to its mother's skirt for fear of losing her in a crowd, Samater in the tight grip of his arm was carrying *their* books, Medina's handbag or Sandra's containing her tampon kit. And the shuttle would spin a curtain of chorus-singers: *Giap/Giap/Giap Ho/Chi/Minh.* A private grievance made public. A shadow at the end of the day is longer than whatever has cast it. The *confronto-scontro.* The *avanguardia degli operai e dei braccianti. Il Maggio Francese.* The summer before the autumn. Medina, Sandra and Nasser sang and participated like everybody else whereas Samater would hold back. Maybe the night before there had been a discussion till the small hours waned and the stars' eyes closed; maybe all four of them had been together with other friends in the trattoria where they met, a trattoria which served good food and good wine but didn't charge exorbitantly. From there they would go to Porto Garibaldi with arms linked, singing *Bandiera rossa* provocatively; the Fascists in their dark shirts would wait in the shade of the palazzi and at times there would be slight scuffles and fist-encounters and the police would rush in on them and they would disperse. Near Via Festa del Perdono, the university within their shout's reach, they would chant and sing and frighten the passers-by like an alarm clock's dawn scream.

> Sow you
> flowery dreams
> during the day
> so as to reap them
> as forget-me-nots at night
> when the fascists are asleep.
>
> Giap/Giap/Giap
> Ho/Chi/Minh!

Giap/Giap/Giap
Ho/Chi/Minh!

An unbroken Ginsbergian howl of commitment, and the leader of the chorus would shout orders, give instructions. A group of young men and women in jeans and near-rags hurling defamatory curses at the institutions of authority, hoping that the government's glassy structure would begin to fall to pieces in reaction to their united cry, the oneness of their fisted arms, young men and women who burned the effigy of the neocrucifix, the heart that one of the young women had been wearing around her neck: the *sacra cuore* had bled to shameful death. Then a mock communion was called, a small prayer was arranged and it was Sandra who led it: "Our Father, Thou art draped in the neon-fragility of plasticity, offer us this day our share of the consumer's goods, protect us, O Lord, from the shower of contradictory cliches." At the Statale of Milan they were organized, and Sandra was a member of the Central Committee. Since Medina and Nasser lived in Piazza San Babila, whenever the *commizi* broke up Sandra and the other close friends in that circle met at their place and would continue where they had left off. The red scarves. The red flags of '68. The challenge to all those institutions in which bourgeois societies invested authority – state, schools, universities and family. Sandra and her parents were at loggerheads and she moved in with Medina and Nasser. The long nights were smoky with the butts of rolled cigarettes and chatty as farewell messages. And when everyone left, Sandra slipped with Nasser into the warm contact of love which didn't exist but which had to be made. She would cry out and awaken Medina in the other room with the joy of her coming, the noise of her arrival. Then Sandra became pregnant. Nasser one morning went with her to a doctor near Piazza Napoli, left her there, and returned the following morning to escort her home. A month later, they were at it again. For Sandra's most memorable nights were those which were stopped, like the holes in a flute, with the phallus of love. When Nasser wasn't there, there was another. Anyway . . . ! The Fascists of Piazza Fontana. The students as rebels, as challengers of the family as an institution, since its main function is economic and of such authoritarian tendency that the Duce had used it as much as Hitler and Stalin had. Sandra developed a slight stoop after she aborted and this appeared to complement Medina's slight waddle. In private, Nasser and Medina had written a poem, each contributing a letter as though it were a crossword puzzle. This was to indicate that their idea of '68 was different from Sandra's and their European counterparts. The poem could be sung to the tom-tom of a drum:

> In Europe and the USA
> it is
> question-time in the halls
> of learning:
> in Southeast Asia
> one listens to the lecture on Ethos of Resistance. . . .

Another unbroken howl. And Medina, Sandra, Samater and Nasser would listen to a re-dramatization by Ginsberg, the master, voicing the owlish howl so loudly that the audience could roll smokable joints out of his mass of curly hair. The Mantra. The *OM* of the Omniscient, the Omnipresent: earthen jars designed to meet the needs of a Kerouac on the move. Sandalwood oil, the skin-paint as repellant. Let no mosquito come anywhere near: malaria is the enemy of mankind. Those were the days of bottle-parties to which anyone came indiscriminately and without invitation. Medina and Sandra would go and buy paper cups – the culmination of a consumer society's idea of cheap disposables. Then would come the improvised festival of guitars. Medina's grand contribution to all this had been the books she bought and lent to everybody, books by Malcolm X, Sartre, Lukacs, Le Roi Jones, Cleaver. And on the wall in her room she had written:

> This is a post-Hollywood farce
> Ionesco acts in it!

And on the wall in the bathroom:

> Listen to the sirens go.
> Quick, ask. How much is the bullet, Monsieur?

But Czechoslovakia's Prague Autumn and the Soviets' invasion of that country shocked her so much she was sick with a high fever. One day, during her convalescence from the painful abortion, one day when she was better and feeling lucid and clear-headed, Medina came to speak to Sandra about a proposed dinner to mark the day she and Samater decided to marry. Sandra wasn't interested in talking about that.

"Fifty-six, do you remember the year 1956?" she suddenly asked.

"I was too young," said Medina. "I can't *remember* something I never knew."

"I'm no older than you, am I? If I can remember, you should be able to. And I can. Very clearly."

"The Suez Canal was invaded by three imperialist powers – France, Britain and Israel. And they were defeated. That's all I could see from where I was. A mirror reflects itself first."

"A host feeds his *guest* first. A mirror sees others who see a reflection of themselves in it. What else do you remember?"

"The Mau-Mau liberation movement struck and made the throbbing heart of British pride bleed: that's another thing I remember. We were flooded with misinformation. That's all I remember."

"They were blood-sucking cannibals. The Mau-Mau. General China, Dedan Kimathi: barbarous cannibals."

"How in hell do you permit yourself to say that?"

"It's how the newspapers described them, the papers that we got. And Moravia, too."

Medina was clearly annoyed. "What was the point you meant to make, Sandra? Come to the point before I lose my temper again."

"Why are you angry?"

"Never mind why. What was your point? What is so important about 1956? Hungary? Is that it, Sandra? Speak up."

"Any nationalistic uprising without sound marxist ideological backing is bound to fail in its attempt to revolutionize and reach the masses. We've seen the consequences. We've seen what became of the Mau-Mau as a national movement, and we've seen Abdel Nasser's failures. A nationalistic imperialist (Nasser) and a tribalistic imperialist (Jomo Kenyatta). But in 1956. . . . "

"The point, Sandra. Come to the point."

Sandra sat up and leaned a pillow against the wall for her head. She took her time. She thought she knew what it was that Medina felt but never said: Sandra always dismissed Africa's political moves and efforts as "neo-colonialist", "imitative", "unstudied and unresearched" or "tribalistic".

"I don't wish to belittle the political significance of nationalist liberation struggles in Africa, Asia or Latin America. But African fascist, neo-colonial dictatorships are a direct result of this total absence of programmed, ideologically sound Marxist thinking. In 1956, unlike the European colonial age of Africa, ideology is at stake. Africa in the early nineteenth century was not equipped ideologically and therefore the capitalist system could overrun their primitive method of self-governing. In 1956, however, the first attempt on the part of the social imperialists to befog international public opinion took place when the Soviets invaded Hungary. My point is that the Autumn of Prague is but the by-product of the question the true Marxists didn't pose themselves or try to answer in 1956."

Medina thought of other possibilities, a number of other examples she could give her guest to prove the culpability of the social-imperialists in their effort to take the leadership of the International Marxist Movement. She could speak of Africa, she could speak specifically of Egypt. But why go so far? They were in Italy:

"The Communist Party in Italy, to begin with. . . . "

The battle began. Sandra had the enraged look of a lioness whose cubs were wounded. Her eyes were red, blood ran to her face and she said:

"Hold it, hold it."

"Yes?"

"Let's keep Italy out of it, Mina."

"But why?"

"You've never understood Italy."

"I've never *what?*"

"You've lived in this country off and on for the past twelve years, you speak the language as perfectly as a native, you've read everything on every bend and curve of its ruins. But you don't understand Italy and you never will. It isn't easy."

"Yet you're talking about Africa. How can you – "

"Hold it, Mina!"

"What the hell! I won't!"

"I'm not talking about Africa. I'm talking about Marxist theory, the

Marxist ideology which is basically European, both in its outlook and philosophical development. Hegel, Marx, Engels, Lenin. They are all European."

Medina was hurt. In an attempt to nurse her friend's hurt feelings, Sandra said:

"Every country has problems and a culture unique to that area. Africa is one such place and Somalia is one such country. Now I can't say that I understand the situation, the problems of Africa (or Somalia) as well as a Somali."

When Sandra felt a lot better, they tried to make up to one another, and in fact for a week Medina kept referring to that conversation which she believed had slightly soured their relationship. A fortnight later, Sandra packed up and returned to her parents' home on the Via del Boccaccio. The two were never on the same good terms as they had been before the confrontation, before that conversation took place. For one thing they now invariably avoided any topic related to the European left and their position vis-a-vis the African continent. The echo most consistently repeated, the voice Medina always heard whenever she encountered Sandra was, *You don't understand Italy, so let's keep it out of our discussions.*

·　·　·　·　·　·　·　·　·　·　·

Three years later. By then, Medina had returned to Somalia and married; by then, Nasser had moved to his Middle East base and he, too, married. Three years, many sleepless nights. Three years and many wakeful dawns. Three years and a thousand evenings heavy with boredom and guilt. Three years, three or four boyfriends. And Sandra was very, very unhappy. She decided to take her life and for that purpose acquired and gulped down enough tablets to kill a whale. But nothing doing. She was still determined, however, to commit suicide. Then, on the margin of her vision, aberrational like the eyes of the future, appeared the *sunnayase* who foretold a future full of love and sun in Africa. She cabled Medina. Could she give her hospitality for a week, a month, maximum two? She would be ever so grateful. Medina said she would try to arrange a visa for her, then she would plan an itinerary for her. They spoke to each other a number of times. Medina through friends arranged a meeting between the Somali ambassador in Rome and Sandra. The ambassador was impressed. He rang his cousin that very day, told his cousin the Generalissimo about a brilliant journalist he had interviewed: a brilliant freelance Italian journalist to whom he would do well to grant an interview. He also mentioned the young freelance journalist's colonial connections: her grandfather had been a Vice-Governor-General of Italian Somaliland. The General was impressed, too. Surprise, surprise. Sandra rang Medina and told her that she had been made *an honorary guest* at the October celebrations of the Revolution, with ticket and a hotel paid for as long as she pleased to stay in Somalia. Another exclusive offer: an interview on the eve of the celebrations. "Unbelievable," was all Medina had said. "Let's wait and see."

Sandra couldn't believe it, either. She was met at the airport by the then Minister of Culture (now the Ideologue), and was whisked off to the hotel and wined and dined and entertained. She was impressed. A chauffeur-driven car, a house with a garden, a maid, an orderly, plus a key to open any door of the Republic. Medina was speechless with shock when they met. Sandra was a disastrous sight. She told her what had happened and what the *sunnayase* had said. The two friends hugged. Sandra sobbed with relief. Medina made a vow to do all she could to help her friend stand on her own feet and be herself again. They embraced tightly and in silence, both feeling and thinking the same thing. Then they stood apart, Sandra taller and still heftier. They were in the flat the "honorary guest" of the revolution had been lent. *I am a guest in my own land,* Medina told herself that day. But she said in the most friendly manner:

"Politics is a multi-chambered palace of passageways and power-cells. Who knows, I may be the one who needs your help, just as my grandfather needed your grandfather. Perhaps it's too early to prophesy."

Sandra threw her hostess a smile, colourful as the dice a challenging child casts to narrow the distance between herself and her rival.

"My grandfather was a colonialist. Your grandfather dealt in slaves. We're different. We may disagree ideologically, you and I. The question may be reduced to whether you are extreme left or I am."

The sun's rays fell on Medina's forehead: a lamp was lit there, a lamp of consciousness. She smiled. "Your grandfather came carrying the light of the civilizing mission of the crucifix," she said. "When its flame waned, Marx lit another. You've come carrying that. You are the spokesperson of a continent just as your grandfather was when here."

A quick glance at her watch. Then Sandra began tidying up the living-room. Medina felt the weight of her presence: maybe Sandra had someone coming, a *guest*. There came over Medina's face an expression of sadness so tranquil one would think she was a person with a secret no one else in the world knew about. Sandra paused for a second and managed to say:

"I'm sorry but I must tidy up the place. I'm expecting someone. A very important person in the government: the most brilliant of government ministers."

"A guest?"

"Yes, a guest. Imagine having guests in a country in which one is a guest oneself. You used to speak of you, the African, as a guest in a century which belongs to Europe and the western hemisphere."

"Him, a guest?"

"Yes, my guest."

"The Minister of Culture. Who would have thought it!" She reached out a hairpin which Sandra had been looking for.

In this century, the African is a guest whether in Africa or elsewhere. A guest. The technology; the ideology; the living cells of power which throb with confidence; the intellectual make-up from which we derive our source of power; the contradictions which breathe life into us. If not a guest, then a slave to a system of thoughts, a system of a given economic re-routing. It was too early to forecast what would happen; but a week after her arrival, Sandra had become the host and they the guest – maybe this sufficiently indicated the precarious position of the African in his own continent. Her years in Europe were just as perilous if not worse: she was always a guest, the other person whose presence gave colour and made the dinner more interesting ("We have a *guest,* a wonderful girl from Somalia"). She remembered those long nights of discussions which in Africa occurred seldom. Atta's people have been guests in America for four hundred years! A guest in Milan, a guest in Mogadiscio. She was a "guest" in the Marxist ideology which she couldn't twist as she pleased for she needed the Soviet or the Chinese or the Yugoslav stamp to give it credibility, she needed the approval of the European intellectual left; in that ideology, at any rate, there wasn't enough space in which she could spread her mat and her exhausted bones. But how could she make Sandra understand all this? How could she warn her of the ideological trap into which she had fallen?

"How are things with you?" she asked Sandra. "How do you fare in Africa?"

"I've never felt so good."

But she wasn't listening to whatever Medina might have said. Where was the maid? Where was the orderly? Someone had apparently said the place was crawling with servants. Had they gone because *he* was coming? For Medina's taste, the place was overcrowded and expensively furnished. Why was Sandra moving these things nervously? Pale traces of dusk; the breeze smelled of monsoon; the ocean wasn't far. Sandra, head up and smiling, was saying:

"It's all a dream. I would never have thought this possible. The generosity of the Somali knows no limits. The sophisticated gentleness. As for the Minister, he has trust in me; he has faith in my ability as a journalist, a faith no one has ever had whether they were friends or editors of journals for which I wrote. It's all a dream. And I'm so happy."

Medina fell silent. She feared her voice would betray the resentment and jealousy she felt, a resentment and jealousy not so much addressed to Sandra but at the Africanness in herself, at her guesthood; if she could, she would have annulled her with her fixed stare of hate. But she caught sight of the joy on Sandra's face. And Medina reminded herself that she was a *guest,* that she should behave herself. In the background of the silence there was a reminiscence. Faint voices of a past: Europe in this hall of mirrors, was talking narcissistically on and on and on and on, whereas Africa was the ghost which never cast back an image, Africa was the spectre without a shadow to reflect, without substance. Sandra went on:

"He says it shouldn't be difficult to convince magazines such as *Afrique-Aste, Africa, Jeune Afrique* and others to commission me for a series of articles on Somalia. Every now and again there'd be an exclusive interview with the General and he would make sure news about Somalia would get to me before it got to any agency."

"And in exchange for that, what do you do?"

"No conditions attached. I should say how things are, write *the truth,* tell the rest of the world about the wonderful revolution here."

"Of course, the revolution first."

"That's right. No strings attached. Just the truth about the October revolution."

"Don't be naive."

"What can he want, Mina?" said Sandra.

"What do you have?"

"Nothing."

"They give you all this for nothing? Don't be naive."

Well! Straight from student politics she had inadvertently walked into the intricate, clannish, tribalistic polemics and politics of Somalia, a country rife with internal intrigues, international conspiracies and local mafiadom. There were the crowned clowns, the tribal upstarts, the genuine "socialists", the befogged persons – all these, and Sandra had walked right into the middle of a scene, with the stage already clayed with the blood of men executed; but a farce was on, and the Russians, tricky as Tarzan, re-wrote the stage-directions for this unactable farce. If Medina whose intellectual makeup was structured on a European philosophical foundation, if she, who had lived in Europe or the greater part of her formative years, couldn't understand Italy – imagine, if Sandra, naive as her vanity, Sandra, who had never set foot in Africa before, could understand Africa in a week, understand it well enough to write about it. . . . Unless the "in" men of the Revolution would dictate it to her and she would sign her name to it, the "in" men who were her political mentors: two cousins of the General, one of whom was the minister whose mistress she had become, the other the country's Ambassador in the Italian capital, the man who made the preliminary introductions and issued the ticket and invitation in the name of the General.

"He said I can write what I please."

"About what?"

"About the revolution."

"You'll write what they tell you to: that's what you do in exchange for all these favours: you put your name to whatever they tell you."

"You never believed I wrote well, anyway, did you?"

"That's beside the point."

"What is the point then?"

Medina reflected for a second or so, then said: "At the day's end, a shadow is longer than the object which has cast it."

"What do you mean?"

Sandra was hanging a portrait of the General on the wall opposite Medina. Had things come to that? Medina would leave before the Minister came, before (who knows !) the General dropped in for a glass of something, himself a guest like her, like the Minister. But she should remind Sandra that she hadn't come to their place for a meal all the time she had been in Mogadiscio. She must before leaving the country.

"No, no. I'm not leaving yet."

"You are not?"

"No. I've never been so happy."

She cast a keen stare in the direction of Sandra.

"That is all the more reason why you should share your happiness with me, Samater and my daughter. Come and have a meal with us, something personal, something local. Let me take you out of this *incestuous circle* of cousins, brothers-in-laws, brothers-in-power. Let me introduce you to the people, give you a true picture, supply you with the other version, the true version these cousins of the General, his brothers- or sons-in-law will not tell you."

"I said, I've never been so happy."

"I thought you would want to be taken out of this incestuous circle. I am sorry but I believe it's very unhealthy for you. You said so yourself; you agreed with me that they were the least interesting, that most of them talk about how old they are, who is older than whom and that sort of thing."

"I repeat, Medina, I've never been so happy."

"Fascists. Exhibitionists. Manipulators of facts and figures for the sake of holding power. Mystifiers of politics. Mass deceivers. And you are happy with this?"

Sandra appeared to be about to rise to the defence of her benefactors, but she remembered the conversation they had had in Milan, and Vigevano and in particular the one about whether or not Medina understood the politics of Italy, whether or not she was in a position to make a comment on local Italian politics. Besides, she didn't know the Minister and his cousin the General sufficiently well; she wasn't familiar enough with their turns of phrase, their names, the way they twisted things, the elegance with which they moved about. So she kept quiet – like a *guest*. For once.

"Why don't we talk about all this when I come to visit?"

Medina got up, gathered her things and said:

"In the house of God, one mustn't blaspheme."

Sandra didn't seem to get that, unless of course she decided not to rise to Medina's provocation.

"I'm looking forward to seeing Samater and your daughter, *Ubax*? How is she?"

"Such an angel. You must come and see her."

For an instant, it appeared they would part friends.

"I'm looking forward to that. I am sorry I haven't had time before."

"That's all right."

Sandra took her to the gate. Peaceful their profiles, smiling their faces, they were back and were together, hand in hand, friends again, no politics, no Africa, no Europe, no ideology to hold them apart. But:

"Unless the Minister, your friend, says that it is not advisable that you see me," said Medina.

Sandra was uneasy like a liar caught at an unguarded moment, like someone reminded of an inconsistency in the anecdote told to a group of enthusiastic listeners.

"He thinks highly of you," she lied. "He said that to me himself."

"So long, then."

They kissed on the cheeks. Medina left, polite as a maid on the day of pay.

The moth, now de-winged, died and its body broke in two. Like a myth, it fell apart, and lay by the flames of the paraffin lamp into which it had flown hero-like, head first. It lay there, it lay dead, a martyred insect, unmourned by its companions that hadn't even begun noticing its absence, its companions that revolved round the light frenziedly like Cherokee Indians preparing a tribal assault on the technology of this century when armed with the weapons of another epoch.

·　·　·　·　·　·　·　·　·　·　·

Four weeks passed and Sandra hadn't called on Medina, Samater and Ubax. The two met professionally in Medina's newspaper office or at press conferences. Every time they ran into each other, Sandra gave an excuse, by turns lame and serious, as when upon her descended parents and a few friends, tickets pre-paid by the government, a tour arranged, a visit to the touristic spots in the southern regions where the sea met the river and the desert at one and the same time; trips up north, Hargeisa, Zeila, and then back. When her parents and her friends were gone, there came a delegation fifty men strong from the Italian Communist party. She was everywhere, her picture was in the papers as she made introductions, as she explained things to the *compagni*, as they lay by the sea to tan, as they were served fresh lobster, an assortment of fish salad to their heart's content. By then, six or seven magazines would publish her articles on *progressive* Somalia and her interviews straight from the "mule's mouth". Then she accompanied the General on a trip across Africa, when the General served as chairman of the OAU. What was she doing travelling with an African head on this state visit? When in francophone Africa, she served as interpreter; and when the General could make himself understood speaking his fractured English, she would change her role and become Press Attaché. Medina learnt of all this with enormous apprehension. Samater hadn't by then been appointed minister; she herself hadn't yet come under attack and hadn't been put under the General's banning order. Somebody suggested she was jealous, resentful of Sandra because she wanted so much to be in her shoes. At this Medina was so disgusted she refused to discuss Sandra and her scandalous affairs. What about the articles Sandra published in foreign magazines? Medina read them since they were the only foreign papers which the censors allowed to enter the country.

"What do you think about her writing?" a colleague at the paper, who many believed was a government informer, asked.

"Muck and cliche-ridden."

"But she gets them published everywhere."

"She writes badly, vulgarly badly, that is why."

"You'll have to explain that."

"Good writing is subversive, bad writing is not."

"What is subversive about good writing?"

"Good writing is like a bomb: it explodes in the face of the reader. Sandra's is flat and as uninteresting as yesterday's gossip. It's repetitive like the speech of a demagogue."

Medina was quite certain this would reach Sandra, and through Sandra the minister and, through the minister, the General. A week later, a different version of the same story was being circulated, a version not attributed to her but to somebody else. The poor man, a journalist colleague, was taken away and never heard of again. Then. . . .

One day, Sandra came uninvited like a princess and brought what she thought was "good news": Medina had been nominated (on her recommendation and the minister's ?) as editor of the only paper of the country, namely *Xiddigta Oktoober*. It was also on this occasion that she hinted that Samater was being considered for something worthy of his qualifications. Soyaan had been dead three months; Loyaan, Siciliano and other friends had been in prison for two and a half months. The other members of their clandestine movement had gone underground. "The General is the drowning man in the proverb who leans and seeks support from the foam. Do you know what I'll do?" she said to Samater. "I'll take it. I personally see this as a challenge to the *movement*." Samater saw it differently and said that there was no point in her taking the job since she wouldn't be in a position to make any radical change. (She sought and received advice from the surviving members of the movement: she must take the job, do what she could to effect any changes within the paper; they had asked nothing of Samater when he became minister, for *the movement* did not give its approval.)

On the first day, the layout of the paper was different, which made everybody content: typographical errors were fewer; there was an editorial, clean, polished and "subversive". On the second, she removed the photograph of the General and the space reserved for his daily wisdom to the nation, and in their place inserted a news item and a stop-press. On the third, she edited the General's speech (speeches of the General were always published unedited and in full and at times the four pages of which the paper consisted would carry no other news) and didn't comment on it in her editorial which was about malnutritional diseases common in that part of the continent. On the fourth day, however, the paper didn't come out: there was a Security purge, Medina was taken for a long interrogation and so were a couple of other journalists. The others who were men were jailed for subversion. She was put under a banning order.

One evening a few days later, while shopping, she ran into Sandra by chance. Sandra's greeting was heavy-handed, almost hostile. Medina deliberately steered the conversation to what had happened.

"I don't understand Somali and cannot read it. So I can't comment on it."

"The layout, the visual thing, the photograph missing – you could see the radical transformation, the *subversiveness* about that, couldn't you?"

"This is a game I cannot take part in."

"What has this incestuous group done to you?"

Sandra said she was in a hurry: "I must be on my way. Love to Samater and Ubax."

Medina did not hear from her until after Samater was appointed Minister of Constructions. For a time, they met every now again, invited each other to parties and meals to which they both knew the other wouldn't go. Then when Medina packed up and left, Sandra called to ask why. And why was she coming today? Did she have any news, good or bad? Had Samater lost his job? Had Nasser been in touch with her? Had the Security confiscated his cassettes?

•   •   •   •   •   •   •   •   •   •   •

"Sandra."

"Hello, Mina."

"How is the Grand Master of Irrelevance?"

"Who?"

"The Grand Master of Irrelevance?"

She wondered if Medina was referring to the Ideologue, her most intimate friend and the cousin of the General, or to the General himself and she asked, making sure she was understood.

"I thought he was the Great Intellectual and Visionary. Is he sufficiently prepared for other designations, personality cult and linked appellations?"

"The General is ill," said Sandra.

"How sad. I always imagined deified personalities were never taken ill like us mortals. What's wrong with him? Old age? Indigestion of power?"

Sandra moved heavily and burdensomely with her slight stoop. But for a second or two they managed to cast aside this gloom like a broken toy when Ubax came in and very politely but formally shook hands with Sandra and allowed herself to be kissed, then left them alone. Medina's smile, like an improvised lie, wouldn't pass the test of time for she was gloomy again and ready to provoke, say wicked things about the *incestuous circle,* and about the General who was taken ill. What if he died? What if he never woke up from his nightmarish sleep? Was the Ideologue the heir apparent or was one of the vice-presidents? The vacuums dictators leave are generally unfillable: would the same thing happen? Medina was thinking as she searched for a drink to offer to Sandra. Idil had probably confiscated all the bottles and hidden them somewhere so that her son wouldn't sin in the same house as she lived in. But after Samater and Idil left the house – what happened after they both left? Sandra wasn't staying for lunch anyway; she had come to say hello to Medina, Ubax and Nasser. Would she at least wait for Nasser? Yes, she would. Was that all she had come for, to say hello and leave? Or to bring news about the General's illness and something else besides?

"Have you heard from Samater?" asked Sandra.

Sandra had not even asked why Medina had packed up and left, why Nasser was in Mogadiscio. And her first reference to Samater was this question. How weird, thought Medina.

"Have I heard from Samater? When and why?"

"A mystery, then."

Medina sat down carefully, cautiously, her eyes fixed on Sandra's movements up and down and the slight hump of deformity on her back, up and down carrying the seed of a secret concerning Samater's whereabouts. Her eyes were wide open and she feared they might break like the windows of heaven and fail her; she feared a tear would after all these years wet her eyelids, that one single shameful teardrop in the presence of an associate member of the *incestuous circle* might erupt through the sown whirlwind of an unharvested seed.

"A mystery? What's happened to him? Tell me."

"He was last seen leaving the hotel just before dawn."

"Leaving? Or was he driven away in a Security car?"

"He was in the company of a woman."

"A woman? A woman other than Atta?"

Sandra was red with rage. Medina couldn't at first understand. Why should she behave so strangely?

"What's so mysterious about being seen with a woman?"

"Depends on who the woman is."

"I don't see how that concerns you, anyway," challenged Medina.

"That bitch. To her, they are her brothers and sisters. She thinks she can exclude me, write me out. The promiscuous bitch. I am whitey, the enemy; I am the one of whom everybody should beware."

However, Medina was calm. She looked upwards and watched Sandra's bulky weight pace up and down again, Sandra blue-eyed and blonde. With her skin tanned, she wasn't as pale, like the sand of the Sahara, as when she came to Mogadiscio, pale and sick-looking. She was big-boned, too, like her mother "whose clumsy body-movements are uncoordinated like an infant's". Her mother's features were ugly "like a felt-tipped pen's faulty following of a badly drawn graffito; artistic, too, like the Pompei-scratchings on a glazed surface under the skin-layer". She had the gait of a mare (like her father) but the short neck of her mother (a neck which "nodded like the mandarin toys Chinese factories were fond of reproducing in billions"). Her parents spoke French to her. ("French is not only a language spoken by a cultured people," her father used to say, "it is a craft.") Little Sandra read Verlaine, Valéry, Rimbaud, Hugo and Baudelaire, and visited France as often as school holidays permitted. She later considered French as the language in which she felt most comfortable, like a palace of aristocrats with high windows, spacious rooms, rocking-chairs and all the bourgeois comforts she had been used to. Her mother was the daughter of a small merchant of small means, a man "whose palms didn't have the colour of potato, thank God!" would boast her mother. And Sandra and she would re-enact an ideological war for the benefit of those around. One day when Medina was there, the two went over the limit, for her mother had added: "Nor were his eyes dusty-grey and hard like the calloused palms of a proletarian. True, they weren't blue and of noble blood like my husband's." The feverish enthusiasm of '68 gave Sandra the courage to leave her parents and move in with Medina and Nasser. Although one thing shouldn't be overlooked: Sandra chose well her hosts who were themselves "guests and temporary residents". To Medina this indicated the temporariness of Sandra and her mother's separation. Further proof lay in this: as soon as she had settled in Somalia, what did Sandra do? She arranged for her parents to visit and see her in this African set-up, happy, loved, appreciated, wanted, a young woman who was on first-name terms with a head of state. Her parents' and her friends' judgement mattered to her. Should one not question whether she was or wasn't grown up enough ideologically, philosophically and personally to sever relations with her parents, their ideas and the bourgeois European upbringing she had had? What about this ridiculous rivalry between herself and Atta?

"Your calm puzzles me, I must confess," said Sandra after a long silence. "It seems you know about Samater's mysterious disappearance. You don't appear in the least bothered by these melodramatic goings-on between him and Atta. Was she the cause of the breakup?"

"No. It's your behaviour that puzzles me. Samater and I have a solid friendship, and a single night's flirtation with you, Atta or any other woman wouldn't upset me. You know better than that. What puzzles me is why you have to bring the news."

"That bitch!"

"I would worry if Atta's role in the plot were not small and insignificant; I would worry if you were being dishonest with me. And I don't see why you should. Is there any other reason why I should worry about his disappearance? In that case, the Security, your friend the Ideologue, and you yourself are the ones whom I blame. Strange, weird things happen when the General is taken ill or is out of the country for a week or a month. Hundreds of people disappear precisely in accordance with instructions from him personally. When he is on the scene again, when he is back or when he has recovered, he wears the by-now famous toothy grin and says that he knew nothing about these disappearances, these imprisonments. So where did you hear the news about Samater's and Atta's disappearance?"

Sandra mentioned the name of the Ideologue.

"Was it he who suggested you come to break the news to me?"

Sandra nodded.

"How naive can you be!"

A silence, heavy and gloomy, fell upon them again. Medina was certain that there had been a plot to have Atta and Samater vanish together so that the scandal created would discredit the notion that he had resigned of his own accord; it would make Samater lose face in the eyes of the public; it would also appear that Atta was the person who had broken up their marriage. Samater's clan would then have no cause to request a revision of the case; finally, Atta would be deported on the grounds that she, a foreigner, was involved in a sexual scandal with a cabinet minister: this would make the Ideologue, the General and many others besides Sandra content. With one single flip of a little finger, the Ideologue was able to turn the tables and win a fabulous hand. But did Sandra realize how she was being used?

"I can hear someone's footsteps moving about in the house," Sandra said, slightly frightened. "Can it be Samater?"

It was Nasser. He had already walked in on them, quiet as a shadow, just like Fatima bint Thabit. Medina's unhappy grin and Sandra's stony expression forbade him to light their dimmed eyes with a flippant remark which was what had gone through his head when he saw them in this grave mood. He and Sandra did not kiss, did not greet each other. Strange? They all behaved strangely. Neither rose to give or receive a kiss. He walked in like a polite student come late for a lecture, tiptoed in and without saying anything took a seat. Sandra and Medina fidgeted in their seats, like students unable to answer questions their examiner asked.

"A day's passing generally warrants change of day, date and page of calendar," Nasser said provocatively.

Medina and Sandra looked at each other, then at him.

"What do you mean?" asked Medina.

"It's all over town, this disappearance of Samater and Atta. Besides, a man called and left a message for you," he turned to Medina. "He didn't leave his name. He said he was a friend."

"What did this man say? Try to remember his exact words."

"'Samater was last seen leaving the hotel just before dawn,' he said. 'He was in the company of a woman, in all probability an Afro-American sister, namely Atta. Just tell her that.'"

Medina noted how very curious it was that the words used by the message-deliverer and those Sandra had used were the same. Sandra stood up and wished she could leave. Medina turned to Nasser and asked:

"What do you think is the meaning of all this?"

He lapsed into Somali so as to exclude Sandra. He said there was no cause for worry. The worst that could happen was some sort of political scandal which would discredit Samater's resignation on a question of principle. Medina said she had thought the same. Then she told him the identical words in which the messengers had delivered their news. She added that she knew the source of the message. Who? She used the Italian word *"ideologo"* to make Sandra curious, make her strain her ears and ask a question. But this did not happen. Nasser suggested they change the subject altogether. He addressed Sandra:

"Whoever disappears sooner or later reappears, dead or alive. So let's not waste time on the details of Samater's or Atta's disappearance. How are you and how are things with you? I hear you are happy and that you're occupied with several journalistic projects at the same time. I hear that you are the highly recommended on-the-spot journalist, on a freelance contract with six or seven different magazines abroad. I hear you are happy and busy. I am glad for you."

She moved about like a sleep-walker. Here she was in the same room with two persons who once were her closest friends; here she was talking about the disappearance of another friend who once was one of her closest friends, another "incestuous circle", a foursome of Medina and Samater as a couple and Nasser and Sandra as another. The circle broke and those who had formed it dispersed like the beads of a broken necklace, running apart, helter skelter, hurrying down the slope as unorganized as a defeated army. With Nasser here, was it possible that he would try to mend the broken string and gather the beads and thread them again? Would she be the bead which had gone astray, the bead which had disappeared under the leg of the armchair? Who would believe that she once was made pregnant by him? Now she was jealous as a baboon and content there was a plot to get rid of Atta. Nasser was saying, provocative as insult:

"I hear you cover the untrod ground with words cast in the pale colour of *revolutionary truth*. I hear you are famous as a journalist and that you work for the quotidinal pleasure of the powerful. Is that true?"

Why were her circles incestuous? She wasn't at any rate the "cordal" bead – she wasn't the centre-point, the focus of the spotlight: Medina was. She and Samater were the "afterthought", the addendum. And when Atta left that circle, she joined another, that of the General and his incestuous oligarchy, a group admittedly less interesting and less stimulating than Medina's. The General's incestuous circle was apparently less homogeneous.

"Samater at least erected monstrous monuments for posterity. Do you believe that the web of words you weave which are poisonous as a spider's spit will be read when the ink has dried?"

Sandra did not say anything. Medina got up and went to answer the telephone which rang in the master bedroom. Ubax came to the doorway and stood there listening to Nasser speak, like her parents, a foreign language which she couldn't understand. She had a stapled set of sheets and was pretending to read them as she turned the pages.

"What is it you are reading?" asked Nasser.

"Chinua Achebe's story 'He'," answered Ubax. "Medina has translated it into Somali for me."

Medina looked at Sandra whom she now saw as a source of annoyance; she struggled hard against showing how much she could hate her. It pained Medina that there was no fellow feeling between them any more, that theirs wasn't a friendly challenge. She was sad she had nothing more to say to Sandra, sadder that Sandra, once a friend, was now a traitor who had betrayed her trust. Nasser was turning similar silent thoughts in his head. Whereas Sandra, unable to stand the quiet surrounding her, rose and left the room.

ELEVEN

Ebla was saying:

"We'll raise the child together if you want. If you don't want to have it, we'll do what is necessary. And, if you wish, we can even find a decent way out of this."

"How?"

"Find a father for it."

"That is an out-and-out insult."

"I didn't mean it to be. I am sorry."

They were in Sagal's room. The walls were bare, no *Queimada* stills and no portrait of Cabral either. But how could they be sure she was pregnant? She hadn't taken a blood or urine test. True, her period was late by at least two days, and she had never known that to happen; hers was punctual as a maintained word. But how could they be so sure? "Women are mysterious as the viscera of Africa," was what she had written to Barbara that very morning. Ebla stared at her daughter as if she were an old garment one did not know whether to save or throw away. Then she said to her daughter:

"Your future is in you. You decide and tell me what to do."

Sagal looked at and touched her stomach: the viscera of unknown qualities, she thought. "I am a woman and everything is possible." She relegated her worries to the fringes of her thoughts.

"And what if it is a false panic?"

"What if it is?"

"Ridiculous."

"If I were you, I would take part in the swimming competition. You can decide at a later date whether or not you wish to go, whether you have the child or abort."

"There is no point in my competing if I know I am going to win. With no Cadar and no Hindiya, competing is no fun. Besides, I have to live with my conscience. Cadar and Hindiya are in jail because they wrote on the walls at dawn, something I've always wanted to. I have a sort of obligation to them, owe them a display of solidarity."

Ebla threw her arms to her sides. "I give up. I don't understand."

"I don't see why you can't. You taught me these things yourself."

"A display of solidarity? Politics and solidarity? Have I taught you these?"

"Yes. Truth must be owned, Ebla. You've made me who I am."

There was a brief pause.

"You arranged something with Amina, didn't you? You have an appointment with her?"

"She will escort me to the venue, yes."

"And you will not take part in the competition?"

"No, I won't."

"Why are you going then? You are not up to something, are you?"

"I wouldn't do anything which might disgrace you, and you know that."

"What does this 'display of solidarity' consist of?"

"Going there and telling the other girls not to take part in the event."

"You mean by organizing a boycott?"

"No, no. Nothing of the sort."

"What then are you going there for?"

"A display of solidarity."

Ebla breathed heavily like a person going up a steep hill. She saw Sagal stooped over something she had written, in all likelihood a letter to a friend. Then they heard the appeal of a chanting mendicant, a man who came as regular as the sun, always at noon. The man chanted the beggar's refrain, asking for alms, asking for a mouthful of something, asking for the fill of his stomach or his tin. Sagal looked up and shouted to him, "Allah's bounties are plenty, but we don't have anything this morning," a set-sentence the beggar had probably heard a number of times that morning. But Ebla remembered that there were last night's leftovers, the rice with beans Sagal didn't come in time to eat, which she could offer the beggar. So she shouted to him to wait a moment. While Ebla was gone to feed the man, Sagal's mind munched the cud of memory, remembering the day she and Amina had called the beggar into the house, given him a seat and some food. After he had eaten his

fill, the two friends took turns to put questions to him. They assured
him that their queries were of a sociological nature and he need not answer if he didn't want to. Where was he from? What had he done before he became an itinerant mendicant, going from door to door,
chanting his blessing from morning till evening? Was he ever married?
Did he have any children? Had he no relatives in Mogadiscio? Why did
he come to this city in the first place? The man gave evasive responses
at first. Then he opened up, he became braver and a great deal friend-
lier. He was a handsome man, with a dignified look and a restful appearance. Even without him changing these rags, one could see that
the face, the way he moved, nothing of him fitted the profession he had
chosen. Why? He was once a rich man, not very rich by the standards
of the city, but one of the wealthiest in his area. He was in his middle
fifties, already an old man, he said, and added: "Look at my head,
nearly all white." Did he have children? Was he ever married? He had
children, fifteen of them, and he had been married five times and never
to more than one woman at a time. He wanted a male heir and so he
tried and tried and tried, and every time he tried, a girl was born. It was
like the gambler in a folktale who would swear that his main intention
was to win back what he had lost or even half of it and as soon as he had
done that he would stop gambling. Fifteen daughters and no son, despite all his attempts, in spite of all that he had paid to fortune-tellers,
to readers of futures, to sorcerers and to men of God. He decided to
contract his sixth matrimony the night his fifteenth daughter was born.
"Then my favourite saint revealed himself to me in my sleep. I told him
my distress and he answered that God had been more than kind to me,
that I was the one who had been ungrateful and that I didn't do anything worthy of my elevated station. 'Why do you think your life will
be accomplished only if you have a son? All children, whether boys or
girls, are a manifestation of Allah's will and His generosity. Are girls not
His creations?' He suggested I repent for my sinful thoughts. I said I
had been to Mecca half a dozen times and that I never, to the best of my
human capability, break any of His canon-laws. 'That isn't enough,' he
said. 'Your arrogance is deeply rooted in the soil of Satan.' What in
your opinion, my saint and intercessor, can I do to win Allah's favour?
'The ungodly wallows in his arrogance and in Satan's swamp, the
saintly are humble and seek the pardon of those whom they have

wronged. Go to your daughters and compensate them with kindness and saintliness, ask them to forgive the hurtful wrongs you've inflicted upon them. Then you must leave your dwelling as empty-handed as when you were born and you must beg for food, lodging and clothing for a period not less than two years. Only then will I show myself to you again.'" How many months had he done? they inquired. He said eight. But he wouldn't say any more. His face now looked ravaged, he didn't have that same restful look as when he started his story; his forehead was like a battlefield. He was still handsome and dignified, though.

Sagal turned and looked at her mother who had just returned, having fed the beggar. She was twenty-one only yesterday, although she looked much older than that today, just as ravaged as the mendicant's face had been when she and Amina had talked to him. She had dark patches of insomnia under her baggy eyes, and her sight had become blurred and unfocusing. Ebla saw the state her daughter was in and couldn't go to the shop, her conscience wouldn't allow her that, so she decided to wait until Amina arrived.

"Come, come. This is not the end of the world," Ebla said.

"Who said it was?"

"Get up. Rise from this unmade bed. Give me your hand." Ebla took her daughter's hand and pulled it.

"Please leave me alone."

"When I was pregnant with you, years ago – "

"I've heard that before."

"I say: this is not the end of the world."

She sat propped up in bed and looked at her mother who tried as best she could to cheer her up. She couldn't lift Sagal's body up from the bed, nor could she lift her spirit from the ravage. A ravine of uncrossable impossibilities separated them. They weren't any longer two clocks which differed in the time they kept. And the question wasn't one of a generational difference or of opinion.

"Has all this to do with the father of your child?"

"What father?"

"Do you know who the father is?"

"Of course, I do."

"Who is he? You haven't told me. Who is the father of your child ?"

"He's insignificant. Like all fathers are. Like mine is. Like Samater is."

"What's his name anyway? Or is he so insignificant you don't want anyone to know?"

"This is *my* child."

"The father, who is the father?" insisted Ebla.

"It's my child and that is what matters."

"And you still don't know whether you want it or not? You should be grateful I am your mother. Many a mother would make things unbearably painful for a daughter who came home pregnant with a fatherless child. So please tell me who the father is."

"Why can't you leave me be!" Sagal shouted.

This shocked Ebla into a peacefulness the like of which Sagal hadn't seen in her in years. She rubbed her forehead and wore a charming smile and said:

"The earth is warm when a seed is buried in it, and a mother is happy when there is a child in her. Be happy as only a mother can be. Be happy as the earth is warm."

"I need a moment of quiet. I must finish these letters."

"I won't say any more," Ebla said and kept quiet but sat on the edge of the bed. "Because I know one thing for certain: that you won't leave me. That is what I've always wanted. To have you near me. And with a child."

Had her mother asked her to abort or get married, had Ebla contradicted her, had she opposed her having the child, Sagal might have taken it as a challenge and fought more determinedly and lethally. Her "you can do what you please" had disarmed her and left her with no choice but do precisely what Ebla wanted her to do in the first place. Some parents know their children's turn of mind better than others and Ebla knew her Sagal as well as any parents might know their child. But what was it that Ebla wanted her daughter to do? Did Ebla know it herself? Now they looked at each other: Amina's voice could be heard, Amina who was talking to the child of the neighbours. Ebla's watch told a different time from Sagal's when each consulted hers. Then they waited for Amina in silence.

· · · · · · · · · · ·

Sown in the sunless soil of a dungeon, a seed, or rather a drop sticky
with the living atoms of germination, just a drop, and nine months
later, a baby in labour, a baby pushing, wanting to come out, struggling to breathe on its own lungs, live its own life independently. Sagal
was alone in her room, and Amina and Ebla were in the other room,
whispering to each other; probably Ebla was covering the same ground
as she had walked with her daughter since morning, studying possibilities, exchanging ideas with Amina who, because she was the same
age as Sagal and one of her closest friends, might elegantly slip in
handy advice, Amina whom Ebla had hoped would see things the same
way as she herself did. Alone and pensive, Sagal held the tampon flat
and stringless in her palm. She threw it up and caught it and talked
to it. . . .

One takes one's unhappiness to the mirror eventually, Medina used
to say and that was precisely what Sagal did. She was in front of the
mirror and saw a head unkempt as an owl-pigeon caught in a drizzle in
the open yard. If she had a child and the child asked the name of its father, what would she say? What did she actually know about the man
who made her pregnant? She couldn't certainly make the same claims
as Mary, the Mother of Cisse, and miracles are seldom seen or accepted; nor was she in the same position as Amina, whose child's pa-
ternity could be traced to one of the rapists if necessary. It was one
thing not telling a man about his own child; but it was altogether another hiding the identity of a father.

But she was weak as the faint whistle of nocturnal insects, she felt exposed like to rain which catches one unprepared. Ebla had said that
they could find a decent way out of this, they could find a father for her
unborn baby – meaning that they could improvise a matrimony between her and another man, the same arrangement Amina's father suggested before she had left his patriarchy. Let the world know that no
pregnancy would chase her into the arms of a man for whom she didn't
care. She had an understanding mother, with an open heart and an
open mind – true, these conditioned one, but the chances that one
might win two out of three hurdles were there; and Ebla, it had to be
said for her, was a love. *Is every drop a grave undug? Is this drop of sperm
my tomb?*

A drop too many, and it multiplies. . . . A drop too many and it would finally form a pool in which she would herself drown, gulp down mouthfuls of water and die. *"Not waving, but drowning"*: Sagal sang Stevie Smith's song of defiance, but it was her heart gave way, the water was too cold, the blood, the responsibility of parenthood was too much to bear. Would they dispatch the little corpse in a shroud of its own or would they bury it with its mother? A child, so far nameless; sex: a girl? Like the hot water your ears lose when you've been in the water too long – would it be something similar to that, say, if she aborted it? Would her womanhood leak warm water like a hot water-bottle if she decided to do away with it? Abort? Abort what? How could she abort a night's lapsus?

She pulled a drawer and put the tampon in there. She took out a pile of photographs tied with a ribbon and stared at one of them: she was in the water, her arm raised, and the camera caught that motion superbly for within the frame of her bent arm, or rather behind it, was Cadar, and just behind her was Hindiya. She didn't know who had taken the photograph, but she could appreciate the inventiveness of the catch-in-action, a moment of history framed and artistically held in still motion (it was the instant she broke the ribbon, the very instant which won her a bronze medal); what's more, this was the arm which never touched the water – and the water never rose to encounter it. Champions meet, lovers too, but.... This reminded her of him, the man whose child she had inside her and she remembered him saying to her apropos of photography, his own profession: "I trap history, catch it in midmotion and frame it in the camera's mind, a mind of stillness, quietness. The present in the past, and the future in the shade of the smile which is remembered and talked about later. I instill stillness in movements. *I suggest, therefore I am a photographer.*" But who was this man? Never mind what she would say to the others. Who was this man?

He was a London-born of Barbados parents, both black and London-bred. His world was the familiar open-ended world of blue jeans and first-name informalities. Five foot eleven, he moved with the ease of the lean-on-the-air-luxuriously-while you-walk Afro-style; one of the legs would remain fixed in position, the palm would be spread out, then tap, touch, and go. There was a cosmopolitan vagueness about his looks.

"Africa is a superimposition of different colours. Fancy this: East Africa is colourfully unimaginative and we needn't bother about Central Africa, which is as colour-blind as the North African bedouin. It is West Africa's combination of colours which made me want to print its parade on the unforgetting lens of my camera."

"What do you think about Somalia?"

"They confiscated my cameras on arrival. And every door is closed with tape red as blood. Permit-cards, permit-cards, permit-cards."

"How long have you been here?"

"Three weeks. I am followed everywhere. Every Somali is afraid to talk to me or help me."

"And what have you seen? Where have you been to so far?"

"Office doors which close in my face, that's all I've seen. Yes, and people with frightened faces, a paranoid Security."

"People, don't you know anybody?"

"People, people, what people? I need a permit to talk to people."

"Have you no friends? No friends among the people?"

"None. And I am bored to death going from the hotel in the morning and spending my days waiting for something to happen, my permit-card to come through. I see all these Europeans who get their work- and photograph permit-cards issued even before they set foot in this country."

"We're a good hospitable people, friendly and generous."

"As people, perhaps. But your government is paranoid beyond re-pair."

"This is a fascist government, suspicious and very discriminatory. You shouldn't confuse the two: the people and the government. You should note the distinction."

"Are you of the people or of the government?"

"I am of the people."

They talked and talked and talked. She decided to take him tempo-rarily out of his caged unhappiness, she decided she would make him aware of the distinction between a basically friendly and hospitable people and the paranoid government which had forced itself upon them by seizing power and then constituting itself as the only legal au-thority in the country. She would take him into her sympathy; she, who *represented* the people and not the government, would be sweet and nice to him. When he was ready to leave, she told herself, he would take with him the memory of this night and of the office doors which closed in his face, and she hoped he would appreciate her effort. They lay down and slept on the starless lawn and they made love. The sun woke them.

Now what was it she had heard about him that made her wish she had had nothing to do with him? Wentworth George had degraded himself and his position and reached a lucrative understanding with the regime: his first professionally taken portrait-photograph since his permit-card was issued would appear in today's paper, someone told her.

Ebla and Amina's voices approached, grew louder and then died down. Ebla was ready to go to the shop. Amina was ready to accompany Sagal to the venue where the competition was taking place.

"You haven't changed your mind, have you?"

"No, no. I am going."

Ebla kissed them in turn. She wished Sagal good luck.

·   ·   ·   ·   ·   ·   ·   ·   ·   ·   ·

Amina had been given the assignment to stay by Sagal and not leave her for an instant, and that seemed to be what she was doing. She escorted her to the changing-room and back, listened to her exchange a few remarks with other girls, remarks that were not only inessential but insubstantial as well. Both had feared this moment and like students unprepared for an exam they had looked forward to it with horror. What would the other girls say? How would they take Sagal's being free when the others were in jail? There was an element of occupational jealousy in all this. If, like Cadar and Hindiya, Sagal wasn't there, too, there might have been a chance for the other competitors who had never won anything in their lives. The girls looked at her with hate and one or two of them said some abominable things which no one with good sense would repeat. In the end, it was Sagal who wouldn't leave Amina for a single instant; she kept a keen eye on her, following as a shadow does its maker. When Amina wanted to go to the bar attached to the Centro Sportivo, Sagal went with her, wrapped in a towel which fitted her like a pram wearing a child.

"What will you have?" asked Amina who was still fully dressed, purse in hand.

"What are you going to have?" The tension in Sagal's voice was sharp like a sword. "I would like something strong, if I may."

"Have it then."

"No, no."

"A can of beer?"

"No, thank you. Just a soft drink."

"Your considerations are pedestrian today."

"That's true."

"What do you care what these simpletons think?"

"Perhaps because I'm too tired to fight it out with them. Look at them – a hateful lot, jealous and envious. But I can understand their hate and that was why I didn't want to come here in the first place. I understand their hate and that perhaps makes it harder to bear. I feel like going to them and saying 'Whatever the outcome of this farce, I won't go, so don't panic.' Imagine: I even thought I might be able to organize a boycott."

"I would describe that as defeatist." .,

Other competitors came in and went out, some who nodded in Sagal and Amina's direction and some who pretended they hadn't seen them. The two girls stationed themselves within speaking distance from them and were speaking loudly to each other about a rumour which had begun to circulate in which it was understood that there was no need to hold the event under the circumstances, that two of the participants would be "nominated". In the hope of hearing the names of the nominees, Amina and Sagal strolled casually past the girls who were talking.

"What would you do if you were nominated?" asked Amina.

"I wouldn't go," replied Sagal deliberately loudly.

Silence. The rumour-carriers walked away, having heard what Sagal had said. They would spread the word the way filthy air scatters germs and disease. Sagal watched a summer fly which was on the counter licking the sugary sweetness of its frontage. Meanwhile, Amina ordered and paid for the soft drinks and the two friends left the bar and walked in the direction of the pool. They took a long route and walked through the parking-space, kicking at the tufts of grass and the low shrubs that gave the place an air of asymmetry. It occurred to Sagal that she was the one in jail, not Cadar or Hindiya. She envied them their tranquillity in that state, she envied them their status, she saw them as heroines of a popular uprising, heroines who one day would have a following. They were the topic of conversation, undoubtedly everyone's favourites. And what was she? She was a prisoner of her own conscience, of a dream, a prisoner of a desire to write her name into history. Sure, she had won this and that medal as a swimmer, as an athlete. But she wanted to be more than that, she thought of herself as someone worthy of greater achievement.

"I still don't see why you wouldn't want to go."

"Some gifts humiliate the receiver while they edify the donor."

"It isn't a gift."

"How very pedestrian of you."

"It was you and Ebla – do you remember? – who convinced me to 'use' my father's influence to get myself and my child the material comforts we needed. And now that you have the chance you've waited for all your life, what do you? You don't pick it up."

"If Cadar and Hindiya were here and I had then won the meet, I might have considered leaving on a government ticket. But Cadar and Hindiya aren't here; they are in prison because they painted walls with writings against the General, something I always wanted to do and for which I envy them. It follows that since there is no other girl talented enough really to compete with me, a political decision is made and pending the approval of the General, I am the nominee, together with any other girl they please. What do you say? Do you suggest that I accept this humiliating offer and be grateful?"

Amina walked ahead whereas Sagal stopped by the pool and stared with horror at the distorted shadow in the water: the picture right in front of her broke up into waves of collated water-motifs, a collage of a kind. Clear as marble, huge as a statue, she froze at the sight of this. A marble statue raised right in the pool to honour the imprisoned heroines, namely Hindiya and Cadar? Vaguely she could hear people speaking about things which did not concern her. A statue of water erected to commemorate a swimmer? She heard Wentworth George say: "Water meaning life, just as the Somali word for water is also *biyo,* which in Greek is the word for life. I cannot think of a people as poetic as the bards in your country." Or had she read that somewhere else? Water meaning *bio* just as the Somali word for *sperm* is also *biyo. I cannot think of anything to say about you.* A pause long enough to lend the drama of the thoughts in her head a meaning.

Amina was standing by her and saying:

"The rumour about the political 'nominees' seems to gather substance. I've heard it more than once."

"Do they mention names?"

"Yes."

"Whose?"

"Yours is one of them."

"And the other?"

"I didn't catch it. The other names change but yours is consistently there all the time."

"I wonder why they would nominate me?"

"Why not?"

At that moment the loudspeakers announced that all participants should remain until the man from the Ministry of Sports and Labour came and until they had heard the ministerial disposition in connection with today's event.

"It offends my pride that anyone thinks I'd accept to be nominated," said Sagal.

"I don't know," said Amina. "I wouldn't if I were you."

This made Sagal mumble a slight curse. Then they looked for a small, quiet corner. She watched a flock of birds which had risen from the hidden horizon and which after a while disappeared into the unreachable unknown of the heavens.

.   .   .   .

"Look," said Amina after a long pause, her voice that of someone shocked.

"What?"

"Look !"

"Oh, that!"

"Who is she?" asked Amina.

"Khadija is her name."

"Yes, yes. But what is she?"

"We used to call her 'the ideal, the puritanical, the pervert'."

"All at the same time?"

Khadija would haul herself down into the water fully clothed and like a soldier changing arms would go in left then right. She would dive in and stay at the bottom of the water out of everybody's view until she had changed.

"This is ridiculous," said Amina.

"It's her puritanical upbringing."

"The way she scuds and scuttles, you wouldn't think she was normal, would you?"

"She is a case."

The expression on Amina's face understandably became rigid; she stared at Khadija as though her life depended on this, her head reclined, her neck, too – like a winch about to hoist an object. A sneeze? Sagal wondered whether to say "bless you" or *"yarxamukallah"* but decided that it should depend on whether or not Amina said *"alxamdulilah"* or "excuse me". In the end she didn't say either for Amina didn't sneeze.

"It is weird, very weird. Why does she do that?"

"Cawra: the body of a woman tempts sin and no one should see it. Khadija shuns the sinful stare of others, whether women or men. She doesn't change with the other girls either, for she believes that there are men hiding just to have a peep at her through a hole in the partition."

"Just as exhibitionistic as if she were nude. Everyone looks at her. I don't see the purpose of it all. If she changed into a swimming-costume like all the other girls, nobody would notice her."

"That is precisely why we refer to Khadija as 'the ideal, the puritanical and the pervert'."

"I understand her puritanical perversion. But why 'the ideal'? In what way is she ideal? Because of her orthodoxy and her strict adherence to the Islamic concept of *cawra?"*

"Not really."

"How then?"

"She is said to have answered the revolutionary call with such devotion she spends her days and nights singing the panegyrics of the General and working day in day out for the Revolutionary Centre of her area."

"Well, well. In that case. . . . "

"The rest is a cornucopia of obscenities and irrelevancies, stories concerning whom she sleeps with. It's not that I give any importance whatsoever to this, but one hears and at times one remembers the oddest of anecdotes."

Amina sneezed so quickly she didn't give Sagal a chance to say anything. In any case, Amina said:

"Beneath this puritanical appearance hides the true woman, the pervert. I bet she says her five prayers daily and I bet she is as soft-spoken as the angel of truth."

"She is the ideal 'revolutionary' woman, submissive as servitude, dumb and dull as a 'yes, *jaalle*, viva Generalissimo'."

They were silent for a second or so, after which Amina spoke, her voice and features showing a strain of nerve and anxiety. She spoke carefully and articulately:

"Is she likely to be one of the nominees?"

"I don't think *they* would make themselves as ridiculous as that."

Whereupon, Amina reviewed for her friend's benefit all the ridiculous nominations made by the General's tribal oligarchy. She mentioned the names of several ambassadors who three or four years before the General's coming to power were nonentities and who were suddenly appointed to ambassadorial or ministerial posts. She jogged her friend's memory and provided her with a longer list of ridiculous nominations, men who were made consuls-general in embassies abroad the day they graduated; men and women who, regardless of previous experience, were allotted departmental positions which made their presence not only irrelevant but also redundant. Of course, Sagal didn't need to be reminded, any more than Amina needed to get this off her chest.

"You've heard anyway, haven't you?"

"What?" said Sagal. "What have I heard?"

"The General is ill."

"How ill?"

Amina looked to either side, made sure no one was eavesdropping on what she was saying. *The paranoia is limitless,* thought Sagal. "Someone says that it's probably the end of him."

"They've said that before."

"No, no. But this is serious."

"What? What is ailing him?"

"Syphilis."

"Are you serious?"

"Syphilis."

"Nomads name their years and seasons 'the year of the drought', 'the season of waterlessness and famine', 'the year of the child-killing measles' or 'the rainy month in which the Sultan died'. We date our memory differently; we think of the General as an institution and date and name things accordingly. 'I remember such-and-such happened when Dheel, Gavere, and Caynaanshe were killed; I remember such-and-such took place when the ten sheikhs were executed. I remember that was when Soyaan was mysteriously eliminated and made a hero; I remember that was when I heard that Samater was nominated Minister of Constructions; or when Medina was put under the banning order which forbade her to publish anything in this country.' Maybe ten years from now, I'll baptize this the day I heard that the General had syphilis."

"No, you won't."

"I won't?"

"You'll baptize it the day you convinced yourself, your mother and me that you were pregnant; the day on which you foolishly decided not to use an air-ticket given to you gratis."

Sagal became restless and was undoubtedly shaken by what Amina had said. Something stronger than her seemed to have taken hold of her. She felt a hard thing take a grip of her throat so much so that she couldn't weep nor could she speak. It was as if she were swallowed up by something bigger than herself, something "enclosed", a room without a door, a road with a certain dead-end, "a whale which never came ashore". Nine months of this, day after day; nine months full of trials and tests to pass. Could she stand it? Amina had passed her own test with no difficulty and for this Sagal was partly responsible. Was Amina going to do the same for her in return? Would Medina and Ebla? She would have to empty her sack first, wouldn't she?

"A propos Samater. . . ."

There was a burdensome look on Sagal's face as she turned to face her friend.

"Yes, what about him?"

"It is possible we may have to name this day 'the one on which Samater disappeared'."

"Disappeared?"

"Various versions of the same story. But he disappears in all of them."

She was no longer the sad, meditative *pensierosa* that she had been a moment back. All that appeared to have gone out of her. She sat up energetically and behaved as though she were ready to go to war if necessary in order to save the life of her friend.

"What versions?"

"For one thing, they say he was seen last in the company of the Afro-American in a car. For another, they say he has been seen swaying drunkenly from wall to wall. In yet another version, they say that the sea has spat out an unidentified corpse."

"What corpse? Whose corpse?"

"A woman's corpse? A man's corpse? No one is sure."

Sagal looked like someone condemned.

"Are you coming with me?"

"Where are you going?"

"To see Medina. Are you coming or aren't you?"

She seized Amina by the arm and dragged her away to the changing-rooms. But while there, the microphone announced the political decision taken and the names of the two girls "nominated" by the Ministry to represent Somalia at the Comecon Meet in Budapest: Sagal and Khadija.

•　　•　　•　　•　　•　　•　　•　　•　　•　　•　　•

When they got to Medina's they found everybody seated in a circle, the air dismally funereal. Medina. Nasser. Dulman. But no Ubax. No one said anything. Silently Amina and Sagal took the empty seats and waited, like everybody else, for something to happen. Every now and

again, Medina or Nasser or Xaddia would stand up and walk round
and round and round like an ant revolving around the corpse of an insect. Amina and Sagal felt like late-comers who arrived after someone
had started telling a story; they sensed that something grave had taken
place although no one had told them anything yet. Dulman, whom
neither had seen for a long time, was there, Dulman who looked as destroyed as Medina; whose cheeks were stained with dried tears; whose
eyes were red from crying. When Medina sat down, Nasser got up to
do his rounds like an officer making sure that the person his firing-
squad had shot was devoid of life. When was it they last met him?
Amina and Sagal had been in their late teens, pigtailed, timid and silent
in his presence. Perhaps he was thinking how fast girls grow; perhaps
he was quoting to himself the Somali saying that a girl's nightly measure of growth was the size of a donkey's ear, and this very thing provided enough justification for girls to be married off at fifteen. Sagal
now wondered if a boy's nightly measure of growth was the size of a
grain of wheat. Nasser nodded in Sagal's and then in Amina's direction
and smiled. That was about the first acknowledgement of their presence and they were both grateful. Sagal almost lost her balance of mind
and was about to say something but checked herself in time. That nevertheless brought about a slight transformation. Amina and Dulman,
in turn, exchanged a greeting of recognition. Dulman and Sagal too.
Then Medina and Amina.

All this in a small way reminded Sagal of a game she and her mother
used to play, a game which consisted of seeing which of the two would
remain silent longer; they used to play it when they had blown out the
paraffin lamp and Ebla was too tired to listen to her daughter retelling a
story from a book Ebla wasn't in the least interested in, or Sagal was too
tired to hear her mother narrate an anecdote about something which
had taken place in the shop that day. But this wasn't a game and no one
was telling any story. *Appunto!* It was this speechlessness which said
more. It was precisely this melancholic silence which spoke to Sagal.

Nasser sat down, and Dulman got up. This was a charade of movement. While going round, Dulman, too greeted and nodded her acknowledgement of their being there. Something communicated to
Sagal that nothing as grave as death had visited the family. At worst,
Samater had done something scandalous, something below him,

something which made Medina, Dulman, Nasser and everybody else embarrassed, something out of character. Perhaps. The absence of Idil impressed upon Sagal's mind that death was out of the question. Jail? His resignation turned down and then imprisonment? Or had he been found drunk and driving dangerously in the centre of the city with Atta as inebriated as he? And where was Ubax? There she came as though she were answering a call, sadly silent, with her thumb in her mouth, unhappy because no one was talking to her or because Nasser and Medina had lapsed into Italian since they were saying to each other things she wasn't adult enough to understand. Dulman took her seat. Now the stage belonged to Ubax who could do what she pleased. She was the person on whom all eyes converged and this made her uneasy, undecided. Then she moved further in and sought solace from the closest, Sagal. She became the thawing warmth whose presence turned the unbreakable ice into water.

"*Ciao*, Sagal!" she said.

"*Ciao*, Ubax!"

They exchanged cheeks. Ubax went to Amina.

"*Ciao*, Muna!"

"*Ciao*, Ubax!"

The room hummed with voices like a classroom left by a teacher for a second or so; voices which spoke hurriedly and urgently – like those of students asking each other, "What is the answer to this? What is the ratio of that? What is the key to this puzzle?" Then silence. A silence which engulfed, concerned and touched all. Ubax stayed by Sagal, quiet as she could be. Medina got up and walked about, her presence that of royalty, her dress, a long kaftan of lilac linen, quietly elegant. What could Sagal say? What could Medina or Amina or Nasser say? Someone was playing a game of death: Soyaan had been silently and elegantly eliminated. There was noise; the bullet, as in Russian roulette, fell into a numbered compartment, and this unique device braced the heart of the duellist, and the drum was beaten ceaselessly, but every time there was a slight pause, a person fell, yes, a person dropped into the design of death or was removed to prison at dawn, and was forced to dance the tarantella of humiliation: it is when you watch the *sfilata* that you begin to miss So-and-so or So-and-so. It wasn't a duellist's game of chance but state policy, defiant as fascism, to kill every challenger, to imprison or, worst of all, to humiliate him or her. When Medina had done her rounds – like a doctor seldom seen in rural areas of Africa and himself infected with the diseases he tried to cure – she, too, sat down. But she didn't look resigned, she didn't appear beaten, she seemed calm as if to say, "Insert another bullet, have the General in person come within shooting range of me and we'll see who falls." Her eyes were burning like witches' cauldrons, her anger was so great Sagal was unable to ask the question she had meant to ask, a question as simple and straight as "What has happened?" Amina and Sagal exchanged a look with question-marks like pendant earrings.

"How did it go, Sagal?" asked Medina finally.

Sagal started, felt her heart miss a beat and for a second or so she couldn't say anything. For whatever came to her mind would sound, she thought, a trifle of nonsense if spoken in this grave situation.

It was Amina who answered:

"She is still the unchallenged champion. She's won again."

Medina looked at Amina accusingly, looked at her with such hardness Sagal was tempted to explain what her friend had meant. Nasser, his voice sweet and gentle and kind, said:

"Congratulations. When will you leave for Budapest?"

"I'm not going," her voice grave.

They all fell silent when they heard this curt response. Sagal regretted she had said it. She felt like someone who, instead of helping, drowned a non-swimmer whose head had for a moment re-emerged for a breath of air. If she tried to explain to those present in the room what her "I'm not going" signified, it would take half of her life to do so. The march-past of faces and memories: what could she say to Nasser to make him understand? What shorthand information could she give Medina to put her in the picture? She didn't want to mention Wentworth George's name or say in this flippant manner that she was pregnant, as if it was no more than a small indisposition. How clever of Nasser to say:

"You'll explain everything later, won't you?"

"Yes."

She smiled briefly but corrected herself just in time. Her expression became wooden and unnatural again. But she wasn't going to push the head of the non-swimmer back into the water: she would let the conversation float. She waited for Ubax to leave quietly before she said:

"Do we have any news about Samater?"

She was evidently agitated and her voice betrayed it. It was Nasser who answered and not Medina to whom she had actually addressed the tail of the question.

"We know nothing or very little."

"Nothing or very little?"

He searched for his sister Medina's signal of approval before he would say any more. When he received it, he went on rather cautiously like a man walking a mined territory:

"The only thing we are sure of is that he was last seen in Atta's company. We don't know where they were heading and in what state."

Dulman sobbed softly and they all looked at her as if to say: "Why are you crying?"

Nasser asked Sagal and Amina what they knew. Amina explained what she knew and where and whom she had got the news from. They compared notes, exchanged ideas on the validity of the information circulating the town.

"The General is ill and that's when the weirdest things happen, and hundreds of people are put in prison. As far as I am concerned, Cadar and Hindiya and their friends are not the ones who wrote those things on the walls of Mogadiscio. It was done by the Security. Just a means of getting rid of the hard core."

Sagal's handsome face set in motion all that it was capable of: she seemed happy one moment, then very sad the following instant. Cadar and Hindiya were not the ones who wrote those protestations on the walls? Did that mean . . . no, that wasn't possible!

"It wasn't the girls they were after," Medina continued.

"Whom, then?"

"They caught bigger fish."

"How do you mean?"

"Twenty to twenty-five potential opposers to the regime have been taken in the purge. The accusation: that they instigated the students to write slogans on the walls and at the same time planned a coup d'etat which was thwarted in time."

"And Samater's role?"

"He was one of the plotters. That's what the Ideologue says."

The air became heavier.

"What about Atta?"

"An American agent serving the interests of imperialism."

Sagal was glutted with gloom, as were all the others, but in addition she feared she would vomit right there and then if she so much as opened her mouth. These were things she couldn't take. She hadn't the guts to face this and worse. Would someone please tell them to stop this charade? Would somebody please stop the roulette wheel which was turning round and round and round? Would somebody loosen the braced drum, confiscate the drumsticks and break them into smaller pieces so they would create no noise and wouldn't talk the secret of the drummer? If this continued for another second, she would faint. The light in her eyes dimmed. All was dark. She was in a tunnel, and with her were Amina, Medina, Ubax, Nasser, Samater, Sandra, and Dulman. She was as sure as death that when they came out of the tunnel one of them would be missing, one of them having been sacrificed, offered as the lamb.

But she woke up with fright. Noise. Someone was saying something, the voice of a woman singing a dirge, an improvised lament in memory of her child. Idil was in the room when she opened her eyes. And all the others save Medina, Idil and herself, were gone. Where had they gone? She got up. She, too, left.

E P I L O G U E

A skyful of bats appeared like pustules on the brow of the heavens and made a hideous noise, the most monotonous, persistent and annoying noise ever heard. They fought in the air, they drove some of the more docile evening birds away. They dived earthwards without ever reaching the ground

"Where am I? What is all this?" asked Samater dazedly.

"You are home," said Medina, "back where we all started from. You are home again, Samater, and so am I and so is Ubax: we are all home at last."

"Home? When did I get back?"

"You were dumped here."

He sat up, or tried to. He held his head between his hands. He felt dizzy, his head was heavy as if from a hangover. He contemplated the ceiling and was silent.

"You've held well," she said. "You've passed the first test of endurance. There will be more. You'll see. And you will pass every one of them. And after you and me, it is Mursal and Mahad's turn."

His eyes looked like a frightened deer's. Then he remembered being dragged across a long, endless corridor. He remembered the ridiculous questioning he had undergone: Who was Atta? What did she want to know? What had he told her? He recalled being hit, he recalled being beaten on the head.

"You've held well. Congratulations!" said Medina.

Samater lifted his head in a manner similar to the way a horse in pain lifts its hoof off the ground, then he dropped back into delirium. He had been in such a broken state when Medina helped him inside, Medina who had whispered something – did she say that the Security had come for Nasser and Dulman? Samater curled himself into a ball, he hid his head between his knees and repeatedly said in a voice of desperate appeal: "Please don't hit me, please don't hit me."

Medina asked herself if Samater had held well, if everything had been futile, if there was any point beginning from the beginning all over again. It seemed an eternity before either of them said anything. She looked shaken but she refused to admit that she was: her voice did not betray her either.

"We've tried. Koschin. Soyaan. Siciliano. You. And me. Now it's the others' chance to try." Then she got up and said:

"Every revolutionary serves a cause greater than he or she. But wait, I'll be back."

There was no denying it: Medina had lost her finesse; her manners had become rough, her language aggressive. Had the systematic sabotage of the Security begun to work on her? Had the prolonged conflict started to make her weary? What about the deliberate postponement of the moment of the inevitable final confrontation? To get to *them*, to break *them*, the General's Security took its time, choosing its victim. Soyaan was dead; Loyaan in forced exile; Siciliano and Koschin reduced to a vegetative state (rumour had it that Koschin was in a mental home); Nasser and Dulman in prison. It was like this: the roulette-wheel turned and every time the ball dropped into a numbered chamber one of *the ten* was gone. Would she hold out longer than any of the others?

She stood in front of the full-length mirror, thinking other thoughts, about how a day grows, like a child: morning, noon, afternoon, dusk and evening; how one could measure on the earth the day's shadow as one marks on a wall a child's height. Then she imagined she was the child who willed not to grow; in the distance a tin drum was beaten and to its rhythm she marched *one-two-three, three-two-one, one-three-two*. . . . She varied the sequence, played with the numerical combination – but made sure she would never get to four.

Yes, she was her own principal opponent. But would they have played differently had the roulette of time been turned backwards and had the dates numbered other compartments? What would she have done had Idil and Samater, to begin with, behaved differently? What if Idil had not suggested that Samater marry that maid? What if, in the first place, Idil had not confiscated his drinks? Or, better still, what would she have done had Samater taken the maid as his lawful wife, since Islamic tradition gave the man the right to marry as many as four women? Most important: how far back in time should all this date from? From when Koschin – the first of the ten – was taken prisoner and tortured? Or from when the General came to power – October 1969? Or should she begin with the day she moved out of the house, this being the very action which brought about all this? A sigh of exhaustion.

She moved away from in front of the standing mirror and now was behind a window which was open and breezy. Sagal. The Somali-American family and their daughter's infibulation rite. Ubax. Xaddia. Nasser's underground poetry and Dulman's collaboration with him. Samater. Amina. Idil. Sandra. Question: why did Medina leave? Employing her language of symbols and metaphors: *She left to dwell peacefully in a notion, find a home in it, a home to which she could bring her life's treasures like a bower-bird other birds' feathers, a room that she could call her own and in which she was not a guest; a home in which her thoughts might freely wander without inhibition, without fear; a home in which patriarchs like Gad Thabit and matriarchs like Idil* (whom she saw as representing the authoritarian state) *were not allowed to set foot.* Why then did she not consult Samater? She had feared he would not condescend to dwell with her in her notion, that he was too committed to compromising with his mother and the General's regime. No doubt she couldn't account for her bold imagination. Nasser, that afternoon, when she gave him a lift to save him from the embarrassment of being picked up by the *pederasts,* had said that Samater (and perhaps he was quoting her) was *the chair* Medina had put in the wrong place, *the chair* someone else came to and upturned. And when Samater awoke, Nasser said, he stumbled upon *the chair* and broke his neck. But Nasser was in prison and so was Dulman. What use? According to law, both Nasser and Dulman, if found guilty, would be sentenced to death. All told, what Medina had done and the humiliation Samater had suffered would be slight as the pain caused by scratching a bee sting.

The door-bell rang. Ubax said she would open it.

·   ·   ·   ·   ·   ·   ·   ·   ·   ·   ·

Xaddia.

"Hello!"

"Nabad!"

To Medina, Xaddia's appearance on the scene just now was discon-certing and disturbing, too. She felt uneasy, as though she were a host upon whom descended a guest whose late arrival made it necessary to re-distribute the portions of a meal; Xaddia's late arrival would require the re-telling of a story already partially told. But where could she be-gin? The two communicated first in silence, then touched slightly: Xaddia's hand clutched Medina's for a brief contact and finally they fell apart. Ubax kept her distance. No one said anything for a long time.

"How is he?" said Xaddia.

"He is asleep."

Xaddia told herself that she would be polite and considerate like a guest who, having arrived late, had no choice but to be content with the portions served. And she remembered a conversation she had with Nasser in Rome, a conversation which now made sense, for Nasser had said: "How much change can one introduce to the landscape, bare as it is, unalterable as it appears? Medina has changed the position of a chair. That is all. She has created a habitat in which she alone can func-tion, she has created a condition in which she alone can live. No room for either Samater or Ubax. How has she done this? She put the chair in the wrong place in the dark. When Samater awoke, he stumbled on it and broke his neck. Remember Barkhadle's favourite maxim: *He does not break who does not compromise.* Samater has compromised with the fascist régime and she hasn't. According to the logic of her construct he will *break* in the end. Medina's maxim: *He is humiliated who breaks.* Presently, Xaddia would ask her; one day. . . .

"When did you get back and from where?" asked Medina.

"Our scheduled flight was cancelled because the General borrowed the aircraft to go to Gabon. I think an OAU meeting or something is taking place there."

"I heard he was ill," commented Medina.

"From Gabon, he will go to Rome to consult a doctor or something, but nothing is clear. We learnt about the cancellation of the flight half an hour before take-off. Ill? He is healthier than a young mule."

"And no one dared tell him that Somali Airlines is an international

company with obligations to its passengers? Whatever has become of
the aircraft the Arabian prince presented to him when Somalia became
a member of the Arab League?"

"The prince offered him a blank cheque, not an aircraft."

The words lingered in the air like the smoke of a New Year bonfire,
heavy with suspense. Medina wanted to know how Xaddia had heard
about Samater, Nasser and Dulman. Xaddia for her part, wished to
learn all Medina knew about Samater. But she had difficulties asking
questions. There was, however, a topic which was taboo – Idil's whereabouts. No one was sure where she was. Xaddia couldn't confirm reports which suggested that she was hiding in the house of a tribal chieftain. What else could either say about her? Nothing. What about Atta?
Xaddia said:

"An airhostess told me that she saw Atta put on a plane going to Nairobi. It was the very airhostess who gave me the news about Samater,
Nasser and Dulman. This airhostess was a former classmate of Sagal's."

"I wonder where Sandra is then."

"The airhostess said that Sandra and the Ideologue were in the VIP
lounge when two Security men were putting Atta on a plane to Nairobi."

"The bitch," said Medina.

For a moment, Xaddia suspected that Medina's strength would become her weakness: the fact that she hadn't envisaged that events
might have taken a different course, it seemed to Xaddia, made Medina
oscillate between silences of inarticulacy and a generic name-calling,
using words like "bitch". An outright admission of failure on her part
might have solved the problem, after all. For Xaddia might have been
willing to open the doors of her mind, Xaddia who had faith in their
friendship, Xaddia who had trust in Nasser's ability to improvise a scaf-
folding on whose framework she and the others could support themselves, Xaddia who had trust in Samater's capacity to love and be loved
regardless of what had taken place. A life with edges rough as the un-
predictable: Xaddia's. She saw no Sagal as continuing her future or
forming a bridge with her past.

Now they looked at each other as they heard the maid's movements
and Ubax's loud appeal to leave her alone; the noise came from the
kitchen in the direction of which neither moved. In silence, Medina

looked out of the window and saw the night possibly as the revealer of all that which the stars might have concealed from everybody else.

"What was the purpose of all this, Medina?" asked Xaddia.

"How do you mean, what was the purpose of all this?"

Medina stared at Xaddia as though she were an unassimilated idea, apparently foreign and undigestible. Whereas, to Xaddia, Medina was unexplainable.

"You would wish this to remain your and Samater's mystery, perhaps?"

Medina nodded. They were survivors of a trauma and they were not ready to tell the tale of the day or the date on which anything happened. Would Xaddia understand if Medina spoke in her usual language of sophisticated metaphors and symbols: a chair misplaced in the dark; Idil in the General; the personal in the political? *For Idil is but a symbol; the General is but a metaphor; etcetera, etcetera.* Would she understand?

"He is back like an item one has pawned and paid high interest to reacquire. But then certain things are generally taken for granted," Xaddia said then.

"Back like an item one has pawned? What are you talking about, Xaddia?"

"When one re-acquires a pawned item, one checks it before taking possession again. Did you do that, Medina? I'll be disappointed if you tell me you did not."

Medina was hurt. But she did her best to hide it.

"You look tired, Xaddia. I suggest you lie down for a while. You can use Ubax's room or if you wish I can ask the maid to prepare the guestroom for you."

"I'm not tired," Xaddia replied, the tone of her voice hard like the stone in her throat. "What makes you think that I am tired?" she said.

This made Medina stop where she was. Then she saw the fire in Xaddia's eyes. It was at that moment that she realized that Xaddia was struggling against the associational prejudice of being lumped with her brother Samater, of being thought of as weak.

"You've no right to say that to me, Xaddia."

"You've no right to destroy our family."

"*Our* family?"

They fell silent.

"I cannot take it any more," Xaddia said.

"What? What is it that you can't take any more?"

"The charade. Your politics. The fact that you will not accept defeat. You are a gambler who having won once thinks that another win is in the offing. You are a habitual gambler."

"You don't understand anything," Medina said.

"No, my dear Mina. And I am not a Sagal or one of those you give a book to read whenever something goes wrong," shouted Xaddia. "So tell me: what *was* the meaning of that charade? Or do you suggest I look it up in some book? A *book for everything.*"

What Xaddia said exploded like a bombshell in Medina's ears and wounded her. She thought: *If only Xaddia could understand that I'm fighting for the survival of the woman in me, in* her – *while demolishing "families" like Idil's and regimes like the General's.*

When Medina didn't say anything, Xaddia continued:

"You pawn and pawn and pawn until there is nothing or nobody left to put up to auction. Yesterday, it was Samater; today, Nasser and Dulman; tomorrow – who knows? – maybe it's my turn; the day after tomorrow, Sagal. When will you stop being obstinate and start seeing reason? Will you never concede or accept defeat?"

"Defeat?"

"Yes. Concede defeat!"

Medina celebrated this with a grin. Then:

"I haven't been defeated yet and I won't concede a point to a regime which doesn't concede anyone the right to exist and live in dignity. A fascist régime is weakest when challenged."

Xaddia's rage gathered into a knot and wedged itself awkwardly and clumsily in her throat, preventing her from speaking her mind. Meanwhile, Medina got up, closed the window and returned to her seat, waiting alert and yet apprehensive. Finally Xaddia's knot came undone:

"Tell me, then. What was the point of the charade in which Samater lost face and his job, my mother her son and dignity, Nasser and Dulman their freedom? What point have you made?"

"I don't see anything so exceptional about Samater losing his job or face; or your mother a dignity which she didn't have in the first place;

or Nasser and Dulman their, what you call, freedom. Others have lost their lives in this struggle against this fascist regime. Others have been imprisoned unjustly. Others have been tortured, humiliated and broken. As for my point: I say the struggle must continue."

"And families must be destroyed?"

Xaddia's attention fell suddenly on Samater's framed photograph which was on the wall and this riveted all her thoughts away from everything else. She decided she would go and visit him in his room. She knew Medina wouldn't deny her this right and she felt consoled. Jiijo, the maid whom Idil had fired but whom Medina had re-hired, entered the room where they had been and the place became swaddled in an odd mixture of perfume of various provenances. The maid wanted to know how many would stay for dinner and whether any more guests were expected. Xaddia said she probably wouldn't dine with them. Then she got up to call on Samater.

·   ·   ·   ·   ·   ·   ·   ·   ·   ·   ·

Thoughts insistent like famished summer-flies wouldn't allow Medina a moment of tranquillity, visiting her brain with a thousand bites which pricked, itched and ached. Is this true, or is that true? Stories about Atta and Samater; stories about whether Dulman broke and blamed Nasser for everything; stories regarding Atta's pregnancy and the fact that behind this sudden expulsion was the Ideologue's (and not Sandra's) conspiratorial hand. Samater as *uomo bruciato*. Nasser: a man caught in the cross-currents of power-politics and Sandra and Medina's polemic. Idil: an itch which provoked a scratch, for Idil never mattered to Medina; she could have got rid of her the day she and Samater came home; Idil's concessions were cheap as a nose-rag and Medina could have bought them easily, she could have paid for them easily, she needn't have pawned Samater. . . . Medina had been serving a cause greater than she.

Theories as facts. Hypothesis as thesis. Sagal had brought these and had come the soonest she could. She was worried about Samater and wondered how he was. Medina said that Xaddia was with him although the last time the maid stole in upon them both were asleep – Samater on the bed, and Xaddia in the chair by the bed.

"And you said you will not go to Budapest, you're decided on that, are you?" asked Medina whose aim was to change the subject. "If you don't go who will?"

"Another girl has been nominated in my place."

"No news about Cadar and Hindiya?"

"None whatsoever."

Above them the electric light burned. The curtains, because there wasn't a breath of wind, remained stiff. In one room of the house which would be haunted by the memory of this week were Samater and Xaddia; in another Ubax and the maid; and in this Sagal and Medina. In one, there was funereal silence; in another, noisy indifference or almost; in this, the two principal actresses paused and posed to each other questions whose responses would one day affect the lives of all those with whom they came into contact this week. Medina considered herself the sole survivor of a traumatic journey; Sagal the only traveller in a dug-out canoe across the agitated waters of other people's lives. Cadar and Hindiya were in prison because they dared rise to the challenge the regime had called them to defy; they too licked their index-fingers wet (as children do) and encountered their challengers at dawn. Nasser and Dulman, on the other hand, defied a martial law and decided to disseminate the country's underground literature.

"Did I tell you that what's-his-name was given twenty-four hours to leave the country?" said Sagal.

"Who is what's-his-name?"

"Wentworth George."

Medina's eyes dwelt a little longer on Sagal's face which flickered like a lamp whose light bent slightly at the forceful wind in the room.

"What in heaven's name for?"

"He was friendly with Atta, they say, and raised his voice at hearing the news about her sudden expulsion. He said he knew the motive behind the expulsion."

"And what was it?"

"She was with child and she told him whose it was."

"And you are with his, aren't you?"

Sagal choked on the answer. Medina followed her eyes. There were Samater and Xaddia in the doorway. Samater's presence filled their vacant look and gave it a meaning. Silently she watched him lean against

the wall, weak with exhaustion. With his free hand, he groped for Xaddia's. And Sagal looked at Medina, then at Samater, and wondered if
she should leave – yes, if all the *guests* should leave. But Medina's gentle
smile and nodding head beckoned her, suggesting she stay.

After a while, the maid holding Ubax's little finger joined them. No
one spoke. It was like a meeting whose chairperson hadn't arrived. Or
rather the silence was heavy like that of a doctor's waiting-room where
everyone is convinced his or her ailment is graver than any other's.
And yet each had a story to tell. *Idil and the General were the absent con-
veners.* Idil who flooded Ubax's sleep with nightmares; Idil who was
the cause of this family upheaval. If Medina hadn't left Samater; if
Samater hadn't been a minister; if he had not been caught in the cross-
currents of internal rivalries; if the Ideologue hadn't hired Wentworth
George to take compromising photographs of Samater and Atta; if
Cadar and Hindiya hadn't been imprisoned on suspicion of painting
the dawn of Mogadiscio with slogans against the regime; if . . . ! Xaddia
had come because she heard the roll-call. Medina? Or Samater for that
matter?

Medina decided she would wait until the night was old, until all the
others were gone. Then she would ask her questions. For instance, did
he know that Nasser had been taken prisoner and would perhaps lan-
guish in jail for years, untried and unheard of, a man without travel
documents? There was the National Security Law of 10 September
1970 (Article 18) which would sentence both Nasser and Dulman to
death for having "spread, disseminated, or distributed reading, spoken
or broadcast matter or information aimed at damaging the sovereignty
of the revolution of the Somali nation." Would Dulman die childless
and (as she believed) unaccomplished in prison? What could be done
for them? Should Medina go to the Yemeni Embassy? Would she go
Kafka-like from door to door trying to prove the unprovable? Heavy on
her conscience were three persons – two of them dead and one as good
as dead; heavy on her conscience was also a Sagal dependent on her in-
tellectually and for advice, for love and understanding; a bridge she
had constructed in her imagination between her own yesterday and
Ubax's tomorrow. She looked at Sagal and received a sweet smile;
Sagal seemed as tired as herself, Sagal who had travelled, although in a
different direction, a traumatic journey full of thorny byways and traps

and betrayals. Medina wondered if she, too, had another traumatic trip ahead of her. She knew she definitely had a long, long way to go to fight for Nasser's release, Samater's rehabilitation and convalescence. First thing in the morning, she would write a letter to Amnesty International, but before that she had to find someone who could give her Dulman's particulars, date and place of birth, etcetera. Medina would also ask Sagal for Cadar's and Hindiya's particulars as soon as possible. She had no doubt Xaddia would be willing to mail the letter herself from Rome. Medina would supplement her intellectual activities – her translations and original writings – with these social responsibilities. With one hand she would revise her translations and continue to write; with the other, she would nurse, medicate and do the social work she had always meant to. A guest, was she still a guest? she asked herself. No, she was definitely no longer a guest in her own country. Sandra, Atta, Wentworth George – yes, time was ultimately a decider. When one has been a guest for a long time, one acquires the right to make slight alterations as to where the chair should be positioned, whether the curtains should be drawn. . . . Medina a hostess? Why, when she altered the position of the chair the house fell in on her and the ground below her shook with seismic determination. No, she wasn't a guest any more. She was a full and active participant in the history of her country.

The journey to the acceptance of roles is final, she thought. Samater. Ubax. And Medina. There wasn't time to tie up the loose ends of the story, though there was a need to tell one another what had happened, a human need to touch the nerve. . . . It wouldn't be difficult to explain to Samater when the others had gone, wouldn't be difficult to put their house in some order.

She got up and softly and silently went to Samater. She took his hand, then dragged him further from the others, yes, from those who qualified as *guests;* then she motioned to Ubax to follow them. The three walked away, refusing to play host to the guests who waited to be entertained with explanations, explications and examples. Medina, Samater and Ubax behaved as though they needed one another's company – and no more.

About the Author

Nuruddin Farah is an internationally recognized author. He was born in 1945 in Baidoa, in what is now the Republic of Somalia. In 1991, he received the Swedish Tucholsky Literary Award, given to literary exiles, and he was the recipient of the German DAAD fellowship in 1990. *Sweet and Sour Milk* won the English-Speaking Union Literary Award of 1980.